THE LOVE OF MY NEXT LIFE

NEXT LIFE DUET BOOK ONE

BRIT BENSON

THE LOVE OF MY NEXT LIFE

Cover Design: Murphy Rae

Editing: Rebecca at Fairest Reviews Editing Services

Proofing: Sarah at All Encompassing Books

Created with Vellum

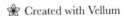 Created with Vellum

THE LOVE OF MY NEXT LIFE

Cover Design: Murphy Rae

Editing: Rebecca at Fairest Reviews Editing Services

Proofing: Sarah at All Encompassing Books

Created with Vellum

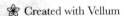 Created with Vellum

PLAYLIST

Love Is a Bitch – Two Feet
Sympathy – The Goo Goo Dolls
Landslide – Fleetwood Mac
My Own Worst Enemy – Lit
Loser – Sueco
I Knew You Were Trouble (Taylor's version) – Taylor Swift
I Think I'm OKAY feat. YUNGBLOOD & Travis Barker –
Machine Gun Kelly
Strawberries & Cigarettes – Troye Sivan
ur just horny – GAYLE
Wish You Were Sober – Conan Gray
Falling – Chase Atlantic
Slower – Tate McRae
Ocean Eyes (blackbear remix) – Billie Eilish
@ my worst – blackbear
Wrong Direction – Hailee Steinfeld
1 step forward, 3 steps back – Oliva Rodrigo
All Your Exes – Julia Michaels
Dress – Taylor Swift
notice me feat. BENEE – ROLE MODEL

i hope ur miserable until ur dead – Nessa Barrett
Never the 1 – ROSIE
Black Balloon – The Goo Goo Dolls
Jealous – Lennon Stella
Moral of the Story feat. Niall Horan – Ashe

Visit my website for the extended playlist.

CONTENT NOTE FROM THE AUTHOR

Please be aware, book one of the *Next Life* duet takes place in a high school setting, which means the main characters are between the ages of seventeen and nineteen. This book contains sexually explicit scenes. All scenes are consensual.

This book also contains some difficult topics that could be upsetting for some readers.

Topics that take place on page are: vulgar language, sexually explicit content*, toxic and unhealthy relationships, underage drug and alcohol use, addiction, physical violence*, bullying, drug abuse and overdose*.

Topics that are referenced but do not take place on page are: suicide*, physical abuse of a child.

*If you require a content-specific chapter guide for these topics, one can be found on my website.

I don't know who needs to hear this, but...
Dump his ass.
You deserve better.

Lennon

"I thought our story was epic, you know, you and me? Spanning years and continents. Lives ruined, bloodshed. Epic."
- Logan Echols,
Veronica Mars, 2x19

Age 9

I FIDDLE WITH THE HEM OF MY DRESS.

It's blue with little white polka dots and a thin lace trim.

I hate this dress. It makes me feel like a little kid. I also hate the black Mary Janes on my feet.

I glance at my reflection in the side mirror, then quickly look away. My braid is loose and messy. There are little pieces of hair already falling out and hanging down by my cheeks. I hate this braid, too. Daddy tried, though, so I keep quiet and watch out the window as the pretty trees and fancy houses breeze by.

Daddy pulls into the parking lot and turns off the engine. Without the radio playing, my heartbeat is too loud in my

1

head. Everything is too loud. He turns from the driver's seat to look at me in the back.

"Ready, Pumpkin?"

I nod. I'm not ready. Not at all. But I smile anyway.

"You look very nice," he says, and I push out the *thank you* he's hoping for. He smiles back. "Okay, Pumpkin. Out we go."

Daddy holds my hand as we walk up the sidewalk, and he pulls open one of the large doors for me. I know where I'm going. We were here last week to sign me up and stuff. Just inside the large double doors is another smaller door, and through that door is the office. I keep my eyes on my ugly Mary Janes the whole way.

"Mr. Washington," a raspy voice greets. "Good morning."

When I finally look up from my feet, I see the smiling face of Principal Townes. She's tall, plump, and very pretty. She's also very nice. She gave me a chapter book to read last week while she and Daddy talked.

"Hello, Lennon," she says to me with a smile. "Welcome back."

"Good morning, Juanita," Daddy says, and he puts his hand on my shoulder and gives me a little squeeze.

"Hi," I say with a quick upturn of my lips, then look back at my shoes.

While Daddy and Principal Townes talk, I stare out the window at the parking lot. Their voices drag and muffle, until I can barely hear them at all. Just the whirring of something mechanical and the clacking of the reception lady typing at her computer. Between the clacks and whirs, some words filter through.

New and *shy* and *quiet*.

Fit in and *time* and *changes*.

I'm sorry.

I drag the toe of one of my Mary Janes across the linoleum and watch as the rubber leaves a filmy, gray streak. Then I use the heel of my other Mary Jane to try and scratch the streak away. It doesn't work, though. I just end up making more streaks.

Streaks like the shadows the blinds made in the study.

Streaks like the rain on the car window as it fell from the dark clouds.

Streaks like the mascara tear tracks as they marred pale, cold cheeks.

My memories are full of streaks, but they're sharp and constant. Unlike the streaks my Mary Janes make on the linoleum. I resist the urge to bend down and scrub them off the floor.

Principal Townes stands from her desk and the movement pulls my attention back to the now.

"Are you ready, Lennon?" she asks softly, and I nod.

"Yes, ma'am."

"Are you excited for your first day?" Her voice is bright and hopeful. I glance at Daddy. His face reflects that hope. He waits for my response: jaw strained and smile tight.

I soften my facial expression. Turn my lips up at the corners once more. I force a lightness into my voice and lie.

"Yes."

I don't miss the quiet exhale of relief that slips from Daddy's mouth, and the sound puts a more genuine smile on my face. I can do this. For him, I can do this.

"Yes," I say again. "I'm very excited."

I give Daddy a hug goodbye and assure him that he doesn't have to walk me to the classroom. He still chooses to wait by the office door and watch as Principal Townes and I head down the hallway. I peek at him over my shoulder a couple times, and just before I follow Principal Townes around a corner, he sends me a small wave. I wave back, and then he's gone.

"This is Mrs. Loftus's classroom, Lennon," Principal

Townes says, stopping next to a wooden door covered in rainbow paper. The teacher's name is taped in large paper letters down the side of the door. I can hear the loud thrum of voices coming from inside the room. A burst of laughter makes me jump slightly. "She's expecting you. Would you like me to walk you in?"

I shake my head. "No, thank you."

"Alright, Lennon. Have a wonderful day, and if you need anything at all, come to the office. Anything at all, okay?"

The concern in Principal Townes's voice is genuine, and so is her kindness. I know it's not pity, and that relaxes my shoulders a little more. I tell her thank you and mean it, then turn the door handle and step inside. The room goes silent when I enter, and my eyes flick briefly over the class before finding the teacher and focusing on her.

Mrs. Loftus is short and skinny, and her dark hair is pulled into a French braid. Hers isn't messy like mine. There are no pieces falling around her face, and I bet it isn't crooked and loose like mine, either. I want to reach up and tug on my hair, but I don't.

"You must be Lennon," she chirps, then she bounces over to me. I keep my eyes on her because I can feel the eyes of all the other kids on me, and I'm not ready to meet them. My skin is tight, and my throat itches. I nod in response, and she places her open palm on my shoulder.

"My name is Mrs. Loftus. I'll be your teacher this year." She moves her eyes from my face to the tables filled with kids. "Class, this is Lennon Washington. She and her father just moved here, and Lennon will be joining us for the rest of the year. Be kind and make her feel welcome."

Mrs. Loftus's hand squeezes my shoulder slightly, and then she gestures to an open seat at one of the tables in the middle of the classroom. I look toward the seat, but before I can take a step forward, my eyes trip over the boy sitting at the table behind mine, and I freeze. He's staring—no, glaring—at me with the coldest blue eyes I've ever seen.

And I cannot move.

My entire body breaks out in chills, the kind I get when I'm going into a Halloween haunted house, or when I have to climb out of my bed in the middle of the night and make my way to the bathroom in pitch blackness. It's creepy and unwelcome and something else I can't understand. Something that twists up my belly and makes my heart beat louder and louder with each thump.

I stand there for seconds, locked in a staring match with this brown-haired boy, and I can hear muffled giggles coming from the other kids. My hands fist at my sides when I feel my cheeks heat, and then he smirks.

It's a small twitch of his lips, but I know it's a smirk. A smile at my embarrassment. Enjoyment at my discomfort. I grind my teeth together, narrow my eyes at him, and take a step forward. One, then another, then another, each one more confident, until I am standing directly in front of him, and his smirk has turned back into a scowl.

I give him one last glare before I turn around quickly and drop into my seat. Mrs. Loftus gives me a packet of materials, explains the directions, then leaves me on my own.

I take a deep breath and spread the packet out in front of me, then take a pencil out of my bag to write my name. I get to the first "n" when my chair is kicked, and my pencil lead snaps right after streaking a gray line up to the top of my paper. I pause and stare at yet another streak, then my chair is kicked once more, harder this time. I whip around and face the boy. He's smirking again, and I glare.

"Stop it," I demand. My voice is quiet when I want to yell. Calm when I want to shriek. I can feel my hands shaking. "Now."

"Make me, *Leonard*," he whispers back, and something

5

about his voice makes the tips of my ears warm. His smirk grows into a full smile, and I can't speak. I just stare. My eyes narrow and my nostrils flare and I'm so, so *mad*, but I say nothing. He cocks his head to the side, turning his crooked smile even more crooked, and without breaking eye contact, he kicks my chair again.

I squeak and grip my hands onto the edge of his table. My knuckles are white, and my eyes burn. But I still say nothing. I don't want to make a scene. I don't want to disrupt the other students.

"Leave her alone, Macon," a sharp, hushed voice cuts in from beside me. "Why are you always such a jerk?"

The boy's eyes leave mine and my shoulders droop immediately, like his look was holding me there, frozen and rigid and burning alive. I look in the direction of the voice and find a girl with unruly, dark brown curls and a scowl directed right at the boy.

"Make me, *Hairy Clairy*," he taunts, and the girl huffs and rolls her eyes.

"That doesn't upset me, Macon," she spits. "Quit bullying the new girl. Pay more attention to the teacher and maybe you won't be so *stupid* and fail *again*."

The girl's voice and expression are both smug, and when I flick my eyes to the boy, *Macon*, his face is blank.

"Shut up, Claire."

"You shut up, Macon."

They stare at each other for a few tense breaths, and then the girl looks at me.

"Ignore him. He's just a jerk," she says to me. I glance back at Macon, but he's not looking at us anymore. He's staring at the paper in front of him. The girl and I turn back around at the same time. "I'm Claire," she whispers and scoots closer. I didn't notice her before, but I guess she's my tablemate.

"I'm Lennon," I tell her, even though I know she already knows. "Nice to meet you."

"Sorry about Macon." She speaks to me while her eyes are on her work as she draws little flowers on the sides of her paper. "He's just angry because he's supposed to be a grade up, but he's dumb."

My mouth drops open at the pointed tone of her voice. She speaks the cruel words as if they are well-known facts. I try to ignore the prickling heat at my back. I know Macon is watching us, or listening, so I lower my voice. He's a jerk, but I don't want to be mean. I also want to know more, even though I don't *want to* want to.

"What happened?" I whisper, hunching forward.

"My mom says he's *lashing out,* but I just think he was born rotten."

My eyes flare, and I stifle a gasp. "How do you know?"

Claire glances sideways at me, her lip curled up, and shrugs. "'Cause he's my brother."

ONE

Lennon

Age 17

"Don't forget your passport," I call over my shoulder as I hear my dad's feet hit the landing. He pauses briefly and jogs back upstairs, without saying a word. I smile and shake my head. I'm not actually sure if he'll need it, but he never corrects me.

He rounds the corner into the kitchen, just as I put the lid on the silver US NAVY travel mug I got him for Father's Day when I was fifteen.

"Thanks, Pumpkin." He wraps his hand around the mug and presses a quick kiss to my head. "Big day. How do you feel?"

I shrug. "The same."

"Yeah? You don't feel older? Wiser?"

I roll my eyes and laugh. "I'm starting my senior year of high school, Dad, not a PhD program." He chuckles, and I watch as he drops down into a chair and puts on his shoes.

"Do I get to know this time?" I lean against the counter and take a bite of my protein bar. He grins and shakes his head. I never get to know, but I always ask anyway. "Okay, then. I'm going with Finland."

He hums and rubs his hand over his chin. "Didn't we already do Finland?"

"Yep, but it's supposedly the happiest country in the world with the cleanest air." I grin and take a sip of my orange juice. "Can never have too much of that."

"Touché." He raises his mug in the air and winks before his face grows serious. "You sure you'll be okay?"

"I'll be perfectly fine, Dad," I say honestly. "I always am. And it's only for two weeks this time. That's a cakewalk."

He studies me. It doesn't matter how many times he leaves me alone. It never gets easier for him.

"Are you sure you don't want to stay at the Davis's? I know Andrea wouldn't mind, and you'd at least have Claire to keep you company."

"Ah, but there's just one small problem with that scenario..." I let the statement trail off, and he sighs.

"Macon," we say at the same time.

"That boy isn't that bad," my dad says. He's always standing up for Macon. "He's just troubled. Just needs a little discipline is all. A father-figure."

"You volunteering for the job?"

He laughs off the question. "I'm just saying cut him some slack. He's had it rough."

"Claire's had it the same, Dad, and she's not *troubled* or *in need of discipline*." I hit him with a stare, and he throws the same look back at me.

"It's been different for Claire, and you know it."

My shoulders slump a little. He's right. I know he is. But as a former "troubled" boy who found solace in discipline, Dad wants to only see the good in Macon.

He'll be looking forever, though, because that boy is nothing but bad.

I pivot and raise a brow.

"Last time I stayed at Claire's for an extended period of time, Macon got high as a kite and then slipped laxatives into our Starbucks."

Dad barks out a laugh, and I bite down on my lip.

"It's not funny, Dad. Macon is a menace. I don't even know how he could have come from someone as sweet as Drea." Dad narrows his eyes at me, and I raise palms, stopping him from scolding me. "I mean *Ms. Davis.*"

"Respect your elders, Lennon Capri."

"Of course, sir."

He gives a curt nod. "If you're sure you'll be okay here by yourself..."

"I am, Daddy. Promise."

"But if you're not?"

"Then I will go stay at the Davis's." I give him the answer he wants. "Or I'll have Claire come stay here." That satisfies him.

He always does this, acts as if I'm the one who's likely to be in harm's way when he leaves. In reality, I'll just be sitting at home doing homework and hanging with Claire. He's the one traipsing around who knows where, doing who knows what, on a dangerous, top-secret mission.

"I gotta head out," he says after taking a look at his watch. He'll likely drive to the base at Little Creek from here, and then from there, I don't know. My skin prickles in the way it always does just before he leaves. Anxiety stirs low in my belly, creating that subtle feeling of nausea I'll have to live with for the next couple of weeks.

He's the only family I have.

I hate this. I've always hated it. But if I tell him that, he'll retire, and then he'll be miserable. I'm not stupid. I know he needs this. Other than me, Dad lives for these missions, this job. So instead of letting the twist of my gut show on my face, I fake it.

"Okay. Claire will be here any minute, anyway." I walk to the sink and rinse out my juice glass, so I have something else to focus on. "Be safe, okay? I'll be here waiting when you get back."

"You be good," he teases, and I huff a laugh. As if I'd ever be anything but good. "I'll be back in two weeks." I nod and bite the inside of my cheek. He walks to me and wraps me in a tight hug, and I grit my teeth and breathe through the desire to cry.

"Hey," he says into my hair, "it's just training."

He says this every time.

I know he's lying.

It might not be a six-month deployment, but I know it's not just training.

I step back and smile anyway. "That's good. Have fun in Finland."

After he shuts the door behind him, my phone buzzes in the pocket of my skirt. I pull it out and check the screen.

"Running late but otw," Claire's text reads. I check the time. We're going to be late for our first day of senior year. I sigh, send her back an "okay," then go to my room.

I stop to glance at myself in the wall mirror, taking note of my dark, navy-blue corduroy skirt and white blouse. I look more suited for a casual job interview than high school. My dark chestnut hair is pulled into a tight French braid, tied off with a small white ribbon, and my face is sporting my usual makeup look—brown eyeliner and black mascara to make my hazel eyes pop, peach cream blush, pink-tinted lip gloss. Claire helped me determine my color palette when we were in 8th grade. I've been loyal to it since. I blink a few times at my reflection, practice a smile, then turn away.

Dropping to the floor by my bed, I pull out the large plastic tote and tug it open. The scent that wafts over me helps to slow the swirling in my stomach.

Parchment and paint and art and *freedom.*

The only reason I can tolerate my dad's extended absences is because, when he is gone, I can paint freely. When he's home, I keep it hidden. I don't want to upset him. He doesn't say so, but I know it makes him nervous. He's always been enthusiastically supportive of everything I've done, except for this. And I don't blame him for being worried.

I'm staring longingly at the contents of the tote when my phone buzzes again. Claire is here. I put the lid back on the tote and shove it back under my bed. Then I hop up and skip down the stairs, grab my bag from the kitchen, and head out the door, locking it behind me.

I'm halfway to Claire's car when I notice a pair of dirty black Vans hanging out the back window, and I can't stop the scowl that takes over my face. Claire's bark of laughter breaks me from my glare, and I resume my walk, my steps heavy and irritated.

I slide into the passenger seat of Claire's car and roll my eyes at her amused smile.

"Sorry, Len," she says airily as she backs out of my driveway. "I'd have warned you, but then you'd want to drive yourself, and I like driving you."

A snarky snort comes from the back seat, and my headrest jolts forward, jostling me and shoving my braid into the back of my head. He kneed it. He's such a child. I stifle a growl.

"Good morning, Leonard," Macon drawls from the back seat, his voice rough like he's only just woken up. I glance over my shoulder and find him sprawled across the back seat with his feet hanging out the window and his black canvas jacket balled up under his head. His jeans are ripped at the knees, his plain black tee is wrinkled, and his blue eyes are closed, but I know if they were open, he'd be making fun of me with them.

"Why are you here?" I ask him flatly. His stupid full lips curve up on one side, but he doesn't answer me because he's rude and probably high.

I take note that his unruly curls, the same color as Claire's, are shaggy and long and falling over his sharp eyebrows. He couldn't even get a haircut before the first day of senior year? He couldn't iron his shirt or wear a nicer pair of jeans?

I flip back around in disgust.

"So sweet for everyone else, Leonard," he croons, then knees my headrest again, and I have to bite back an *ouch* from the force of it. "Why are you always such a bitch to me?"

I grit my teeth, just as Claire reaches into the back seat and punches him hard in the thigh. He grunts and draws his knees to his chest, hitting my headrest again, and jostling me forward. Again. This car ride is going to give me a concussion.

"Jesus Christ, Claire." He growls, and Claire snorts.

"I told you, you weren't allowed to talk to her," she spits. "*She's* welcome here. *You're* a charity case."

Macon pulls his jacket out from under his head and tosses it over his face, grumbling something about PMS and bitchy sisters.

I side-eye Claire.

"*Why* is he here?" I repeat, and she sighs. I can't tell if she's more annoyed with me or him. It had better be him.

"Our angel boy '*swerved for a raccoon*' and drove his car into a ditch," she says, using one hand to air-quote '*swerved for a raccoon*.'

My jaw drops and I whip around to stare at him.

The only thing Macon loves is his car. He actually *worked* to buy it, and Macon is the laziest person I've ever met. I think the only reason he works at the town grocery store at all is to pay for insurance and gas.

"You totaled your car," I gasp at him, but he doesn't respond. Claire speaks up, instead.

"It's just the front bumper. Nothing terrible, but it's in the shop for the next week." My shoulders relax as something like relief washes over me. At least he didn't lose the only thing he cares about.

"Don't worry," Claire adds, "he'll be driving himself by Monday."

"How did I not know about this?" Claire usually tells me everything. One of her favorite topics is complaining about Macon. She shrugs.

"I didn't know until this morning. I guess it happened super late on Saturday, and he had it towed and taken care of without telling Mom."

Something about that leaves me unsettled, but I don't know why, and I don't speak again until we're pulling into the senior parking lot.

I grab my bag from the floorboard and climb out, but before I can swing my backpack strap over my shoulder, my braid is yanked back, and Macon's body is pressed against my side from behind. I freeze. He lowers his face next to mine. I can feel his breath on my neck. He smells like spearmint toothpaste, weed, and something spicy.

"Have a good day, Leonard," he rumbles, and I stifle a gasp when his lips brush against the shell of my ear. I grit my teeth and fist my hands at my sides, angry about the goosebumps that appear on my skin. Then he's gone, pushing past me and loping up to his group of delinquent friends. Sam, his off-again, on-again fuck buddy, slides her arms around his waist and sends me a death glare before sucking his face off. I guess they're on again.

"He's disgusting," Claire muses as she steps up next to me. I hum in agreement, then consciously remove the snarl from my face. She turns to me with a mischievous smile. "Ready, Bae?"

I smile back and loop my arm through hers. "Ready, Bae."

. . .

My classes are what I expected. AP this and AP that. The same faces I see every semester, have seen every year since 9th grade, with a cast of the same teachers. When you only take AP and honors classes in a small school, your circle doesn't change much.

I have lunch with Claire, which is nice. I narrowly avoid a not-so-accidental collision with Sam that would have resulted in my white blouse covered in ketchup, which I consider a win. Usually, I'm not that lucky. But it's the last class of the day that has me bouncing in my ballet flats.

Senior free period.

I've got more than enough credits to graduate with honors. Because of that, I've earned the coveted free period. Dad thinks I'm using it as a study hall. I didn't correct him.

I head to the back of the building, toward the arts wing, and the closer I get, the more relaxed I feel. I pass the gym, the sound of squeaking tennis shoes slips through the doors, but I keep my eyes in front of me. In the cooking class, it smells like charred cake. The clanking of tools can be heard coming from the shop and wood working classes. But it's the scent of paints and clay and charcoal pencils, and the sound of a classic rock song drifting through the door at the end of the hall that has all of my attention.

I'm practically skipping by the time I reach it.

It's not a study hall. Not at all. It's way better.

"Lennon," Mr. Billings—or Hank, as he wants us to call him—greets me from his place at the back of the room. His flannel sleeves are rolled up and his arms are splashed with clay water as he sets up the pottery wheel. He's my favorite teacher. Has been since freshman year, though I've never actually taken a class with him.

"Hi, Hank!" I chirp. "Thank you so much for letting me spend my free period in here this semester."

"Of course, Lennon." He grins, showing off coffee-stained teeth through a rusty red beard. "I've already set you up a station in the corner," he gestures to an easel next to a table, and on the table, I see brushes and watercolors piled on top. "But you can move it to wherever."

I walk toward my station.

"Oh, no, this will be perf—" I start to say, but I'm cut off when a familiar boy with ripped jeans and messy curls comes lumbering out of the supply closet behind Hank. My smile drops from my face. Macon has two bricks of gray clay in his hands, and when he spots me, his eyes narrow.

"Oh, Lennon," Hank says, "I forgot to mention that you'll be sharing the period with Macon this semester."

My earlier fondness for Hank goes up in flames. He's Judas now. Brutus. Traitor. Allowing the enemy to taint my sacred space. I'll never forgive him.

"*You* earned a free period?" I snarl, and watch as Hank's face twists up in surprise at my tone while Macon's transforms into a cocky grin. He's always liked bringing out the worst in me.

"What if I said I just wanted to spend time with you?"

He's taunting me, his voice sarcastic, as if the idea of anyone wanting to voluntarily spend time with me is hilarious. My mouth tightens and my eye twitches. His smile flattens.

"Don't worry, Leonard. You won't even know I'm here."

I roll my eyes and turn to my station, foregoing the stool at the easel and sitting instead at the table.

"Is this going to be a problem," Hank asks slowly. I want to say yes. I was under the impression this would be *my* time. I don't even look at him when I answer.

"No, sir," I say curtly, just as Macon drags out a "nope."

I do my best to tune them both out.

I focus on the paper in front of me and let music from the stereo be the only sound that my ears register. I want to free paint today, so I use a smaller sheet of watercolor paper and don't bother sketching anything first. I sort through the tubes of paint, select a few colors that call to me, and pluck out a couple brushes. My earlier irritation with Hank cools a bit when I realize he's already set me out two jars of water and a roll of paper towels.

I maneuver all the supplies until they're arranged in an arc around me in the way I prefer, then take a brief moment to appreciate the clean, fresh set-up. I smile softly, but as I reach for a brush, my skin prickles with fire, and I whip my eyes to Macon's side of the room.

Sure enough, he's watching me with a furrowed brow, eyes the color of the hottest flame. I cock my head to the side and study him for a moment. Macon is sitting in front of the pottery wheel and Hank is sitting next to him. Hank is talking about something, gesturing wildly to the wheel and the clay, and Macon nods but doesn't take his eyes off me.

Is Macon learning how to make pottery?

He raises a dark brow, then flicks his eyes down to his side. My eyes follow and I release a sigh of irritation when I see what he wanted me to see.

His middle finger.

Macon is flipping me off. He is *such* a child.

I turn my attention back to my work, and I don't look at him again for the rest of the period.

I clean my station five minutes before the bell and am out the door with a quick goodbye to Hank right as the period finishes. I'm walking as briskly as I can, without all-out jogging, but the familiar slap of dirty Vans on the linoleum grows louder the more ground he covers.

I feel like the prey in a horror movie.

Within seconds, Macon is sidling up to me. I tighten my

books to my chest, just as he yanks on my braid. Spearmint and weed and spice.

Caught. If this were a horror movie, I'd be dead.

"Why doesn't anyone know you paint?" His question makes my shoulders stiffen.

"I don't."

"Sure looked comfortable in there *painting.*" I stare forward and don't answer, but he doesn't take the hint. "I've taken art every semester, and I've never seen you in a class."

My eyebrows shoot up, and I don't mask my surprise. "You take art?"

"Never tried to hide it. Unlike you."

"I don't hide it. I've never had space in my schedule for an art class," I state. It's true. I've been too busy with honors and advanced placement classes. I took intro to graphic design to fulfill my arts credit because it was safe and wouldn't upset Dad.

Curiosity hums through my body despite my disdain for Macon, and I can't resist asking. "So...pottery?"

He shrugs. If he's surprised by my interest, it doesn't show.

"Thought I'd give it a try." He pauses and glances down at me quickly. "And Hank is kind of doing me a favor."

I wait to see if he's going to elaborate, but he doesn't. Instead, he catches sight of Sam and waves to her before turning to me.

"Tell Claire I'll catch a ride home with Sam." His lips curl into a devious grin. "Gonna fuck her in the janitor's closet before she drops me off."

My jaw hangs open in shock, and he laughs out loud.

"God, you're too fucking easy," he snarks, walking backward, and I scowl. "Later, Leonard," he shouts so everyone in the hallway can hear him, and then he turns and jogs to Sam. She flips me off just before they walk away.

TWO

Lennon

"Hey, girls," Claire's mom greets us from the kitchen as we walk through the door. "How was school?"

"It was school," Claire says, rounding into the kitchen and pulling herself up onto the counter. She snags an apple from the basket next to her and underhands it to me, then grabs another for herself. "Annoying but necessary."

I laugh at her assessment and so does Andrea. "You're so cynical, Claire. What about you, Len? How was school?"

I smile at her and give her the answer she wanted from her daughter.

"It was good, Drea. I like my classes, and I've got a senior free period last, so every day will end on a good note."

At least I *hope* it will. So long as a certain "troubled" boy leaves me alone.

Andrea is pleased with my answer. I wait to see if she'll bring up Macon's schedule, maybe mention something about his free period, but she doesn't. And in order for me to start the topic, I'd have to tell her that I'm spending my free period in the art room. I definitely don't want to do that.

"Your dad is gone for a bit, right, Len?" Andrea asks

20

instead, and I nod. "Did you want to stay here while he's gone? You know we'd love to have you."

"Oh, no, that's alright, Andrea. I'm good at home." Her face falls and Claire groans.

"*Leeeeen,*" Claire whines around a mouthful of apple. "Please? You know you'd rather be here than at home all alone." She pokes her lip out, and I force a smile.

I wouldn't, actually. I'd much rather be in my own bed, in my own room, with my paints and my music. I chew on my lip and force a smile.

"What if I come stay the weekend?" I offer. Her shoulders perk up. "I don't want to live out of a suitcase the first week of school," I tell her, and it's not a lie.

I also don't want to sleep on the twin air mattress in her bedroom, or share the Jack and Jill bathroom with her and Macon. And I definitely don't want to be in the room right next to Macon's, so I can hear him sneaking out in the middle of the night.

Or worse, sneaking Sam *in.*

I suppress a shudder as his words at school pop back up in my head, and my thoughts are invaded by a visual of Macon screwing some faceless girl in the janitor's closet. Right next to a mop bucket and one of those large brooms the maintenance crew push around.

In my mind, Macon is still fully clothed, but the ragged breathing coming from him as he pumps into the girl, and the way his one hand presses into the wall for balance, makes my heart race and my cheeks heat.

"...pick up your stuff after school on Friday." Claire's voice regains my attention, and I blink out of my daydream...day nightmare?

"Sounds good," I say, and Claire hops down from the counter and tosses her apple core in the trash.

"We're gonna go upstairs for a bit, Mom. You work

21

tonight?"

I put my uneaten apple back in the basket, then follow Claire toward the stairs, keeping my attention on Andrea.

"I am closing and have inventory tonight," Andrea says. "I have to leave in twenty and will be back late, but I'm off tomorrow."

Andrea is a manager at a large department store. She's worked there for as long as I've known the Davises, but she started as a retail clerk. She worked her way up and was promoted to manager two years ago. Macon bought her flowers and cupcakes to celebrate. It's literally the only kind thing I've ever seen him do.

"Don't work too hard," I tell her, and she winks at me.

Claire tells her mom she loves her, and we head upstairs to her room. As soon as we cross the threshold, she shuts the door and hits me with a guilty look. My back goes rigid.

Not again.

"What?" I ask nervously.

"Don't be mad," she says, nose scrunched in an attempt to look apologetic. She's not. She never is.

"Just tell me," I demand.

"Promise you won't be mad, first."

I tip my head to the ceiling and close my eyes.

"Fine," I say into the air, "I won't be mad." And even if I am, I won't tell her.

She claps excitedly, and I bring my eyes back to her face. Her triumphant grin sets my teeth on edge.

"Josh invited us to a party, and I told him we'd be there." Her words are rushed, her eyes so wide and giddy that I can't help the upward turn of my lips.

Claire has been crushing on Josh since eighth grade. They made out once sophomore year after a football game, but he acted like nothing happened the next day. I don't like him at all, but Claire does.

I'll give it to her, he is gorgeous. Quarterback of the football team with a dazzling smile and thick eyelashes. He's a regular small-town American hero. And of course, he's a jerk.

"He invited *us*?" I push her, and she scrunches her nose up again.

"C'mon, Len. Everyone knows we're a packaged deal," she says, all but confirming my suspicions. Josh didn't invite *me*. He invited *her*. I'm just being dragged along...

"And I suppose you want me to be DD?"

"Lennon," she whines, "you don't drink anyway. I'm not saying I'll get wasted, but I'll need a drink to take the edge off my nerves. You know how I get around Josh."

I snort a laugh and she glowers at me. She's not kidding. She's a tongue-tied, bumbling mess around the Golden Boy.

"Claire," I try to reason, "it's a *Monday*."

I don't know why I bother even pointing it out. She won't care. Not like I do. As if on cue, she waves her hand in the air, dismissing my statement.

"Please, Len? It's not like you have to worry about curfew with your dad gone, and my mom won't be back until like four." She folds her hands under her chin and bats her "blackest black" coated lashes. "*Pleeeeeeease?*"

I don't even have to say anything. She knows the moment I cave, and she bounces up and down with a laugh.

"Thank you, thank you, thank you, Lenny C. You're the absolute best bestie I have."

I roll my eyes. "I better be your only bestie."

"Okay, I'll take you home to change and get ready, and will pick you up around ten. Good?"

I screw up my lips. "I need *six hours* to change?"

She turns her back to me and walks into her closet. "Maybe you can wear that denim skirt I got you for your birthday? And a black cami."

That denim skirt is distressed to hell. Frayed at the hem

23

and ripped under the back pocket. If I move a certain way, you can see my underwear. And my camisoles are meant to be worn under blouses. She knows this.

Before I can protest, she pops her head out of the closet with a pointed stare.

"You have no reason to say no, Len. Your dad isn't here to care what you wear. You can dress like you're actually a seventeen-year-old high school student instead of a twenty-eight-year-old businesswoman."

Then she disappears back into her closet.

I *like* how I dress. Sure, Dad approves, and I like that Dad approves, but I like my style. I like looking like a "twenty-eight-year-old businesswoman." It gives me confidence, and it doesn't hurt that I don't bring attention to the parts of my body I'm insecure about, which is all of it. Modest businesswoman is my aesthetic, and I like it that way.

I don't bother arguing, though. Claire is like a dog with a bone when she wants something, and tonight, she wants to dress me up like a seventeen-year-old Barbie doll.

"Fine," I relent. "I'm gonna go."

"Want me to drive you," she calls from the closet, but makes no move to come out.

"No, it's fine. It's just two blocks."

"Kay! See you at ten!"

I let myself out the front door and make my way to the sidewalk. I'm halfway home when a loud muffler and louder music come toward me. When I glance up, I recognize Sam's red coupe. It passes me, heading toward the Davis's house. I start to release a sigh of relief, but then the car pulls a U-turn and rolls up next to me. My relief was premature.

A quick glance to the side shows me that Macon is driving, Sam is hanging out the passenger window, and there are two other people in the back seat. Probably Macon's other stoner friends, Julian Rogers and Chris Casper. I keep walking, but the car slows to a crawl to keep up with my pace.

"Hi, Leonard," Sam calls, her voice sickeningly sweet and followed by a chorus of sniggers. "How was your first day?"

I force a tight smile.

"It was good, Sam," I say, because the decorum that's been drilled into me since birth demands that I respond politely. "How was yours?"

I glance back at the car briefly. Her grin is actually a sneer. A viper posing as a friend. She knows she's not fooling me, so I don't know why she gets such a kick out of the act. I flick my eyes past her toward Macon. His attention is on the road. His defined jaw is tight, but he's relaxing back in the seat. One hand on the steering wheel and the other hanging out the window, completely carefree and uninterested in my exchange with his fuck buddy.

I stare a little harder. Narrow my eyes slightly. I will him to look at me, hoping maybe he'll have some decency and drive away, but his head stays locked forward.

"My day was great," Sam says, drawing my attention back to her. "The end of the day was even better." She winks at me, and I realize she's probably referring to the janitor's closet. I don't respond. "It's hot out, Leonard. You want a ride? You gotta be gross and sweating."

"No, thank you," I say tightly. "I'm good."

She leans forward and holds something out of the car door.

A styrofoam cup. A slushie from the gas station. Red, from the looks of it. My shoulders lock up, and I pick up my pace. Sam laughs.

"You want some of this to cool down? It's real good."

"No, thank you."

"Oh, I insist, Leonard," she sing-songs, and then she throws it at me, hitting my ankles and making me stumble forward. The smell of alcohol hits me hard—it was a spiked slushie, apparently—and the cold liquid coats my legs and dots my skirt.

I suppress a growl and catch myself from tripping over the cup. The sound of cackling assaults me, then a fake "sorry" is yelled, right before the car speeds off.

I hate them.

I hate them all.

I hate Macon the most.

I breathe through my nose to will away the angry tears, then I bend over and pick up the cup to throw away at my house. My legs are stained red, my ballet flats covered in the sticky juice, and there's even some spots on my shirt. My white blouse is probably ruined.

When I get to my house, I toss the slushie cup into the outside garbage bin, then head inside and straight for the shower. I scrub my legs roughly, but the red slushie stain still shows faintly on my pale skin. God, Sam is such a bitch, and Macon is a dickhead. I don't know why they hate me so much, but the feeling is mutual.

I give up on my legs, wash my hair and face quickly, then turn off the water. I dry, pull my wet hair into a French braid, then throw on an old US NAVY tee and sweats. As soon as I drop down next to my bed, the tension in my body melts away. I tug the tote back out and bring it downstairs to the kitchen table.

It will take me thirty minutes to get ready for the party. I've got a good five hours still. I'm going to paint.

Something angry and moody.

Frustrated and isolated.

Something therapeutic.

CLAIRE PULLS UP TO MY HOUSE AT EXACTLY TEN. HER promptness speaks to her excitement. Claire would be late to her own funeral.

I lock the house and make my way to her car, and she lets out a wolf whistle.

"Dang, Len," she says when I climb in the passenger seat. "You look hot. Those knee-high tights are very *good girl gone bad*."

I snort a laugh. Thanks to Sam's slushie bath, I look like I have hives. I had to wear the tights to cover the red stains on my shins and calves. Since my ballet flats looked stupid with the tights, I'm wearing my black suede booties.

It's actually a cute outfit.

If I could put a cardigan over the cami, I'd be all set.

"I wish I had your boobs," she says with a pout, and I roll my eyes.

"Why? You actually *have* boobs. Mine are practically microscopic." It's the same thing I always say when she does this. She's sporting a perky C-cup and I weigh in with barely a B.

"Yeah, but you can go without a bra, if you want." She gestures to her chest. "I gotta keep these bad girls contained."

I laugh and she smirks, looking a lot like Macon, before narrowing her eyes and studying me critically.

"You gonna keep your braid in?"

"I was planning on it," I say, but she reaches over and pulls the ribbon from the end, anyway. Using her fingers, she releases my hair from the French braid and tousles it, so it falls in waves around my shoulders. Then she ties my black lace ribbon around my neck like a choker.

"There," she says, and she smiles proudly. "What would you do without me?"

I roll my eyes and smile back, but I don't answer. She's my best friend. My only friend, really. Without her, I'd be sad and lonely and lost, most likely.

Claire prattles on the whole ride to Josh's house. He lives in the country on a farm, so I'm not surprised when she pulls up and the entire road and drive are lined with cars, a big bonfire blazing in the back about fifty yards from the bigger house. I can't help the thought that the fire probably should be farther away, but these kids think they're invincible.

Claire parks behind some huge Ford truck.

"I'm so nervous," she says, her hands clasped tightly in her lap. "How do I look?"

"Boneable," I state, and she barks out a laugh. "Just...remember you don't have to do anything you don't want to do."

"Oh, trust me, I won't." She bounces her eyebrows at me, and I laugh with her. Claire isn't a virgin. Not by a long shot. I'm technically not either, but she's way more experienced than I am.

We climb out of the car, she locks the door, and hands me the keys.

"Let's do this, Bae." She holds her arm out to me, and I loop mine through hers.

"Lead the way, Bae."

Inside the house, Claire makes a beeline for the kitchen, where we find three coolers full of cheap beer. She turns up her nose at the beer and opens the fridge.

"Bingo," she says, and pulls out a spiked seltzer, opening it and taking a big gulp. "Let's do a lap."

I walk with Claire, arms linked, around the house, and she stops to talk to basically everyone. She's much more popular than I am. Part of it is because she's grown up here. She's been to school with all these kids since kindergarten, and I'll always be the outsider who showed up in the middle of fourth grade.

But the other part, probably the bigger part, is that Claire is just more likable. She's got one of those personalities that draws people in. She's witty, she's stylish. She's outspoken when she wants to be.

And I'm...*amiable.*

Polite.

Nice.

No one *dislikes* me—well, except for Sam and Macon, but I don't like them either—but no one really *likes* me either. They can take me or leave me, makes no difference to them.

Claire laughs and flirts, and I smile and speak when spoken to. My outfit draws a few appreciative glances, but otherwise, I might as well be one of the bangles on Claire's wrist.

"Oh my god, he's coming over here," Claire whisper-hisses at me, breaking me from my staring contest with the wallpaper. I glance at her, then follow her eyes.

Josh.

All-American sparkling smile on his face as he pushes his way through the house, eyes stuck like a tractor beam on Claire. I can feel her vibrating.

"Deep breaths," I whisper back. "You got this."

"I got this," she repeats, and then flashes a Miss Virginia Teen smile just as Josh steps in front of us. "Hey, Josh," she chirps. "Thanks so much for the invite."

"You havin' a good time?" He flicks his eyes from Claire to me, then does a double take. His eyes drop from my face to my camisole, down my body to my shoes, then back. When Josh's eyes linger long enough to make me uncomfortable, Claire jostles me and speaks up, getting his attention once more.

She gets him talking about school, then flashes me an annoyed look that I don't quite understand. Is she mad at me because he was leering?

No. Definitely not.

I fold my arms over my chest anyway.

I'm lost in my thoughts again when Claire nudges my arm. I glance at her, and she's got that giddy smile on her face and Josh's arm slung over her shoulder.

"I'm going to go sit with Josh at the bonfire," she says, then flares her eyes at me slightly. I get the hint. *She's* going to the bonfire. I am *not* to follow. I nod.

"Have fun," I tell her. "I'll be here."

"You sure you don't want to come, Lennon," Josh asks, and Claire laughs nervously.

"That's not really her scene, right, Len?"

"Yeah," I say slowly, "I'm not really a fan of bonfires." Claire's smile grows with my lie. She mouths *thank you*, then tugs on Josh's arm.

"See you in a bit, Lenny," she says, then she and Josh turn and walk away, leaving me to just...stand around by myself.

I head back to the kitchen and rummage through the cabinets until I find a glass, fill it with water from the fridge, then wander over to a corner and plant myself in it. I pull out my phone and open my e-reader, settling in for a few hours until my services as designated driver are needed.

Soon I'm overcome by the smell of spearmint and weed and spices, but emphasis on the weed, and my hackles rise just seconds before a familiar body presses up against my side.

"Where's your braid, Leonard?" Macon asks, his mouth hovering just above my shoulder. I tell myself it's so he can be heard over the music. I whip around to face him and flinch a little at how close our faces are. The bloodshot whites of his eyes make his blue flame irises pop, and paired with his harsh dark eyebrows, he's even more unsettling up close. I school my face into a façade of boredom before speaking.

"Why? Mad you don't have something to yank on?"

I realize my mistake the moment his lips curve up into that wicked, crooked smile.

"Actually, Len, I think I could wrap this around my fist just fine."

He reaches up and fingers a wavy strand of my hair as he speaks, and I swat him away. His laugh makes my neck and ears burn, and I grit my teeth against the desire to hit him harder.

"There she is," he croons, teasing eyes bouncing between mine, and takes a step toward me, backing me into the corner. "You angry, Leonard? Am I pissing you off?"

I huff, but I don't answer. He steps closer and puts his hands on the wall above my head. The smell of weed coming off him is overpowering.

"Jesus, Macon, how much did you smoke?" I curl up my lip in disgust. "You smell like you hotboxed the car on the way here."

"You know what hotboxing is, *Astraea?*" he taunts. I bristle, but he laughs me off. "Close. Try the basement bathroom."

I shake my head. "You're unbelievable." His smile widens and he shuffles forward an inch more, then lowers his lips to my ear.

"When you gonna be sweet for me, Lennon?" he whispers, his hot breath making me shiver, and I feel his fingers trail down my arm, leaving goosebumps in their wake. "Or did you use up all your fake smiles today and only got scowls left?"

"Back off, Macon," I grind out, and shove at his chest. He doesn't budge. Just chuckles, and I can feel the vibrations of it under my palms. I don't know why I don't remove my hands, or why I don't shove harder.

I just...don't.

Instead, my fingers curl into his shirt, digging my nails into the muscle underneath, and he hums, dropping his head to my shoulder.

"There she is," he says, and his voice is rough and deep, his lips dragging over my neck with each word. He nudges my choker with his nose, and my eyes clamp shut.

I grab fistfuls of his shirt, unsure if I want to pull him closer or push him away, when he bites my neck and sucks on it hard. I gasp at the pain and shove with all my strength, bringing my knee up into his gut for good measure.

He grunts and jerks away, laughing hysterically when he almost falls on his ass. He swings his eyes to me, and his laughter dies when he sees my hand cupping the spot on my neck he just assaulted. He straightens himself, either unaware or uncaring of the attention we've garnered from the others in the room, then stalks back toward me.

I plant my feet and square my shoulders, prepping for attack. When he's within distance, he shoots his hand up and grabs my wrist.

"Let me see it, Len," he says, the emotion in his eyes unmistakable yet completely unreadable. I'm paralyzed, unable to process everything I'm seeing pass over his face. Concern, maybe, for hurting me. Lingering humor. Exhaustion. Anger. But there's something else. Something that heats my blood and quickens my breath. He licks his full lips and locks his eyes back on mine. "Show me," he says again, more forceful this time, and gives my hand a tug.

It's the tug that spurs me back to action.

"Let go of me, Macon," I demand.

I jerk my arm back, ready to kick or push or scream if I have to, but at my command, he drops my wrist and takes a half-step back. We don't say anything else. We just stare at each other, chests heaving. I wonder if his heart is pounding as hard as mine. His eyes drop to my lips, and instinctually, I wet them with my tongue. His jaw tightens, and he moves to close the distance between us once more, but before he can, arms wrap around his waist from behind and Sam's face appears next to him.

"Hey, baby," she purrs up at Macon, and he slowly unpeels his eyes from me to bring his attention to Sam.

I don't know what I was expecting him to do but flashing her a dazzling smile and planting a sloppy kiss full of tongue on her bright red lips wasn't it. It makes my chest ache and my throat burn. I can't stop the way my face twists up in anger.

"Hey, baby," he says back. "Was just telling Lenny here how much I like her socks."

At that, Sam looks down at my legs, then promptly bursts out laughing.

"Oh, Leonard," Sam says in the breaths between laughs. "Why ever would you need to wear those?"

She clutches her stomach as she laughs, and when I glance back at Macon, he is staring at me with a blank, bored expression. But his lips twitch just the tiniest bit when I narrow my eyes at him.

They know that my legs are splotchy red and stained from whatever the hell was in that slushie cup. They might have even planned it. And this, whatever this was that just happened between me and him, was just another of Macon's twisted jokes.

I hate him.

I glare daggers at them, my teeth clenched so tight that my jaw aches. My free hand is fisted as the other presses tightly on my neck. Macon lets his eyes drop back to the fist at my side, and his lips curl into his crooked smirk.

"There she is," he says proudly, looking back at me and biting his lip before saying, "there you fucking are, Lennon Capri."

He winks, then walks away with Sam hanging off him like a bitchy barnacle, leaving me confused and speechless, with an aching neck and tiny nail cuts in my palm.

I hate him. I hate him. I hate him.

It takes me a half an hour to get my heart rate back to normal, and I hide in Claire's car for the rest of the night. She texts me around 3:15 am, and I have her back in her bed before Andrea comes home.

There's no sign of Macon.

THREE

Macon

"WAKE THE FUCK UP, DICK."

The demand is punctuated with a few pounds on my closed and locked bedroom door. Each pound adds to the throbbing in my head. I roll over, feel around blindly for something to throw, and whip the first thing I grab.

It hits the door with a hard smack, and Claire shrieks on the other side. I can't help the laugh and peek one eye open to see what my weapon of chance was.

A shoe.

A *woman's* shoe.

Wtf?

I jolt up and immediately feel like I've been attacked by a cast iron frying pan. Or knocked out by the bouncer at Club FLEX again. Pressing my palms to my temples, I try to ignore Claire's nagging, and gingerly open my eyes to scan the other side of my bed, then the floor next to it. When both turn up empty, I heave a sigh of relief.

No sign of Sam, or anyone else. Don't know how the fuck the shoe got here. My dick doesn't feel like it fucked last night. I remember it getting sucked, but I don't think I fucked anyone.

"I'm serious, Macon," Claire shouts again. "I know you want to fail out of high school and live up to your potential of being a deadbeat suck on society, but I promised Mom I'd at least get your dumb, lazy ass to school, so get the fuck up!"

God, she is such a fucking bitch.

I roll out of bed and pull on some clothes, tossing back some Tylenol from my nightstand. A bump would work better, but Sam hasn't been able to steal any more from her dad. Instead, I dig a joint out of my nightstand and light it up, blowing the smoke out my window and spraying air freshener at the same time. I get three hits in before fucking Claire is pounding on my door again. I put out the joint and slip it into my almost empty pack of cigarettes, then shove the pack in my back pocket with the plan to finish the joint at lunch.

If I have to spend last period with Lennon again, I am gonna need to be buzzed.

Thinking of Lennon makes me think of the party, and thinking of the party gets me half hard and pisses me off. She's such a fucking phony.

Claire pounds again, and I swing the door open, just as she shouts in my face.

I glower at her, then push past and head down to the kitchen. Mom's already got coffee made, and as soon as I step in the room, her face falls.

"Macon, are you high?"

My shoulders tense, and I refuse to look at her. I hate disappointing Mom. I just don't know how to not.

"I'm goin' to school, Mom. I'm doing my homework like a good boy. I'm showin' up to work on time." I pour myself a cup of coffee and down half of it, burning my tongue and throat. "I'm nineteen. I can handle myself."

She sighs. She's sick of this conversation.

"Nineteen or not," she begins, and I finish.

"I'm still under your roof. I know, Ma. Fuck, I get it, okay?"

I turn around and find both Claire and Mom watching me. Mom with sadness, and Claire with disgust. I flip Claire off and walk to my mom, pulling her into a hug.

"Don't worry about me, okay? I got me, and I won't let you down."

She squeezes me tighter, then lets me go. "I sure hope so, Macon."

She tells us to have a good day at school, then takes her coffee and goes into the living room. Immediately, Claire turns on me.

"What the hell is wrong with you, Macon?" she seethes. I don't answer because I know it's a rhetorical question. Claire thinks she knows exactly what's wrong with me. She whips around and marches out the door.

Some siblings, who have been through what our family has been through, are close; they bond over the shared loss and become best friends despite their differences.

Not me and Claire.

She hates me. She *blames* me.

And honestly, I agree with her.

I throw myself into the back seat of Claire's car and toss my jacket over my face. She turns up her shitty music because she knows it irritates me. Fuck, I miss my car. Monday cannot come soon enough, for multiple reasons.

When I feel the car turn and move into park, I hold my breath. The drive was too quick for us to be at school already, which can only mean...

I pull my jacket off my face and sit up.

Sure as shit, here comes fucking Lennon bouncing down the path from her house to our car. Gray skirt and a baby-pink button down. And that damn braid.

Un-fucking-believable.

When she climbs in, I fling myself back down and groan.

"Figured you'd want to drive yourself instead of ride with me, Leonard," I hiss, and watch her shoulders stiffen.

"She tried," Claire speaks up in her place, "but she can't say no to me."

I can hear the smug smile in Claire's voice, and I scoff. Of course. Because Lennon doesn't say no to anyone. Lennon is too *nice*. Lennon bends over backward for everyone.

Everyone except me.

I smirk to hide my disgust and take note of the silk scarf tied around her neck. I remember my lips on her, my teeth. I must have marked her good if she's got to wear something other than makeup to hide it. It makes me hard.

I jab my knee into the back of her headrest, making sure to hit it right in the middle, so it knocks into that schoolgirl braid of hers. I hate that fucking braid.

"Nice scarf, *Astraea.*" Her delicate jaw tightens, and I can see the muscles twitch like she's grinding her teeth. Good. My smile grows. "Why you wearing that, huh?"

"Shut *up*, Macon." Claire groans. "Jesus, why can't you just leave her alone."

"It's fine," Lennon says. "I can ignore him for the next ten minutes. He's *nothing*."

Her words are like a punch to the gut, so I jab my knee into her headrest again, and she lets out a little growl. I smirk. There she is. I pull my jacket back over my head.

"Why did he call you *Astraea?*" I hear Claire ask Lennon quietly. Then I hear the tiniest amused laugh. Lennon's.

"She's the Greek goddess of purity and innocence," Lennon says. "Celestial virgin."

Claire snorts. "Innocent, maybe," she jokes, "but virginal and pure? Definitely not."

My fists clench at my sides and my heart kicks hard into my rib cage. I barely register Lennon telling Claire to shush through the sound of blood rushing in my ears. What the fuck does she mean, *definitely not?* I pull my coat off my face and glare at Lennon, the embarrassed shade of pink on her cheeks —the same one that usually amuses me—makes my vision blur with fury. When Claire parks in the senior lot, I'm out the door before the girls can even unbuckle their seat belts.

It's only Tuesday, and I'm already sick of this week.

I head straight for Sam. She's standing with our friends, Julian and Casper, but I ignore them and grab on to her waist, pulling her body hard against mine and taking her mouth in a kiss. My anger pours into this kiss, battling with her tongue and biting hard on her lip. Her taste is familiar, cigarettes and cinnamon gum, and I try to force myself to focus on just that. On her body, and her tongue licking at the inside of my mouth.

But Sam digs her nails into my side, and Lennon invades my brain. Standing trapped in that corner last night at the party. Wearing that black tank top that showed zero cleavage, and those fucking knee-high socks.

And her hair.

I might hate her hair down more than I hate it in a braid.

I groan into Sam's mouth, and she presses harder into me. I back up and grab her hand, keeping my eyes off her face and swollen mouth.

"C'mon," I say, and tug her behind me. She giggles. The sound grates on my nerves. I pull a little harder, so she picks up her pace. I practically drag her behind the school building toward the shed that holds the football equipment. She's panting by the time we reach it.

I unlock the door with the key I stole from Coach Schultz, and I push Sam inside.

It takes seconds to have her front pressed against the wall and her pants down to her ankles. I pull a condom from my wallet and roll it on, then mentally exchange cigarettes and cinnamon for rose-scented shampoo and soap. Sometimes peppermint, too, when she's stressed about school and sucks on mints like an addict.

I close my eyes and replace short, blonde hair with long, chestnut brown. In a braid that I untie and unravel myself. In waves that I wrap around my fist and yank. Pink, soft lips. Hazel-green eyes. Freckles.

I come in minutes. Pull out, discard the condom and zip up before Sam even has her pants to her thighs.

"Jesus Christ, Macon, thanks for nothing," she snaps, and I scoff as she does up the buttons on her jeans. "You could have at least gotten me off first."

I shrug and pull the pack of cigarettes out of my pocket, plucking out my joint and lighting it up.

"You know where your clit is," I say after a drag. "You coulda rubbed one out on your own."

She snarls at me and swipes my joint, taking a long drag and blowing the smoke out her nose.

"This arrangement might not be working for me anymore, Macon," she threatens, and I huff out a laugh.

"Then how will you piss off Senator Daddy, *Samantha*?" I take the joint back and put it out gently on the wall, so I can stick what's left of it back in the box with my last two cigarettes. "I bet Seth Travers would eat you out for hours if you asked him to."

The glare she hits me with would make a better man cower. I just roll my eyes. Seth Travers is in the marching band and captain of the math club. He's also Sam's neighbor.

"You're a fucking asshole," she spits, flinging open the door and marching out into the blinding sun.

"Not the first person to tell me that today," I shout at her, and she throws her middle finger up at me before disappearing back around the school.

I close my eyes and drop my head back on the wall. The bell rings in the distance.

Fuck.

I'm late for U.S. History. Mrs. Pardy is going to skin me alive.

My high is nearly gone by the time last period rolls around. I finished my joint at lunch, but I should have held out a little longer. I'm too sober to deal with Lennon Capri Washington.

I arrive to class a few minutes early, just like yesterday, so I have a minute to appreciate the art room without Lennon's smell engulfing everything. I head straight to the closet and grab some clay and an apron.

"Macon," Hank greets me from his desk, "how's your day been?"

"Fine, Hank," I lie, and take my seat at the pottery wheel. He eyes me curiously, cocking his head to the side.

"Are you high?"

I sigh. "Barely."

"You can't be——"

"I know," I cut him off, irritated he would even suggest it. "I don't do that anymore. I haven't for two years." I meet his eyes, so he can see my sincerity. "I will never show up there in any condition except stone sober."

He regards me for a few more seconds, then nods.

"You've got boxing tonight?" he asks, even though he already knows. He makes the schedules for the rec center because his husband, James, owns it. Hank knows exactly what I teach and when, but I nod anyway.

"And pottery starts next week," I say, nodding at the pottery wheel. He picks up on my not-so-subtle hint—leave me alone and let me practice—just as Lennon waltzes in. Hank winks at me, and some of the tension bleeds out of my muscles.

He won't say anything around her. He knows how important it is to me that no one knows. Not even my mom.

I started volunteering at the Franklin Youth Recreational Center when I was sixteen.

It wasn't exactly voluntary.

I'd been caught tagging a random house, and rather than press charges, the owner agreed to let me off with an alternative. Volunteer at his rec center, and I wouldn't have to go to juvenile court for a suspected hate crime. It wasn't a hate crime. I had no idea who lived in that house, but the threat alone was enough to make me accept James's offer without hesitation.

After a year, and after I stopped showing up high as shit, James started paying me, and I was able to quit my job stocking shelves at the supermarket. It was going great until my dumb drunk ass drove my fucking car in the ditch. I called James instead of Mom, and he and Hank helped me out. They wanted to tell my mom, but since I'm nineteen, they, thankfully, left it up to me. I do have to start teaching another class at the Center to pay them back for the tow, though.

Pottery.

Hence why I'm spending my free period learning the basics of working the wheel. It's fine. I don't know what the fuck else I'd do, anyway. Get high, probably.

I watch Lennon as she walks to her table and sits. She keeps her eyes off me, but mine zero in on the scarf around her neck. Her moves are practiced and precise as she sets her paints and brushes out in front of her, like she's done this a thousand times.

My legs itch with the need to go over there. To watch her paint.

I bet she's fucking brilliant at it. Lennon doesn't know how to fail.

When she catches me staring, she sneers, and I smirk before looking away. I spend the rest of the hour trying, and failing, to make a simple bowl. I'm supposed to teach a bunch of ten-year-olds how to throw clay next week, and I can't even make a bowl. I'm going to have to stay late this week at the rec center and practice some more, so I don't make a complete ass of myself.

One thing I've learned working at the Franklin Youth Recreational Center: kids can be real dicks. If I suck at this, they'll gladly let me know.

I finish cleaning my station and washing my hands seconds before the bell, so I'm right behind Lennon as she speed-walks out the door.

Because I'm an addict, I sidle up next to her and match her pace.

"You gonna take that scarf off for me, Leonard?" I taunt. "I want to see my artwork."

Like always, she stays quiet. It makes me madder than usual. I move closer to her and lower my voice.

"Does it hurt? Can you still feel me?"

I can see goosebumps rise on her pale skin and she tries to walk faster; I keep up just fine.

"Want me to give you a matching one on the other side?"

"Shut it, Macon," she whispers, her voice quiet but full of venom as we walk up to her locker. I lean my shoulder on the locker next to hers as she undoes her padlock. She turns her body, so I can't see the combination, but I already know it's her mom's birthday. I open my mouth to tell her as much, just as some prick from the football team moves next to her.

"Hey, Lennon," he says, and his grin shows off two stupid dimples that I know for a fact the girls in school die over. Lennon's shy smile tells me she's no different.

"Hey, Eric," she says back. She hugs her bag to her chest and looks down, then back up at him through her lashes, and I can't hold back my scoff.

"Don't you have practice, Masters?" I cut in, and he flicks his attention to me. He widens his eyes, tries to give me that universal *bro back off I'm running game* look, but I cock my head to the side and stare him down, instead.

"On the way to practice now," Eric answers. He looks back down at Lennon. "I was hoping maybe I could talk to you for a minute?" He smiles tightly back at me. "*Alone.*"

"Yeah, of course," Lennon says airily, like she's breathless over this douche. "I was just, um..." She shuts her locker and locks it up. "Walk with me?"

He puts his hand at the small of her back, and they head toward the doors that lead to the parking lot.

"Use a condom, Leonard," I call to her, forcing humor into my tone. She glares at me over her shoulder.

"Don't you have a janitor's closet to visit?" Her voice is a hiss, but I laugh and send her a wink.

"Why are you always thinking about my dick, Leonard?"

Her jaw drops and her eyes bounce around the hallway. People are watching, some are giggling behind their hands, and Eric moves his palm from her back to her shoulder, then pulls her body smoothly under his arm. He says something to her, and a soft smile replaces her shocked expression. My chest is on fire. Just before they walk out the doors, I shout something I know will infuriate her.

"Eric, ask Leonard what she's hiding under that scarf." I make sure my voice carries, so everyone can hear me. "Maybe she'll let you see my handiwork."

They both freeze for a second, just long enough that I know my words hit how I wanted, then they continue out the doors without a backward glance.

I make my way through the parking lot and head straight for Sam, Julian, and Casper. The way Sam glowers when she sees me tells me I probably can't use her as a ride to work, and I sure as fuck am not riding in the car with Claire and Lennon.

Sam says something to the guys and then storms off, just as I reach the group.

"The fuck did you do to her this time?" Casper asks with a raised brow. I shrug, but don't answer. I didn't do anything she shouldn't already expect.

"One of you guys wanna give me a lift to work?" I pull my cigarette pack out of my pocket, open it, then sigh when I remember I smoked the rest of my last joint at lunch.

"Why don't you ride with Claire?" Jules asks, holding a fresh joint out for me. I grab my wallet, pull out some cash, then exchange it for the joint.

"Thanks, man," I grumble as I put the joint in my box and slip it back into my pocket. "Can't ride with Claire cause there ain't enough room on her broom."

The guys laugh and Casper hooks a thumb in the direction of his truck.

"I'll drop you at work," he offers. "Gotta leave now, though, cause my shift at the hardware store starts in twenty." He starts walking to his truck and I follow.

"Later, Jules," I call behind me. He waves, and when I turn back around, my eyes land on Lennon's from across the parking lot.

She's facing Eric, and he's talking to her, but her attention is on me. I stare back, and she narrows her eyes, but the moment is broken when Eric reaches down and tucks a stray strand of hair behind her ear. And she fucking beams up at him like he's the second coming of Christ and she's an evangelical Sunday school teacher. I watch in fury as she says something back, then nods, and he leans down and kisses her on the cheek.

On the fucking cheek.

I'm a split second from rushing across the lot and tackling him, but then he walks away, leaving Lennon gazing dazedly at his retreating form.

I want to fucking barf.

I hop in Casper's truck and we're silent for the ten-minute drive. He drops me at the supermarket, and I wait for him to turn the corner before I cross the street and walk the two blocks to the rec center.

I've got to run a boxing class for a bunch of eighth graders, and then I'm gonna work the bag myself until my knuckles bleed.

FOUR

Lennon

"So, what did he say, Lenny? Read it out loud."

There's a Friday night Lifetime movie marathon on Claire's TV, and she sits cross-legged on her bed with a bag of popcorn in her lap. I'm on the air mattress on the floor munching on Oreos. We used to sleep in the same bed when we had sleepovers, but we prefer to have our own space now.

"He asked if I'd go out with him tomorrow," I say, rereading the text message on my phone. I glance back up at Claire. "What do I say?"

"You say yes, dummy. Eric Masters is fucking gorgeous, and he's a running back so you know he's in shape." She winks, and we both laugh. "And *mayyybe* you mention doubling with me and Josh?" Claire bats her eyelashes at me, and I shake my head.

"I thought you guys just made out and he said he '*wasn't lookin' for anything serious right now.*'" I make my voice low and douchey for that last part, making Claire giggle in spite of the shitty topic.

"Yeah, he said that, but doesn't mean we can't still hang

out." She throws some popcorn in her mouth and chews. "And if you date Eric then I have a more accessible way in."

My face drops.

"You are not whoring me out to Eric Masters so you can get more time with Josh," I deadpan.

"I'm not!" she protests. "I didn't tell Eric to ask you out. He likes you. I'm just trying to take advantage of your advantageous situation."

She waggles her eyebrows and I shake my head. She's incorrigible. I don't even know if I like Eric, but I guess going on one date is as good a way as any to find out.

"Fine," I relent, and shoot a text off to Eric. We agree he'll pick me up at 7 pm tomorrow for dinner and a movie. Boring. Standard. Predictable.

"Yay!" Claire squeals, clapping her hands in front of her. Some popcorn spills onto her bed from her bouncing, but she doesn't care. "And your burn is looking better, too. You should be able to cover it with makeup easy."

She gestures to my neck, where my "curling iron burn" is in the early stages of healing. I force a smile.

"Yeah, that's lucky."

"Next time you decide to try and curl your hair, though, maybe let me do it," she adds. "That's what you get for always wearing your hair in a French braid. You don't even know how to work a curling iron."

She laughs at my expense, and I join in, mostly because I'm just glad she and Eric bought my *I'm so clumsy and silly that I accidentally burned myself with a curling iron* story. It's the oldest lie in the book, but because I'm innocent ol' me, they bought it.

It's much better than the *I was mauled by my best friend's delinquent pothead brother, and I maybe liked it a little more than I should have* truth, anyway.

"Wanna go through my closet so I can pick you out

something to wear?" Claire asks, but I immediately shoot her down.

"Claire, you know your clothes don't fit me. My hips are too big, and my boobs are too small." Sometimes I think she offers to do stuff like this just so she can feel better about herself. I work hard to mask the insecurity I feel, especially being best friends with a bombshell like Claire, but it's exhausting.

"I'll wear something of my own. Something *me*. If he doesn't like it..." I shrug, and Claire lets out a dramatic sigh.

"You're no fun."

"I never have been," I say, half-joking. "Why start now?"

"What are you doing Sunday?" My shoulders tighten at her change of subject.

"On Sunday? Nothing. Why would I be doing something on Sunday?" I say it slowly and keep my eyes on the television, but I still worry that it sounds fake. Claire pops more popcorn in her mouth before responding.

"I dunno. Before you set up that date with Eric, you told me you wanted to be home early on Sunday." She takes a sip of her Diet Coke before adding, "I figured that meant you had plans."

"Oh, no. Just some college application stuff."

She hums, buying my lie, and refocuses on the movie. We watch in silence for a while when her phone starts to buzz on her nightstand. I check the time on my own phone. It's one in the morning. Who would be calling her at this time?

I watch her check the Caller ID, and then her face twists with irritation.

"What?" she barks into the receiver, waits a moment, then rolls her eyes. "Put him on, then."

I raise a brow at her, and she mouths, *Macon*. Then she looks at the ceiling as the voice on the other end of the phone tells her something she doesn't like.

Huh. He hasn't ridden with us since Tuesday, and he hasn't so much as looked at me in free period the rest of the week. What's he gotten himself into tonight?

"Why can't one of you bring him?" Claire asks. "Have Sam take him back to her place."

Another pause. Then a groan.

"This is bullshit, Casper."

Casper? I thought she was talking to Macon.

"Yeah, fine," she huffs out. "We'll be there in fifteen."

She hangs up the phone and gets off her bed, stomping toward the door.

"C'mon," she says as she leaves the room. "We gotta go pick up the dumbass."

Two minutes later, I'm sitting in the passenger seat of Claire's car, wearing nothing but sleep shorts, my oversized Fleetwood Mac tee, and flip flops. No bra. No panties. No braid. She drives all the way across town in silence, her fingers white-knuckled on the steering wheel, her face scrunched into an angry scowl.

I want to ask what's going on, where we're going, but I don't.

We take Old Courthouse Highway out of town, heading toward the fairgrounds. There's no fair right now, and the racetrack only runs on Thursdays and Saturdays. It's Friday. When Claire pulls up on one of the dirt roads that runs the perimeter of the property and turns off her headlights, my worries are confirmed.

Freaking Macon. I swear, if we get arrested for trespassing, I will murder him.

"Don't tell me we have to hop the fence."

Claire doesn't respond. She just surveys the fence until she finds what she's looking for. Without talking, she marches up to a section of chain-link, crouches down, and pulls it up, creating a four-foot hole.

"In you go," she says flatly. I stare at her blankly. No way in hell does she expect me to crawl through that hole. I'm not breaking and entering. I'm not going to freaking jail. I tighten my lips and shake my head no. She sighs, then wordlessly turns and crawls through the hole herself.

Great. Now I'm a bad friend.

Freaking Macon.

I sulk up to the fence, pull up the broken section, and crawl under, getting my knees and feet and pajamas filthy with dirt. I jog to catch up with Claire as she makes her way to a big building. It's usually the livestock barn when the fair is here, but instead of going inside, she weaves her way around the back. The muffled voices grow louder and louder until we run almost smack into a group of Macon's friends.

The bad kids, basically.

Chris Casper, the guy Claire was on the phone with, spots us immediately and hurries toward us.

"Hey," he says quickly, "follow me."

He turns and leads us to another, smaller building, and then behind it, where we find Julian, kneeling on the ground next to Macon.

Macon, who has a bloody lip and a bruised cheek, and is currently lying in the dirt. The whole area smells strongly of vomit and weed, and I choke back the reflex to gag.

"What the fuck is he on?" Claire asks, putting her hands on her hips and staring daggers at Macon. At her voice, he opens his eyes and tries to focus on us, then lets out a slow gurgling laugh. The sound makes my skin crawl, and I wrap my arms around my torso to try to avoid shaking.

"Fuck off, Claire," he slurs. "Get the fuck outta here."

"Just beer and weed," Julian pipes up, answering Claire's question, but she shakes her head.

"It's never just beer and weed anymore," she says, and my head jolts back.

"What?" I say, bouncing my eyes between Claire and Julian, then Macon. "What do you mean 'it's never just beer and weed'?" They ignore me.

"It was this time," Casper says. "I swear. I was fucking watching him."

Macon groans and curls into the fetal position just as Sam creeps around the corner. Claire catches sight of her and juts out her finger, pointing right at her face.

"You," she growls. "What the fuck did you give him?"

"Nothing he didn't want," she snarks back. Macon groans again, then laughs.

"Nothing I didn't want, Claire," he spits out.

"You're so fucking stupid, Macon," Claire says, disgust dripping from every syllable, and Macon laughs. He just keeps laughing and groaning, alternating between the two. It's such a disturbing sound that it makes me want to cry, but Claire stomps up to him and kicks him hard in the shoulder. He coughs out a laugh.

"Chill, Claire," Julian says, and I step forward.

"C'mon, Claire." I put my hand on her shoulder. "Let's just get him home."

Claire shrugs off my hand and kicks Macon again, harder this time, and he grunts, rolling his face into the dirt. He mumbles something that sounds like *leave me the fuck alone,* and Claire lets out a sardonic, hollow laugh.

"Next time, do us all a favor and OD," she hisses, and my jaw drops.

"Claire," I gasp, but she doesn't even look at me. Instead, she looks at Casper. "I'm taking your truck. I'm not letting him puke in my car. Sober the fuck up and bring my car to me in the morning."

She tosses Casper her keys, and he does the same, not even

bothering to argue, then she just turns and walks away.

"She's such a fucking bitch," Macon says into the dirt.

"I know, man." Julian grunts as he uses Macon's floppy, useless arm to try and hoist him over his shoulder. He manages to get Macon in a fireman-type carry and slowly starts in the direction Claire stormed off. "Fuck, you gotta lay off the brownies, bro."

Macon snorts and mumbles something like *fucking stacked, dick.* Julian just rolls his eyes and pats Macon's thigh. Casper and I walk quietly alongside Julian, listening to him pant and heave as Macon hangs lifeless. I hate it. I can't stop searching Macon's face to make sure he's breathing.

"She didn't mean that," I whisper to the guys, to myself. "She doesn't want Macon to OD." She couldn't have meant that. She doesn't know the gravity of what she said.

The guys stay quiet, and Casper glances at me. Gives me an apologetic look. Like I'm naïve. Like I don't know my best friend. And I say nothing.

Julian and Casper have to lay Macon out flat and pull him through the hole in the fence. If the situation weren't so fucked up, it might be funny. Then they lift him carefully and slide him into the bed of the truck. Claire is already sitting in the driver's seat with the radio blaring.

"Hey, Len, could you—" Casper starts, but I'm already pulling myself into the bed of the truck with Macon. I give Casper a tight smile, and he mouths a thank you.

"You're gonna be cold," Julian says, then pulls off his hoodie and hands it to me. I take it gratefully and pull it on. It's a nice night, but driving down the road in the open bed of a truck is going to be freezing. I don't even care that the hoodie smells like weed.

"Thanks, Julian. Chris. Just...thanks."

"You can call me Casper, Lennon," Casper says, and I smile, just as Claire puts the truck in drive and takes off.

I position myself next to Macon with my back against the cab, then try to maneuver him so he's lying on his side. At my touch, I feel his body vibrate. I rub his arm lightly to try and comfort him, and he inches his way up, so his head is in my lap.

I move my hand from his arm to his curls and gently run my fingers through them. I've always wanted to see what his hair felt like. It's impossibly soft. So much so that I'm almost jealous. He makes a sound like a whimper, then presses his face into my lower belly. I can feel his breath through my shorts, heating the spot between my legs, and I freeze.

"Hmmm," he hums against my body, then inhales deeply, making me blush crimson. He slides one of his hands up the leg of my shorts, and I slap my hand over his, just as the tips of his fingers graze my naked hip. He lets out a bark of laughter, then passes out.

I keep my fingers on his pulse point the entire drive back to his house.

When Claire pulls the truck up to the curb and gets out, she comes back and hoists herself up on the back tire, scowling at Macon.

"How are we going to get him inside?" I whisper.

"Leave him out here," she says. Her voice is tired. Unfeeling.

"We gotta keep an eye on him, though," I reason, and she shrugs.

"Let him choke on his own vomit."

"Jesus Christ, Claire. Quit saying stuff like that."

She hops back off the tire and turns toward the house.

"I'm going to bed," she says as she walks away. "If you want to stay with the druggie, be my guest."

I just gape at her until she disappears behind the front door.

After a while, I drift asleep with my back against the truck cab and Macon's face resting on my thighs. The sun is just starting to rise when I'm awoken by the faintest touch stroking my neck.

I flutter my eyes open and am met with Macon's piercing blue ones. I hold still as he runs his fingers over the bite mark he left on Monday night.

"*Astraea*," he whispers, dropping his eyes to the bruise on my neck. He moves his hand from my neck to my hair and twirls a strand around his index finger. "Sweet, sweet Lennon Capri."

He locks his eyes with mine and we just sit there, staring. It's the weirdest feeling, this connection. This *spark*. I'm barely close to understanding it when he jolts up quickly, throws his torso over the side of the truck, and pukes everywhere.

FIVE

Lennon

I left Claire's early on Saturday, under the guise of wanting to "prep for my date."

Really, I just didn't want to run into Macon.

I'm still shook from the whole scene on Friday night. Claire's behavior. Macon's..._whatever._ I don't know how to process it all.

My date with Eric went fine. We got along really well. We went to dinner at a steakhouse in Suffolk, then out to see the new blockbuster movie. He put his arm around me in the theater and walked me to my door. Kissed me on the cheek before I went inside. Asked me to go to a party with him next weekend.

For Claire's sake, I agreed.

Today is the day I've really been looking forward to, though. Sunday.

I double check my appearance in the mirror. My black slacks and light gray flutter-sleeved blouse are perfect, down to the creases. My nude pumps make me feel a little older than I am. My hair, of course, is in its usual braid.

It might be overkill for this interview, but I want to make a good impression.

I grab my leather satchel with my resumé and portfolio, and make myself walk, instead of run, to my car. As soon as I turn it on, my phone hooks up to the Bluetooth and Stevie Nicks's voice floats through the speakers.

I take a minute to rest my head back on the seat and soak it in. I love my car. I love driving. I only ride with Claire because she doesn't like being a passenger unless she's drunk. If it were up to me, I'd drive everywhere.

I put the car in reverse and pull out of my driveway, then turn in the direction of downtown. After about fifteen minutes, I'm pulling into the parking lot next to an old brick building. It used to be the Franklin Elementary School, but when they built a new one, about ten years ago, this building was purchased and turned into a rec center. It doesn't look like much from the outside, but it's a community staple.

I take three deep breaths, check my makeup in the mirror, then head inside. As soon as I step into the office, I'm greeted by the owner.

"You must be Lennon," James Billings says. "Your guidance counselor called me on Friday. Come on in."

"Thank you," I say with a genuine smile as he ushers me into one of the chairs in front of his desk. His desk is stacked with papers and his bookshelf is just as cluttered. A single, lonely fern sits on top of a filing cabinet, and there are framed pictures everywhere. James and his husband, Hank, who also happens to be my art teacher, smile happily at the camera. In some, they're surrounded by kids from the center. In others, it's just them.

"Did your guidance counselor tell you about the program?" James asks, pulling my attention away from the photos. I nod eagerly.

"She did. You're starting some art classes for the kids. You're looking for volunteers to help teach them."

"That's right," he says. "Before now, it's been athletic stuff. Boxing, dance, yoga. But my husband Hank has been campaigning for art classes for the last few years, and we finally got some funding for it. We're excited."

"I'm excited. I'd really love to be part of it," I say honestly.

"Your old after-school activity ended, is that correct?"

"Yes. I used to be on the Scholastic Bowl team, but our advisor retired last year and none of the other teachers stepped up to take over." I shrug. "They're all pretty loaded with work already, as you know."

He sighs and nods in agreement. Since his husband is a teacher, he gets it.

"Well, the art classes will be Tuesdays and Thursdays. You'd be good to teach classes—painting, drawing, whatever else you decide—on those days?"

"Yes, definitely." I'm so excited I could leap from my seat. I have to press my palms to my legs to keep them from bouncing.

"Great." He claps his hands together and stands up. "Let me show you around."

"Wait," I say, confused, "you don't want to see my resumé?"

He chuckles. "Lennon, we're thrilled to have you. Your guidance counselor gave me a rave review, and if you say you can teach art to middle schoolers, I believe you. As long as you're okay with it, you'll start Tuesday."

My smile is huge, making my cheeks hurt, but I nod frantically anyway.

"Yes, I'd love to. I can't wait."

"Well, let's do a tour." He waves his hand out the door, and I follow.

James takes me through the gym, where the various athletic activities take place, introducing me to any volunteers and kids we meet along the way. He shows me the rooms they use for yoga, tutoring, and a few other things. The cafeteria. The storage rooms. And then finally, the room where I'll be teaching.

I love it before we even step through the door.

It doesn't matter that it's filled with a bunch of mismatched tables and smells of dust.

I can already see it full of kids with paint brushes and pencils making art.

"Does it matter what I teach first?" I ask, glancing at the shelves in the back of the room holding supplies.

"It's totally up to you," James says, then gestures to the back. "Those are the things we were able to get with the grant money, as well as some stuff that was donated. Feel free to dig through and make a plan."

I nod, already walking toward the shelves. He tells me he's going to head back to the office then asks if I'll be alright by myself. I tell him yes, without looking up from a box full of paints. He leaves, and I spend the next hour sorting. Planning. Organizing.

There's a good amount of stuff in here. Enough for me to cover different mediums for probably the next few months. That's likely Hank's doing. I wonder why he didn't tell me about the volunteering positions. He knows I paint, but I had to learn of this opportunity through my guidance counselor. The thought annoys me briefly, then flits away as I lose myself in art supplies.

I've finished scoping things out and am wandering back the way I came, peeking into classrooms as I go, when I hear music coming from a room farther down the hall.

"In Your Eyes" by Peter Gabriel.

It's one of my favorites.

I make my way there on light feet, not wanting to disturb

the person in the room, but when I peek around the door, the breath wooshes from my lungs, and I freeze, stunned.

It's Macon.

Shirtless Macon.

Shirtless Macon working behind a pottery wheel.

The first thing I notice is that the front of his curly hair is pulled back in a little pink butterfly clip, which should look ridiculous, but it doesn't. He's crouched over slightly, and he's chewing on his lip as his focus stays on the wheel between his legs.

I let my eyes trail over his sculpted bare shoulders, to the strip of brown leather hanging around his neck like a necklace. His naked chest is dotted and smudged with gray, and it takes a second for me to realize his left pectoral is covered with a tattoo. I squint at it for a few breaths, trying to make it out. The defined muscle is covered with a clock. And script of some sort, but I can't read it. My attention catches on his small, brown nipples, and something about that makes the hairs on the back of my neck tickle.

I haven't seen Macon shirtless since I was thirteen, he was fifteen, and our parents took us to the beach for the weekend.

He's definitely not built like a fifteen-year-old anymore.

That is *not* the chest of a fifteen-year-old.

I drag my eyes down to the clay he's working and stare at his hands, the surgical scar on his left wrist, his rigid forearms. He's covered in wet, gray clay, and it glistens as he uses deft fingers to shape what looks to be a large bowl. His clay-splattered biceps bulge as he attempts to work the bowl to his liking. It's rough, from what I can tell. Uneven. Kinda floppy. But his determination doesn't waver.

Not until the music starts to skip, and I realize there's an old CD player sitting on a table, just a few feet from the door.

When Macon glances up at the CD player, our eyes meet,

and his flare wide. His hands slip, the bowl folds in on itself, and I turn and run.

"Lennon, wait," he calls from behind me, but I don't stop. I don't even know why I'm running, but I keep going as fast as my heels allow me. He catches up to me in seconds.

I'm almost to an emergency exit when Macon's hand wraps around my arm, covering my skin in cold, slick clay, and he spins me around until my back is pressed against the wall. His eyes frantically search my face, as if first confirming that I am, in fact, Lennon, then he releases my arm and steps back.

"What are you doing here?" he asks. He's not angry, but he's flustered. Like I'm not welcome here. I raise a brow and put my hand on my hip.

"What are *YOU* doing here?"

He puts his hands up, turning them over and back to show off the clay, then gestures to my arm.

"Sorry," he says, referring to the handprint he smudged on my skin. I shrug off his apology.

"I'm going to be volunteering here," I rush out. "Art classes on Tuesdays and Thursdays."

He clamps his eyes shut and drops his head back. He mouths something at the ceiling, then brings his hands up to his head and presses on his temples. I don't tell him that he's gotten clay all over his face and hair. I'm sure he knows.

"What's wrong?" I ask. He's obviously distressed. He shakes his head then hits me with a look I've never seen on his face.

Vulnerable. Anxious. Desperate.

"You gotta swear you'll stay quiet," he says, his voice low and secretive. "You can't tell anyone. Not my mom. Not your dad. Not Claire. Fuck, especially not Claire."

I shake my head. "What on earth are you talking about? What can't I tell them? You planning to smuggle drugs in that bowl?"

He snorts at my joke, but the seriousness returns immediately.

"Swear it," he insists, and I roll my eyes. "Please, Lennon."

"Fine. I won't tell anyone you like to make pottery at the rec center."

"I work here, Len. I teach boxing, run basketball scrimmages, and do janitorial shit throughout the week. And now I teach pottery on Thursdays."

I gape at him. "Huh?"

"I work here," he repeats.

I shake my head. "I thought you worked at the supermarket down the street?"

"Nope. Here. For like three years now."

He grins like he's proud he's stunned me, and I run the information through my head. He works here. Has for years. And his family—everyone, as far as I know—thinks he works in the back at the supermarket. I screw my face up in confusion.

"Why don't you want anyone to know?" I ask, and he blows out a breath.

"Can't you just keep quiet and leave it at that?"

"No. I need to know why I'm keeping this secret."

He studies me for a minute, eyes narrowed, and I narrow mine right back. He sighs like he's over my bullshit, and I grin.

"I started working here because I spray-painted a giant ejaculating dick on the side of James and Hank's house."

My jaw drops and he throws up his gray palms.

"I didn't know who lived there, I swear to god. Was gonna tag up every house on the street, but James caught me on his security camera. Instead of pressing charges, he let me start volunteering here. Then the volunteering turned into an actual paid job, and I quit the supermarket."

"Oh my god," I say, and he smirks.

"That's nothin'," he says. "Wanna know why I'm teaching pottery?"

I nod, because what can I even say? Of course, I want to know.

"You know how I ran my car into the ditch?"

"Yeah..."

"I didn't swerve for a raccoon like I told Mom. I was high as fuck. I called James and he came and got me and had my car towed to the garage. I'm working off the tow charge. I just don't want to bother my mom with this shit. I disappoint her enough as it is."

I can't fully comprehend what I'm hearing. I knew Macon was trouble, but vandalizing houses? Driving while high?

"Macon...you could have gotten killed," I scold. "You could have killed someone else."

"Yeah, I know, okay?" he spits. "It was fucking dumb. I'm a fucking idiot. I know that. James already laid into me. It won't happen again."

The tense set of his jaw and the utter guilt I see in his eyes make me change the subject.

"Why can't you just tell your mom you're working here?" I ask. "You get paid. You don't have to tell her why."

"No," he shakes his head rapidly, "definitely not. She'll ask questions and I'll have to answer them. I can't lie to her face, Len. You know that. And then Claire will find out, and she'll ruin it."

"No, she wo—"

"She *will*, Lennon," he insists, cutting me off. "Claire will fucking ruin it, and she will tell everyone. She'll make it something it's not, and then people will show up here. My friends." He sighs. "I just..."

"This place is important to you," I finish for him. "You want to keep it for yourself."

He doesn't respond, but I know I'm right. And after seeing how Claire behaved on Friday night, I'm also not sure he's wrong about her. It hurts to consider; I feel like I'm betraying my best friend, but I don't blame Macon for wanting to keep this from her.

The thought makes my stomach roil.

"Well," I say, after a minute of silent staring, and hook my thumb toward the exit. "I guess I should probably go."

He flashes me that crooked grin, and I, once again, become very aware of the fact that Macon is shirtless and covered in clay with his hair up in a cute little butterfly clip. I will my cheeks not to flush and keep my eyes fixed firmly above his neck.

"And I should probably get some more practice in; otherwise, those kids are gonna call my ass out on Thursday."

I nod, give him a little wave, and head toward the door. Just before I push it open, Macon calls out to me.

"You gonna let me know why you don't tell anyone you paint?" he asks, and I pivot just enough to see his face.

"Nope," I say with a small smile, "and if you want me to keep your secret, you'll keep mine."

He laughs—a genuine, amused laugh—and it makes my stomach do a little flip thing.

"You'll keep my secret either way," he says confidently.

I purse my lips and study him.

"What makes you so sure?"

His smile grows, and he shakes his head before saying, "because that's just the kind of girl you are, Lennon Capri."

I fold my lips between my teeth, then push through the door, leaving him standing shirtless and clay-covered in the hallway.

SIX

Lennon

On Monday when Claire picks me up, I sling a duffle bag with a week's worth of clothes into her trunk before climbing into the passenger seat.

I caved. She knew I would.

The cab lacks the distinct smell of spearmint, weed, and spice, instead filling my senses with Claire's cucumber melon air-fresheners that she stuck into the vents of the car.

"Morning," Claire says as I buckle my seat belt. "I'm so glad you decided to stay. Mom is too. She got those protein bars and the OJ you like."

My chest warms. I might not want to be at Claire's this week, but Andrea always goes out of her way to make me feel welcome.

"She didn't have to do that," I tell Claire, and she laughs.

"You know how she is. I think she wants you as a daughter. If she could trade you for Macon, I think she totally would."

She says it jokingly, but my brow furrows, bringing me back to the weekend.

Do us all a favor next time and OD.

I try to shake away the cruel sound of her voice, but it still slithers over my skin, cold and disturbing.

"Claire..." I start, then trail off. She glances at me quickly before looking back out the windshield.

"What's up?"

"Friday...when you said it's never just weed and beer..." She sighs, and I watch her jaw tighten as I continue, "What did you mean?"

Her lip curls in disgust. "Mom found cocaine in his room about a month ago."

I gasp, my first thought is why on earth would he have cocaine. My second is how the heck could he afford it. She nods in agreement at my distress.

"I'm pretty sure he's also taking pills, but I don't know what." She shakes her head. "He's not even discreet about it. I've seen him straight up pull a loose pill out of his pocket and take it dry. Told me it was ibuprofen, like he thinks I'm an idiot."

I chew on my cheek and then clamp my eyes shut at the onslaught of thoughts.

"Why is he doing it?" I ask. "He's gotta know the risks."

Claire shrugs like she doesn't really care. "He was born fucked up, Len. Always has been. Like he's got a death wish and doesn't care who he brings down with him."

I stare at her profile. "Could you put him into rehab?"

She scoffs. "And who would pay for it? In case you haven't noticed, Lennon, we're not exactly swimming in money like you."

My jaw drops at the vitriol in her tone, and I don't even know what to say. We're not *swimming in money*. Not at all, but there isn't space for me to talk or correct her because she just trudges forward.

"Besides, you can't force someone to clean up. If they don't want to do it on their own, it won't work."

"Do you think he's depressed? Suicidal?"

She sighs, not saying anything else, but the complete and utter apathy she's displaying makes me physically ill, and I suddenly have the urge to hug Macon.

I stay quiet until we get to the school, then do a quick scan of the senior lot when we park, my eyes stopping and sticking when they land on Macon's group of friends. Casper and Julian are standing with their backs to me, but Macon's tall form is leaning on the trunk of his 1981 Dodge Charger, giving me full view of his wrinkled black tee and holey black jeans. When he first got the car, I thought it was hideous. The black paint was faded in places and the wheel wells were speckled with rust, but Macon was obsessed with it. I have to admit, it looks a heck of a lot better now than it did two years ago.

I watch Macon interact with his friends, looking for I don't even know what, but he laughs and jokes like usual, his crooked smile showing just a tiny peek of white teeth. When Sam sidles up next to him and throws her arms around his waist, my mouth twitches with the need to turn down. She flicks her eyes to me, then whispers something in Macon's ear. His brow furrows slightly, then slowly his full lips spread into a wide grin. His eyes drag up and meet mine, and for the briefest of moments, my breath catches in my throat. Then he says something to Sam, and she cackles in response. Claire's windows are up, and the radio is still on, but I swear I can hear the grating sound of her laugh.

Once again, I'm the subject of one of their lame jokes. Any thought I had that Macon might be offering an olive branch turns to ash.

"God, I hate that girl," Claire says, making me jump slightly. I turn toward the driver's seat and see that she's watching the same thing I am.

"I'm pretty sure she's the one giving Macon all that shit. Thinking she can drug him up enough to love her or something." Claire sneers, then looks away, turning off the engine. "She'll be his dealer forever. Macon doesn't have a heart."

At lunch, Josh and Eric surprise us by dropping their trays onto the table next to Claire and me. Josh throws his arm over Claire's shoulder, and I have to stifle a laugh at the excited way her eyes flare. She's trying so hard not to giggle, and it's adorable.

"Ladies," Josh says, flashing his Golden Boy grin at me before focusing all his attention on Claire. Eric sends me a small smile and mouths, "hi." I mouth, "hi" back and then look down at my plate to hide the too-wide smile threatening to break.

"Hey, guys!" For as nervous as she is, Claire's voice is smooth as silk. If you didn't know her, you'd never be able to tell her heart is beating in overdrive. "How was your weekend?"

"Mine was great," Eric pipes up, sending me another smile, but this one is more suggestive, and it makes my cheeks heat.

"Mine, too," Josh says. "I know yours was good."

Claire laughs, gearing up to flirt, and I tune it out. *I know yours was good* tells me all I need to know about the direction of their conversation.

"Are you thinking of coming to our game Friday?" Eric asks me as our friends talk. He darts his eyes from my face to his plate and back. He's nervous, and that's flattering. It eases the tension in my shoulders a bit.

"I am," I say softly. "The first home game of the year? I'll be there with my school spirit bells on."

He grins and holds my gaze, making the tips of my ears and the back of my neck prickle with nerves. Having his undivided attention is exciting, but unsettling. I hold my breath.

"Would you want to wear my away jersey?" he asks, and my jaw drops.

Me. Wear the star running back's jersey? To a home game?

"You don't have to," he backpedals, misreading my shock for disinterest. "I just thought I'd ask. It's cool."

"No, no," I stutter out. "It's not... I'm not..." I close my eyes and take a breath, then start over. "I would love to wear your jersey. Thank you."

When I open my eyes again, his smile is stretched over his face and it's contagious. I laugh once, then again, and he bites his lower lip.

"Okay, cool. I'll bring it tomorrow for you."

"Okay," I breathe out, then look back at my sandwich. "Sounds good."

Josh and Eric leave, saying they have to spend the rest of lunch with their coach, and in their absence, Claire's stare is hot on the side of my face.

"What?" I ask, meeting her wide eyes.

"Eric Masters asked you to wear his jersey on Friday," she deadpans.

"I know." I take a bite of my sandwich, stalling. "Weird, right?"

"I mean, you went on one date. *One.* He kissed you *on the cheek.* And now you're wearing his jersey." She balls up a napkin and tosses it on top of her uneaten lunch with a huff.

"I know..." I'm not exactly sure how to respond to this, and at my silence, her shoulders drop, and she spins in her seat, so her knees are touching my leg.

"I'm sorry," she breathes out. "I'm jealous and acting like a bitch."

I laugh. "You want to wear Eric's jersey?" I joke, and she rolls her eyes, nudging my leg.

"I just feel like I'm getting nowhere with Josh. I like him so damn much, Len, but I feel like I'm competing for his attention with basically every other girl at school." She shuts her eyes and groans. "Ugh, I sound so fucking disgusting."

"No," I say, and pat her shoulder lamely, "you only sound a little disgusting."

Her eyes spring open and her mouth drops on a loud, surprised laugh, then she bats my hand away. I laugh with her, and then shake my head and hit her with a serious look.

"I know you've always liked Josh but remember your worth. You are so friggen great, Claire. You deserve someone who makes you feel *seen*, not glanced over."

She bites her lip and looks at her hands, which are now folded in her lap. I place my palm on her fists and squeeze.

"Demand to be treated the way you deserve, and walk away if he doesn't give you that," I say sternly.

"It's not that easy," she whispers, and I squeeze her hands again.

"It should be."

She takes a deep breath, gives me a tight, closed-lipped smile, then turns back to her food.

"So how did Sunday go?" she asks, changing the subject. I freeze. *What does she know about Sunday?* "Did you get your college stuff done? You still wanting to go to VCU?"

I release a slow breath. Right. I told her I was doing "college stuff."

For a second, I want to come clean with her about what I was really doing. Claire would gladly keep my secret from my dad; I've kept much more damning things for her in the past. There's no reason to hide my painting, or my new volunteer position at the rec center, from her.

But then I remember Macon.

His plea for me not to tell anyone, *especially* Claire.

Macon, who doesn't deserve my loyalty in place of Claire.

Macon, who goes out of his way to make me feel like crap.

Macon, who is struggling with...*something*.... Who obviously needs...*something*.

And then I remember Claire's words on Friday. Her behavior this morning. And I make my decision without further hesitation.

"Yeah, VCU is my first choice." I try to make my voice excited. "But I'm probably going to apply to a few others just in case."

"Noooo," she whines, "no out of state. I can't afford it and we have to go together. No way I can brave college without my bestie."

"You could always apply for scholarships," I tell her, and she snorts. We've had this conversation before.

"With my GPA? Schools are more likely to pay me to *NOT* go to their school."

"Well, if you get enough of *that* money, you can pay your way anywhere!"

She gasps and swats my arm again, the earlier tension about Josh forgotten, and my guilty silence is buried just enough that I can ignore it for now.

SEVEN

Lennon

I'M WIPING DOWN TABLES AFTER MY SECOND ART CLASS AT THE rec center when I feel, rather than see, someone leaning on the doorframe.

I look up and find Macon. His sleeveless shirt is covered in clay, and his hair is back in that little butterfly clip. My face stays blank, not at all excited to see him, and it makes him smirk.

"Why watercolors?" he asks randomly, and I shrug.

"Why do you care?" I ask, then stand up straight and cross my arms over my chest.

I've been staying at Claire's all week, and I've barely seen him. He was absent from class Monday and Tuesday, and when I saw him running a basketball scrimmage at the center on Tuesday night, he barely spared me a second glance. Today and yesterday, he didn't even breathe in my direction, except for grunting a stupid laugh when Sam made a comment about my outfit in the hallway.

I don't know why it stings, but it does.

"Curious," he says with a shrug. The shrug makes the defined muscles in his arm jump, grabbing my eye, and I notice

71

a few smears of dried clay on his bicep. It makes my throat tighten, and I have to swallow a few times before speaking.

"It's unforgiving," I say honestly, and he cocks his head to the side in interest. "It's a beautiful medium, and the techniques can be difficult to master. And when you make a mistake, it can't always be easily erased. Most of the time, you have to build on it or transform your original design to accommodate it."

I shrug and go back to wiping down the table. I don't mention anything about my mom.

"Like life," Macon muses, and I pause, considering his comparison.

"Yeah, I guess. Kind of like life."

"So, you like watercolors because they're beautiful, difficult to master, and unforgiving?"

"Yeah," I say. I grin at the table, refusing to look up at him. "It's my love medium."

I hear him hum and go silent. When I look back up at the doorway, he's gone.

"How do I look?" Claire asks, then spins in a circle so I can survey her appearance. Tight black jeans, tight green crop top, and dark brown curls cascading in glossy ringlets down her back.

"Gorgeous, as usual."

She smiles, and the painted numbers on her cheeks pop. Josh's football number in our school colors. She tried to get me to paint Eric's on mine, but I put my foot down.

I'm already wearing the jersey. I don't need face-painted numbers, too.

Speaking of the jersey...

"So, you gonna put it on?" Claire gestures to the wad of

mesh fabric I'm holding balled up in my lap, then laughs. "Just put it on, Len. Stop being ridiculous."

I huff and stand up from where I was sitting on her bed, then tug the jersey over my head. It's big around my shoulders and arms, but a little more snug around my hips and backside. It's also long, reaching about mid-thigh.

"I know you won't, but you could probably rock that as a hot mini dress," Claire says as she studies my outfit. I roll my eyes and hold my tongue. "Here, let me just..."

Claire moves me around and messes with the hem of the jersey, adjusting the length and cinching it at the back somehow so that it fits better.

"How'd you do that?" I ask as I spin in front of the mirror. I actually really like the way I look in this jersey, which I wasn't expecting. It makes me smile bigger. My dark wash high-waisted jeans look great too, adding to the illusion of an hourglass silhouette.

"Hair tie," Claire answers. "Simple."

"Huh." I check myself out once more, fingering my loose French braid. I tied a green and gold ribbon around the end, and Claire put shimmery gold shadow on my eyelids. "It looks kinda good, doesn't it?"

Claire snorts. "We're hot. Let's go."

I follow Claire down the stairs, noting the eerie quiet coming from behind Macon's closed door. He's not the type to show up to football games. Is he at the center tonight?

I shouldn't even care.

I don't care. Not at all.

"We're leaving, Mom!" Claire yells, as we hit the landing.

"Be back by curfew," Andrea shouts back from somewhere in the living room.

"Always am, Mom. Love you."

"Love ya, Drea," I call out, and Andrea pokes her head into the hallway with a smile.

"Love you both," she says. "Have fun and be safe," she adds, and I follow Claire out the door.

The bleachers are already packed when we get to the field. It's a warm night, but there's something decidedly *fall* about high school football games. Makes me want to wear a scarf and drink cider. It makes me want to paint a forest full of reds and oranges and yellows.

I trail behind Claire as she weaves up the bleachers. She takes a seat dead in the middle, right on the 50-yard line, then pats the empty spot on the aluminum bench next to her. I plop down gracelessly and try to ignore the prickling feeling of eyes on me.

I know it shocks people. It shocks me, too, honestly.

Me. Lennon Washington. Wearing Eric Masters's football jersey. Surreal.

Claire chatters on about the game, the other team, the party after. I smile and nod and chime in when expected. When our team takes the field, she stands up and claps, and I do the same. When Josh throws our first touchdown, Claire jumps up and down along with the crowd, while I celebrate in a much more subdued manner.

When Eric rushes for a touchdown, I cheer along with everyone else, proud to be wearing his jersey. When he runs along the sideline of the field, stops in front of Claire and me, and points directly at me with the football in his hand, my heart flips, my breath hitches, and I can't stop the smile from spreading over my face. A ref blows a whistle, Eric tosses the football to him, and then he gives me one last look—one last flirtatious smile, beaming through the facemask of his helmet —before turning around and jogging back to his teammates.

"*Whaaaaat*," Claire says with a grin, "was *that?*"

I shrug and bite my lip, trying to tame my giddy expression. Claire nudges me with her elbow and giggles, which starts me giggling, and it's not until my laughter has calmed that I notice

Chris Casper watching us intently from the bottom row of the bleachers.

The rest of the game goes by quickly, and we win 48 to 21. Claire drags me off the bleachers and convinces me to wait with her in the parking lot for the guys to come out of the locker room. It feels like an hour goes by before Josh and Eric come waltzing out, bags slung over their shoulders and hair wet from their post-game showers.

"Good game," Claire says as Josh slides his hand over her shoulders. "You did great."

"Thanks, babe," Josh says, and Claire nearly swoons at the pet name.

"Are you coming to the party?" Eric asks, and having his full attention makes me nervous. In a good way, I think.

He reaches toward me and lightly grabs the hem of his jersey, rubbing the material between his thumb and forefinger before giving me a soft smile. My cheeks warm and I have a hard time keeping eye contact. I smile and nod, then bounce my gaze between his face and Claire's.

"We're going to head there now," I tell him. His answering smile is beautiful. Genuinely happy. Genuinely interested. I clasp my hands together behind my back to keep from fidgeting.

"You want to just follow us?" Josh jumps in, and Claire and I agree.

The ride to Josh's house is short and full of nervous energy. Claire won't stop tapping the steering wheel. Even I have to restrain myself from messing with the hem of Eric's jersey, touching the place that he touched just moments before.

I think I have a crush. Maybe.

I'm excited. Having Eric's attention on me is new and thrilling, though a bit unnerving. And confusing. I can't quite wrap my head around it, but I think I like it.

I picture the way he looked, and the way I felt, when he

stood on the football field and pointed at me with the football. My heart speeds up as I replay his actions when he kissed me on the cheek after our first date and think about his brown eyes and his kind smile.

But then those rich brown eyes and kind smile morph into ice blue orbs and a troublemaking smirk. It shocks me at first, and I fist my hands on my thighs. I see Macon, shirtless and covered in wet clay, with his unruly mop of curls pulled back with a sparkly pink butterfly clip.

The unwanted invasion makes me angry, and I screw my eyes shut to try and force him out of my head.

"You okay?" Claire's voice makes me jump, and I whip my eyes to the driver's seat. She's darting her attention back and forth between me and the road, her face etched with concern. "Do you have a headache? Are you carsick? I have ibuprofen."

I shake my head and force a smile.

"No, thank you," I breathe out. "I think I'm just a little tired."

"You want to go home?" she asks, but her tone is reluctant. Even if I wanted to, I couldn't disappoint her like that.

"No," I say brightly, "but thank you for offering."

Claire smiles then, and bounces a little in her seat as we turn onto Josh's road.

"Just a few hours, okay? We'll be home before curfew."

I roll my eyes. "You're never home before curfew."

Her grin is conspiratorial. "We'll sneak in, and no one will be the wiser."

I shake my head. She gives Macon so much shit, but she's just as bad about some things. She's just better at hiding it.

We park on the road in front of Josh's house, and I hold my hand out for the keys the moment Claire cuts the engine. She eagerly slaps them in my palm. We climb out of the car and lock arms, then make our way up the long drive. Josh and Eric pulled into the driveway, so it's just Claire and me.

We enter the house and go to the kitchen, just like last time, and Claire pulls a seltzer from the fridge. I'll come back for a glass of water in a bit. We do a lap. Claire flirts and gossips with whomever she can. I smile and nod, fielding questions about my relationship with Eric. People who usually don't pay any attention to me are suddenly very interested in my life and who I might possibly be dating.

"We're just friends," I repeat, and each time I'm met with skeptical looks. I don't acknowledge them. How can I elaborate on that question for them when I'm not even sure myself?

When Eric and Josh find us, I'm relieved for all of fifteen seconds. Then Josh whisks Claire away to do *whatever*, and I'm left alone with Eric. My back is to the wall by the stairwell and he's leaning over me, engulfing me in the scent of leather that tickles my nose.

"Thanks again for coming tonight," he says, his eyes intent on mine. "I think I played better knowing you were in the stands."

I laugh and roll my eyes. It's so cheesy, and so obviously a line.

"Yeah, okay," I tease. "Like the star running back needs a good luck charm."

He bites his lip with a grin and shrugs. "You never know. It felt different."

I glance down and calm the twitch of my lips to stretch wider. Being complimented by Eric is weird. Being flirted with is even weirder. It fills my stomach with butterflies and my brain with fuzz.

"I guess I should come to some more games, then," I say quietly. "Just in case."

He reaches out and toys with the end of my braid, brushing the ribbon through his fingers. I brace for a tug that doesn't come.

"I'd like that," he whispers, and leans forward slowly.

He's going to kiss me. I panic.

I lick my lips and dart my eyes around the room. People are watching. A lot of people. I don't want my first actual kiss with him to be here in this crowded room full of gawkers. My shoulders tighten and anticipate his lips on mine, but they never land.

Instead, I jump forward with a yelp as cold liquid sloshes down my back. The smell of beer fills my nostrils. I whip my eyes to the stairs to find Sam cackling down at me, an empty red cup in her hands.

"Oooops," she slurs. I rapidly scan behind her for an ice blue glare, but I don't find one.

"Real nice, Sam," Eric growls, and he brushes his hand down my back in an attempt to swipe the beer off. He's unsuccessful. The alcohol has already saturated the jersey and my tank top underneath. "Fuck, my jersey is going to reek now."

"It was an accident," she purrs. "But the smell might be an improvement for Leonard. You should thank me." He glares at her as she slinks away.

"I'll go clean up in the bathroom," I say under my breath, and Eric looks back down at me with sympathetic eyes.

"Upstairs, end of the hall on the right," he tells me with a nod. "I'll find you something else to put on."

"Thanks."

I push through the crowd of people and weave my way up the stairs toward the bathroom. No sign of Sam, thank god. I close the bathroom door behind me and lock it, then rest my head on the wall. Closing my eyes, I take a few steadying breaths. What a disaster.

But I'm strangely relieved, in a way. At least I avoided the public kiss.

I slip the jersey over my head, then my camisole, and stick them under one of the sinks on the dual vanity. I soak them in warm water and wring them out, trying to at least get some of the beer out before they're washed. I glance in the mirror and huff a laugh.

Ridiculous.

I'm standing in a nude bra in the quarterback's bathroom, cleaning beer out of the running back's away jersey because my best friend's brother's bitchy girlfriend decided to dump her drink on me. For the second time in as many weeks, too.

Luckily, Sam missed most of my braid, and the band of my bra isn't too wet. I dig through drawers until I find a washcloth, wet it with warm water, then run it over the back of my neck and shoulders as best as I can.

I smell like Bud Lite.

I'm attempting to clean the middle of my back when a door on the opposite side of the bathroom, not the door I came in, opens.

"Someone's in here," I start to say, but the person steps in anyway and shuts the door behind him. Macon.

I drop the washcloth and cover my chest.

"Get out, Macon," I hiss. He leans back on the door with a smirk, then hooks his thumb over his shoulder.

"Josh's room," he says, explaining the second door.

"Why were you in Josh's room?" I ask, then frown. He distracted me. "Get out."

"I sell weed to him sometimes," he says, like it's nothing, then turns toward the toilet. He reaches for the button on his jeans, and I whip myself around and throw my hands over my face. The sound of him peeing infuriates me, but also makes me feel...*strange*. Odd at the weird intimacy of the moment. I don't like it.

"Gross, Macon!" I shriek. "You could have warned me. You could have asked me to leave."

He flushes and laughs, then I hear the sink turn on as he washes his hands.

Thank *god* he's washing his hands.

"You can turn around now," he drawls, so I do, covering my chest once more. "It's just a dick, *Astraea*."

I scoff. "You can leave now," I sneer.

He doesn't budge. Instead, he takes a step toward me.

"Nice bra," he says with a chuckle, and I narrow my eyes at him.

"Yeah, well your girlfriend dumped beer on me," I spit, then bristle more as his smirk widens. "I have to wash my freaking clothes in the sink, and Eric is finding me something else to wear."

The smile drops off his face, his blue eyes flaring with irritation.

"Eric Masters is a tool," he says, and I grit my teeth, my jaw so tense that it makes my head hurt. He flicks his eyes to the sink, where the jersey is soaking, then back to me. "And you look like Tool Bag Groupie Barbie in that jersey."

My jaw drops and my hands turn into fists. I'm practically vibrating with fury.

"Shut *up*," I growl, and he takes another step toward me. "I do not."

"You do," he says plainly, then drags his eyes from my face to my chest. "You look much better without it."

I can feel the flush spread from my ears to my neck, then to my collarbone. I can't tell if it's anger or embarrassment or both.

"Fight back," he says when he looks back at my face. I can feel his eyes on the tightness of my jaw. "Use your fucking voice, *Leonard*."

My fingernails are cutting into my palms with how hard I'm clenching them, my chest is tight from the force of my locked arms. I stay quiet, and he takes another forceful step toward me, leaving only inches between our bodies.

"Quit being so fucking nice." He growls. His taunting voice

is low but full of irritation. Of anger. "Are there no real thoughts in that pretty head? Gonna stay quiet when you fuck the football team, too? You just a polite groupie Barbie, Leonard?"

He cocks his head to the side, his eyes bouncing between mine, then reaches up and tugs hard on my braid.

"Nice, polite, *boring*, gang bang Barbie."

I explode, slapping his hand away and giving his chest a hard shove, so he falls back a step.

"Shut *up*, Macon," I spit. "Do you ever shut up? You're such an asshole. Just because I give a shit how other people feel. You wouldn't understand. You're not capable of empathy. You're so fucking selfish."

I take another step forward and shove him again.

"If you weren't so busy getting high and screwing everything that walks, maybe you'd care a little more about being nice. But you don't care about anyone but yourself. You're a miserable asshole. You just want everyone else to be miserable with you, and I hate you. I. Hate. You."

My chest is heaving, my eyes narrowed into slits, and I watch as Macon's nostrils flare and his jaw tightens. He gives his head a small shake, then another, before descending upon me. His hands grip me hard at the waist and his mouth attacks mine, searing me with a forceful kiss.

My hands fist into his shirt as I'm hit with a wave of lust and confusion strong enough to knock me off my feet. When his tongue swipes over my lower lip, I gasp and shove him away.

"What the hell was that?" I wipe my mouth with the back of my hand and glare at him. His eyes stay on my lips. "What the hell, Macon!"

"You're finally acting on your impulses with me, Lennon," he grinds out, panting. "Don't stop now."

There's something about the way his attention stays on my

lips, like he's desperate for them, or the way his voice is rough with an emotion I don't quite understand, that makes my feet move without my permission. My fingers slide into his hair as his big hands wrap around me once more. Our bodies slamming together; our mouths colliding gracelessly.

There's nothing *nice* about this kiss. It's not polite or gentle. It's rough, almost violent.

His hands grab at my bare skin, squeezing and pulling in a way that will leave red marks. It hurts as much as it feels good. His tongue invades my mouth, tangling with mine like it's fighting for dominance. Conquering.

I pull hard at his curls, and he growls into my mouth, pushing me back up against the door and pulling hard on the waistband of my jeans with one hand as the other palms my breast, tweaking my nipple through the fabric.

My brain is static.

My heart pounds in my rib cage, and I release a whimper as he undoes the buttons on my jeans and rubs his fingers over my underwear. I widen my stance and suck in my stomach on instinct, giving him room to explore.

He slides his hand into the cotton fabric, and I press my head back to the door, my mouth dropping open. He drags his teeth over my jaw and groans when he swipes his fingers through me. I don't know when it happened, but I'm wet, and my body tingles at his touch. He sucks and laps at my neck as he presses a finger into me, and I release a strangled, nearly silent cry.

"Yes?" he asks against my skin.

"Please," I whisper back.

There's so much happening everywhere that I'm not sure what specifically I just consented to. If it's to the slow way he's started pumping in and out of me, or to the way he just pulled down the cup of my bra, exposing my breast. If it's to more.

I don't care. In this moment, I want it all.

He crouches, leaving hot, open-mouth kisses on my shoulder, collarbone, and the swell of my breast. When his lips close over my nipple, I whimper again and pull tighter on his hair, pressing him into my body. I feel him start to slip a second finger inside me when there's a knock on the door at my back. Macon and I freeze.

"Lennon?" Eric's deep voice comes from the other side of the door. Macon's eyes meet mine; mine are flared wide with fear while his are hard and narrowed. He shakes his head no, but I ignore him.

"Yeah," I answer, and Macon removes his hand from my pants quickly. My brow furrows as I study him. He folds his arms over his chest and glares at me as I fix my bra and rebutton my jeans.

"I brought you a shirt," Eric says. "I took it from Josh's sister's room. She's at college, so I don't think she'll care."

I can hear the smile in his voice, and my stomach twists. I might be sick. I feel so guilty, and when I look back at Macon, I know he can tell.

"Thank you," I say to Eric. "Give me just a second."

Macon takes a step toward me and grabs my waist. I shake my head and scrunch my eyebrows, mouthing *NO*, but he ignores me.

"He doesn't touch you," he commands in my ear. Goosebumps prickle my skin, my body wanting to melt back into him, but I shove his chest instead.

"You don't get to tell me what to do," I whisper back.

He grabs my braid and yanks it, exposing my throat, then presses his mouth to my sensitive skin. I freeze.

"He doesn't fucking touch you, Lennon." His lips ghost over my pulse point, and my whole body shivers. I feel him smile against me. "We're not done."

He turns and leaves out the same door he came, without another word, but his threat lingers.

EIGHT

Lennon

It's well after ten in the morning when I wake up on the air mattress in Claire's bedroom. A glance at her bed tells me she's still out cold. Her hair is a mess and last night's makeup is smudged.

I frown.

She would hate me if she knew what happened at Josh's last night.

She'd definitely kill Macon.

I don't know who she would be angrier at.

I was so shook up after my encounter with Macon that I told Eric I had a headache and spent the rest of the night alone in Claire's car, agonizing over what happened. She stumbled into the passenger seat around two, and we snuck into her bedroom just before three.

Two hours after her curfew.

I laid awake for another two hours listening for Macon, but I never heard him come home.

My body burns when I replay what happened in that bathroom. The way my nipples harden at the memory of

Macon's mouth on my skin confuses me, and then I grow angry with myself.

This is Macon. Claire's brother. My tormentor.

Deadbeat pothead who apparently now pops pills and vandalizes houses for fun.

I try to think of Eric, to go through the things about him that I like, but I'm overcome with guilt and have to push him out of my head. Macon did this just to mess with me. I'm sure he left that bathroom and went straight to Sam to laugh about it.

And I'm here stressing out over all the people I could potentially hurt.

I hate him.

I get up and make my way to the Jack and Jill bathroom that Macon and Claire share and spend the entire time brushing my teeth on the defensive. I don't know if Macon is in his bedroom on the other side of the bathroom door, but if the knob so much as jiggles, I'm sprinting out of here.

Luckily, I'm in and out without trouble.

I leave a brief note for Claire, telling her I have homework and I'll call her later, then I grab my bag and quietly slip out of the house. I heave a sigh of relief the moment I close the door behind me. I know Andrea is off today, but I'm glad I didn't run into her. I don't think I could face her after last night. Not yet.

Macon's hands. Macon's mouth. Weed and spice and spearmint.

We're not done.

I shake my head to get the images out of it.

I make the short walk to my house, trying to think of anything but Macon and the bathroom, and when I finally turn the corner onto my block, I break into a sprint.

Dad's 4Runner is in the driveway, which means he's home a whole day early. I pay attention to nothing else, zeroed in on our front door, unlocking it and kicking off my shoes in record time.

"Daddy!" I call through the house, barreling into the kitchen where I expect to see him drinking a protein shake in his workout clothes. I screech to a halt and burst into tears when he's exactly where I want him to be.

"Hey, Pumpkin," he greets with a smile, grunting a little when I tackle him in a hug. He squeezes me tightly and chuckles. "I guess you missed me?"

I sniffle and nod into his shoulder. My emotions are such a mess.

"Just a little," I say on a laugh. I pull back and look at him, surprised to see him still wearing pajama pants. I raise a brow. "Late start?"

He laughs. "Got in late, so I slept in."

I smile. He deserves to rest. God knows what kind of stuff he had to do over the last two weeks. I drop my arms and step back, then something strange registers in my head. I lean back in and sniff his shirt.

"Lavender?" I ask when I pull away. His face is blank. "Why do you smell like lavender?"

"You tell me." He shrugs. "You're the one who insists on doing the laundry."

I roll my eyes.

"That's because you shrink everything," I say with a laugh. Then I walk to the refrigerator. "You want eggs? I'll cook, and you can tell me all about your trip."

I glance back over my shoulder, and he raises an eyebrow that says, *nice try, kid*.

"*Fine,*" I relent. I knew better than to ask. "Then, I'll cook and tell you about my first two weeks of senior year."

"That sounds great."

I smile as I pull out the egg carton and frying pan. I freshen up Dad's coffee then get to work at the stove, rambling to him about my classes and my teachers. I let myself relax into the familiarity of it. The comfort.

I breathe easier when Dad's home. He's here. He's safe. My little family is intact. And nothing else matters.

I TELL MY DAD I'M STUDYING AT THE LIBRARY.

I tell Claire I'm studying at the library.

The only person who knows the truth is the one person I'm avoiding.

Yesterday, he tried to approach me in the hallway a few times, but I managed to always be with Claire or Eric. In free period, I could feel his eyes burning holes into my face.

He even threw a small ball of clay at me.

I kept my eyes on my paper and refused to acknowledge him.

When the bell rang, he was out the door immediately, and I haven't seen him since.

But just because Macon skipped free period today doesn't mean he won't be at the rec center tonight. In fact, I'm certain he'll be here.

I check in with James when I arrive and keep my head down as I walk past the gym. The squeaking of shoes and the bouncing of balls tell me there's a basketball scrimmage going on, and I'm sure that if I let myself peek inside, I'd find Macon playing coach with a whistle around his neck.

I don't peek inside.

I go straight to my classroom and set up for today's class. I'm letting the kids illustrate their own comics this week, and I think they're going to love it. I decided to cover some drawing and sketching before we do paints, and it's been working really well so far.

As the kids start to arrive, thoughts of Macon and Eric and

Claire are put into a box and shoved out of the way, so I can focus on this art class. Just as I thought, the kids really enjoy the project, and by the time class is over, I'm not ready to go back to my real life.

I want to live my secret for a bit longer.

I shut the door to the classroom, move to the back corner, and lay out some paints, brushes, and paper. They're not my preferred brands, but they'll do. I pull up the music streaming app on my phone and decide on a playlist, hitting shuffle.

And then I paint.

I don't have a picture in mind, but after a few minutes, the direction becomes clearer.

Guilt. Anxiety. Lust.

An abstract depiction of the emotions sitting heavy in my stomach and clawing at my throat. Dull greens and grays with hints of blue, blending and swirling, until there's no real beginning or end.

Abstract impressionism tends to be my favorite style to paint, but there is nothing tangible about how I'm feeling right now. No defined image to grasp. Just a mess of emotions that I don't quite understand.

So, I do what I always do.

I put it on paper and try to make it into something beautiful.

Or, at the very least, to expel it from my body.

I'm not sure how much time has passed when the door opens, catching my attention. I look up from my paints and watch Macon slip into the room. Our eyes lock, but neither of us speak.

He walks silently toward me, rounds the table, and sits down softly in the chair beside me. I watch him as he studies my painting. I try to identify the emotions that pass over his face. It feels like forever before he finally lifts his attention off my work and meets my eyes.

"Will it bother you if I stay?" he asks, his voice soft and sincere. I blink twice, speechless, but he doesn't shy away from the silence. He waits for my answer.

Somehow, I know nothing but words will satisfy him.

"No," I say after a moment, "you won't bother me if you stay."

He gives me a small nod, then settles back in his chair to watch me paint.

"YOUR PLAYLIST IS A GOOD ONE," MACON SAYS AS WE WALK TO our cars an hour later. It's not what I expected him to say, but I'm grateful that he doesn't comment on my painting. For so long, it's just been meant for my eyes. I'm not used to someone else experiencing my art.

"Thanks. I was feeling some indie folk-pop tonight."

He hums into the night air, and we take more steps in silence, the asphalt crunching under our shoes.

"You have kind of an eclectic taste in music," he muses again as we reach my car. I laugh, unlock the car door, then turn to face him. I study him for a moment, weighing my secrets, before deciding to come clean with one of them.

"I blame you for that," I tell him honestly, and his lips purse and his eyebrows scrunch in confusion. I laugh again and his lips twitch into a playful smile.

"The first time I had a sleepover with Claire, you were listening to Fleetwood Mac, and I fell in love with the song 'Sisters of the Moon.' The next time I came over, you were listening to Cake. The time after that, Wu-Tang Clan."

His eyes are so wide, his smile so big that mine stretches to match, and I have to look away from him or I'll lose my nerve. I shrug to play it off.

"It was always something different, almost always something I liked, so I started taking notice. Started looking forward to hearing whatever your music choice would be. No matter how much you pissed me off or teased me, I was still excited for the moment you'd turn on your music."

I huff out a laugh.

"Then Claire would complain that it was too loud, and you guys would get into a fight, and Drea would make you turn it off. Then, eventually you got headphones. But before the headphones..."

I trail off, and he chuckles. When I look back up at him, he's closer than he was before. My breath catches in my throat and my laugher dies. He reaches over and fingers the end of my braid.

"Well, Lennon Capri," he whispers, moving his hand from my braid to brush a stray piece of hair behind my ear, "you're welcome for giving you great taste in music."

I roll my eyes and scoff playfully, then open the car door.

"Go home, Macon," I tell him with a smile. "I'll see you tomorrow in free period."

I try to hide the hopeful tone in my voice. I'm a little disappointed in myself for it being there at all. This is *Macon*. But...I don't know...

I'm hopeful, regardless.

"See you tomorrow, Leonard," he answers with a smirk, then he turns on his heel, walks across the street and heads down the block toward the supermarket. I know he parks his car there, since everyone thinks that's where he works, but I don't know what his plans are for the rest of the night.

Is he going to get high? Will he at least be safe if he decides to drink? Is he meeting with Sam?

The last one bothers me the most, and I hate it.

On the drive home, I listen to "Sisters of the Moon" three times and tell myself that what I feel for Macon is platonic. My concern is that of a friend.

Maybe Macon and I are becoming friends.

And I'm not at all jealous.

"GOOD MORNING, DAD," I SAY CHEERILY. HE SITS AT THE counter drinking his coffee with a tablet in front of him, no doubt reading some sort of news source. It's so nice to see him here after two weeks filled with the niggling reality that he could not return.

"Morning, Pumpkin." He smiles at me over his coffee cup. "You driving yourself or is Claire coming to scoop you up?"

I grab a glass from the cabinet and the OJ from the fridge, filling my glass to the brim.

"Claire will be here soon," I tell him before taking a drink. Then I smile. "She knows you're home, so she'll probably come in to bother you."

"She's no bother." He chuckles. "With as much time as you've spent together growing up, she's like a daughter to me."

I smile at the thought, but then reconsider.

"You know, Dad," I say, "I love Claire and all, but I'm glad she's my friend and not my sister. I don't know if I could handle living with her 24/7."

Before Dad can reply, I hear the front door open and flash him a grin.

"Speak of the devil," I joke, just as Claire comes barreling into the kitchen and tackles my dad in a hug. He grunts and acts like he's lost his balance, but we both know he's faking it.

"Sir, hello, Sir," she greets when she pulls away. "You an admiral yet?"

She raises an eyebrow at him as she walks to me and steals my juice. When Dad doesn't answer her, like usual, she shakes her head and pretends to be disappointed.

"Slacker."

Dad barks out a laugh and his eyes crinkle at the sides,

drawing my attention to the other fine lines on his face, the silvering of the hair at his temples.

My dad is still young, but this life has aged him. Sometimes I forget that.

He and my mom got married young and had me younger. But even after becoming a single father in his twenties, my dad still managed to complete his master's degree in international affairs and excel in his military career. He's technically a reservist, now, but I know there's more to it that he doesn't tell me. Six-month deployments are difficult on any family, but they're almost impossible for a single parent. After Mom, Dad had to take a giant step back from the career that he loves.

Claire teases him about being an admiral all the time, despite the fact that he's far too young, but I think, deep down, it bothers him that it's an honor he'll likely never achieve. Maybe if it weren't for Mom...

If it weren't for *me*.

I pull myself out of my thoughts and tune back into Claire and Dad's conversation. She's telling him about school and how she needs me to go to an in-state college with her. My dad laughs her off.

"Has Lenny told you about Eric yet?" Claire blurts, and I widen my eyes in shock at her as Dad whips his attention to me.

"Who is Eric, Lennon?" he asks, his voice curious and his eyebrow raised.

I send Claire a scowl. She sends me a very Macon-like smirk.

"He's just a friend, Dad," I say, and before Claire can out me anymore, I come clean. "We went on one date last weekend, and he asked me to wear his away jersey to the home game on Friday. He's kissed me on the cheek. The end."

"Hmmm." He studies me, and I brace myself for what I know is coming. "I want to meet him."

My shoulders fall, and I sigh.

"Fine."

"And maybe we should make an appointment with Dr. Evans," he adds, and I cringe.

"Dad," I whine, and Claire giggles. I shoot her another glare, and she covers her smile with her hand. I look back at my dad and school my face into the picture of sincerity.

"I promise that if it comes to that, I'll talk to you. But it's not necessary right now."

He nods, and the tension in my body loosens.

Claire has been on birth control since she was fifteen to help with her periods, and she's already had sex, so she told me all about how that first appointment went. I luckily haven't needed birth control—with the exception of that one time—so I'm holding out as long as possible.

Stirrups and speculums and some new doctor all up in my business? No thanks.

And despite my promise, my dad doesn't know about my first and only experience with sex, and I'm going to keep it that way. The next time it happens, I'll do it the right way. The first time, I'd rather forget.

"Well, either way, we'll need to see Dr. Evans soon. Before you graduate," he says slyly. I cock my head and stare him down.

"Why?" I ask. He takes a sip of his coffee and keeps his face blank. "What are you up to?"

He stays silent, letting the anticipation build. I narrow my eyes and put my hands on my hips.

"Dad."

He shrugs and takes another sip before speaking.

"I just think a checkup would be smart before you spend the summer with Becca," he states, calmly and coolly, like he hasn't just given me the one thing I've been begging for, for years.

"Really?" My heart is racing, and my smile makes my cheeks hurt. I glance at Claire. She's frowning, so I look back at Dad. "You're letting me go to England?"

"I've been talking to Becca," he says slowly. "We think it would be the perfect time. Before college. And you're older now..."

He lets his statement trail off, and I give him a tight smile. We don't really talk about it, but he's stopped watching me so closely since I turned seventeen. In reality, the age doesn't matter much, but it made him feel better when I made it through my sixteenth year without any markers.

"You're leaving for the whole summer after graduation," Claire says, breaking my eye contact with Dad. I look back at her to find she's frowning harder. If that's even possible. "I thought we were going to go on an East Coast road trip."

My face falls. Claire's been talking about a graduation road trip since we started high school.

"Claire," I say slowly, "I know. I'm sorry. But..."

"But Lennon hasn't seen her aunt Becca in almost eight years," my dad cuts in. Thankfully. "And Becca wants to see her only niece. Letting her spend the summer with her aunt is my graduation and birthday gift to Lennon."

Claire scowls, but I can tell she's accepted it. My dad's word is still law.

"Fine," she pouts, and I launch myself at him.

"Thank you, thank you, thank you," I say as I hug him tightly. He laughs and pats my back.

"You'll leave after graduation, and I'll fly in for your 18th birthday in July."

"Thank you, Dad," I say earnestly, trying to keep the tears from my eyes. "Seriously."

I know how hard this will be for him. I know he's probably agonized over it. It's going to hurt him and he's going to worry...

But...a whole summer with Aunt Becca in England.

She's an artist. She paints like me, but she also draws and sculpts and welds together wacky statues of salvaged metal. She's been featured on news channels and in magazines, and she knows several famous painters. And I've seen pictures on social media of the little village where she lives outside of Brighton. It's the perfect blend of quaint and quirky. Fun. Beautiful.

I haven't seen her since I was nine.

I've wanted to visit ever since.

"Of course, Pumpkin," my dad says quietly. "I want you to be happy. You know that."

I kiss him on the cheek. "I love you."

"Love you most," he says, then lets me go. "Now go to school, you delinquents, before the truancy officer comes knocking."

Claire snorts. "You're so old."

He waves her off with a grin. We tell him goodbye and head to her car. She spends the whole drive to school lamenting the fact that I'm "abandoning" her for the summer, but even her bad mood can't bring me down.

I'm going to England this summer. I've never been so excited.

I TRY NOT TO, BUT THE MOMENT WE PULL INTO THE SCHOOL parking lot, my eyes scan for Macon. I find him immediately leaning on his car with Sam plastered to his side.

My stomach twists.

Seeing him with her after what happened Friday night bothers me, but I think I would have gotten past it if it weren't for what happened last night at the rec center. Him watching me paint. Telling him about his influence on my music tastes. I just thought...

I'm not sure what I thought.

I scold myself. Temper my scowl when Sam rests her head on Macon's chest. The same side as his tattoo.

I bet she knows what the tattoo is.

She probably was with him when he got it.

"I know," Claire says. "He's so gross." She turns off the engine and we climb out of the car.

"Pretty sure he had Sam over on Sunday while Mom was working. His whole room smelled like weed, and when he finally came out for dinner, he was so high he could barely stay awake."

She keeps her eyes forward as we pass, refusing to even look at him.

"Mom cried, and then spent the rest of the night in her bedroom on the phone."

Despite my better judgment, I glance back over my shoulder. Macon's watching us with a frown.

"I hate him, Lennon," Claire says. "I really do. I don't care that he's my brother. He's fucked up my family and he won't stop until it's well and truly broken."

My first instinct is to defend him, but I stop myself. Instead, I reach out and grab her hand and give it a squeeze.

"I know," I whisper. I don't know what else to say, so I don't say anything. I just let her be angry and tell her I love her when we part ways to go to our lockers.

"See you at lunch," she says with a smile, so I smile back and nod.

Eric is waiting for me at my locker, and the sight of him warms me up and sends ice through my veins at the same time.

He's gorgeous. He's kind. He's a good guy.

We're not dating. Not really. But I still feel so freaking horrible. I feel like a cheater.

"Hey," he greets, and takes my bag when I stop in front of him. I smile and unlock my locker.

"Hey," I say back, then take my bag from him to exchange out books. I take a deep breath when I finish and turn to face him. "I have bad news."

His face falls. "Is everything okay?" he asks. "Are you alright?"

His immediate concern for me makes me feel even more like a jerk. I shake my head and force a smile.

"Yes, I'm fine," I say quickly, "but my dad wants to meet you."

Instead of arguing or running in the opposite direction, Eric smiles.

"I'd love to meet your dad," he says, and my lips break into a grin.

"Really?"

"Really."

"What would you say to," I suggest tentatively, "coming over for dinner?"

"That sounds great."

His voice is so genuine. *He* is so genuine. My crush grows as fast as my guilt.

"Weird question," he interjects as we walk in the direction of my first class. Eric has started walking with me in the halls whenever he can, and I'm still not used to the stares.

"Shoot," I tell him.

"Does your dad drink? You know, if I were to bring him something..."

I fold my lips to keep from smiling, then side-eye him curiously.

"Not often, but when he does, it's bourbon."

Eric nods. "Any particular kind?"

My smile breaks, full teeth, and my eyes squint as we stop at the door of my class.

"Expensive," I tell him playfully, and he grins back.

"Have a good day, Lennon," he says. "I'll see you in a bit."

He walks backward, keeping his eyes on me, pinning me to the spot with his gorgeous smile, until he turns the corner and disappears.

"That was disgusting," a deep voice taunts in my ear, and my shoulders shoot up.

I whip around and hit Macon with a glare.

"You're disgusting," I hiss. I move to walk into the classroom, but he grabs my wrist and pulls me into his chest.

"He doesn't fucking touch you." His voice is a growled command, and I spin around and shove him off me.

"Like Sam doesn't touch you?"

His face shows a flicker of shock, and then he smirks slowly. I lean in close, so only he can hear me, and jab him in the chest with my finger.

"*You* don't fucking touch me," I say, and then I turn my back on him and go into class.

It takes me the first thirty minutes to calm my racing heart. I don't take a single note. I don't retain anything. And then we're given a pop quiz and I'm almost certain I fail it.

Freaking Macon.

This is all his fault.

NINE

Macon

"Do we have to listen to this," Sam complains from her spot on the couch. I don't respond. She's ruining my high.

I keep my head dropped back and my eyes closed as Casper changes the song. On my left, Julian taps my arm, and I tilt my head just enough to see where he's holding the joint. I grab it and bring it to my lips.

"I don't want to spend the whole day in Casper's garage again," Sam complains, louder this time, and I groan. We ditched after lunch. I tried to get out without Sam knowing, but she has the good weed...

"Do you ever stop bitching?" I ask her. It's rhetorical. I know the answer.

The couch shifts to my right, and I can feel her crawling up next to me. She slides her arms over my shoulders and brings her lips to my ear.

"Let's go to my place," she whispers. I snort and tilt my head away from her. She presses a kiss to my neck. "I just got some stuff," she adds, and that grabs my attention.

I peek my eyes open and glance at Julian. He's lying on the futon in the corner. He looks like he's sleeping. I check in front of me, hoping for the same, but Casper's alert and watching. His brow is furrowed, and he gives a slight shake of his head.

Judas.

I know he's been talking to Claire. He thinks I don't know about his fucked-up obsession, but I do. He acts like his concern is for my benefit. It's not. No one is concerned about me. Casper just wants to fuck my sister. I narrow my eyes at him briefly then tilt my head to Sam.

"What kind of stuff?" I ask, and she smiles suggestively.

"Good stuff."

Her grin is the opposite of innocent. Her lips almost too full and too red. Too unlike the lips I want to see. I tug her forward and kiss her anyway. She bites my lip hard, reminding me of violent kisses in a hidden bathroom, and despite my high, my dick jumps.

"Let's go." I stand gingerly, mastering the spinning in my head, and grab Sam's hand. I don't look at Casper or Julian as I walk out. I don't say anything. I hear Sam tell them we'll see them later, but I'm already climbing into the passenger seat of her red coupe.

I recline the seat and close my eyes.

She gets in the driver's side, leans over and does my seat belt. I hear her click her buckle and turn on the engine.

"Wake me up when we get there," I tell her, and then I pretend to sleep for the rest of the drive.

Sam's parents are gone when we get to her house, but that's not surprising. They're never around. I trail her through the front door, up the stairs, and into her dad's office, where she proceeds to pop open a wall safe, covered by a canvas family portrait of Sam, her parents, and her older brother, Chase.

As she rummages through the safe, my eyes find the lens of the tiny security camera hidden within the crown molding in the corner of the room. I stare it down as if it matters. Knowing it's there always makes me uncomfortable.

"I told you to stop worrying about that," Sam says. I look at her as she raises her middle finger to the camera. "It only activates if the code is entered incorrectly, and even if they did watch it, they don't fucking care enough to do anything about it."

She sneers in the direction of the camera once more, then walks out of the room, leaving the wall safe hanging wide open.

Sam goes into her bedroom and drops down on the bed. She gestures to the mattress next to her, so I take a seat, and she spreads some "good stuff" out in the space between us. I survey it.

A few small baggies of white powder and various pills, all of which I'm familiar with, lie about on the bedspread, but my eyes fall on a separate, slightly larger bag and I study it. Inside are capsules filled with more white powder and a few sheets of colorful blotter papers. I glance from the bag back to Sam.

"That's new," I say with a raised brow. Her dad doesn't usually have hallucinogens. He's strictly blow and pain pills. We usually get our weed and Molly from some chick in Suffolk.

"It's not from Dad," she says with a smile. "I scored it from one of Chase's frat buddies. It's like LSD."

I eyeball it. The twitch in my fingers to grab it, the desire to place a tab on my tongue and let it dissolve, to crack open one of the capsules and snort the contents into my bloodstream, makes me clench my hands into fists.

"*Like* LSD?"

"Yeah," she picks up the bag and opens it, then pulls one of the smaller baggies filled with capsules. "Synthetic research drugs. I guess they're stronger, though." She removes a capsule and holds it out for me. "The guy gave me a bunch to let my friends try."

"You mean he's making you his drug mule," I correct, and she shrugs. She doesn't care.

I consider the capsule between her fingers. Stronger than LSD sounds like a good time, but it also sounds like a bad fucking idea. I don't know Chase's friend, but if he's anything like Chase, I wouldn't trust him to dose my drugs.

I brush her hand away and reach for the oxy instead.

The second it's in my mouth, I feel my shoulders loosen. I close my eyes and imagine the pills sliding down my throat. Pretend I can visualize them dissolving. Watch the drug enter my vascular system and my heart pump it into my waiting limbs.

Everything starts to slow down the way I like it.

I hear Sam moving, baggies rustling and a drawer closing, and then the mattress dips as she climbs on top of me.

On instinct, my palms grip her legs. I squeeze and rub them as her lips and tongue drag over the skin of my neck. She messes with the button on my jeans, and I slip my fingers under the hemline of her shorts. I massage the flesh on her thighs. I try to pretend it's softer than it is. That it's more plush.

Her hand dips into my jeans and strokes my dick over the fabric of my boxer briefs. I groan into the air when she squeezes my shaft. I move to grip her waist, but it's too small and feels wrong in my hands, so I move them back to the thick spot on her thighs. I massage and squeeze, thrusting my hips into her palm as she presses hot kisses to my neck.

With my eyes closed, I do a good job of pretending, but once Sam's mouth lands on mine, her taste is unavoidable, and I lose all interest.

I stop the kissing and move her off me, then I stand.

"What the fuck, Macon," Sam says, her eyes wide with shock as she wipes her mouth with her hand. I rebutton my pants and adjust the semi my dick is sporting.

"You owe me from Sunday, and I'm not in the mood," I say flatly, and her face falls. I should feel like an asshole, and maybe I do, but the pills are starting to kick in and with them comes the numb.

"Fuck you, Macon," Sam whispers. I can hear the hurt in her voice, but I feel nothing. I don't know why she's upset. I'm the one acting like a whore paid in drugs. I turn around and walk toward her door.

"She's never gonna want you," she says, louder, just as I step into the hallway. "You're wasting your time."

"I don't know what you're talking about," I call, without looking back at her.

But I do know.

I know exactly what she's talking about. It would take a hundred more oxy to make me forget it.

I put my headphones in, point my feet in the direction of my house across town, and walk. At some point in the journey, my playlist takes on an indie folk-pop sound, and instead of turning down the street to my house, I let my legs carry me to Lennon's.

I stop just to the left of her house, the two-story building seeming just as stately and proper as it always does with its white stone façade and large, black-trimmed windows. The lawn and shrubbery are perfectly manicured, and I smirk at the thought of Lennon's dad on his knees pulling weeds and pruning peonies in between top-secret SEAL missions. I take two steps toward the front door, then stop in my tracks when I notice the expensive blue truck in the driveway.

My lip curls in disgust as I take in the football number decal in the back window.

Fucking Eric Masters is here to meet Daddy.

I waltz up to the truck and peek through the tinted windows. A gym bag, some schoolbooks, a reusable coffee thermos in the cup holder. Minimal trash. Nothing worth stealing. Figures. Eric Masters is a damn boy scout and exactly what Trent Washington wants for his baby girl, I'm sure.

Instead of going up the path to the front door, I move around the side of the house and walk toward the backyard. There's a tree in the back that I know for a fact reaches to the window of Lennon's upstairs corner bedroom.

Claire used to use the tree to sneak out when we were younger. She'd ask to stay over at Lennon's and then sneak out to see whatever guy she was dating at the time. I don't think Lennon has ever done it, but she was always willing to cover for Claire until Mom extended our curfew, making it easier for my darling sister to sneak in and out of our own house.

I've never once told my mom about the shit Claire gets up to. I don't want to hurt Mom any more than I already do. But Claire gladly tattles on me every chance she gets.

My sister is a grade A bitch who hates me.

My mom is a saint who doesn't deserve the bullshit I put her through.

I stand at the base of the tree and look up at the branches.

I'm not totally sure that it is going to hold me, but I'm still fairly high and extremely horny, so I grab hold of one branch, then another, and steadily pull myself upward, until I'm looking through the window into Lennon's tidy bedroom.

The window and screen both lift smoothly, and I slip inside without incident.

The room smells like her. Clean and crisp, soft and beautiful.

Roses, like her shampoo. And paint, like her obsession.

I haven't been inside Lennon's bedroom in years, but it doesn't look like it's changed much. Pictures are tacked to a bulletin board above a white wooden desk, and I study each one.

Pictures of her and Claire ranging from age nine to seventeen.

Pictures of her and her dad. In some, he's in uniform, but in most, he's wearing civilian clothes.

My eyes catch on a picture of a young Lennon with a woman who looks exactly like her, and even though I've never met her, I know instinctively that it's her mom, Susanna. Lennon is maybe five or six in the picture, her chestnut hair in a tight, perfect French braid tied off with a pink ribbon, and she's smiling up at her mother with a missing front tooth. Susanna looks just like Lennon today. Same brown hair. Same hazel eyes. Same sweet smile. I'm so lost in the similarities that I almost miss the paintbrushes in their hands, and the smudges of paint on their cheeks.

My brow furrows. My brain is fuzzy from the pills, but something feels significant about this.

Another picture grabs my attention.

One of Claire, Lennon, and me from a few summers ago when Trent and Mom took us to Virginia Beach. We're all in swimsuits, and Claire is smiling at the camera with her arms thrown around Lennon in a hug. I'm staring down the camera with my hands in my swim trunk pockets, looking every bit like I don't want to be there. But Lennon?

Lennon almost looks like she's looking at me.

And she's smiling.

I pull the picture from the bulletin board and shove it in the back pocket of my jeans without thinking, then crack the door, so I can hear downstairs.

Laughter filters toward me. Some deep, some airy. Lennon's dad and Eric seem to be hitting it off, from the sound of it, and Lennon is loving it. My stomach twists, and anger surges through the haze in my head.

Fuck Eric Masters for ruining my high.

I shut the door and kick off my shoes, then toss myself onto Lennon's bed. Her rose scent blankets me once my head hits the pillow, and I fall asleep seconds later.

. . .

105

"WHAT THE HELL ARE YOU DOING HERE?" A SWEET VOICE hisses, and I pop one eye open to find the most gorgeous sight.

A shocked and angry Lennon Capri Washington.

She's so fucking hot when she's pissed.

I smirk just to watch her jaw tense.

"Macon," she demands, putting her hands on her hips and drawing my attention to the bouquet of flowers she's holding.

It's big. Expensive. I look it over. Try to find something wrong with it, but I can't. It's actually pretty perfect. Vibrant and colorful. Unique. Artistic. Very *Lennon*.

Fucking Masters.

"Where's all your paint shit?" I ask her without moving. I keep my arms folded behind my head, which is resting on her pillow, and my ankles crossed.

"What?" She blinks, and I smirk again.

"Your paint shit," I repeat. "Where is it?"

Her eyes bounce between mine, then she drags her gaze from my face to my feet and back. I let her look, and give her space, let her adjust to the sight of me in her room. On her bed.

Fuck, I know I'd need a minute if the situation was flipped.

"My paints..." She trails off, then her eyes drop to the floor. "They're put away."

I sit up slowly. I don't take my attention off her. Her face is full of guilt and longing.

"Your mom used to paint," I say, and she nods, keeping her eyes on the ground. "That's why you keep it from your dad?"

Another silent nod.

"I'm sorry," I whisper, and she finally brings her hazel eyes to mine. The sadness guts me, and I instinctively move toward her. Her eyes grow wide, and she bites her lower lip. I reach up and use my thumb to pull her plush lip away from her teeth, then rub gently over the red mark. "Don't do that, *Astraea*."

"It upsets him," she says to me, and I guess it makes sense, but it still pisses me off.

So his daughter's passion reminds him of his dead wife? So the fuck what.

She's dead. Lennon is here.

"You shouldn't have to sacrifice what you love for someone else," I say firmly, and her soft eyes harden.

"It's not a sacrifice. I love him, and when you love people, you're glad to do things for them," she argues. "You don't want to cause them pain."

Her words hammer at my chest. Every syllable an accusation. I read between the lines.

She doesn't think I care about my family. She thinks I don't care that all I do is hurt them. She told me so in the bathroom at that party. I'm a selfish, miserable asshole.

And I can't even defend myself. She's right.

The way the muscles tense in her jaw and neck tells me she's prepped for a fight. She won't get one. Of all the ways I'm selfish, she's the most damning.

Without taking my eyes off her, I bring her braid over her shoulder and pull the ribbon off the end, then I shove it in my pocket with the picture I stole.

"I hate this fucking braid," I grind out, using my fingers to undo the strands.

She doesn't move, but the way her eyes flutter shut when I reach her nape spurs me on. Gently, I thread my fingers through her hair. When her lips part on a sigh, I give in to impulse and make a fist, tugging her hair at the root. She gasps and her eyes fly open, one hand coming up to grip my wrist. I walk her back slowly until she is pressed against her bedroom door, then I push my body into hers.

She opens her mouth to speak, but nothing comes out. I wait as she licks her lips. Takes a breath and clears her throat. Then she tries again.

"Why do you keep pinning me to doors?"

Her voice is the sexiest rasp, and I have to bite back a groan. I smirk instead and bring my lips to the shell of her ear.

"Maybe I need to make sure you stay where I want you," I say, then bite down lightly on her earlobe. She arches her body into mine, and I blow out a slow sigh through my nose. Holding back. Waiting. "You gonna run, *Astraea*?"

She brings the fisted hand at her side up and grips my shirt, then tightens her other hand around my wrist, but her words stay locked up.

"You know I like to hear that pretty voice," I taunt, pressing into her just enough so she feels my hard dick. "Give me that big girl voice."

She swallows and licks her lips again before saying, "I won't run."

There she is. The words are difficult for her, laced with frustration, but she says them. Forces them out. I can't tell if she's nervous or if she hates herself a little for wanting me. I want to bristle, want to feel offended, but I'm used to being the guy girls want in secret. Only Sam's ever flaunted me, and that's less pride and more spite. Some fucked-up, mommy-daddy issues rebellion.

I can't waste time being upset about the inevitable.

"Tell me to leave, and I'll go," I tell her.

It's honest. I've never been more honest. My heart thunders in my chest. I hold my breath until she answers.

"Stay," she whispers.

My mouth is on her instantly, my tongue impatient to war with her tongue. My lips desperate for her lips.

She's an addiction.

My worst fucking addiction.

I recognize it in the way my fingers tingle, the way my brain fixates. The way I want her is a compulsion, a craving. I don't care about the consequences the moment my hands are on her. I clamp my eyes shut against the guilt and let my hands push her skirt to her waist so I can dig my fingers into the soft flesh of her thighs and ass. I groan again and pull her harder into my body.

Lennon doesn't miss a beat before her hands are in my hair, tugging and scratching her fingernails against my scalp.

I knew she liked my hair long. Those scowls and scoffs are because she hates liking it.

I push that thought out of my head with the rest of them, then spin us around and walk backward, until I'm sitting in the purple bowl chair in the corner of her room and she's straddling me. Our lips never break. These violent, angry kisses are just as relieving as they are punishing.

I deserve the punishment. It kills me that she thinks she does, too.

But the whimper she releases when I thrust against her center makes me fucking weak, and I use her ass cheeks to guide her movements, rocking her back and forth until she's grinding on me in a way that makes us both pant and moan.

She starts slowly, moving tentatively as she finds her rhythm.

"Fuck, Lennon." My hands are gripping her so hard as I meet her thrust for thrust. "Fuck, baby."

When she pulls her lips from mine and drops her head back, I know I'm in trouble. The grip in my hair tightens and her movements speed up, dragging her hot pussy over my jean-clad erection. I grunt and halt my thrusts.

The feeling of her on me is almost too much, even with my jeans and boxer briefs acting as a barrier. When I think about the fact that her skirt is pulled up to her bra and only her cotton panties are keeping her from coating my jeans in her pussy juices, I have to bite my lip and white-knuckle the edges of the chair.

She starts making these little noises. Her mouth hanging

open and her pretty face tilted to the ceiling, she whimpers and gasps, whispers *yes* into the air.

I've never seen anything so intoxicating. So worthy of obsession.

I try to hold out. I try to rip my eyes from her body, pray to a god I'm pretty sure doesn't exist that she'll just fucking come before I blow in my pants. I want to see her come.

I need to see it. Hear it.

Fuck, I would kill to feel it.

The thought alone brings me to the edge, and I have to punk out.

"Baby," I plead, gripping her hips again with firm hands and stilling her body. "You gotta stop."

Her lower lip pokes out and her brow furrows in disappointment, and I laugh. Then I grab her hair and pull her to me so I can kiss that pouty mouth.

"Why," she says against my lips. My smile is euphoric and embarrassing and fucking cheesy as hell.

"You keep going and I'm gonna come in my pants," I confess, and her mouths curls up into a devilish grin, making me laugh again.

"Let me take care of you." I bring my hand to the front of her panties, find her clit, and rub on it. She cries out, then slaps a hand over her mouth. Her hazel eyes are curious, shocked. Her pupils blown out so wide I would swear she was rolling.

I rub it again, with more pressure this time, and she groans.

I crook one finger into the crotch of her underwear when a knock raps at her door. We both freeze.

"Lennon?" her dad calls into the room.

"Yeah?" she answers. Her voice is hoarse and sexy. I try to slip my fingers back into her panties, but she slaps her hand over mine and shakes her head frantically.

"I just wanted to say goodnight," Trent says before

sounding the death knell of my hookup. "I really enjoyed meeting Eric tonight."

Lennon's eyes close and she grimaces.

"I'm glad, Dad," she croaks.

Fuck. I gently slide her off me, then stand up and slip on my shoes.

"I really think your mom would have liked him," Trent adds, hammering the last nail in my coffin.

"Me too, Dad." She swallows hard and hangs her head, her attention falling on the bouquet of flowers lying in the middle of her bedroom floor. She doesn't look back at me. "Love you."

"Love you too, Pumpkin. Sleep tight."

Neither of us dare speaks until his footsteps fade down the hall.

"You need to leave," she whispers. I sneer at the shame in her tone.

"I'm already on my way out," I spit back. She whips her eyes to me, humiliation replaced with indignation.

"You don't get to be mad at me about this," she rushes out. "*You* climbed through *my* window. *You* pounced on *me*."

"Pounced?" I scoff. "Like I'm some predator and you're prey?"

She shrugs with a look of dismissal on her face. "If the shoe fits."

"Bullshit, *Leonard*." I take a step toward her and relish the way her eyes flare. "You feel guilty for cheating on your jock boyfriend? Fine. But don't act like you didn't want this just as much as I did."

Her mouth drops open, face flushed, and she averts her eyes back to the flowers.

"He's not my boyfriend," she argues, and I choke on a humorless laugh.

I turn my back on her and walk toward the window,

stopping briefly to snatch the bouquet up from the ground. I shake the flowers over my shoulder, hard enough that petals fall off and litter the carpet.

"Maybe you should tell him that, then."

I drop the bouquet out the window and swing my legs out after it, climbing down the tree branches without another word. When I jump to the ground, I aim my feet for the flowers and land with a thud, then drop the crushed bouquet in the trash bin at the curb on my way home.

TEN

Lennon

It didn't surprise me when Macon ruined the beautiful bouquet Eric had brought me.

That's what Macon does. He ruins things. He sows destruction and chaos. I don't know how much he can help it, actually.

I *am* surprised to find a new bouquet waiting for me when I unlock my locker the next morning. I smile immediately and a laugh escapes my lips, an impulse I'm too stunned to analyze. I know without a doubt the flowers are from Macon.

I was mad at him when I woke up this morning. Furious. Now I can't stop smiling.

It's a gorgeous display of daisies, roses, and Queen Anne's lace. Some sprigs of blue delphinium, some lisianthus blooms. Flowers I only know about because I took a week-long floral arrangement class at the college last summer. The bouquet is absolutely beautiful, and so many questions flash through my head as I admire it.

How did he get my locker combination? When did he get these flowers if he left my house after nine last night? How could he afford them? How did he get them into the school this early?

I feel his eyes on me first, and when I glance up, Macon is on the other side of the hallway, leaning against the wall with one foot propped up beneath him.

His eyes smolder, the hottest blue flames, and a shiver runs down my spine when his full lips quirk up at the side. I'm about to head to him—to do I don't know what—but I stop in my tracks the moment I see Claire's face, shining with delight from the locker next to mine.

I hadn't even realized she was standing there.

"Are these from Eric?" she squeals excitedly, bouncing on her toes.

"Oh," I stutter, "um..." I flick my attention back to Macon, but he's gone. I glance at the vase, and my eyes catch on the note sticking up from the blooms.

whoops
not sorry.
- M

IT'S SCRAWLED IN THIN, MESSY SCRIPT, AND I RESIST THE URGE to laugh despite my agitation. Even Macon's handwriting is chaotic.

I reach up and snatch the card, shoving it awkwardly in my bag with a forced smile.

"Yeah," I lie. "Dinner went well."

"Ugh," she groans, and I change out my books and slam my locker shut before Eric decides to pay me a visit and catches sight of the flowers he definitely didn't buy. "I wish I could get Josh to meet my mom, but he's kind of parent-phobic."

I snort and change the subject.

"How is chem?"

"Blows," she groans, "but so much better with your notes. Thank you so much, Bae."

"Of course, Bae."

Claire is taking chemistry this semester, and she's struggling. I took chem sophomore year, so I gave her all my old notes. She used to make fun of me for hoarding my binders from every semester of high school, but she's not laughing now that she's benefiting.

"You want a study buddy tonight?" she asks, just before we part ways in the hallway, and I freeze. My mouth drops open, but nothing comes out.

Tonight.

I'm supposed to be "studying at the library," which is code for volunteering at the rec center. With her brother.

If it were just my secret, I probably would tell her the truth. But knowing that it could somehow rat out Macon... I just...

"I can't..." I hedge, "I, um, promised Dad I'd do dinner with him."

Claire groans. "You just did dinner with him last night with Eric."

"Exactly." I laugh and hope I don't sound as slimy as I feel. "It was with Eric. Dad wants to debrief, just him and me."

"Fine, bitch." She sighs dramatically. "See you at lunch."

I just lied to my best friend twice in the span of five minutes. Both times it had to do with the brother she despises, and those lies don't even come close to the rest of the crap about him I'm keeping from her.

I sink into my desk and drop my head into my hands.

What the hell am I doing?

I STOP IN MY TRACKS WHEN I WALK INTO THE ART ROOM.

Instead of the pottery wheel sitting in front of the storage room, it's been moved to the corner where my station sits. No Macon yet. Just the pottery wheel. I keep one eye on the door to my right as a I slowly make my way to my work space.

I know he's in there. I can feel it.

I sit down slowly and start arranging my materials, the basket of paints already sitting on the table for me. It could have been Hank, but I have a feeling it was Macon.

Two jars of water, too.

I pull my sleeve of brushes from my bag, and Macon emerges from the doorway of the storage room. He's carrying clay and he's changed from his regular black shirt into a ratty old band tee with the sleeves ripped off.

I recognize that band tee. He used to wear it all the time when we were freshmen.

The Doors.

That shirt is why I know every song on their 1996 Greatest Hits album.

I don't take my eyes off him as he walks toward me, but his eyes stay down. He walks slow, his face blank. Like he's bored. He's probably high. When he takes the seat next to me, though, he doesn't smell strongly of weed.

It actually troubles me more. Pills don't have a smell.

I focus on the spicy scent of his bodywash instead, the faint hints of lavender giving me pause and calming me at the same time. I watch as he straddles the pottery wheel, then takes something off the hem of his shirt and uses it to hold back the front of his shaggy curls.

The butterfly clip.

Then he wets the throwing surface before unwrapping his clay and setting it on the surface of the wheel. He rolls the clay around a few times, kneads it in a way that makes the veins in his hands and forearms pop, then glances at me over his shoulder. Our eyes connect and he smirks, then he winks at me, causing my lips to part and my breath to hitch.

He looks back at the wheel, picks up the clay and slams it on the surface, then starts spinning the wheel with a pedal by his foot. He scoops water from the basin and wets the clay, using his hands to smooth the sides.

More veins and muscles. Slick, gray clay coats his skin, covering his deft, strong fingers, and I'm brought back to the night in the rec center hallway and the gray handprint he left on my arm. The coolness of it. The way it tightened as it dried on my drive home. The inexplicable desire I had to leave it there and not wash it off.

Then Macon uses the middle and pointer fingers on both hands to press slowly into the top of the spinning clay, creating a hole.

I have to look away, then.

The warmth I feel in my stomach and lower, the thoughts of those hands on me, those fingers inside me. I squeeze my eyes shut and work to control my breathing.

Jesus, this is ridiculous.

This is *Macon*, and I'm suddenly acting like some horny, obsessed idiot.

He's making a freaking bowl. It's not pornographic.

But in spite of myself, I can't stop peeking at him as he works. The rest of the class period, I paint and peek. He mostly keeps his eyes on the clay, but every so often, I feel him, the burning prickle of his blue gaze. When I glance at him, our eyes meet and flit away, meet again. It's a playful dance, shy yet magnetic. Uncertain and unavoidable. Thrilling and new and igniting something in my chest that's hot and consuming.

The connection I feel with him...

...It's art.

My painting today is a series of grays and tans, with hints of bright, burning blue. Wet and dry techniques, smooth fingerprint type lines. Veins. Muscles. Curls. A broken clock.

Sharp edges and hard truths.

Macon.

We clean up before the bell without speaking. He changes back into his black t-shirt. We've gone the whole period without saying a single word. We walk slowly, side by side, down the hall to our lockers. I drag my feet for reasons I don't want to admit.

"You're talented," he says to me, breaking the silence.

"Oh," I stutter, "I'm not... I've got a lot to learn. I just play around with it."

"No," he says firmly, "you're talented, Lennon." He grabs my wrist and pulls me to the side of the hall. "You shouldn't hide it."

I bristle, teetering between distressed and defensive.

"Take the fucking compliment, Len," he demands. "You don't have to put everyone else's feelings before your own."

The authoritative tone in his voice makes me angry. I feel scolded, but fend off my impulse to cower and apologize. Not with Macon.

Never with him.

"That's great coming from you, Macon," I spit. "You put your feelings before everyone's."

He stares at me, blank-faced, his eyes bouncing between mine, and it makes me self-conscious. What is he thinking? Why can't I read him?

He reaches up slowly, pulls my braid over my shoulder, and takes the ribbon off the end, shoving it in his pocket. The second one he's stolen.

"You're talented, Lennon," he says again. "And you know it."

I stare at him, trying desperately to make sense of the thoughts swirling in my head. I break eye contact because I can't think straight when he's focused so intently on me. I glance at the ground, then the ceiling, then down the hallway. When my eyes fall on Claire, heading our direction, I panic. She's talking to Josh and hasn't seen us yet, so I grab Macon's wrist and pull him into the nearest room.

I don't even have time to care about the urinals on the wall because I'm freaking out.

"What?" Macon asks. "What's wrong?"

"She can't see us," I rush out, and his face falls. He stalks back to the door and peers out, then turns around and hits me with a glare.

"*Claire?*" he says indignantly. "You don't want *Claire* to see us? We were fucking talking, Lennon. It's not like I was sucking on your nipple with my hand down your pants."

"She can't know about that," I say quickly, panicked. "No one can."

His jaw drops and he jerks his head back, then laughs. A humorless and sinister chuckle.

"Of course," he says slowly, walking backwards toward the door. "I'm just a miserable asshole, right? A fuckup. A druggie. I don't care about anyone but myself." He stops just before the door, his face void of emotion. "Nice and polite Lennon Washington would never be with someone like me. Claire Davis wouldn't allow it."

Then he opens the door and exits, leaving me silent and staring at the now empty spot on the floor where he was just standing.

Macon doesn't come to see me after my class at the rec center. I stay painting well into the night, waiting. He never comes, and I can't ignore the guilty prickle creeping over my skin.

I think I messed up.

ELEVEN

Lennon

"No more, please, I beg you," Claire moans from her spot on her bed. Her legs are propped on the headboard, her head teetering on the edge, and her arms are thrown over her face.

She's so dramatic.

"We've only done half the notes," I say with a laugh. She's got her first test in chem on Monday, and she bribed me with Andrea's strawberry shortcake to help her study. I should have known half the job would be dragging her through the work.

"It's torture," she says. "I hate chemistry. It sucks."

"Yes, it does, but you need it to graduate, so ovary-up and finish these notes," I tell her sternly. She takes her arm off her face and rolls her head in my direction.

"Can we snack first?" She bats her eyelashes. "*Pllleeeeease?* I need sustenance or I might pass out."

I roll my eyes, but I slide the binder off my lap and stand up from the floor, where I've been sitting. Claire claps her hands with joy and bounces to her feet.

"Yay!" She practically skips to the door, and I follow. When she hits the landing, she shouts for Andrea. "Mom! We need to feed Lennon! She won't stop complaining!"

My jaw drops and she sends me a smirk over her shoulder. I swat at her, but she dodges and runs down the stairs. When she rounds the corner and is no longer in sight, I halt my steps and back up several feet.

Silently, I press my ear to Macon's door, straining to hear something. Anything. But there's nothing.

I haven't seen him since the bathroom incident at school. He's been completely MIA, and it worries me.

I hurt his feelings, and that wasn't my intention. I meant what I said: Claire can't know about any of this Macon and me mess. But... I can't stop the feeling I should apologize. Explain myself? Give him...

...Oh god. The "it's not you, it's me" conversation.

I scoff at myself and jerk away from his door. This is absolutely ridiculous. I don't owe Macon anything. It's not like I'm the one who pursued him.

He cornered *me* at that party.

He burst into that bathroom on *me*.

He climbed through *my* window.

I didn't ask him to buy me flowers. I didn't ask him to come and watch me paint or tell me I'm talented. I'm not the one stealing his ribbons, or whatever.

I'm innocent in all this.

The moment I think the word, his voice invades my head, and I cringe.

Astraea. Greek goddess of innocence and purity. He thinks he's so freaking clever.

Well, I took that honors English class, too, and he obviously didn't pay as close attention as I did. He forgot something. *Astraea* is also the goddess of justice, and I think it's time I served up his.

"Lenny!" Claire calls up the stairs, making me jump. "C'mon. Mom made shortcakes."

"Sorry," I say as I hurry down the stairs, "I had to use the bathroom."

And I also made up my mind to fight fire with fire.

"Um, excuse me, who are you and what have you done with my bestie?" Claire asks from the driver's seat. I smile and shrug it off, feigning confidence I totally don't feel.

"Just wanted to step out of my comfort zone tonight," I tell her as I buckle my seat belt.

"Eric isn't going to know what's hit him," she says with a laugh and waggles her eyebrows suggestively, then pulls out of my driveway. I shrug that off, too. Eric isn't exactly who I'm concerned with. "I did damn good with that shirt. You're welcome."

I smooth my hands down my dark wash, skin-tight skinny jeans and try to ignore the chilled air reminding me that a significant portion of my upper body is exposed. Claire bought me a white silk halter top for my birthday last year. The back is scooped low, the hem cropped short, and the material is almost-but-not-quite see-through.

I told her there was no way in hell I'd ever wear it.

I'm eating those words tonight.

"Don't celebrate yet..." I say, and she side-eyes me. "I have a request."

"Okaaaay."

I fidget with my fingers since the hem of my shirt is above my bellybutton and take a breath.

"Well, you know how I hate going to these things..."

"Yeah?"

"And I only really go for you," I say honestly. "I'd rather be at home watching a movie or reading..." *Or painting.*

"I know, Len," she says defensively. "I appreciate you

coming with me. But you have fun. You can't even act like you don't."

I don't argue even though she couldn't be more wrong. I could give her a rundown of the last two parties we attended, but that's a terrible idea, so I don't.

"I was just wondering if you could DD tonight," I blurt out, then wait.

She stays silent. Taps her fingers on the steering wheel. The longer she goes without talking, the more irritated I get. I never ask for anything. She drags me to these things all the time and I'm always her babysitter. This one time—

"But, Len," she breaks the silence, "you know how hard it is for me to socialize at these things without having a drink." I grit my teeth and roll my eyes out the window. "You don't even like alcohol."

"Claire," I begin, my voice flat, ready to argue my point, "I just think tha—"

"Okay, fine, Lennon," she breathes out. "Fine. I'll DD tonight, but you owe me."

I force a smile and agree. I don't point out how, if we're doing a tit for tat sorta thing, she's way more in my debt than I am hers.

But I only want to antagonize one Davis sibling tonight, and that sibling isn't Claire.

We're quiet the rest of the ride to Josh's house, and when Claire parks on the road and climbs out, she makes a show of taking the car keys and shoving them in her clutch.

"Thank you," I say, and she shrugs, so I change the subject. "Looks like the guys are back."

I note several of the football players' vehicles on the road, which means they're back from the away game. Just the mention of Josh melts away some of Claire's icy front.

"Do I look okay?" she asks nervously, and I nod.

"You look hot. You always do, but definitely tonight."

She smiles, then frowns.

"Sorry I'm such a bitch," she says, then wraps me in a hug. I laugh, and it's genuine. She's so moody and stubborn. She always has been. But she's also a cream puff. "I'm just so freakin' nervous."

"Forgiven and forgotten." I pull away and hook my arm with hers. "Let's go."

Like every other party, we head to the kitchen, but this time, I'm the one cracking open a seltzer and taking a sip.

"This is disgusting," I say after I swallow. "It's worse than that sparkling-flavored water. I didn't even know that was possible."

Claire laughs as I take another drink.

"Well, disgusting or not, you're a lightweight, so go slow," she says, and tugs me toward the back deck. "Let's post up and let the guys come to us."

I haven't seen any sign of Macon or his goons. My head's been on a constant swivel since we got here. The deck gives a pretty good vantage point of the yard, but I can't make out anything more than silhouettes of the people down there, thanks to the giant bonfire. I swear it's bigger than it was last time. They really shouldn't have it so close to the house.

The longer I stand staring at the bonfire, the more uncomfortable I become. I feel so out of place. I want to wrap my arms around my stomach or tug down the hem of my shirt. I want to go home and put on pajamas, actually. I take another sip of the nasty seltzer, wrapping both my hands around it like a little kid with a mug of cocoa.

I'm cold, wearing a glorified washcloth to cover my breasts, and I'm drinking possibly the grossest beverage ever. It's like a fuzzy burp.

This was such a dumb idea.

Before I can tell Claire I've changed my mind, that I want to go back to my house and watch reruns of '90s sitcoms, Josh comes and whisks her away, leaving me awkwardly staring after them with a fake smile as she giggles off into the distance. I thought she would want to stay with me since I'm drinking and she's not. I never drink. I thought maybe she'd at least want to give me some support or something. I'd have stayed with her.

I frown and uncertainty prods at my brain. I'm losing my nerve and feeling very alone.

Taking my eyes off Claire's retreating form, the other Davis catches my attention. Macon is pressed against a tree with his tongue down some random girl's throat. It's not Sam. I clench my fist, spilling some of the seltzer all over my hand. I watch, teeth-clenched, as the girl runs her hands up and down Macon's arms. When she shoves her hands into his hair, I feel murderous.

But his hands never leave her waist. I stare at his hands, study his fingers. I could probably paint them from memory, for as much time as I've spent watching them recently. They're loose where they sit on the band of the girl's jeans. Not gripping or pulling. Not rubbing or massaging. Not slipping under barrier clothing to caress naked skin.

They're just...resting there. Like they're killing time or boredom.

"There you are," Eric's voice interrupts my voyeurism, and I turn my head toward him. He walks through the sliding doors and crosses the deck to stand next to me. I take a deep breath and force another smile.

"Hey," I say brightly, "how was the game?"

He doesn't answer. He just smiles and gives his head a little shake, glances down my body quickly, then runs his hand through his hair. It's shy. Cute.

"Sorry," he says, his smile turning embarrassed. "You just,

126

uh. You look really nice, Lennon. You look pretty. I mean, you always look pretty, but tonight, it's a different kind of pretty."

Now it's my turn to smile. My cheeks and ears blush as I laugh quietly at his nervous stammering. There's something empowering about rendering a gorgeous boy speechless, especially when that boy can have any girl he wants.

"Thank you," I force out, grabbing for the hem of my shirt, then forcibly folding my hands behind my back. "Claire bought me this shirt for my birthday last year."

"Remind me to thank her." Eric's voice is playful, but his gaze runs over me tentatively, then flits away, before dragging back. Like he wants to look longer but doesn't know that he should. It's sweet.

So unlike anything Macon would do.

Macon stares. Unashamedly. *Rudely*.

Eric's attention is like a gentle breeze tickling my skin.

Macon's is a forest fire consuming me in flames.

I flick my eyes back over my shoulder, but Macon and the make-out girl are gone, so I focus on Eric.

"I never see your hair down, but I like it." He reaches out like he's going to push my hair behind my ear, but then he drops his hand and slips it into his pocket. "Sorry," he chuckles. "I'm so nervous right now and I don't even know why."

"You don't have to be nervous," I tell him honestly, then take his hand and give it a squeeze. His dimples pop when he grins, and it makes me hyperaware of how close we're standing. I drop his hand. "Tell me how the game went."

Eric talks about football, then school, and I smile and laugh when appropriate. I give good small talk. I'm the perfect mirror when I need to be, and he's the perfect gentleman. Kind, respectful, flattering. I could love him, I think. If I let myself.

When I finish my drink, Eric offers to get me another one, and I say yes. The moment he leaves, my back heats.

"What the actual fuck are you wearing?"

Macon's voice is mocking, and I spin around to find him leaning on the deck railing with a lit cigarette between his lips. His hair is mussed, like someone just had their tacky manicured nails in it. The collar of his shirt is stretched out, but that could just be because Macon is a slob.

I put my hands on my hips and face off with him.

"Clothing," I answer flatly.

"You look ridiculous."

My mouth wants to drop at his sneer, but I catch myself and tighten my jaw. I want to cover my body. The parts of myself I don't like flash in my head, all of the ways I'm exposing my flaws. I almost cower, but the disgusted curl of Macon's upper lip only fuels my rage.

"*Eric* likes it," I say, and hope it sounds more confident than I feel.

Macon closes the distance between us in three steps.

"That douche likes it because he can see your nipples and wants to titty-fuck you." He growls, then blows a stream of smoke out of the side of his mouth.

The smoke makes me angrier than his words. I snatch the cigarette and stub it out on the railing.

"So what if he does?" I spit. He steps closer, pressing me into the railing. His pupils are giant. I don't know if it's because of the dark or because he's on something.

"You so desperate for attention that you gotta dress like an actress in a cheap porno?" He fingers the strap of my halter and I swat him away. "You wanna get titty-fucked, *Astraea*? Just ask."

"Don't call me that." I shove at his chest to hide the embarrassed tint on my cheeks. "Don't touch me."

"Didn't care I was touching you when you were dry-humping on my dick," he says loudly.

"Macon," I gasp, and whip my eyes around to make sure

no one heard him. He chuckles, and I have to swallow back a growl. "Go back to your backyard bang and let me get back to my *date*."

His eyes narrow and his nostrils flare, but then he barks out a laugh.

"You jealous, Leonard?"

"Never," I say through my teeth.

"Didn't think you were a jersey-chasing groupie," he taunts, and I smirk through my rage.

"Well, I always knew you were a worthless loser."

My voice is cloying, and I'm staring him down when Eric appears over Macon's shoulder with my new seltzer.

"Here, Len," Eric says, handing me the drink, then turns to Macon. "Hey. Is there a problem?"

"Macon was just leaving to get high," I snarl, then turn to Eric. "Thank you," I tell him sweetly, then pop the tab. I move to take a drink, but the seltzer is ripped from my hand and tossed into the yard. "What the hell, Macon?" I shout.

"Dude, what was that for?" Eric asks, but Macon blows him off and points at me.

"You're done drinking," he scolds, then looks at Eric. "She's done drinking."

"I'll do whatever the hell I want!"

"You will not drink, *Astraea*," he says again, his voice low and stern. It stirs something deep in my belly, further stoking my anger.

I'll show him *innocence* and *purity*. He thinks I'm so darn easy to mess with. Thinks he can touch me and tease me. Abandon me for days and then put his hands on other girls. He thinks he can make me a joke. This time, I'll be the only one laughing.

I stand on my tiptoes, so we're almost nose to nose, and whisper, "watch me," then push past him and storm into the house. I find a group of football players taking shots and swipe one.

"Thank you," I say quickly, throwing back the shot before they can protest.

Then I gag.

"Oh my god, that's terrible," I force out, and the group laughs. I fan my face and shake my head.

"Want another?" a burly guy asks, and I nod and hold out my hand.

He gives me another shot, and I take that one too. I gag again.

"Ugh, it doesn't get any better," I cough out, and they roar with more laugher.

"Masters, your girlfriend don't like liquor," someone calls out. I want to say I'm not his girlfriend, but an arm wraps around my shoulder, and I glace up to find Eric holding out a bottle of water with a grimace.

"It's nasty," he says in my defense, and I nod in agreement. I twist the lid off the water and take a giant gulp, my head already starting to spin, then glance over Eric's shoulder. Macon is glaring at me from the corner, so I grab another shot glass, flip him off, and don't break eye contact until the demon liquid hits my tongue.

I cringe, but I don't gag this time. Why the hell do people drink this stuff for fun?

"Let's dance," I say, my words starting to slur, but I'm determined to win this one. To make Macon...I don't even know. Jealous? Angry? To make him feel even half of what he makes me feel. The thought ignites a spark of joy in my chest. I grab Eric's hand and pull him through the house toward the music.

I move my body to the song with Eric's hands on my waist. I block out the thought that, right now, I am every stupid "unpopular girl" stereotype in every teen movie who gets drunk at a party and makes an ass of herself. Will I dance on a table and hit my head on a chandelier? Will I vomit on someone's shoes? I can't bring myself to care.

The beat switches up, and I slow my movements, giving Eric my back and gliding myself over his front. His hands grip my hips and pull me closer. I press into him and lift my arms behind my head, so I can thread them around his neck.

Everything starts to feel heavy and warm, like moving through bath water. I can feel the music like it's instructing my moves. I close my eyes and see every note in paint strokes. It's beautiful and fascinating, and I want to laugh.

So, this is what it's like being drunk. I kind of get it now.

I feel lips on my neck, a slow exhale dancing over my collarbone. I lay my head back on Eric's shoulder and turn my face to his, but before his lips touch mine, he's ripped from my hands, and I'm jostled forward. I spin around just in time to see Eric stumble back, then Macon throws me over his shoulder.

"Put me down!" I screech, using one arm to cover my chest and the other to beat on his back. I thrash about, twisting back and forth in the fireman's hold. Briefly, I'm reminded of Macon at the fairgrounds and the way he was dangled lifeless over Julian's shoulder, but that thought flits away. "This isn't funny!"

"Dude, Davis, put her down, man, what are you doing?" Eric shouts from behind us, a small hint of confused humor in his voice.

"Stay out of it, Masters, or I'll hit you so hard you gotta sit out next game," Macon threatens over his shoulder. Eric throws up his palms and stops in his tracks.

"No! Macon," I yell, hitting him again. "Put me the fuck down! Put. Me. Down!"

"Shut the fuck up, Lennon, Jesus Christ," he scolds, and I thrash and hit him harder. "You want me to drop you on your fucking head?" he shouts, then a sharp crack sounds through the air and over my skin, my ass burning. "Quit fucking moving."

"You just smacked my ass," I screech again and pound on his back. It vibrates with a laugh. "Put me down you big...stupid...fucking...dummy!" He snorts and smacks my ass again.

"I said you were done drinking, Lennon. You're going home."

The word *home* stills me. Instant calm. Instant cooperation. I do want to go home. I want to go to sleep.

"Claire's DD," I mumble, and prop my elbow on his back, so I can rest my chin on my fist. My head bounces with each step, and I pretend I'm riding a horse.

We get closer and closer to the bonfire, and then Macon stops in his tracks. He groans.

"What the hell?" I hear Claire yell. "Is that Lennon? Put her down, asshole!"

"Claire, are you fucking drunk?" Macon asks, and I jolt up. I try to push up with both hands, but my shirt starts to fall over my face, so I clamp one arm over it again. I should have worn a bra. This shirt is the worst.

"No," I say, trying to see over his shoulder, "she's DD."

Macon smacks my ass again, making me yelp, and Claire yells something at him.

"Real fucking nice, Claire," Macon says, using the hand not holding me hostage to pull something out of his back pocket. "Real responsible."

Macon turns and walks away, giving me a view of a very angry Claire glaring at us with a plastic cup in her hand.

"I'm just buzzed," Claire argues, and I huff, my alcohol-addled brain trying to make sense of the situation. She drank? No. She was DD. She promised. She wouldn't do that. Friends keep their promises. My jaw drops, but she says nothing to me.

Macon's talking to someone. Not to me and not to Claire.

He makes his way down the long gravel driveway with Claire stomping after us, and when we get to the road, Chris Casper is waiting in his idling truck. My head pounds, and the smell of exhaust turns my stomach.

"Gonna barf," I mumble, and I'm lifted and spun until I'm on my knees with someone holding my hair back as I puke into the ditch.

It tastes like the shots, but worse.

I take it back. I don't get it. Drunk is bad. The bath dance wasn't worth it.

Someone rubs my back until I've heaved up the entire contents of my stomach, then hands me a bottle of water. I drink the entire thing.

"Thanks," I whisper.

"Yeah," Macon says, then he helps me up and slides me in the front seat of Casper's cab with Claire climbing in after him. I glance at the clock on the dash. It's only eleven-thirty. I groan.

"Dad'll be awake," I mumble, dropping my head on the shoulder next to me. Mint and weed and spice.

"Fuck," Claire says, and I feel Macon's exasperated sigh.

"Mom works tonight. We'll go back to our house, and you can text Trent and tell him you're staying there."

His shoulder rumbles under my head. I feel a hand squeeze my thigh and I reach for it, wrapping my hand around the thick wrist and rubbing my thumb up and down the scar there. I listen to the sound of the engine and focus on the smell of Macon's shirt.

"Wake up," Macon whispers, brushing my hair away from my face. "Need me to carry you?"

I shake my head no and climb out of the car, then stumble. Macon catches me, just before I fall on my face. With a laugh, he scoops me into his arms.

"C'mon, drunk ass," he teases. "You're gonna be so fucking hungover in the morning."

I don't even know where Claire or Casper are. Behind us? Next to us? All I know is Macon's breathing and his arms and his hard chest. I bet that tattoo is right under my cheek. I want to know what it says.

Macon unlocks the door easily, despite cradling me in his arms, then walks silently through the hall. Just before the living room, he stops in his tracks.

"Fuck," he says, and I open my eyes to my dad's murderous glare.

It all happens in slow motion.

My first instinct is to apologize, to explain, but then I notice Drea standing behind my dad with her hands covering her mouth, her eyes wide with shock. This is her house. Why is my dad here? It's only eleven-thirty.

Then I see the open bottle of wine on the coffee table. Two glasses.

Then the scent of lavender. A candle. The same kind Drea burns to relax after work.

The lavender.

Lavender.

Why do you smell like lavender?

I glance back to my dad, then to Drea.

It clicks.

"You guys are sleeping together," I state.

Andrea gasps and looks at Macon. "You told her?"

"No, but you just did," he states flatly, and I move my eyes to him.

"You knew?"

His brow furrows as he looks at me. *Guilt.*

His arms tighten around my body, reminding me I'm still being held bridal-style against his chest. He opens his mouth like he wants to apologize, but Claire walks in behind him and gasps. She says something, and I can tell from her tone that she's just as shocked. She pieced it together quickly. She must not be as drunk as me.

"How long?" I whisper to Macon, and he cringes. *Long,* then. My stomach swirls. I open my mouth to speak, to inquire, but I throw up all over him instead.

TWELVE

Lennon

THE MOMENT I OPEN MY EYES, I SLAM THEM SHUT AGAIN.

My head pounds and my mouth tastes like barf-coated cotton. *Glamorous.* I groan and roll over onto my stomach, sinking my head into my hands.

It's the squeak and give of the air mattress that releases the flood of images from last night.

Shots with football players. Dancing with Eric. Hanging upside down from Macon's shoulder. Claire drank when she said she wouldn't. I vomited in a ditch.

I...vomited on Macon?

And then the big one hits.

Dad and Andrea. The candle. And Macon knew.

I get up slowly, babying my fragile head, and walk into the bathroom, leaving Claire snoring in her bed. I take the ibuprofen from the medicine cabinet and pop two in my mouth, bending over and drinking straight from the faucet to wash them down. I use the toothbrush I leave here to brush my teeth, which helps me feel marginally better. Then I barge into Macon's room, ready to hurl questions or insults at him, but he's not there.

The bed is unmade, and it smells faintly of weed, but he's gone. I can't tell if he slept here at all.

I make my way down the stairs and into the kitchen, finding my dad sitting at the table with his hands folded in front of him. I halt and tilt my head to the side.

"Did you sleep here?" I ask. He shakes his head.

"I came over this morning."

I look away and walk to the coffee pot, sending up a thank you when I find some already brewed. I fix a cup, blow on it, then take several sips before finally turning to face the music.

Dad's face is stern, and any other time I would feel ashamed. I hate disappointing him. But not this time.

"You drank last night," he says, and I nod.

"You gonna punish me?"

His mouth hitches the tiniest bit at the corner, and he shakes his head.

"I think the way you're feeling right now is punishment enough."

I roll my eyes, then flinch at the pain the motion causes. I take another sip from my coffee and meet my dad's stare.

"How long?"

"We've been seeing each other regularly for about a year," he says. The steadiness of his voice irritates me and reminds me that he's been trained for interrogation. I huff.

"So before that you were just fucking?" I spit, and he jolts.

"Lennon Capri," he scolds, and I cower a bit under his tone. I bite my tongue on the apology I want to utter, though. I'm not sorry. I glare back at him and wait. His shoulders fall. "We were never *just fucking.*"

Surprise tickles my throat and my eyebrows jump up. My dad *never* cusses.

"When did it start?" I whisper, and for the first time, I see a hint of shame on his face.

"A few years ago," he hedges.

"*When*, Dad," I force out. When he speaks again, his voice is contrite.

"Since Virginia Beach," he says, and my jaw drops.

That was nearly five years ago. I try to comb through my memories of that trip, but nothing stands out. It was just my best friend and her family coming on vacation with me and my dad. Dad and Drea have always been friendly, but there's never been any sign to suggest...

"Why didn't you tell me?" I ask. "Why did Macon know and not me?"

"I don't have a good answer for that," Dad says slowly. "I didn't want to confuse you or affect your friendship with Claire. For a long time, it was just you and me, and after your mom, I didn't want to disrupt your normal. And Macon, well, he was just in the wrong place at the wrong time."

"Oh my god," I whisper, thoughts of Macon walking in on my dad and his mom make my skin crawl.

"Just kissing," my dad clarifies, as if that makes it less weird. "Around Christmas."

"That's almost a year ago!" I shout. "And you were here last night, why? Because you knew Claire would be gone and you guys were sneaking around? Is that why you suggested we stay at our house last night?"

"Lower your voice," he says sternly, and I take a deep breath and grit my teeth. "I was here last night because Andrea had a difficult conversation with the kids' dad, and I came over after to console her and be a good friend. I planned to go back home after."

I snort at *friend*. I don't mention the wine or the candle. I didn't think my dad would lie to me about something like this, but our whole relationship revolves around secrets. I feel angry and betrayed and guilty all at once.

"There's something else," he says slowly, and I whip my eyes back to him. His face is blank.

"Don't tell me you want to marry her," I whisper.

"I've been thinking about it for a while," he confesses. "We were going to come clean about our relationship over winter break, and I was going to propose after you graduated."

I blink at him. I blink again. I stare hard, and I don't speak.

"I love her, Lennon."

The vulnerability and sincerity in his voice breaks me, and I start to cry. He stands and walks to me, pulling me into a hug, and I wrap my hands around his large, muscled torso and cry into his shirt. I breathe in the familiar scent of our laundry detergent, and the faint hints of lavender hit me like a frying pan over the head. God, I was so stupid. I start to laugh.

"The lavender," I say between laughs and sobs, and he chuckles. "I never connected the two."

He rubs my back and rests his chin on my head.

"I'm sorry this is how you found out, Lennon, but I'm not sorry for falling for her."

I pull back and smile softly through my tears.

"I know," I choke out. "I love her too. She's easy to love."

He smiles. "She is." He releases me and steps back. "I'm going to head back home, but Andrea and I would like to have a family dinner, all of us, to start getting used to the situation. Since you all know, now, there's no reason for us not to publicly date."

"Okay," I force out.

I'm okay with it, I am, but I don't miss how he never once *asks* if I'm okay with it. *There's no reason*, he says, all but admitting my opinion about this relationship doesn't matter. The realization tastes bitter.

My fingers itch for a paintbrush, but *my* secret is still a secret, and it's going to have to stay that way. At least for a little while longer.

"Oh," my dad blurts before he leaves the kitchen, "I forgot to tell you. Eric came by the house this morning to check on you. Brought you some flowers. He's a nice kid, Len. I'm glad you found him."

I flatten my lips between my teeth and breathe through my nose.

"Thanks," I say after a moment. "Me too."

Dad leaves me standing in the kitchen with my secrets swirling around me, taunting me. Reminding me that I can't be angry with my dad for lying, because I'm the biggest liar of us all.

I head back upstairs to change after another cup of coffee. When I get to Claire's room, she's awake and sitting upright on the bed.

"So..." she starts, "Virginia Beach, huh?"

I sigh. "Yep. You were listening?"

"All of it," she says with a nod, then screws up her face. "It's so weird that our parents have seen each other naked."

"Ew, Claire." I close my eyes and shake my head to get the thought out.

"When they get married, do I have to call Trent, Daddy?"

"Eeeew, Claire, please never call him daddy."

She barks out a laugh, then gasps.

"Does this make my crush on him taboo?"

"Claire! You're not allowed to crush on my dad," I squeal, to which she laughs harder.

"Well, no, definitely not now that he's gonna be my *daddy*."

I groan and face-plant onto her bed while she giggles. I don't say anything. I just let her tire herself out, and soon she flops down next to me and sighs.

"There is one cool thing, though," she breaks the silence. I hum in response. "We're gonna be sisters," she says.

Her voice is giddy, and for a moment, I feel it. The excitement of having a family again, one that's larger than just me and Dad, makes me hopeful. No more spending missions and deployments worrying by myself. No more loneliness.

Bigger holiday and birthday celebrations. Family meals. Family vacations. *Family*.

Claire might be a lot sometimes, but aren't all sisters? I love her like she's family already. This will just make it official. I turn my head to her and smile.

"That'll be cool," I say honestly, and then she bursts my fragile bubble.

"I'll finally have a sibling that matters," she says wistfully, and my stomach drops to my feet. I don't say anything, and soon, Claire falls back to sleep.

I make my way down the block to my house, wearing my jeans from last night and one of Claire's pajama shirts. It's the closest I've ever come to a walk of shame. I'm not sure where the halter I was wearing went, but I'm okay with never seeing it again.

I'm halfway up my driveway when my phone rings. I don't recognize the number, so I send it to voicemail. A text comes in immediately after.

It's Casper. Answer the phone.

It rings again, and I answer it.

"Chri—er, Casper?"

"Hey, Lennon," he says quickly. His tight voice makes me stop walking, three feet from my front door. "How fast can you get to Chesapeake?"

I'm not sure what I expected to find when I pulled up to the address Casper sent me a half hour later, but a drunk, stumbling Macon, throwing eggs at a very large, very expensive looking two-story brick house wasn't on my list of possibilities.

Casper was adamant—*do not tell Claire*.

Now I understand why.

I put the car in park, just as Macon bends over and picks up a bottle of brown liquor, takes a long swig, then hurls it at the house. It hits the brick with a loud SMASH, narrowly missing a large picture window, and I'm out my door and running toward him before he can throw anything else.

"Come out here, you motherfucker!" Macon screams at the house. "Deadbeat son of a bitch! COME OUT HERE."

"Macon," I shout, grabbing his arm just as he tries to throw another egg. "Macon, stop!"

He shakes me off and I fall back on my ass. He throws the egg, hitting the front door right in the middle.

"Go home, *Leonard*," he yells over his shoulder, picking up another egg from a carton at his feet. I jump up and dart forward, stepping on the carton and crushing the last few eggs with my ballet flat so he can't throw any more of them.

"What the fuck?" he shouts, whirling on me. "Stay the fuck out of it, Lennon!"

"You're going to get your dumb ass arrested," I hiss, just as the door to the house opens and then slams. I look up to see a very angry older man on the front steps. He's scowling, vibrating with fury, and he has a phone in his hand.

"Go home before I call the police," the man says. I'm terrified, but Macon laughs.

"Call 'em," Macon slurs, then bends down and picks up the carton of crushed eggs. I grab his arm and tug him toward my car.

"Please don't call the cops, sir," I plead. "He's done. He's not in his right mind. I'm taking him home. We'll pay for the damage."

"I'm not paying this fucker for shit," Macon sneers, shaking me off again. When my hold on him breaks, he throws the crushed egg carton, hitting the wall beside the man, and stalks toward him. When he's close enough, Macon swings, punching the man right in the face. The man falls back, and Macon falls on top of him.

I scream and rush forward. Macon grunts words with each punch.

Deadbeat. Selfish. Asshole.

For a minute, I think he's recounting the insults I threw at him last night.

"Macon, stop it, please," I say, my voice shrill with fear, my eyes stinging with tears.

There's blood on the man's face. On Macon's hands. The man is struggling, hitting Macon's torso, thrashing back and forth as Macon wails on him. I've never seen a real fight before.

"Please, Macon," I cry. "Please!"

Macon stops, pulling back to look at me, and the man lands a punch on Macon's jaw, the sound cracking over the lawn and laying him out flat on the fancy stone pavers. I collapse next to him, scanning his face to assess his injuries. His lips are busted and bleeding, the swelling already noticeable, and his jaw is bright red from the punch.

"Go home, Macon, now," the guy commands through pants, and my eyes jump to him in shock. He looks worse than Macon. His eyebrow is split open, along with his lip, and he already has a black eye forming, making his piercing blue eyes look...

Just like Macon's.

My hands tighten on Macon's arm when I realize who just punched him. Who he just beat up. His dad.

The more I look at him, the more shocked I become. Macon looks *just like* his dad. The height, the hair, the eyes. Even the cruel tilt on his full lips is the same. This man in front of me is what Macon will look like in thirty years, if he ever gets his shit together. Cuts his hair. Wears slacks and button downs.

Corporate Macon.

Business Macon.

"She didn't deserve that," Macon seethes, making me

jump. I pull my attention away from his dad and look down at him as he struggles to sit up. "I'm the fuck-up. I'm the one you hate. You don't get to fucking punish them."

He swipes at the blood on his lip with his hand, smearing it on his chin. Some of it drips onto his black shirt and disappears.

"If you come back here, I'll press charges. Vandalism. Assault. Battery." The man throws his finger out at us, and the sneer on his face is a carbon copy of the one I've seen many times before on Macon.

"You're nineteen," he continues slowly. "I'll make sure they throw your punk ass in prison."

"But this is your son," I say in disbelief.

"Don't fucking remind me."

The man turns around and stomps back into the house, slamming the door behind him. It's not until he's gone that I notice the little boy, maybe six or seven, peeking out at me from the picture window. Blond hair, but with unruly curls just like Macon's.

I stand up and give Macon's arm a tug.

"C'mon, let's go," I say, and he shakes me off again and stands on his own.

"Go home, Lennon," he grumbles, "stay out of this."

"Too late for that," I huff. "Casper called me and begged me to keep you out of jail, and your drunk ass needs my help, so get in the fucking car."

"Fucking Casper," he grunts, but he doesn't argue anymore.

When he's buckled in my passenger seat, I head back the way I came, driving us out of the expensive, daunting neighborhood.

"How'd you get here?" I ask, glancing at him briefly. He's slouched in the seat with his eyes closed, holding some tissues to his lips to stop the bleeding. I might have to take him to get stitches.

"I drove."

"You *WHAT*?" I screech, ready to slam on the brakes and beat the crap out of him myself. "You're *wasted*! You said you—"

"Chill, Lennon, fuck," he scolds. "I was sober when I drove. My car is at the liquor store. I walked from there to Daddy Dearest's house."

I heave a sigh of relief. It's still not good. But it's better than I thought it was two seconds ago. I look at him again. He's obviously in no condition to drive. If I bring him home, he'll have to come back and get his car at some point. But I don't want Claire or Drea, or heck, even my dad, to see him like this.

I'm hit, once again, with this deep, urgent worry. A familiar anxiety clawing desperately at my mind and chest.

Macon needs *something*. I'm not sure what. I doubt he knows either.

But if he doesn't find it, he'll seek it out with pills or alcohol or sex. Probably all three, and the reality makes me sick to my stomach. I look at him, his hunched, broken form in my passenger seat. How is this talented, strong, beautiful boy so haunted?

I picture the absolute disgust, the hatred, in Macon's dad's eyes just before he stormed back into his house. The way Claire talks about him like he's wasted life. Andrea's tears.

Don't fucking remind me.

Do us all a favor next time and OD.

He's just troubled.

Oh, Macon. Suddenly, I want to cry, but I swallow it back and school my face.

I make the decision without consulting him. I just punch the address into my GPS, then hook my phone to Bluetooth and turn on my Fleetwood Mac playlist. With the music playing and the GPS set, I head toward the interstate, taking the East ramp instead of the West.

When Macon cracks his eyes open fifteen minutes later and realizes we're not heading back to Franklin, he sits up and turns in his seat to look at me with his eyebrow popped.

I glance at him and smirk.

"Go back to sleep, loser," I say with my eyes back on the road. "I'll wake you when we get there."

THIRTEEN

Macon

W⒣ᴇɴ Lᴇɴɴᴏɴ ᴘᴜʟʟs ᴜᴘ ɪɴ ꜰʀᴏɴᴛ ᴏꜰ ᴀ ꜰᴀᴍɪʟɪᴀʀ ʜᴏᴜsᴇ, I can't stay quiet anymore. I turn in my seat and stare at her.

"What's this?" I ask, hooking my thumb over my shoulder at the four-bedroom beach house we stayed in during our Virginia Beach vacation a few years ago. It looks the same.

Lennon holds her finger up, silencing me, while she types on her phone. So, I wait. Thirty more seconds. Sixty. Just before we hit four minutes and I lose it, Lennon puts her phone in her lap and smiles at me.

"Luckily, it wasn't rented since the tourist season is over," she says, as if that tells me anything.

"Okay...?"

"Well," she says with a shy shrug, "I just rented it for the night. Obviously, we can't stay here overnight, but we can use it to fix this—" she waves her fingers in a circle around my face, "—and hang out until you've sobered up enough to drive your own car home."

Warmth spreads in my chest, but I don't let it show.

"We couldn't have just hung out at a park or some shit?"

She rolls her eyes. "Shut up and get out of the car, Macon."

I smirk, but the motion causes a flicker of pain when my lip cracks. I lick at the blood and do what she said. I unbuckle my seat belt and trail her up the stairs, where she punches a code into the door. It unlocks with a whir, so she pushes it open, and I follow her inside.

"The furniture is new," she says absently, walking around the living room and lightly touching everything. The couch, the chair, the strategically, hand-picked books on the built-ins. She drags her fingertips over every surface, testing it out, feeling it, in the same odd way she always has. I'm fascinated in the same consuming way I've always been.

She wants to touch everything. To experience it all.

I just want to touch her.

She turns to where I'm standing in the doorway and her smile drops away.

"Shit," she whispers. "Be right back."

She walks past me and heads back to the car, pops the trunk, and pulls out a red plastic box. I laugh when I see what it is.

"Oh, shut up," she says with a huff. "Go sit down. You're a mess."

I snort and roll my eyes, but I follow her direction and stumble onto the couch as she kneels in front of me. She pops open the travel first-aid kit and rummages through the contents, pulling out some antiseptic wipes, band-aids, and a tube of anti-bacterial ointment.

She sits back on her ankles and studies me, her eyes flitting over my injuries. My eyes stay trained on hers. She rips open one of the antiseptic wipes.

"This might sting a bit," she whispers. Her breath fans over my cheeks. I don't feel a thing as she uses the wipe to dab at the cut on my lip. Just the pressure of her delicate, talented fingers and the vibrations of her closeness. I work to keep my breathing even, secretly pulling her rose-scented shampoo into my lungs with each inhale.

Her brow furrows.

"This looks bad, Macon. You might need to go to a hospital."

I shake my head slightly, just enough to let her know I won't go, but I don't speak. I've been in worse fights. Had more serious injuries. My wrist aches just at the thought. This split lip is nothing. It will heal quickly on its own.

"Fine," she says with a sigh. "Just let me..."

She cleans the blood off my lips and chin, then puts some anti-bacterial ointment on the cut. She prods at my jaw lightly, and I hiss.

"Sorry," she says quickly. "It looks nasty. It's already bruised and swollen. I'm going to go see if there's anything we can use as an ice pack."

She hops up and walks into the kitchen. I hear a door open, drawers rustling, and then she's back with a balled-up dishtowel in her hand.

"Bingo," she says. "The fridge has an icemaker."

Instead of handing me the ice, she kneels back in front of me and presses it to my jaw. The chill hits me, and my eyes fall shut. We're quiet for a moment. Me breathing her in, her holding me together.

"So that was your dad," she says finally. Inevitably.

"Yeah."

"He's..." she trails off, so I finish for her.

"A dick."

She laughs, but she doesn't argue.

"He told Mom he's not going to pay for Claire's college," I tell her. Her face folds into sorrow.

"No," she whispers, and I nod.

"It wasn't in the custody agreement, but it was something

he always said he would do." I shrug off the fury. "He changed his mind."

She shakes her head, confused.

"I didn't even realize he was still part of your lives. You never see him or talk about him."

"Cause we don't fit into his perfect little life with his perfect little family," I say honestly. I try to sound unaffected, but I fail. "He still paid child support, though. Until Claire turned eighteen."

Hush money, is what it should be called.

"Anyway, he's decided he's done with us for good, now. Claire's eighteen, and the honorable Phillip Morrison has relinquished all financial responsibility."

"Wait..." she says, glancing at the ceiling in thought. "Phillip....the lawyer from the radio commercials? The injury defense attorney?"

"One in the same."

"Dang."

"Yeah."

She doesn't say it out loud, but I know what she's thinking. He's loaded. If you couldn't tell from his fucking McMansion on the man-made lake, you'd know from his cheesy fucking radio ads that play on every station in Virginia. Dick could afford to pay for Claire to go to college ten times over, and it wouldn't even make a dent in his bank account, but greed doesn't give two fucks about who it hurts.

"Poor Claire," she whispers. "Poor Drea. That must have been the difficult conversation my dad must have been talking about."

I scoff.

"It was hardly a conversation. He sent my mom one text. One. And then ignored all her calls until flat out blocking her."

I take the icepack from Lennon, so I can sit back on the couch and rest my head on the cushions. I hold it to my jaw and close my eyes. I feel her move onto the couch beside me, but she doesn't speak.

"My mom can't afford to pay for Claire to go to college. She's going to have to take out fucking loans, and she probably won't even qualify for financial aid because *he's* her fucking father, and he's one of the richest fucks in the state."

I let out a humorless laugh.

"It's fine," I say sarcastically. "She'll just be another person drowning in student loan debt when she graduates."

The whole situation makes me want to punch something. Or take something.

"I'm sorry." Lennon takes my free hand in hers and squeezes. I flip my hand and thread my fingers through hers. The touch makes my shoulders relax.

"I wish he was dead," I confess. When Lennon doesn't speak, I realize my mistake and cringe. "Fuck. I'm sorry, Len. That was insensitive."

"No," she whispers. "It's okay. You're angry. I get it."

"It's just...to know that he lives thirty minutes away and wants nothing to do with us?" I swallow and breathe through my nose. "At least your mom didn't leave you by choice."

When she doesn't speak, doesn't make a noise, I turn my head toward her and open my eyes. She's staring at our clasped hands and chewing on her lip.

"Hey," I whisper and give her hand a squeeze. When she looks up at me, my stomach falls to my feet and my heart falls with it. I've never seen her look so haunted. So empty. "What? What's wrong?"

"You know how my mom died?" she asks, her voice flat.

"She was sick..." I say slowly. It's what my mom said. I always assumed it was cancer or something. When Lennon flinches, I know I'm wrong.

"My mom had bipolar disorder," she whispers. "She'd have these mood swings. Dad says they started around the time she

151

turned sixteen. My dad and her were together all through high school. Did you know that? They were high school sweethearts. He knew her before...*Loved* her before."

She pauses and swallows. Licks her lower lip.

"One time I came home from school, and she'd painted half the living room bright yellow because she wanted our house to be like the sun. The next day, she couldn't get out of bed and stayed there for a week."

I put down the icepack and turn, so I'm facing Lennon, but I never let go of her hand. Her lips are pursed, and her brow is furrowed, staring at something on the floor.

"She was better for a while. Got help. But she would get worse when Dad would leave. Six-month deployments are hard, you know?"

I squeeze her hand again, but I don't speak. I save the space for her voice. It's her story.

"He was already five months into a deployment when she overdosed," she whispers, and my heart stops. "A bottle of vodka and a bottle of pills."

She squeezes her eyes shut as tears leak through her lashes. I pull her to my chest and hold her tight. She buries her face in my neck. I let the implications sink in.

Five months into a six-month deployment.

Meaning Lennon had to have been the one who...

Fuck, and she was only nine.

I rub her back and let her cry into my shirt. I run my fingers through her hair. Press soft kisses on the top of her head. I do everything I can think of to comfort her, short of taking her pain into my own body so she can be free of it.

If I knew how to do that, I would.

"Is that why you don't let Trent know you paint?" I ask after a while.

"Yeah," she says against me. Her lips tickle the skin on my neck as she talks. "I used to paint all the time, but I could always feel him watching me. Waiting. Like I was this ticking time bomb."

She sits up and makes eye contact with me. The wet, red-rimmed look of her eyes makes the green in her hazel irises seem almost ethereal.

"My mom painted. She was so talented. But in her moods..."

Lennon pauses, grappling for the words. She looks back at the carpet, stares at it for a few moments, then finally brings her eyes back to me.

"You could kind of tell by her paintings. The colors she'd use, the speed at which she'd paint. You could tell when she was heading for a crash."

She shrugs.

"I was tired of Dad trying to read into my work that way. Not seeing my paintings as art, but as warnings. I don't know, as if they were harbingers of my impending mental illness, or something. It made him so anxious. I could tell he hated it."

"Do you think..." I start to say, but then stop. I don't have to finish. She knows what I was going to say.

"I don't know," she whispers, concern or embarrassment or both coating her words. "It can be genetic. I read that signs typically start anywhere between eighteen to twenty-nine, but my mom's started at sixteen. They got worse when she had me, but then they got better for a few years. Things improved when she was on my dad's health insurance because she got a proper diagnosis and treatment. Therapy and meds. It's why he enlisted. But..."

She trails off and doesn't finish. I don't push.

I've always had a lot of respect for Trent. He's one of the only people who has never treated me like a complete fuck-up. He treats me better than my sperm donor. I didn't know about everything he went through with Lennon's mom, but now that

I do, I respect him more. And for Lennon to have gone through this as a kid? Shit.

"I'm sorry," I say, though I know it's not enough.

I hate that phrase. *I'm sorry.* But what else could I possibly say? It happened, and it's fucked up that it happened, and I *am* sorry.

"Thanks. Me too," Lennon says, then she reaches up and starts pulling her hair into a French braid. "Wanna go sit on the beach?"

I nod, but I don't take my eyes off her hands. Her talented fingers twist and loop strands of her long, brown hair until it's all in an immaculate braid hanging down her back. She ties it off with a ribbon that she pulls off her wrist. It's practiced and perfect. You can tell she's been braiding her own hair for years.

"Why do you always braid your hair?" I ask as she stands up and walks through the house toward the door that leads to the beach access.

"I just always have," she says with a shrug. "I like them."

"But you don't though," I challenge. She raises an eyebrow. "I don't?"

"No," I tell her. "You hate your hair in a braid. You've hated it for as long as I've known you."

"Yeah..." She blinks and messes with the hem of her oversized t-shirt. "Well...my mom always used to braid it."

I don't say anything else until we're seated on the beach, our shoes off and our toes dug deep in the sand. I lean back on my elbows and watch her watch the ocean. Her eyebrows are scrunched, deep in thought. I give her shirt a light tug to get her attention.

"Hey," I say softly, "I should have told you."

She turns to me and studies my face, bouncing her eyes between mine, checking for a lie.

"It's okay."

154

"Is it really okay, or are you just saying that to avoid confrontation?"

I already know the answer, but she needs to own that shit. She purses her lips and blows a puff of air through her nose.

"It's not," she says finally. "It makes me angry that I was left in the dark about this. You should have told me."

"I know." I sigh. "Trent asked me not to. He wanted to be the one to tell you. It was his place to tell you, not mine. But after the first month passed..."

I sit back up and rake my fingers through the sand, plucking up a shell and tossing it into the water.

"I should have told you, and I'm sorry."

She nods and her lips curve up just slightly.

"Forgiven," she says. I'll take it. "They want to have a *family dinner*," she uses her fingers to make air quotes, "but at least I'll have some time to get used to it."

"I am glad they're together. Mom deserves someone great, and your dad is a really great guy."

"I'm glad, too. It's kind of weird, though."

I snort. "Imagine walking into the kitchen at one in the morning, high as shit, and seeing his tongue down her throat. I thought I was on a bad trip."

"Oh, gross." She groans, and I laugh.

It's the first time I've really laughed in a while, sitting here on the beach alone with Lennon. So much in my life is fucked up, but here with her, it's easy to pretend. I hate myself a little less when Lennon is around, even on days when she hates me enough for the both of us.

"Hey." I nudge her shoulder. When she turns her head and locks her gaze with mine, I reach out and trace her jaw with my knuckles. She leans her head into my touch and my heart speeds up. "Thank you," I whisper. "For this."

"Of course." Her voice rasps, and she bites her lip. I can't resist.

I'm an addict with poor impulse control.

I take my thumb and rub it across her plush lower lip, smoothing the mark from her teeth. Her lips part in invitation, and I slide my hand to her neck and pull her into me. Her mouth lands on mine without hesitation, like she was waiting for this. Like she wants it as much as I do.

Our last few kisses were angry, rushed. I make sure this one is slow, sliding my tongue over hers in the smoothest caress. The contact stings my cut, the pressure causing an ache in my swollen lip, but I welcome it. I kiss her harder until I feel the cut break open. I want it to hurt more. Her fingers tighten in my shirt, but she pulls back.

"Wait," she forces out. "We shouldn't. You're going to be my *brother*."

I chuckle. I can't help it. I press my forehead to hers and smirk.

"But I'm not your brother right now, am I?"

I wait. Restrain myself. Slowly, she smiles and shakes her head no, then she's pulling me on top of her in the sand, kissing me with more fervor than before. Speeding up the slow pace I'd set. Tugging on me until her legs are wrapped around my waist and my hand is up her shirt and pulling down the cup of her bra. I pinch her nipple, and she arches into me, letting out the sweetest little whimper.

"You like that," I say, and pinch it again, harder this time. Her whimper turns to a low groan, and I smile. "Tell me you like it, Lennon."

I pull back and she chases my lips, but I stay just out of reach.

I do it again, and the way her mouth falls open on a gasp and she pushes her chest into my hand is so god damn sexy that I can hardly believe it's really happening. Fuck.

I press my hips into her, showing her how hard she's made me.

"Tell me you like it, Lennon," I rasp, and the roughness of my voice surprises even me.

"I like it," she pants out. "I like it."

I kiss her again, moving my mouth from her lips to her jaw, then pulling her shirt up so I can take her nipple between my teeth. I circle my tongue around it, suck, and then bite down, just enough so she can feel it. Just enough that she gasps and bucks her hips into mine.

I grunt at the contact. She'll be absolute fire when we fuck.

She'll turn me to ashes, and I'll gladly burn.

I'm unbuttoning her jeans when her phone vibrates in her front pocket.

"Don't answer it," I say, pressing open mouth kisses to her belly while she writhes under me. She lets it go to voicemail, and I smile against her skin. I trace my tongue over the hem of her panties and move my hands to the band of her jeans. I'm about to pull them over her hips when the phone vibrates again. I groan and drop my head to her stomach as she pants.

"I have to," she says. I take her phone out of her pocket and hand it to her without moving. My head bounces when she laughs, and I can't help but smile. I hear her type something and she sighs. "It's a text from Claire."

Of course, it is. I look up at her, resting my chin on her pelvis.

"And?"

"And apparently family dinner is tonight."

We don't speak as we lock up. Lennon drives us back to Chesapeake and drops me at my car in the liquor store parking lot.

"See you at six," she says. Her voice is sad. Her mouth has been stuck in a small frown since the text.

"Hey, it's okay," I tell her. "It's just a dinner. You'll have time to adjust."

She forces a smile and nods, so I climb out of the car and wave goodbye as she drives away. I unlock my car and rest my head on the headrest. I run back through the events of today. I itch to open the glove box and light up the half a joint I've got stashed in there, but I don't. Instead, I put my car in drive and pull out of the parking lot and head home sober.

When I pull into the driveway, Claire is waiting on the front steps, and she looks murderous. Fucking great. I drop my head on the steering wheel once, then again, and take a deep breath. I turn the car off and get out.

"What the fuck did I do this time?" I say as I close the distance between us. I notice her eyes are red, and it looks like she's been crying. For a brief minute, I worry something happened to Mom, but then Claire stomps toward me and clocks me right across the face.

My hand shoots up and covers my jaw.

"What the fuck, Claire," I shout.

"I hate you," she growls. "I hate you."

"Yeah, well what else is new."

Fuck, she hit me good. Right in the spot that's already bruised from my fight with our father.

"He's not paying for my college," she yells, and I sigh. Mom told her. "This is all your fucking fault." She shoves at my chest.

"How the fuck is it my fault?" I yell back. She shoves me again.

"You fucking hit him? You threw eggs at his house?" She tries to punch me again, but I step back, and she swings at air. "You're not fucking twelve anymore. Jesus Christ, when are going to grow up and think of anyone other than yourself?"

"I went over there *after* he punked out of paying for your

college, Claire," I tell her. "It's not my fault he's a fucking prick."

"Mom called him and *begged*, Macon," Claire seethes, and my stomach drops. "She fucking cried on the phone with him."

"You'd let her do that?" I spit.

Mom *hates* talking to our father. He's a manipulative asshole and makes her feel like shit. Claire would let Mom subject herself to his bullshit over a couple grand for in-state tuition?

"I can't believe you'd make her call him over this."

"I didn't make her do shit," Claire says through her teeth, angry tears streaming down her face again. "This is *my college*, Macon. My *future*. Just because you don't have one doesn't mean you get to fuck up mine. She got him to reconsider! He was gonna pay half and then you went over there, and you fucking ruined it!"

Fuck.

Do I even bother telling her that he's full of shit? That he wouldn't have done it? He was just jerking Mom around like he always does. Making her crawl to him just so he can kick her lower.

"I didn't ruin anything, Claire." I shake my head and laugh at the sky. This is real shitty karma. "He's a prick and he's always been a prick."

"I hate you," she hisses again, wiping tears from her face. "He should press charges and send you to prison."

Her eyes are full of hatred. The same I saw in my father's eyes a few hours ago. The same I see in mine every morning.

"Why can't you just die," she whispers. "Everyone would be better off."

The words hit how she intended. Right in the middle of my chest. Low in my stomach. And the voice in my head, the one that tells me all the time what a fuck-up I am, repeats them.

My gold-star father has said more than once that I'm the reason our family is fucked. Couldn't stay out of trouble, even as a kid. A bad seed or whatever. Suspensions starting in first grade. Failing tests. Fighting kids twice my size and getting my ass beat. Being held back a year.

He was always such a dick to me because I was an embarrassment to his Ivy League education. Time-outs didn't work. Insults didn't work. Hitting me didn't work. Locking me in my room for entire weekends didn't work.

Instead of falling in line, I lashed out harder.

Something in me is broken. Something crucial, and I don't know how to fix it.

Now he has a new family.

If it weren't for me, Mom wouldn't have to work so hard. Claire wouldn't be such a bitch. She'd have her college paid for. I'm fucking everything up without even trying.

Claire's sinister laugh pulls me from my thoughts.

"You're un-fucking-believable," she chokes out. "Screw you, Macon."

She stalks to her car without another word and drives off toward Lennon's house. And fuck, I can't even let her have that. I'll ruin that relationship, too, because I can't stay away. I never could.

I walk inside and the house is silent. I go searching for Mom and find her on the back patio with her head in her hands, her shoulders shaking.

My fault. My fault. My fault.

I go to her, to hug her, to apologize, but when she hears me coming, she sits upright and her eyes fall on my bruised jaw, my split and swollen lips. Her face scrunches, and she lets out a sob.

"Oh, Macon," she cries, then drops her face back into her hands.

I don't say anything. I just back away and go straight to my room and lock the door. I dig through the top drawer of my dresser until I find one loose oxy, but it's not enough. It never will be enough.

"Fuck." I ball my fists and press them into my eyes. Tug at my hair to feel anything other than this fucking desperation. "Fuck!"

I pop the pill in my mouth and swallow. I try to imagine it working. Try to summon the numb. But nothing happens.

I squeeze my eyes shut against the sting, breathe through my nose against the failure.

The first time he hit me replays in my head. The first time he kicked me when I was down. The first time he grabbed my arm so hard it left a bruise in the shape of his hand. The crack of bone. The barrage of hissed insults and threats.

The look on Mom's face when she found the bruises on my side and stomach.

The way she cried when she learned they didn't happen at school. That it wasn't an accident that broke my wrist.

The way she blamed herself. *Why didn't you tell me? How did I miss this? How could I let this happen? I'm sorry, Macon. I'm sorry. I'm sorry.*

I put my hands to my head and press hard on my temples.

I don't want to see the argument again. I don't want to see him hit her again. I don't want to remember packing our things in the middle of the night, moving to a shitty motel, dealing with Claire's wails.

She was always a daddy's girl.

I took that from her.

My stomach churns with the need to vomit, but I don't want to lose the only oxy I have. I can't lose the numb.

I pick up my phone and send a text to the last person I want to see, but the only person who can give me what I need right now.

FOURTEEN

Lennon

IT'S STUPID THAT I'M STRESSING OVER WHAT TO WEAR.

I know that.

It's just dinner.

It's even stupider that I'm looking at every outfit I choose, wondering what Macon would think of it. I shouldn't care about what Macon thinks of how I dress. I never have before. I certainly shouldn't now that he's almost certainly going to be my *brother*.

Gross.

But then Macon's words from earlier flash through my mind. He's not my brother right now...

I keep seeing his eyes on the beach right before he kissed me. I keep feeling his hand around my neck. His lips on my stomach. His teeth on my nipple.

I keep fantasizing about where things were headed before Claire interrupted.

Claire.

God, this would break her if she found out. She would murder us both. Am I betraying our friendship by crushing on her brother?

Oh my god, I'm crushing on her brother.

My brain short-circuits for a whole minute. How? How did this happen? How did one free period turn into...*this*? I run through everything. The art room. The rec center. Pottery and paint and Macon.

And I cannot. Stop. Smiling.

I hide my face in my hands, pressing on my cheeks to try and tame the ridiculous grin. Shit. This is bad. This is so bad.

I peek through my fingers at the clothes in my closet. I should just wear what I normally would wear and leave it at that. I should put my hair in a braid and text Eric back and forget about this stupid *whatever* with Macon.

Ugh, but I don't.

I pick out a top that fits a little snug and a skirt that sits a little higher on the thigh. I leave my hair down in waves. I do it all with the hope that Macon will like it. Because it's also exciting, this crush. I've never gotten butterflies before. No one has ever made my heart kick up so fast I thought I'd pass out. No one has ever touched me the way he does.

No one has ever made me feel everything so strongly.

I put the outfit on and look at myself in the mirror. I smooth my hands down my blouse, stopping at my waist the way he does, then grip my hips just slightly. I run my hands down my thighs, inching the hem of my skirt up slowly.

"Lennie," a sob comes from my doorway, and I flip around to find Claire standing there with mascara smeared down her cheeks and red splotches on her face and neck. She's a mess. My first thought is to apologize—she's found out about Macon and she's come to end our friendship—but then she walks to me and wraps me in a hug, nearly collapsing.

"Shhh," I whisper, confused. "What's wrong, Claire? What happened? Is everything okay?"

"Everything is ruined," she cries. "My dad pulled my

college fund because Macon went to his house drunk and beat him up."

I stiffen. That's not how it happened.

What do I do? Tell her I know? Correct her? Inform her that her sequence of events isn't right? Macon went there *because* her dad pulled the college fund. In his own misguided way, he thought he was standing up for her.

"He's fucked everything up for me again, Lennon," she says.

I know she's wrong, but I stay quiet and rub her back. Her tears are soaking through my blouse, but I don't let go.

"God, why does he have to be so horrible? If I didn't have you, I'd be miserable. What am I going to do without you this summer?"

"I'm sorry," I whisper. I am. In more ways than she realizes.

Because I'm falling for her brother, and she's going to hate me if she ever finds out.

"I DON'T EVEN WANT TO SEE HIM." CLAIRE GROANS AS SHE drives us back to her house. "I might stab him with a fork if he even tries to look at me."

I force a laugh. "That would make for an interesting dinner."

I've spent the last hour listening to Claire complain about Macon. It's not unusual, but for once, I couldn't join in. She didn't notice.

As soon as we turn onto Claire's street, the sight of Macon's Charger makes my pulse quicken. I have to physically keep myself from bouncing in my seat.

I want to see him.

Even after everything with Claire, I want to see him.

We've got time. He's not my brother yet, I tell myself. It assuages the tiniest bit of guilt.

We head into the house and the smell of pasta sauce and garlic immediately makes my mouth water. I've always loved Drea's cooking. That will be one plus if Dad and her eventually get married. Dinners will always be fantastic.

When we round the corner, the table is set and Dad and Drea are dancing around each other in the kitchen, stirring a pot of sauce and sprinkling cheese on homemade garlic bread.

"It smells amazing," I tell them. I look around for Macon, but I don't see him.

"It's almost ready," Drea announces. "Claire, will you go get Macon?"

Claire glowers at her mother's back, and I send her a tight smile.

"I'll go get him," I offer, and Claire mouths a thank you. I am a terrible friend, but I hurry up the stairs anyway.

I rap on his door and wait. Nothing.

"Macon?" I knock again. Still nothing.

I try the door, but it's locked, and my heart starts to race for an entirely new reason. Flashes of gray, of streaked mascara and dried vomit play like a movie reel through my memories, and I'm not breathing when I run through Claire's bedroom to get to Macon's through the adjoining bathroom.

"Macon?" I call into the dark room. I'm too scared to turn on the light. "Macon."

There's a lump on his bed, and I slowly walk toward it, praying to anything that he's okay. That it's not what it could be. He wouldn't. It couldn't happen to me again.

I chew on the inside of my cheek as I reach out with trembling fingers to pull the covers back, and I release a relieved cry when it's just a pile of pillows underneath. My legs collapse, and I fall to my knees, dropping my head onto his comforter.

"Oh, thank you," I whisper. "Thank you." I close my eyes and breathe, giving my tears a minute to dry. It's okay. He's okay.

Then reality sets in and my nerves jump again.

Where is he? I take out my phone and text him.

Hey. Family dinner?

I wait. Stare at the screen and will the text bubble to pop up. It doesn't.

You coming? Your mom made pasta.

Another minute. Still nothing. Unease prickles at my neck, and my throat goes dry, but I push all thoughts about where he could be and who he could be with out of my head.

He wouldn't do that to me. I'm sure of it.

"He's not up there," I tell Drea when I get back to the kitchen. My heart squeezes when her face falls.

"Oh," she says, then glances at the clock on the stove. "Well, let's go ahead and get started. He's probably just running late."

I fake a smile and nod.

"I can't wait to taste it." It wouldn't have been a lie five minutes earlier. Now my tongue tastes like heavy, thick ash in my mouth.

We sit down and fix plates. We make small talk. I tell my dad I was studying today. Claire makes fun of me for studying so much. I don't miss the way Drea and Dad look at each other, or the way Dad rubs her shoulder and squeezes her hand whenever he can.

I wish I could ignore it, but I can't.

I also can't ignore the way the minutes tick by on the clock. The plates slowly empty. Drea grows more and more upset. Then she and Dad share a look.

"It's okay," she says quietly. "Let's do it. I'll fill him in later."

My shoulders tense. "Do what?"

166

"Well, we have an announcement," Drea says, then smiles at my dad. My stomach turns, and I clench my hands into fists.

"Don't make us wait," Claire squeals, bouncing in her chair with excitement.

Another smile. Another hand squeeze. Another pause.

"Just tell us," I bark out, and Drea's eyes flare with hurt. "Sorry," I whisper. I don't look at my dad. I know he's disappointed.

"We're getting married," Drea says, then slides something on her ring finger and holds up her left hand, flashing a shiny new diamond.

"Yay!" Claire beams. She jumps up and rushes around the table to hug her mom, then my dad. I'm frozen in place. "Congratulations!"

"And we're moving in together," Dad adds, and my heart falls to my feet. "We're moving in two weeks, and we want to have a small ceremony over Christmas."

No. This is a joke. Two weeks? Christmas is only two months away.

No.

"You said graduation," I interrupt. "You said you'd propose after graduation."

"Yes," my dad says, his voice slow. Like I'm a wounded, scared animal he's cornered. I suppose I am. "But since you all know now, we didn't see the point in waiting."

"Why?" I ask, my voice rising. I bounce my eyes between Dad and Drea frantically. "Why rush? Are you pregnant? Did you get her pregnant?"

"Lennon Capri," my dad scolds, and I flinch at his tone. I can feel Claire's and Drea's eyes on me. I close mine, try to breathe, but I can't.

I'm going to have a panic attack.

"You said graduation," I repeat. "You said we'd have time to adjust."

I bring my hands to my head and push on my temples.

"You said. You lied. You just spring this on us after lying for years and expect us to be okay with it right away and you don't even keep your promise to give me time to adjust."

"Lennon," Drea says. Her voice is sad, but I can barely hear her over my rapid breathing.

I need air. I need space.

"I need to go," I blurt out, standing abruptly and knocking the table with my legs. The dishes clank. Water sloshes. "I'm sorry. I have to go."

I rush out the front door and jog down the block. About halfway, I screech to a halt and hinge at the waist, directing my breaths between my knees. The pressure in my head releases just enough that the blood rushing through my ears isn't as loud. My fingers tingle. My toes tingle. I stand back up slowly, so I don't pass out.

It's then that I hear a car idling and loud music playing.

Somehow in my foggy brain, I know what it is before I look, but I look anyway.

Sam's car is parked at the curb, muffled music surrounding it, and there's a jumble in the passenger seat. A mess of bodies.

I walk closer.

No. I'm *pulled* closer.

I don't even think. I just walk. And when I get to the car, I pull the door open. I'm hit with a cloud of weed so thick, I have to wait a moment before the scene before me comes into focus. When it does, I wish it hadn't.

It's Sam straddling Macon. Their lips are swollen. Macon's shirt is stretched.

His pants are undone.

"Leonard," Sam screeches, "you fucking creep." She adjusts her shirt. "Get the fuck out of here!"

"Macon," I say, but his head stays down. "Macon," I say

louder, my voice cracking. He ignores me, and it makes me furious. These are angry tears.

"Macon!" I scream and push his shoulder. I push it again harder.

Sam is saying something, calling me names, climbing back into the driver's seat.

But all I can see, all I can focus on, is Macon. The way he rolls his head back against the seat, then slowly turns in my direction. His face is blank, his eyes glossed and red. I choke on a sob, my hands fly to my face. His swollen lips. His mussed hair. His dead eyes.

"Why?" I ask.

"Get the fuck out of here, *Leonard*," he says, and it guts me. I let out a sob, then another.

And then I laugh. Because I'm such an idiot.

I swipe angrily at my tears, but they don't stop falling. I laugh again.

"I hate you," I tell him. I put every ounce of feeling into it. "I. Hate. You."

"Feelin' is mutual, bitch," Sam taunts from the driver's seat.

For a brief moment, I think Macon will stand up for me, but he doesn't. He just closes his eyes and rolls his head away from me.

"Go," he says into the air.

So, I go.

I REFUSE TO TALK TO DAD. I TELL HIM I NEED SPACE AND I'LL talk to him when I'm ready.

I don't apologize for my behavior tonight. I don't think I'm sorry. For once, I don't want to placate anyone just to avoid a conflict.

I'm hurt and hurting. I'm angry with my dad. I need to sit with that, and so does he.

I paint for hours. Picture after picture of angry, violent strokes, sad and sorrowful shades. Each painting is a different fragment of my broken heart, a different stage of grief, but I never reach acceptance. I'm stuck oscillating between anger and depression, skipping over bargaining entirely, until eventually falling asleep.

And then I circle back in my dreams, and denial comes to me.

The sound of my window sliding open wakes me, but instead of sitting up, I close my eyes tighter and roll onto my side, giving him my back.

"Go home," I say into the darkness.

Macon doesn't respond. I just hear him, feel him, close the distance between us.

"Go home, Macon," I force out, my voice hoarse and ragged with tears. "I don't want anything to do with you."

"I know," he says, but he keeps walking until I can smell his spicy scent and notice it's missing the lingering sweetness of weed. He sits on my bed, then lies down. I feel the bed dip when he lays his head on the pillow. I keep my back to him.

"I'm so sorry, Lennon," he whispers. The pain in his voice makes the tears welling in my eyes fall down my cheeks. "I'm so fucked up. I keep hurting everyone. But I can't stand knowing I hurt you."

I try to swallow back a sob, but I fail, and instead, my body shakes with it.

"I'm so fucking sorry," he says again. "Please tell me how I can fix this."

In spite of myself, I roll over and face him. In the moonlight and the glow from my alarm clock, I can just make out the cut on his lip and the bruising on his jaw.

How was that only a few hours ago? We were just on the beach this afternoon.

"Please, Lennon," he pleads, reaching out and pushing a

piece of hair behind my ear. My tears fall harder. "I'm begging. I can't lose you. I keep fucking everything else up, but I can't lose you. *Please*, Lennon."

"Why?" I say, and he clasps his eyes shut. "Why go to her? Why were you in that car? After everything today..."

I trail off. I know I sound pathetic. It's not like we were dating. He never promised me anything, but I can't stop.

"I don't know," he says finally. It's not what I want to hear. "I wish I had an answer, but I don't."

"That's not good enough, Macon." I shake my head and the pillowcase scratches my wet cheeks.

"I know. Don't you think I know that? I don't want to be like this. I don't want to hurt you. But since you've got Eric—"

"Don't you dare," I interrupt. "I don't *have* Eric. I didn't go to Eric today. After the beach with you, I went home. I picked out an outfit I thought you'd like. I went to dinner at your house, excited to see you, only to find you hours later fucking Sam in her car!"

My voice is so angry, rasping in the loudest whisper I can manage, and it hurts my throat.

"We didn't fuck," he defends. "I swear to god. I wouldn't do that to you."

I laugh out loud, sardonic and hollow.

"Oh, but making out and letting her hump you in the passenger seat is okay?"

"No." He shakes his head. "It's not okay. You're right. And I'm so fucking sorry."

He reaches out and takes my hand. I don't pull away, and I hate myself a little bit for that.

"Why did you go to her, Macon?"

I see the moment he gives. His face falls slack and his eyes close. He takes a deep breath.

"I was buying some pills from her," he confesses into the darkness. My heart breaks. I don't mention that buying shouldn't involve sex and touching and kissing and whatever it was they were doing in that car.

"You have to stop taking those," I say, instead. "My mom...She didn't...I couldn't..."

"I know." He scoots closer and pulls me to his chest. I bury my face in his shirt and take a deep inhale. "Let me make it up to you. Please, Lennon." He pulls back and tips my chin up. "I can't lose you."

I don't stop him when he brings his lips to mine. When I taste tears, I don't question who they belong to. I don't move away when he wraps his arms around me. I don't pull back when he slips his tongue into my mouth.

I kiss him back.

I kiss him back, and I cry, and I let him hold me, and another part of me breaks. I pull him closer and push away the screaming in my head.

He presses his forehead to mine, our rapid breaths mingling.

"It'll never happen again," he says. I shake my head. "I'll fix it."

"You can't," I tell him honestly. "I don't think I can trust you."

"I'll fix it," he says again. He kisses me sweetly, his soft lips slowly gliding over mine. "I promise. I'll make it up to you."

I don't say anything. I don't respond at all. If I open my mouth, I don't trust what will come out of it.

He presses one last kiss to my lips, and then he disappears out my window, leaving a dent in my pillowcase and a hollow feeling in my chest.

WITH MONDAY MORNING COMES A POUNDING HEADACHE AND suffocating anxiety.

I don't want to go to school. I don't want to face Sam or Claire. I don't want to know which Macon I'll get today, if he's even there at all.

When my phone buzzes in my skirt pocket, I head out the door to meet Claire. She's on time, which means she's eager to talk. I wanted to drive myself, but she begged. I climb into the car in silence and put on my seat belt.

"Hey," she says. Her eyes are on my face, studying me, so I force a smile.

"Hey."

"You've been avoiding me," she says quietly. I shrug.

"I've been avoiding everyone."

It's not a lie. Had Macon bothered texting at all yesterday after creeping out of my window, at close to four in the morning, I would have ignored him, too. I think. I hope.

"I know it's a lot," Claire says. "It's been just you and your dad for a long time, and this whole change is really sudden. I didn't understand why you were so upset about it at first, but I talked to my mom, and I think I get it now."

She takes a deep breath and grabs my hand.

"But I think we need to be excited for our parents. They deserve happiness."

I know she's right, but her words feel patronizing. When you've spent your entire life being selfless, being scolded on the importance of it chafes. Don't I deserve to be happy, too? Don't I deserve a little warning before my whole life changes?

I pull my hand out of Claire's grip.

"I don't want to talk about this right now, Claire," I tell her.

"Okay," she whispers after a moment. Then she puts the car in drive, and we head to school.

Macon is nowhere to be seen when we pull in the lot. Neither is Sam. A visual of them in that passenger seat invades my head, and I prepare myself for the worst.

173

"Hey," a low voice greets me as I climb out of the car. I look up into deep brown eyes and a warm smile.

"Hey, Eric." I focus on his dimples. "How was your weekend?"

He chuckles a little and grabs my bag, slinging it over his shoulder.

"I feel like I should be asking you that," he jokes. "I stopped by Saturday morning, but your dad said you were sleeping over at Claire's. I was gonna take you out for a hangover breakfast."

My smile is genuine. The first one in what feels like years.

"Thank you, Eric," I say. "That was very sweet."

He shrugs it off, but it's true. Eric is sweet and kind. He's thoughtful. Caring. He would never do anything to hurt me. He certainly wouldn't get high and hook up with someone hours after...

No. Nope. Not going there.

"It was a little weird, though, Davis carrying you off like that," Eric says tentatively, and I want to groan at the mention of Macon. I keep my face blank. "But I guess since he's Claire's brother, and you guys' families are close, he's just...protective..."

He keeps his eyes on me as his statement trails off, asking without asking. The hope I see there kills me, but what do I say? Actually, Macon's been fucking with my head for weeks now, and I think I have a crush on him that might kill me?

No. I definitely can't say that. So instead, I force yet another tight smile and nod.

"Yeah," is all I say, but it makes his grin widen and his dimples pop, and I feel smarmy.

"So," he continues, distracting me from my self-loathing, "I was wondering if you'd want to get together tonight and study for the calculus test?"

He's nervous asking. It's not a date, I tell myself. And he really is so kind.

I really do think I could love him if I tried.

"Would you mind coming to my place?" I ask, and he smiles like he's surprised. "We could order a pizza?"

"Yes. Definitely." He nods eagerly, like one of those silly sports bobblehead statues, and my smile stretches wide. "I can be there at seven? I'll come right after practice." He pushes his hair back and laughs. "I promise to shower first."

I giggle. A real giggle. "Okay. Sounds good."

He walks me to my locker and leans on the one next to mine as I turn the lock.

"It's a date, then," he says excitedly. "See you later."

I watch him walk away. The farther away he gets, the more my smile fades, until he's turned the corner and I'm frowning at nothing.

I turn back to my locker and pop it open, then stare at what I find inside.

A ceramic mug.

It's rough and unpainted, obviously just from the kiln. The handle is a little wobbly, the mouth of the mug is uneven. It's more of an oval than a circle. But it's a mug, and it's handmade. And inside of it is a sticky note. I read it without breathing.

please don't give up on me

♥M

On impulse, my lips twitch at the corners with the need to smile.

Damn you, Macon.

I scan the hall for him, flicking my eyes from corner to corner, but if he's watching me, I don't see him.

I go through the day without a single Macon sighting, though I pass Sam in the hall a few times. Her scowl tells me she's holding a grudge from the weekend. I don't care. I've been angry with Sam since she stepped on my science diorama in sixth grade. She thinks that just because her dad is a senator, she can treat people like crap and get away with it.

As far as I'm concerned, she can stay mad.

I'm relieved when I walk into free period and find the pottery wheel by my station. Just like last time, I can feel him in the room. I sit down and set up, noting the paints and water that's already been put out for me, and seconds later, Macon emerges from the storage room.

Just like last time, we don't speak.

We spend the whole week like that, then the next. Me painting, him sculpting, in complete silence. Just the clinking of my brushes in the jars of water and the whirring of the pottery wheel. He comes to sit with me after my classes at the rec center, too. He watches me paint, and we listen to music. We don't even say goodbye when we part ways at night.

It's peaceful, despite the niggling worry that he's trying to lull me into a false sense of security. It makes everything easier to ignore. Easier to deny.

We don't mention what happened. He doesn't apologize again. We just create and exist comfortably in the silent space together.

It's funny, actually.

He's so adamant about me using my voice, but Macon and I definitely seem to work better together without words.

I put the mug he made me on my dresser with the post-it note inside.

When the movers come to pack up our house, I wrap the mug in bubble wrap and place it safely in my backpack, not trusting anyone else with it.

When I unpack my things in my new room, in the new house across town that I now share with Claire and Macon, I put the mug on the top shelf in my closet. I tell myself it's to keep it safe, but really, it's to keep it hidden from Claire.

I dislike my new room. The house Dad and Drea bought together is nice, but it doesn't feel like home. It's all happened so fast that I had no time to sort out my thoughts other than panic and denial. Dad is happier than I've ever seen him, though, so I say nothing.

When he looks at me, I fake the same smile I've always faked, and he buys it like he always has. He's trained in interrogating criminals, but he still can't seem to read me.

"Dinner!" Drea calls up the stairs.

She's ecstatic. Between her and Claire, I've been in positive energy overload. My dad's excitement is more muted, but it's still there. In every deep chuckle, every sidelong glance. I know he's completely in love with Andrea, and I'm trying so hard to be happy for him.

I walk to the mirror above my dresser and quickly put my hair in a braid.

I practice a smile. I smooth down the front of my shirt, then take a deep breath.

I'll adjust to this. I can love it for my dad. For Andrea. I practice one more smile, then head out into the hall, running smack into Macon.

He's leaning on the wall outside my door. Waiting for me.

He glances over my shoulder into my room and smirks.

"No tree," he says quietly, then nods in the direction of his room down the hall, "but I think we can make this work."

He turns and trots down the stairs, leaving me staring at his back and trying to calm my racing heart.

This is going to be interesting.

FIFTEEN

Macon

"YOU LOOK SO HANDSOME," MY MOM SAYS FROM BEHIND ME AS I stand on the dais in front of the wide mirror in the tux shop. Tuxedos aren't my jam, but I do look pretty fucking good.

I straighten my jacket and smooth down the lapels.

"I do look good, don't I," I say with a smirk. I watch her in the mirror as she laughs.

She's so excited. She was never married to my father. She was just a kept woman for a few years, working her ass off to help put him through law school while he fucked around on her. If anyone deserves the wedding of their dreams, it's my mom.

She stands and comes up behind me, looping her arm through mine and resting her head on my shoulder.

"You look so grown up," she whispers, her voice cracking. "I still remember when you were just the sweetest little eight-pound chunk with a mop of curls and the biggest blue eyes I'd ever seen."

She sniffles, and I snort.

"Don't even start crying now." I groan playfully. "No

memory lane detours, please. I much prefer the six-foot version of myself. This version doesn't shit his pants."

She laughs and swats my chest, then wipes tears from her eyes.

"Didn't ever think I'd be here," she says with a smile. "My baby boy walking me down the aisle as I marry the love of my life."

Her voice cracks again, and I pull her into a hug.

"You're going to be a beautiful bride, Mom," I say as I squeeze her. "I'm honored to be the one giving you away."

She pulls back, places her hands on my cheeks, and looks me straight in the eyes.

"I love you, Macon," she says seriously. "I love you always, no matter what."

I swallow the lump in my throat and nod. I want the words to stick. I want to focus on the sincerity in her voice. The love in her eyes. But all I can think is, *she shouldn't.*

She shouldn't love me no matter what because all I've done is let her down. Put her in danger. Hurt her.

I'm obsessed with her future stepdaughter, for fuck's sake.

The more she loves me, the worse I'll hurt her.

I'm hardwired to ruin things. I can't change it. It's only a matter of time before she's crying over something else I've fucked up. At this rate, it's likely going to be sabotaging her relationship with *the love of her life* because I can't keep my hands to myself.

But I'm trying. Fuck, I'm trying. With an addict, it's not *if* they'll relapse. It's *when.*

"I love you too, Mom."

"Go ahead and get changed," she says as she releases me from the hug. "We've got to meet Claire and Lennon for lunch."

"Oh," I say casually, "I forgot to tell you, I picked up a shift, so I have to bail on lunch."

It's a lie, but it's one she happily buys.

Picking up shifts at work is something a responsible person does. She wants to believe I'm responsible. In truth, I don't trust myself around Lennon, especially not in front of my mom.

I was able to hide it so fucking well in the past, but I've fucked that up, too.

I've touched her now. Tasted her. And like usual, I can't control the cravings.

"Well, don't work too hard," Mom says with a smile. "I'll wait and walk out with you."

"Okay." I nod to the dressing room. "I'll be right back."

After changing, paying for the alterations, and setting up a pickup date for the tux, I wave goodbye to my mom from the parking lot. When she turns the corner out of sight, I pop the glove compartment and pull out my pack of cigarettes.

Only cigarettes in it now, unfortunately.

I slide one out and slip it between my teeth, then flick my lighter and bring it to the end of the cigarette. The cherry glows bright red as I take a long drag. I hold it in, savoring the burn until I can't anymore, then blow the toxin through my nose.

The nicotine relieves the smallest hint of tension. I flex my fingers in and out of a fist and try to think of anything other than the pills sitting in Sam's dad's safe.

I fail.

I finish the cigarette and drop the butt out the window, then light another.

I actually hate cigarettes.

I run through my list of options. I could go to the rec center. Pound the bag for an hour or throw some clay. I've been getting pretty decent at the wheel. I've been wanting to try and make a vase for my mom as a wedding present. Maybe get Lennon to paint it.

I think Mom'd like that.

I flick the cigarette out the window and pull out of the lot. I park behind the supermarket, just in case, then jog down the street to the center. I pop into the office and say hey to James when I get there. Tell him I'll be with the bag for a bit and to come get me if he needs help with anything. Then I head to the gym.

The center is a hive of activity at all times, but especially on weekends. Sometimes I'll help out when James needs me, but he usually keeps me scheduled weeknights. Those are harder to fill with the regular volunteers. I'm a willing pawn.

I'm not surprised to find that my favorite bag is free. It's the one that's beat to hell and duct-taped in more places than not. Everyone wants the new ones, the ones without rips or tears. Not me. If I'm going to spend time beating the shit out of something, I want it to resemble me in every possible way. Flawed. Broken. Anything but perfect.

I didn't think to pack any gym clothes, so I'm gonna have to do this in jeans and a t-shirt, but it's fine. I pull on some gloves, and after the first jab, I start to relax. I do three-minute rounds, starting with a basic jab-jab-cross sequence. I switch up each round on the fly, adding ducks and pivots, hooks and counters, pulling from drills I use when I teach and building on them. Each round gets more challenging, physically and mentally.

I'm sweating and panting after ten minutes and deliciously sore by the end of the hour, but I'm still keyed up.

I head to the room where I teach pottery and try to throw a vase, but everything about it makes me think of Lennon, and thinking of Lennon makes me fucking crazy. I can't sit behind the pottery wheel these days without needing to feel her next to me, and needing to feel her fills me with guilt and self-loathing.

I'm such a selfish prick.

I try to ignore it. I try to throw and think of nothing but

the clay, but I can't get my vase to hold shape. It keeps collapsing in on itself.

I feel like I'm collapsing in on myself.

It's basically a shitty metaphor for what a terrible son and brother I am.

I clean up and storm out, not bothering to say goodbye to James. The dude is too intuitive. If he sees me all twitchy like this, he'll find something for me to mop.

I pull my phone from my pocket as I stalk toward my car. I dial and it's answered on the third ring.

"Yeah?"

"You alone?" Julian laughs at my tone.

"You still hiding from Sam?" he asks. I roll my eyes at the humor in his voice.

"Fuck you, Jules." I climb in my car and turn the key. "You got weed? I'm out."

"Yep," Julian grunts. "Sam's got some better shit, though. We're going to the fairgrounds tonight if you wanna come."

"Pass," I say, turning my car in the direction of Julian's house. "But I'm on the way over. I've got cash."

I hang up without waiting for a response but kick myself for it when I pull up to the curb five minutes later.

"What the fuck?" I groan. Sam's stupid fucking red coupe is parked in Julian's driveway. I'm going to fucking murder him.

I wait for a minute. Consider my options. I could go see Josh, but the chance he'd nark on me is too high now that he's boning Claire regularly. I don't want to drive to Suffolk and see the hippie chick, and Casper never buys weed. He just puffs when we pass.

"Fuck," I mumble under my breath, then turn off the engine and make the death walk to the house.

"The prodigal son returns," Julian says when I enter the backyard. He and Sam are lying on sun loungers around his pool. It's too cold to swim.

"Thanks for the warning, douche," I deadpan. I walk up to him and drop some cash on his chest, paying no attention to the she-devil next to him. "Appreciate it."

Julian snorts, then grabs the cash and heads inside. I turn to follow him, but Sam's voice stops me in my tracks.

"Have you fucked her yet?"

I roll my eyes. "Jealousy doesn't look good on you, Samantha."

"Jealous?" She scoffs. "Honey, I've had you. I can't wait for her to see what a lousy fuck you are."

I bark out a laugh, then stalk toward her lounger. Her eyebrows lift higher which each step I take, until my hands are braced on the arms of the chair and I'm leaning over her.

I take my time. Watch her chest rise and fall with pants. Note the way her lips part *just so* and her tongue peeks out to wet them.

"Lousy fuck?" I repeat, then drag my knuckle down her jaw. She gasps as if on cue. I move my thumb to her mouth, pressing it between her lips, and she sucks just like I knew she would. She swirls her tongue, laving the pad of my thumb, doing her best to imitate a blow job.

My dick doesn't so much as twitch.

I pull my thumb out of her mouth with a pop, then smear her spit over her lower lip.

I lean closer, leaving just inches between our faces, and wait.

She breaks sooner than I expected, rising to close the distance between us. I step back just before her lips land, my smirk turning to a sneer.

"I'll make sure she reports back on our *lousy fuck*, then," I say. "Since you're so invested."

She growls, slamming her hands into the cushions on the lounger, just as Julian comes back outside with my weed.

"You'll be back," she says through clenched teeth. "I'm the only one who can give you what you need, and you know it."

My chest aches and my fingers itch to shake her, to pat her down for loose pills. I wouldn't even have to do much to get some. Make out in her car. Some groping. It doesn't even have to be sex. I could probably get away with just letting her blow me. Pills for a week, probably.

But then I see Lennon's face. The hurt I caused. The anger.

I hear her voice crack. *I hate you.* Feel her tear-soaked pillow. Taste the salt on her lips.

And I fucking hate myself, too. For my weakness. For my selfishness.

Julian stands next to me and slaps the bag of weed to my chest. I snag it, then I hit Sam with a dead stare.

"Not anymore."

I turn and walk out of the backyard without another word, and I hope like hell she didn't see through to the truth in my words.

When I get to the new house, I climb out my bedroom window and onto the roof. This place doesn't feel like home, yet. I don't know if it ever will. The place I feel most comfortable is leaning on the door jamb outside of Lennon's bedroom. Waiting on her, like always.

The second-best place is right here on the roof.

I slap my sketchpad and pencil on the shingles next to me and open the baggie. I send a silent thank you to Julian when I see that he included two joints with the bud. I toss my grinder back inside the window and spark up. I lie back, close my eyes, and pull the marijuana deep into my lungs.

It's so much fucking better than cigarettes.

I smoke half the joint and make myself stop, stubbing it out carefully before slipping it and the other joint into my pack.

Then I prop my body against my window, flip to a blank page in my sketchpad, and create.

"Mornin'," I say gruffly as I step into the kitchen, giving my mom a hug and kissing her on the head.

"Good morning, sweetie," she greets back.

I glance at the kitchen island where Claire and Lennon are sitting. Claire is scrolling through her phone with her middle finger brandished in my direction—*charming*—but Lennon gives me a small smile.

"Morning," she says, then focuses on her juice. I drag my attention away from her and back to my mom.

"Where's Trent?" I ask, pouring a cup of coffee. This whole Beaver-Cleaver-Happy-Family morning routine is weird as fuck, but I'm trying my damnedest to fall in line.

"On base," Lennon answers, pulling my eyes back to her. "He's had to be there early all week."

"Admiral training," Claire jokes, and Lennon rolls her eyes. We may not be allowed to know the details of Trent's job, but we all know he's not about to be an admiral.

"We're still going to have a family dinner tonight, though," my mom chimes in, handing me a package of S'mores Pop-Tarts.

I rip open the package and take a bite out of them, just right into both of the pastries like I always do, but halt mid-chew when I catch the look Lennon is throwing me.

"What?" I mumble. My mouth is full of Pop-tart, which makes her scrunch her nose up even more.

"You're just gonna...tear into 'em like that?" she asks. "Just...go to town on 'em without toasting or anything?"

My lips curl up. She's so fucking cute. I take another bite.

"I take every opportunity possible to raw dog."

Lennon spits juice out of her mouth, Claire groans something like *oh my god that's disgusting*, and my mom hits me so hard in the stomach I almost choke.

"Fuck, Ma," I laugh out, wrapping my arm around my torso and jumping away from her. "It's just a joke!"

"You do not talk to your sister like that," she scolds, and everyone in the kitchen freezes. My mom's hand flies to her mouth and her eyes go wide, and then she giggles. Then Claire giggles.

Lennon and I don't join in on the glee.

"We're gonna be sisters!" Claire squeals, then throws her arms around Lennon in a hug. Lennon laughs, but it's fake as fuck, and she darts her eyes away from me.

"Can't wait," she says. She pats Claire's back then shrugs out of the hug. No one but me seems to notice how uncomfortable she is, or if they do, they just don't fucking care.

"Oh, Mom," Claire says, "can we do family dinner tomorrow? It's the last home game tonight, and the players' girlfriends are running concessions."

Lennon's back goes ramrod straight.

"And that affects you two *how*?" I ask, and Claire scowls.

"I'm covering a shift for Josh, and Lennon is covering a shift for Eric." Her voice is so smug, and I have to breathe slowly through my nose. "We're wearing their away jerseys and everything."

I stare at Lennon's face, but she won't look at me.

"Oh, that's so fun," my mom says. "We can definitely move family dinner to tomorrow night. You don't work, right, Macon?"

"Nope," I say quickly. "I'm off."

Claire and Mom talk some more, but I tune them out. I stare at Lennon instead. I will her to look at me, but she doesn't. She drinks her juice and scrolls her phone, so I take out my phone and send her a text.

Say you have to get something from your room.

She freezes when she reads it. She even stops chewing her toast. I watch and wait for her to text back, but she doesn't. For a minute, I think she's going to ignore me entirely, but then slowly, she slides her phone into her pocket and stands up.

"I'll be right back," she says to the floor. "Forgot something."

Then without looking at anyone, she walks out of the kitchen.

I hoover the rest of my Pop-tart and down my coffee, then put the mug in the sink.

"Gotta piss," I say, and Claire gags. "See you later."

My mom sighs, she's over my shit, and I kiss her on the head again before leaving the kitchen and heading upstairs.

I bypass the bathroom and slip right into Lennon's room.

"You're not allowed to be mad at me about this," she hisses the moment I step into the bedroom.

"Oh, no?" I stalk toward her. "Doing concessions as Eric's *girlfriend*? I thought he wasn't your boyfriend, Lennon."

"He's not," she argues, folding her hands over her chest. "I said yes to be—"

"*Nice*," I mock, cutting her off. She stomps her foot and her jaw tenses.

"You're not my boyfriend *either*, Macon," she snips, and it pisses me the fuck off because it's true. "I can do whatever I want."

"I said he doesn't touch you."

The fury in my voice is barely restrained. I have to fist my own hands to keep them from shaking. I'm fuming, and I fully recognize I'm being a total asshole.

I've made it a point to keep my distance from Lennon for weeks now, and I've fucking hated it. I've held my tongue as best I can. I've kept my hands to myself despite the fact that having her sleeping just feet from my bed every night is killing me. Having to shower in a bathroom filled with her bodywash is fucking with my head. The only time my skin stops crawling is when she's sitting next to me with her paints, but even then, it physically hurts not being able to touch her.

Every single second my hands aren't on her is a wasted lifetime. Every minute I'm not kissing her is a silent, painful death.

But she's Claire's best friend.

She's going to be my mom's stepdaughter.

She's Trent's pride and joy.

She can *never* belong to me, but I'll be mother-fucked if I have to sit back and watch her waste time on Eric fucking Masters.

"He doesn't touch you," I repeat.

"Yeah, well, you haven't touched me either."

The retort is whispered but hurled at the same time. An accusation, and from the looks of it, she hates that she went there. She's shown she cares, and it snaps my restraint.

I close the distance, wrap my hand around her neck, and pull her to me. Her lips crash into mine without hesitation. She opens for me immediately, and our shared groans mingle the moment our tongues touch. I walk her back until her legs hit the bed, then I push her onto it and cover her body with mine, without breaking the kiss.

Her legs part and wrap around my waist, and I use my hand to shove her skirt up past her hips. I grip her thick thigh and squeeze.

Fuck, the things I want to do to this body.

"Macon," she sighs when I drag my lips from her mouth to her jaw. She presses her body into me, rubbing on my hard cock, and I groan against her skin.

"We can't," she pants out, but she doesn't stop moving on me. Doesn't stop teasing my dick with her heat. "We can't do this. It's wrong."

"Lennon," I rasp between kisses. "Shut up."

She huffs out a laugh, and her hands tighten in my hair. I move down her body, pressing kisses everywhere possible. I pull her shirt up to her neck and kiss the swell of her breasts, tugging down one of the cups, so I can suck on her nipple. I trace my tongue along the outside of her stupidly cute, little belly button. I push her skirt up so its sitting under the band of her bra and bite those fucking sexy hip dips.

"Oh my god," she cries, and tries to tighten her thighs around my shoulders. "Are you doing what I think you're doing?"

Her voice is shocked, but her blown pupils and quivering body are aroused.

"What do you think I'm doing, *Astraea*?" I ask as I move lower, then press a kiss to her panty-covered pussy.

She hisses, but instead of answering, she tightens her grip in my hair. I lick her over her panties, and she whimpers.

"You think I'm going to tongue-fuck you?" I taunt, licking her again. "Is that what you think I'm going to do?"

"Are you?" she asks between pants.

I chuckle, taking my finger and slipping it past the crotch of her underwear, swiping through her wetness and biting back a groan. I hook my finger in her panties and tug them to the side, revealing her glistening pussy.

"Fuck me, Lennon," I rasp, dropping my forehead to her inner thigh and clamping my eyes shut.

Of course, she'd have a beautiful fucking pussy. Of course, she fucking would.

"Macon," she whines, and my dick aches. She wiggles again, and I open my eyes and look up into her face. Propped on her elbows, Lennon's hazel eyes are wild with need and watching me with rapt attention. I press a kiss to her inner thigh, and she bites her lip.

My heart is racing so fucking fast, it's going to leap out of my damn chest.

"Lenny!" Claire calls from somewhere in the hall, and Lennon and I whip our heads to her door. I hear the footsteps pounding up the stairs, but I can't move.

"Len, we're gonna be late!" Claire calls again, closer this time. Lennon's body is rigid, and we're both frozen in place.

I glance at the handle on Lennon's door.

Unlocked. *Fuck.*

Then—*bang, bang, bang*—"Let's go!"

More footsteps, moving away this time, then a door opening across the hall.

The moment we realize that Claire went into her own bedroom, we spring into action. I jump off Lennon and help her up, tugging her skirt back into place.

"Coming," she yells, pulling down her shirt and shoving me into her closet, just as the door to her room flings wide open. I plaster myself to the wall behind a row of clothing.

"Sorry," I hear her say with forced brightness. "Let's go."

They leave the room, shutting the door behind them, and I slide to the floor and drop my head in my hands. I work on slowing my breathing, calming my pounding heart, and then I get up and let myself out quietly.

I might have to go through the entire day with a raging case of blue balls, but I've also got a smirk I can't shake off.

Lennon and I might have been cut short, once again, but we're not done.

And next time? I don't care who interrupts. I'm not stopping until she comes.

SIXTEEN

Lennon

I skipped free period.

Kind of.

I sent an email to Hank and told him I had a meeting with my guidance counselor. I lied. I spent the entire free period hiding in the girl's bathroom. Which honestly was stupid because if Macon were to come looking for me, he'd have no issue with checking every girl's bathroom in the school.

Still, it makes me feel a tad bit protected.

When the bell rings, I practically run to my locker hoping I can miss Eric, but I fail. He's waiting for me with his jersey in hand, and his smile is so bright. So kind.

I am a terrible, terrible human.

"Hey, Lennon." Deep dimples and straight, white teeth.

"Hey, Eric." Tight lips and a black, black soul.

He hands me his away jersey. I take it and hug it to my chest.

"Thank you. Good luck tonight!"

Eric moves in like he's going to kiss my cheek, and I step away from him. The confusion on his face makes me feel about two inches tall.

"Sorry," I lie. "I think I'm coming down with something. Don't want to get you sick."

"Oh!" The gratitude that replaces the confusion makes me feel even lower. "Thank you." He takes a step back, putting more distance between us. "If you don't feel well, stay home and rest. I'll understand."

God. He's so freaking nice. I don't deserve someone like him, not after what happened this morning in my bedroom with my soon-to-be stepbrother. My thighs clench at the memory, and I have to actually shake my head to get rid of it.

"No, it's okay," I say. "I'll see you later?"

Eric leaves just as Claire appears. She's already wearing Josh's jersey, and from the way she's bouncing, she feels like a million bucks.

"Why aren't you wearing that?" she asks, gesturing to the jersey. I roll my eyes and slip it on over my shirt. She smiles, satisfied. "I told Coach we'd do the set-up, too."

"Why?" I scrunch my nose as I throw my books in my bag. "We're already working shifts, and we're not even actual girlfriends. Why can't one of the real girlfriends do it?"

"*Len*, c'mon." She pokes out her bottom lip. "I just think it would be nice, ya know?"

"Or you think it will win you brownie points with Josh," I counter, and she smirks. "Why do you need brownie points when you're already giving him exclusive access to your whole lady bakery?"

"Lady bakery," she squeals with a laugh. "That's terrible."

I shrug and smile. I'm proud of my joke regardless of how terrible it was. I open my mouth to tell her to remember her worth, to not give more than she gets, but then I bite my tongue.

Even thinking the thoughts makes me feel like the world's biggest hypocrite, so I don't say anything at all. I've had nightmares about Sam and Macon in her car. Every time I see her, I get anxious that she's going to meet up with him. I can pretend all I want, but I don't trust Macon, and I haven't forgiven him, yet I still let him do what he did this morning. And I still want him. I'm a disgusting, pathetic cliché.

I help Claire set up the concession stand and listen to her talk. She complains about chem. She talks excitedly about our parents' upcoming wedding. She asks about college stuff.

Claire's worked with one of the guidance counselors to perfect her college applications, and she's pretty much accepted the fact that she's going to have to take out a ton of loans since she refuses to go to community college.

I haven't told her yet, but my dad has already mentioned offering to pay for Claire and Macon's post-high school educational plans. Not that Macon has any. I told Dad as much, but he waved me off with a *well, just in case.*

"I can't believe they're going to Greece for their honeymoon," Claire says as she fills the fridge with sports drinks and soda. "Your dad is like a real-life prince charming just sweeping Mom off her feet."

I laugh a little at the visual and try to fight the frown. Dad and I have always talked about traveling after I graduate. Instead, he's sending me to England to stay with Aunt Becca. I'm excited to go, but now I can't help but wonder if part of the decision was made to get me out of the way for his new marriage.

He said he was going to propose after I graduated.

Is he hoping to ship me off so he can have some alone time with his new wife?

"And who leaves right after a wedding?" Claire adds. "I thought people at least waited a few days or something, but they really said *we're not wasting time*, going with that small afternoon wedding and evening flight."

I laugh again, not taking my eyes off the candy bars I'm lining on the counter.

"At least your mom let us pick our own bridesmaid dresses."

"Yeah, 'cause what does it matter?" Claire snorts. "There's gonna be like five people there. We could wear pajamas, and Mom wouldn't care. She just wants to jet off to Santorini, so she can bone your dad in a Grecian villa on the sea."

"Ewww, Claire," I groan, throwing a Snickers bar at her, "Stop."

She holds her belly as she laughs, and I shake my head. She's ridiculous.

We finish setting up and wait for the first shift of concession workers to show up. Me and Claire are working later. Her shift is at the end of the first half and mine is at the end of the second half, but we agreed to do the shifts together, so we're both basically working two. I don't mind, though. I don't care if I miss parts of the game. Football is boring.

Which is why I spend most of it zoned out and scanning the stands.

I tell myself I'm not looking for Macon.

I know it's a lie.

I try like hell not to wonder where he is, not to worry about whether or not he's with Sam, but I can't. I can't stop. I'm jealous and worried, and I hate it.

Claire's concession shift is slow because, apparently, the game is "intense," and no one wants to leave the stands, so we spend most of the time talking. Well, she talks. I listen and laugh when appropriate. At halftime, the PTA moms come and kick us out, so we walk the track around the football field, and she talks some more before we move back to the stands for the second half to start.

When it's time for my shift in the concession stand, Claire asks if it's okay that she stay and watch the game instead of helping.

"It's such a close game," she pleads. "I don't want to miss

it. And no one is going to the concessions right now. Not when it's so close."

"Claire," I sigh, "I didn't even want to do concessions at all. I don't want to sit in there by myself."

"You don't even like football," Claire says with a huff. "And I need to have something to talk to Josh about after. That cheerleader from West was posting about him all over online, so I want to stay ahead of the competition."

I open my mouth to argue, to tell her how ridiculous she sounds and how she's being a crappy friend, but then I bite my tongue. Who the hell am I to say those things now?

"Fine," I say with a forced smile. "See you after."

"Thank you! I love you!" she shouts as I leave.

When I get to the concession stand, I tell the girl working that she can leave, and then I make myself comfortable with my phone. Claire's right. The game is neck and neck. Nobody is going to come to concessions to buy stale nachos with bright yellow, globby cheese and overpriced cans of soda.

I pull up a book on my e-reader app and try to tune out the cheering coming from the bleachers, but not even two pages into my book, the door to the concession stand opens. I smile, assuming it's Claire coming to help me out of guilt, but when I turn around, it's the other Davis sibling.

"You're not supposed to be in here," I say quickly, and because he's Macon, he laughs.

"I thought you were past caring about what you should and shouldn't be doing."

My cheeks heat immediately, and I glance over my shoulder to make sure no one is close enough to hear us. We're alone. Everyone is glued to the game. When I turn back to him, he's closer, and my breath hitches.

"What do you want?"

I wince at how breathless I sound and the crackle in my voice. I straighten my shoulders to seem more composed, but he smirks, which means I failed. He takes another step closer, then another, until he's directly in front of me. A finger's reach away.

"The same thing you want," he says, the piercing blue of his eyes pinning me to the spot.

It doesn't matter how many times I get this close to Macon. His presence shocks and excites me like it's the very first time. Every thought in my head is silenced until I'm hyperaware of the sound of his breathing and the rapid beating of my heart. He reaches out and pulls my braid over my shoulder, slipping the ribbon off the end and shoving it into his pocket. Number three.

I don't breathe. I don't move, except for the tiniest tilt of my body toward him. It's not intentional. It's like I'm pulled, but I don't resist. I welcome it, just like I welcome his fingers wrapping around the back of my neck and the tug of my lips onto his. I welcome the bite of his teeth on my lower lip, the caress of his tongue over mine, the press of his body into me.

I was hoping he'd come here.

I think I knew he would.

I bring my hands to his head and slip my fingers into his hair, his soft curls exactly what I've been craving all day. I ignore the guilt and the warning bells, and I pull him as close to me as possible, until there's no space between our bodies. No room for air or doubt or reality.

Just us.

Just him and me.

He backs me up slowly and pushes me against the counter. My back is to the football field and the bleachers full of fans, but all I care about is Macon. His hands and his mouth. He pulls away, nipping at my jaw, sucking on my neck, then dropping to his knees in front of me.

"What," I pant out, "what are you doing?" I look behind me, then back down at him. He smirks.

"Finishing what I started." He slides his hands slowly up my thighs and under my skirt. I clamp my legs together, halting his hands with my own. My eyes are wide, my mouth dropped in surprise.

"You can't," I say, and his amused smirk grows. "People will see."

He knocks on the underside of the counter.

"No one's gonna see me," he says. "You just gotta act normal."

He slides his hands between my legs and pushes them apart, and damnit, they open for him. Without any resistance.

He brings his index finger to his lips.

"Shhh," he whispers. "Be a *good girl*, Lennon Capri."

I don't miss his mocking tone, but I'm too dazed to call him out on it. He slips my skirt up my thighs, pressing a kiss to one, then the other, before inching the fabric up over the curve of my ass.

I glance behind me again, making sure that no one can see, but there isn't a soul close to the building, and the counter reaches to just above my waist. Hot breath heats my center, and I look back down to see Macon with his mouth covering my panties and his eyes on my face.

I gasp. The feeling of his tongue massaging me through the cotton barrier is somehow more erotic now than it was this morning, and this time, he doesn't tease. He uses his finger to pull my underwear to the side and swipes his tongue over me. I moan, then clap my hand over my mouth. He licks me again before closing his lips around my clit and sucking, never breaking eye contact.

"Oh my god," I whisper.

His usually piercing blue eyes are so dark, sapphire instead of topaz, but just as depthless and breathtaking. My thighs quiver. I can't handle the sight of him in front of me, on his knees for me, with his mouth on my body. His palms cover my backside, and he pulls me firmer against his face, flicking his tongue over my sensitive, swollen skin.

"Macon," I gasp, and his groan vibrates between my legs. One of his hands leaves my body as he reaches down and grips the bulge in his jeans. It makes me hotter, thinking of him touching himself. His hand on his erection, stroking himself as he licks me.

I tug on his hair. I want to writhe on him, and the thought makes my breaths grow shorter. I pulse my hips, just a little, to test it out, and the feeling makes my vision spark white.

"Fuck," Macon says with glistening lips, pulling back just enough to speak. "Move on me just like that," he rasps as he slips a finger in me. I have to bite the insides of my cheeks to keep from crying out.

I open my mouth to speak, to say I don't even know what, but laughter behind me breaks through the haze in my brain. It's closer than it should be, and I glance over my shoulder to see two students heading our way.

I grab Macon's hair and pull, dragging him away from my body.

"You have to stop," I say frantically. "Someone's coming."

He smirks, his full lips shiny and wet with my arousal.

"Yeah," he rumbles, "*You.*"

He grabs my hips and turns me, so I'm facing the approaching girls. I recognize them. Alana and Sarah. They're juniors, and I've had a few classes with them in the past. Alana is nice enough, but Sarah is a gossip and loves drama.

God, they cannot know what's happening in here.

I push my waist against the wooden counter and try to straighten my skirt, but my hands are halted by Macon's as he shoves his body between my legs, wedging himself underneath the overhanging countertop.

His lips close back over my clit, just as the girls stop in front of the concession stand. I gasp and dig my fingers into the counter so hard I almost break a nail, and the girls eye me with concern.

"Hey, Lennon, are you okay?" Alana asks, and all I can do is nod and force out an *mmhmm*.

"You sure?" Sarah chimes in. "You're all red and kinda sweaty."

I feel, rather than hear, Macon laugh, and I use more strength than I have available to jut my knee out. It hits hard muscle, and he lets out a satisfying grunt at the contact. I want to laugh, but he sucks hard on my clit, and I have to bite back a cry instead. The girls glance at the countertop, as if trying to see through it.

"I'm fine," I say with a forced smile.

"Okaaaaay," Sarah says, dragging her eyes from the countertop to my face. "Well, can we get two bottles of water and two caramel candy bars?"

The candy bars are within reach, so I grab two and toss them on the counter. Macon swirls his tongue faster around my clit and slips his finger back inside me and I swallow a moan. The drink case is behind me on the far wall. There's no way I can walk to it right now. The way Macon tightens his hold on my thigh tells me he wouldn't let me even if I wanted to.

"No water," I gasp out, and the girls gape at me.

"It's right there," Sarah argues, pointing to the drink case.

I shake my head and clamp my eyes shut. More pulsing of his fingers. More flicking of his tongue. A graze of teeth. A vibrating hum. The pressure at my core builds rapidly, threatening to explode, and all I want to do is move on him. I want to force my fingers into his curls and pull, but I can't with Alana and Sarah staring at me like I'm a creepy science experiment.

"It's warm," I tell her. "Broken. Probably contaminated."

"Oh, gross."

I nod but can't bring myself to pry my eyes back open.

"Just take the candy," I say. "On the house. For the inconvenience. No water."

Macon slides in a second finger and my body lurches forward as he does something new to my clit with his tongue. My eyes fly open just as the girls jump backward.

"Leave now," I beg. My voice is a rasped cry. "Please," I say again, and they start walking backward.

"Sure," Alana says, "uh, feel better?"

The cheering from the stands gets louder, thankfully, and the girls turn around quickly to hustle back to their seats. Macon's tongue swirls around me then flicks at the sensitive bud of nerves between my legs.

"Oh fuck," I groan. He uses the hand not thrusting inside of me to grip my ass and move my hips in a slow pulse. I follow his lead, finally moving on him the way I wanted. I barely register the buzz from the bleachers, the mounting excitement from the crowd. I speed up and so does Macon, thrusting and swirling as I drag my swollen core back and forth over his wicked mouth.

"I'm going to come," I say, and I feel him hum. "Oh, god, Macon. I'm gonna... I'm gonna..."

My voice cuts off with a choked cry, my body bowing forward until my top half is lying on the counter and my thighs are clamped tightly around Macon's head. Blue flames dance in and out of my vision as my climax roars through my body. Goosebumps rise on my skin as sweat dots the back of my neck.

I hear Macon chuckle, feel him press a kiss to my inner thigh. I breathe in through my nose and out through my mouth and wait for the fuzziness to clear from my limbs.

The blood whooshing through my ears makes it hard to notice the sound of the crowd at first. The announcer shouts something through the loudspeaker, something that sounds like

Eric Masters, and I push myself off the concession stand counter to look toward the field.

Everyone in the home section of the bleachers is on their feet, jumping and waving and cheering. There's a commotion on the field, a huddle of players, someone lifted on shoulders. I blink a few times.

We must have won.

Then I watch as the player on the team's shoulders is put back on the ground and starts to run toward me.

"You've got to be fucking kidding me." I groan when I can read the number on Eric's jersey. I don't even have time to kick Macon out. I just tug my skirt down over my ass and stand up straight, plastering a smile on my face just as Eric skids to a halt in front of the concession stand.

"We won," he shouts, reaching over the counter and planting a kiss right on my lips. I freeze, but he doesn't notice. He pulls back, his dimples competing for attention with his bright white teeth. "Did you see? I just made a seventy-yard touchdown. There are scouts here," he says quickly through pants.

I force a smile and nod, even though I didn't see anything because I was too busy coming with Macon's tongue on my clit.

Oh shit. Macon.

I stiffen. He's not between my legs anymore. I swipe my foot out in front of me to see if I can find him but get nothing.

I clear my throat.

"Congrats," I say to Eric. I take a step back so he can't kiss me again and try to peek under the counter.

"Are you coming to the party?" Eric asks, bouncing on his feet. I nod. "You want to—" He stops suddenly as Macon emerges from beneath the counter. Eric's head cocks to the side. "Davis?"

Macon ignores him.

"Fixed it," Macon says, unwrapping a candy bar while he speaks and taking a bite. He looks at Eric and hooks his thumb toward the drink case. "It was broken," he deadpans. "Warm, contaminated water."

I look back at Eric and try to look innocent.

"Thanks, Macon," I say quickly.

"Oh, you're *very* welcome, *Astraea*," Macon says. I clench my hands at the teasing tone in his voice. I swear to god if he tells Eric what just happened here...

"Uh, Davis," Eric says. His brow is furrowed as he stares at Macon. "You've uh, got something..."

Eric gestures to his own mouth and chin, and my eyes go wide. I whip my head toward Macon and sure enough, his face is still a glistening mess, covered in, well, *me*. My mouth drops open, mortified, and weirdly turned-on.

Macon looks from me to Eric, and his lips twitch at the corners.

"Hmm, sorry," Macon says, swiping his fingers slowly over his chin before slipping them between his lips and sucking on them. "Messy eater."

I'm still gawking at him, my cheeks and ears burning red, when he winks at me, nods goodbye to Eric, then saunters through the door and out of sight.

SEVENTEEN

Macon

I TURN DOWN THE JOINT JULIAN OFFERS AND WAVE OFF THE beer. I'm not ready to lose the taste of Lennon on my tongue.

I had to jerk my dick in my car like a horny kid after leaving her in the concession stand. Not my finest moment, but fuck if I was gonna walk around with a raging hard-on the rest of the night. As it is, just the flashes of memory have me sporting a fucking uncomfortable semi.

I've been watching her all night as she makes small talk and weaves in and out of groups of people. Claire's been sticking close, and that pisses me off. I don't know if Lennon asked her to or if it's just Claire's bitchy sixth sense to fuck with my happiness, but I haven't been able to get close to Lennon since we got to this stupid party.

"Hello! Earth to Davis." Julian's irritated voice makes me drag my eyes off Lennon.

"What?" I spit, and he rolls his eyes.

"Keep eye-fucking your stepsister and everyone at this party is going to know about your obsession," he says, and I sneer at him.

"Shut the fuck up, Jules," I bite out. "She's not my stepsister."

"Basically is," Casper chimes in with a grin, and I flip him off.

"And I'm not obsessed," I argue, aware and hating that I sound like a petulant child.

"Yeah, okay." Julian snorts. "That's why you have whole-ass sketchbooks fucking f—"

I punch him in the arm hard enough that he stumbles backward, choking out a laugh just before stopping himself from falling on his ass. He throws his palms up at me in surrender with a dumb fucking grin. I settle myself back against the wall and let my eyes wander to where they want to be.

Fuck Jules and Casper. They act like I'm embarrassed or ashamed of my fixation on Lennon. I'm neither of those things. I have entirely different reasons for keeping it quiet, but those reasons are taking on water and my logic is about to capsize.

Lennon has been doing a great job of keeping her eyes off me, but she's also been keeping her distance from Eric, so my irritation is tempered for now. My fists clench when I think of the way he leaned over the fucking counter and kissed her after the game tonight.

Lennon thinks I didn't see him, but I did. If the jock would have looked down, he'd have seen me, too. The only thing that kept me from launching myself at the prick was knowing Lennon wouldn't want to make a scene, so I made a more subtle statement. More for her benefit than for his.

I'm playing the long game.

But if he tries it again, I'll knock his empty head clean off his Ken doll body.

Someone nudges my arm, tries to pass me something, but I wave it away. Nothing else is tainting these lips until they're back on Lennon. I stare at her. I know she feels me. She always does. I will her to look at me, but she doesn't. She'll keep ignoring me all night because she's a brat, but I'm tired of waiting.

"I'll catch up with you guys later," I say to Jules and Casper.

Julian groans and mumbles some smart-ass comment, but I'm already weaving through bodies to reach the other side of the room. I maneuver so I'm behind Claire and smack in Lennon's line of sight. I step right in front of her so she can't pretend she doesn't see me, and I smirk when she startles.

Yeah, brat, I know you've been ignoring me.

I pull a cigarette from my pack and slip it between my lips, then nod to the door leading outside. Her brow furrows, and her eyes jump from me to Claire and back.

Claire is talking to some cheerleaders. She's not paying any attention to Lennon, like usual. When Lennon pulls her bottom lip between her teeth, I know I've won. I nod once more to the door, telling her to follow, then I turn and walk outside.

I push through the crowd and head into the yard, stopping about halfway between the house and the bonfire. I lean against a tree that's in direct view of the door, then take the cigarette out of my mouth and put it behind my ear. When Lennon comes out, it'll be easy enough to spot me.

I pull the thriller I've been reading up on my e-reader app while I wait, and when I hear footsteps crunching over the fallen leaves, I click off the screen and slip my phone into my pocket before looking up with a smirk.

The smirk turns into a scowl when I see blonde hair instead of brown.

"Go the fuck away, Sam." I groan, sighing at the night sky. "Why can't you take a hint?"

She laughs and closes the distance between us, then puts her hand on my chest. It makes my skin crawl.

"I just wanted to let you know that my dad was home this week..."

She lets the statement trail off. She doesn't have to explain. I already know what it means. When Senator Harper is home, his safe becomes a veritable pharmacy. Then he jets off to wherever, leaving his stash for his kids to raid. There's no way he doesn't know that Sam and Chase know the combination to his safe, and it's never made any sense to me. What kind of parent would knowingly supply his kids with drugs?

"I don't care what Senator Daddy left for you or what kind of Mommy issue demons you're trying to exorcise with the bad boy across town, Samantha."

I take the cigarette out from behind my ear and put it back in my mouth, sparking it up with my lighter. I mourn the loss of Lennon immediately, but my skin itches and I need it to stop.

"I told you to fuck off and leave me alone. I'm done being your rebellion." I pull the nicotine into my lungs and blow it out my nose. "Start whoring yourself out to your neighbor or something if you're so hard up for dick."

She growls and digs her nails into my chest. They bite into my skin through my long-sleeve shirt, and I slap my hand over hers to make her stop.

"So, you're just done?" She sneers. "Goody two-shoes Lennon Washington pays you the tiniest bit of attention, and you're just throwing me out like trash?"

She presses into me, and I close my eyes against the overwhelming urge to shove her. I understand why she's upset. She's used to being discarded, and it sucks. I can relate.

"What about all the shit we've been through? *Years* of friendship," she says, twisting the knife in my gut with her words.

Guilt sets in as memories of late-night conversations and tears and arguments flash through my head. Me and Sam used to be best friends before things got all fucked up and confused. Before the pills and the powder and the sex.

She takes her other hand and pounds it into my chest, so I grab that one, too.

"You promised you wouldn't abandon me," she says, her voice softer. Younger. And my heart fucking sinks. I'm such a dick. I'm no better than my father.

I look down at Sam, see the glisten of tears in her eyes, and for a second, I want to pull her into a hug. I want to apologize. I want to tell her that I didn't lie on that day at the clinic when I promised I wouldn't leave her side. I meant it when I said I'd get her out of that fucked-up house with her father's fucked-up friends. I want to tell her she can still depend on me. That I'm still her friend.

But then I think of Lennon.

I see her face outside of the car when she found me with Sam. I hear her crying, and the sound mixes with my mom's tears, and Claire's tears, and my own fucking tears, and I know I can't keep my promise to Sam.

I can't keep any promises, apparently.

But I have to try for Lennon.

I'm addicted to Lennon Washington, and Sam has to be collateral damage.

"Sam," I say softly, squeezing her hands into my chest, pleading that she'll understand. "I just...*I can't.*"

She shuts her eyes on the tears and bites her lip.

"Please," she begs. "We can stop with the pills. It can be totally straightedge. No touching. Nothing. You're my only friend. You're the only one who knows." She presses her forehead into my chest. "*Please*, Macon."

I rest my chin on the top of her head, giving her another second before I have to pry her off me, but then I hear more leaves rustle and a gasp. My eyes fly open to Lennon's shocked face.

Rage and pain war in her expression, and I push Sam away from me.

"Lennon," I say, and she takes two steps back. Her eyes fall to Sam, who is still gripping onto my arm despite me trying to shake her off.

"This?" Lennon breathes out. "This! Did you want me to see this?" She takes two more steps back, and I shake my head.

"No," I say quickly, "you weren't supposed to see this."

She scoffs and the first tear falls down her cheek.

"So, you were planning to, what, get it over with, with your whore *before* I came out here?"

"Oh, fuck off, Leonard," Sam seethes. She lets go of my arm and stalks toward Lennon.

"Don't, Sam," I warn, but she ignores me.

"You think you've got something with your *brother*, Leonard?" More slow steps forward, but Lennon doesn't budge.

"Shut up, Sam," Lennon whispers, and Sam laughs.

"Samantha, get the fuck out of here," I growl. When I reach for her arm, she yanks it away and hits me with a glare.

"Don't fucking touch me," she hisses, before turning her attention back to Lennon. "You're a challenge, Leonard. A chase. The good girl cliché that every guy wants to fuck for bragging rights."

Lennon shakes her head. "You're wrong."

"Sam, shut the fuck up," I shout.

"You haven't fucked yet, have you?" Sam says, ignoring me, closing the distance between her and Lennon. "That's why he's still stringing you along. He'll lose interest once you spread your legs."

Lennon looks over Sam's shoulder at me, her eyes both accusing and questioning.

"She's wrong, Lennon," I say, but I can tell she doesn't believe me.

"Fuck him, then," Sam taunts, drawing Lennon's attention back to her face. "Fuck him and see if I'm lying." Lennon's jaw tightens and her hands fist at her sides. Sam takes one more step and opens her mouth. "Go ahead and be a slut for your bro—"

Lennon punches her.

A closed-fist hook to Sam's jaw that makes her stumble backward. Sam pauses for a split second, then shrieks and launches herself at Lennon. I move to stop her, to restrain her, but I only make it two steps before Lennon lands a jab to Sam's face that makes a sickening crunch.

Sam screams and falls back into my chest. I just catch sight of the blood gushing down her face before she clamps her hands over her nose. It's broken. It has to be broken. Lennon just broke Sam's nose.

"You're a fucking psycho," Sam yells, her voice garbled through her hands and the blood.

"Shut *up*," Lennon growls, advancing on us. I take a step back with Sam to avoid any more violence, and Lennon glares at me before looking back at Sam.

"I don't give a shit who your dad is, Samantha Harper," Lennon says through her teeth. "You know who my dad is? He's a Navy SEAL, and he taught me how to break a bone without breaking a sweat. You *ever* talk to me like that again, you ever *touch* me, and I'll make sure your face is so messed up, you'll never be in another cheesy campaign video."

My eyes go wide and my jaw drops. Lennon looks from Sam to me.

"Both of you stay the hell away from me."

Lennon turns and stalks toward the road, so I let go of Sam and run after her.

"Lennon, stop," I shout, grabbing her arm. Lennon turns

on me and swings, but I jump back, and she misses. "Jesus Christ, Lennon, let me explain."

"No," she spits. "Fuck you, Macon."

"It's not at all what you think," I plead. "You didn't see what you think you saw."

"Don't you gaslight me, asshole." Her voice is shaking with anger. I have never seen Lennon this mad. "I saw her *plastered* to you. I saw her face in your chest and her hands in your hands and your fucking lips in her hair," she says. "Don't tell me I don't know what I saw!"

"Nothing fucking happened!" I yell, aware we're drawing a crowd.

"She was all over you!"

"I was handling it."

She laughs again. That hollow, sardonic laugh that I've come to hate. Then her face crumples, and she covers it with her hands. I walk closer. She's crying, and I hate that more than the laugh. I'd rather have her pissed at me forever than hurt and crying.

"Lennon," I whisper, reaching for her, but she steps away. She takes her hands off her face and my chest cracks open at the sight. Her hazel eyes are red-rimmed and swollen, her face covered in tears. She's still beautiful, but she's broken, and it's my fault.

"I just punched Samantha Harper because of you," she whispers through her tears. "I broke her nose." She squeezes her eyes shut and swipes at the tears on her face. "I hate the person you're making me. I hate who I am when I'm with you, but I hate how I feel when we're apart."

Fuck. I step toward her again, needing to touch her, but she backs away from me and shakes her head, holding her palms up at me. I halt my steps.

"When you're with me, you're exactly who you're supposed

to be," I say. I mean every fucking word. "We are *exactly* who we're supposed to be when we're together."

"You've made me a liar," she forces out on a sob, then her face transforms into an angry scowl. "I'm lying to *everyone* because of you!"

Her disgusted tone, her accusation, makes my shoulders stiffen. I grit my teeth.

"All you ever do is lie," I say through my teeth. "You're a *liar*, Lennon. You've *always* been a liar." She opens her mouth to argue, but I cut her off. "At least now you're lying for yourself instead of everyone else."

She closes her eyes against the steady stream of tears, and we stand in silence for a few breaths. I wait. Like I always have, I wait for her words. I'm always waiting on Lennon.

When she finally speaks, I want to burn everything to the fucking ground.

"This is done, Macon," she says calmly. "You and me, whatever this was, is over. Leave me alone."

I take another step forward, ready to tell her no way in hell are we over, but she puts her hands up again.

"Please," she croaks. "Please."

My feet turn to lead. My breath stops.

"*Please*," she says again, and I give up.

I nod once, then feel my heart shatter as she turns and walks away.

EIGHTEEN

Macon

"This is the lamest bachelor party I've ever been to," I say to Trent after taking a sip of my soda.

He chuckles. "How many you been to?"

"Besides the point," I say with a shrug. "I could go to a million after this and this will still be the lamest."

He chuckles again and raises his soda to his mouth, just as his friend sits in the hard plastic chair next to him. His name is Joe. He's Trent's best man. I'd never met him before today.

"The kid's right," Joe says. "Bowling is lame. I thought we'd get strippers."

"Yeah, Trent." I nod eagerly. "Where are the strippers?"

Trent shrugs, then stands and walks to the little machine thing that spits the bowling balls out after they go down the lane.

"I like bowling," he says, then proceeds to throw a strike.

I don't think there's a single thing this fucker can't do.

"You just don't want to be hungover tomorrow," I say to Trent as I walk up to take my turn. He nods.

"That too."

My ball goes into the gutter. My score in this game is

pathetic. I turn around and glare at Trent and Joe as they laugh at my shitty bowling skills. This bachelor party sucks.

I want to smoke a joint and sketch on the roof, not throw a bunch of gutter balls at Franklin Bowling Alley with Trent and his old as fuck military buddy. I want to wander through the house and hope like hell I get a glimpse of Lennon that isn't across the dinner table and tainted with fake smiles and forced pleasantries.

She's transferred out of our free period and quit the rec center.

If I'd have known she was going to do either, I would have done it first. I hate that she's given up two things she loves because she can't stand being around me. She won't talk to me except to appease our parents. She won't look at me until she has to. She won't show me a shred of emotion, and I'm losing my patience with her.

I've given her space and time. I've been respectful. But if I have to be on the receiving end of one of Lennon's fake as shit nice girl smiles one more time, I'm going to explode. The fire in her hazel eyes is dormant. I want to see her jaw tighten, her fists clench. Fuck, anything except this polite, placating bullshit.

"—for tomorrow?"

I glance up and find Joe and Trent staring at me expectantly.

"Huh?"

"Have you decided if you're bringing a date," Trent repeats slowly. "For the wedding tomorrow."

"Oh." I throw myself into my chair and shake my head no. "Nah."

"You sure? Claire and Lennon will have dates," he says, and I bristle. "You could invite one of your friends instead?"

"Nah," I say again. "I'm good."

I take a drink of my soda. There's going to be roughly twenty people at the wedding tomorrow. One of those people will be Eric. I'm actually really proud of how I handled the news, considering I watched it all go down at the dinner table.

Claire hinted that she wanted to bring a date. Mom and Trent said it was fine. Claire told Lennon that she should bring Eric. Lennon declined. Mom and Trent agreed with Claire. Lennon caved.

The whole thing was awkward and infuriating, and the fact that no one picked up on Lennon's screaming discomfort still pisses me off. Almost as much as the fact that she agreed to bring Eric fucking Masters as her date to our parents' wedding.

I drink the rest of my soda and pretend there's liquor in it.

If I don't get to smoke a joint soon, I'm gonna lose my fucking mind.

The thing is, I really like Trent. I like this Joe guy, too. I don't entirely hate bowling. But I am anxious as fuck about tomorrow. I have to sit through a wedding ceremony and a formal luncheon while Lennon is dressed like a goddess and hanging on the arm of her no-neck football dick date. And I have to behave. I can't touch her or talk to her or even look at her in any way that could suggest anything other than brotherly affection or else I risk ruining my mom's special day.

"You wanna do another game or head out after this?" Joe asks Trent, and I hold my breath. Trent glances at me and then barks out a laugh that makes my lips twitch up at the corners. I roll my eyes.

"We can head out," Trent says. He throws his arm around my shoulders and gives me one of those side-hug, back-pat things before dropping his arm and taking a step back. "I think Macon here has been tortured enough."

I can't hold back my grin. It's such a *dad* move.

Or at least, it feels like a dad move.

I guess I wouldn't really know.

I laugh and shake my head, but I don't argue. It's obvious I'm not having a blast, so I switch out my ugly bowling shoes for my Vans and slip on my jacket. Mom and the girls got a suite at the hotel in Suffolk, so I won't run into Lennon until tomorrow.

I wish I could say it makes me feel better, but it doesn't. Not having her around fucks with me just as much as having her around. I'm going to spend the whole night wondering what she's doing and who she's doing it with, which is why I plan to smoke a ton, drink a bit, and fill another sketchbook up with drawings of her eyes and hands and lips and that stupid fucking braid.

When Julian found my sketchbooks a couple years ago, he fucked with me for weeks. Not because I had sketchbooks filled with Lennon, but because I had sketchbooks filled with *parts*. Pages of eyes and eyebrows. Of lips making various expressions. Hands creating different gestures.

Why don't you ever draw a whole person?

This is some serial killer shit, right here.

He didn't realize that it was Lennon until he saw the braids. Each one tied off with a different fucking ribbon. That was my mistake, assuming he was too high to make the connection.

He thinks I only sketch her in pieces because I'm trying to keep my feelings for her hidden, but that's not why.

I only sketch Lennon in pieces because I'm not worthy of the whole. I'm not good enough. I'd fuck up a full rendition, so I stick to perfecting her in parts.

"I'll see y'all bright and early tomorrow at the Hyatt," Joe says as he walks to his car in the bowling alley parking lot.

I was worried he'd come back to the house and want to bond and do bachelor party shit like, I dunno, smoke cigars or play poker or something. I'm relieved when he doesn't. I'm not surprised, though. For being a badass Navy SEAL, Trent's kind of boring.

I smile and glance at him in the driver's seat of his

4Runner. This whole situation sucks for me, but I'm happy for Mom. She deserves a good, boring guy.

"Thanks for coming with tonight, Macon," Trent says, breaking the silence. "I know it's not your idea of a good time, but I was glad to have you there."

His words kind of surprise me, so I shrug and blow it off.

"Sure," I mumble. "Thanks for the invite."

Trent nods, and it gets quiet again. I wait for him to turn on the radio, but he doesn't. Something else is coming. I can feel it.

A scolding? A warning? Some sort of chest banging alpha show of dominance?

I sit up straight and ready myself. It won't be the first time a father-figure has laid into me. I'm pretty good about hiding the hurt now. When Trent takes a breath and opens his mouth, my lips tighten, preparing to bite my tongue and take it.

"You're a good kid, Macon," he says, and my jaw drops. He glances at me and chuckles. "You are," he insists. "I know you've had a rough go, and you haven't always made the best decisions—"

I snort. Understatement of the year, and he doesn't even know half of it.

"But I see you," he continues. "I see how much you love and care for your mom and Claire. I see how hard you work. I know you're smart and talented, and I know that where it counts, you're good and kind. You've been forced into a very difficult situation, but you're a good kid, Macon, and you're going to be a good man."

I swallow hard and clear my throat.

"Thanks," I rasp.

It's not at all what I was expecting. Now I'm waiting for the other shoe to drop.

"I want you to know that I love your mom very much," he

says. "I'm going to do everything in my power to make her happy."

"I know," I say honestly. If I know anything, it's that Trent Washington is head over heels for my mom, and he'd do anything for her.

"I also love you and Claire. I'm so happy that you're going to be my family, and even though I'm not your biological father, I hope someday you can come to see me as your dad."

Fucker is going to make me cry.

I take a deep breath and nod. I don't know what to say, so I say nothing. I stare out the front window, then slide my palms down my thighs and grip my knees so I have something to do with my hands as Trent starts talking again.

"One last thing," he says with a small laugh. "You can come to me for anything. Anything at all. If you're in trouble, or confused, or if you just don't want to be alone with your thoughts, I'm here for you, okay?"

"Okay," I say quietly, squeezing my eyes shut against the sting. "Thank you."

He reaches over and pats me twice on the shoulder, turns on the radio. He inches up the volume on a Goo Goo Dolls song and sings along under his breath as we drive back home. We don't say anything else.

For the millionth time since I learned about my mom and Trent, my gut twists.

I want to see Trent as a father. Fuck knows he's a billion times better than the man whose DNA runs through my body. I want him to look at me like a son he's proud of and treat me like I'm worth something. Under any other circumstances, in any other life, I would welcome Trent as my dad. I would *want* it.

But in this life, I can't.

If he knew about my sketchpads, about where my mouth and hands have been, he would never look at me the same again. If he knew how I think of his daughter. How I crave her. My father's looks of disgust and hatred invade my mind. I drop my head back on the headrest and close my eyes.

When we get back to the house, I tell Trent goodnight and climb the stairs to my room. I pull the vase I made Mom as a wedding present out of my closet and stick it in the frou-frou gift bag I bought, making sure to stuff a shit-ton of tissue paper inside of it. I sign the card, wishing Trent and Mom everlasting marital bliss or whatever, then I grab my joint and my sketchpad and climb out onto the roof.

I spark up and lie back, letting the cold December air prickle at my feet through my socks. Goosebumps cover the naked skin on my arms. I take a long drag, hold it in, then blow it out slowly into the night. I let the weed tame the itch for something stronger.

It's only a matter of time before this all explodes in my face.

WE GRAB COFFEE FROM STARBUCKS BEFORE WE GET TO THE hotel, and Trent sends me to the room being used as the bridal suite with the coffees in a drink holder and a note he wrote for Mom.

I don't walk into the room, don't even glance inside, but I can feel Lennon anyway.

I wait in the hallway as Mom reads the note. She cries, then laughs as she curses Trent for almost ruining her makeup, even though she doesn't have any on yet. Her hair is curled and swooped into this elaborate twisty thing and she's wearing some sort of silk robe with flowers on it. Her makeup gets done soon, she tells me, and she won't put on her dress until very last.

"You look beautiful, Mom," I tell her honestly, and she smiles, wiping tears off her cheeks.

"Thank you, Macon," she whispers. "I feel beautiful."

I smile and pull her into a hug, being careful not to smoosh her hair. I tell her I'll meet her downstairs in three hours, then I leave her to finish doing whatever it is brides do on their wedding day. If it's anything like what the groom does, she's pacing back and forth a lot and flipping between ESPN and Family Feud on the hotel television.

Trent's a fucking wreck, and it's kind of hilarious. I wonder briefly if he was this ridiculous when he married Lennon's mom, but I don't ask. I just laugh every time Joe cracks a joke about how Trent is an anxious ball of nerves, then laugh harder every time Trent threatens to murder Joe.

When it's time, we make our way down to the banquet hall, where they'll have the ceremony and the luncheon. Trent heads toward the officiant, and I walk to the alcove, where I know Mom will be waiting for me. I weave through the guests, most are just work friends of Mom and Trent, and deliberately ignore Josh and Eric. They're here in suits because they're Claire and Lennon's dates. I grit my teeth and focus on my task.

With every step I take closer to the alcove, my heart kicks up faster.

I know Lennon is waiting with my mom and Claire. It's been more than twenty-four hours since I've seen her, and it's actually painful. I haven't had to endure more than eight hours without a Lennon sighting since we moved into the new house, and I've gotten used to the constant fix. As I turn the corner, my body relaxes, and I inhale.

Roses.

Mom's bouquet, yeah, but also Lennon.

I look at my mom first.

"You look so beautiful, Mom," I tell her again, and she fans her face.

"Don't say anything else," she warns. "I cannot cry. I cannot."

I laugh at the same time Claire and Lennon laugh, drawing my attention to where they're standing. I dance right over Claire and focus on Lennon. She's gorgeous, and my chest tightens.

Her hair is in one of those twisty deals just like my mom's, but Lennon has sprigs of baby's breath pinned into hers. She's wearing a dress of emerald green, and I know the moment our eyes connect, I'll be a goner.

I force myself to look away. Back to my mom. To Claire, even.

"You nervous?" My mom flares her eyes at me, then snorts. "Okay, forget I asked," I joke. "But if it makes you feel any better, Trent is an excited mess. Twice I had to keep him from storming down here and starting the wedding early."

Mom's laughter is light and giddy. I notice the change in the ceremony music and check my watch. My mom is chewing on her lip when I look back at her.

"Ready to go get your man?" I say with a grin, crooking my arm out for her to grab. She loops hers through mine and nods.

"I am," she whispers.

"Well, let's go get him, then."

The ceremony is short and beautiful. Mom cries. Claire cries. Lennon cries.

Hell, I think even Trent's eyes well with tears. The only time I am close to crying is when Lennon catches my eye from across the aisle as the officiant instructs our parents to begin their adventure of marriage with a kiss.

The green in her hazel eyes is so bright, magnified by her emerald dress, and I can see every emotion pass through them. I can see them, and I can feel them. Happiness and sorrow. Joy and jealousy.

I'm a terrible, terrible son.

Just like in rehearsal, I walk with Claire down the aisle after the ceremony and Joe walks with Lennon. We go to the courtyard to take pictures while the hotel and catering staff switch the banquet room from the ceremony to the reception set-up. It doesn't take much. Mom and Trent opted for a low-key luncheon rather than the traditional reception party. They're going to eat, mingle, then jet off to Santorini for two weeks.

I thought I would be able to make it through without incident, but the moment Eric sits next to Lennon and puts his arm around her, I go rigid. I glare at them from across the table as they laugh with Claire and Josh.

Eric trails his finger up and down Lennon's arm and she stiffens, but he doesn't notice. Why does no one see her discomfort but me? Always. She needs to stand up for herself, but she doesn't. Where's the fearless girl who isn't afraid to speak out? She's never held back with me.

When Eric takes his arm off Lennon, I start to relax, but then he slips his hand under the table and, judging from the way Lennon flinches, he places it on her thigh. I give her two seconds to say something, to move his hand or her leg, or hell, to loosen the fuck up.

She doesn't. So, I do.

"You're making her uncomfortable," I say, my voice low and directed at Eric. He glances at me, confused.

"What?"

"Your hand, Masters." I sit up straight and gesture to Lennon's lap. "She doesn't like you feelin' her up."

"Oh...I..." Masters looks at Lennon, who is gaping at me.

"Shut. Up. M—" Claire starts to say, but I point my finger at her.

"No," I tell her sternly, silencing her, then I look back at Masters. "Move your fucking hand."

To his credit, Eric looks to Lennon with concerned eyes.

"Am I making you uncomfortable?" he asks softly, and I hate that I respect him in this moment. Lennon chews on her bottom lip before forcing a small smile, then shrugging.

"Yeah, a little," she answers. Eric's shoulders fall, and he puts his hand in his own lap. "I just... I'm not really..."

"No," he shakes his head, "you don't have to explain. I apologize."

"It's okay." She nods. "Thanks." She flicks her eyes from Masters to me.

I nod and stand from my seat. I need something. I'm not going to make it through the next two hours sober. I walk to one of the catering staff, a younger kid wearing black skate shoes with his catering uniform, and flash him a fifty-dollar bill. It was supposed to go to Jules for weed but desperate times.

"Can you swipe me a bottle of champagne?"

He looks from me to the money and back. He doesn't even hesitate.

"Meet me in the courtyard in, like, two minutes," he mumbles, then he disappears from the banquet hall. I walk to the courtyard, and the kid appears a minute later with two bottles of champagne.

"It's cheap," he says with a smirk. I chuckle and slip him the fifty, then he goes back to work.

I lean on a pillar in the courtyard, just out of sight of the entryway and pop open the bottle. I take a drink and wince. I hate the sweet, fizzy shit, but it's gonna have to do. If I thought I could get away with a joint at my mom's wedding, I'd already have one between my lips. So instead, I drink the first bottle slowly. I let myself enjoy the haze that blankets my body as the liquid disappears. I close my eyes and drop my head back on the stone and try to think about nothing but summoning the numb.

Before I realize it, half of the second bottle is gone, and my head is floating. There's music coming from inside the banquet hall, signaling the end of the meal, and when I stand to head back inside, I regret not finishing my lunch. I put a hand on the pillar to steady myself and focus on the bite of cold in the December afternoon. It's only a few weeks until Christmas and the weather is finally starting to feel like it.

Once I think I can walk without swaying, I head back to the wedding.

Mom and Trent are dancing to their wedding song, but I seek out Lennon. She's watching her father and my mother with a soft smile on her face. She's happy. I want to be happy, too.

Then Masters puts his arm around her again, and she turns her smile on him.

All thoughts of happiness disappear.

I stay in the corner for a few more dances. I watch Eric twirl Lennon around the dance floor like a fucking tool bag and I want so fucking badly to cut in. I almost do. Twice. But then I remember that I'm drunk, and this is my mom's wedding, and Lennon is now officially my stepsister.

I keep repeating it.

Stepsister. Stepsister. Stepsister.

Instead of calming me down, it pisses me off more. Eric pulls Lennon close on a slow song and she rests her head on his stupid chest. I turn back to the courtyard and down the rest of my champagne.

I need this fucking day to be over.

When it's time to send Mom and Trent off on their honeymoon, they change out of their wedding clothes, and we line up with flower petals to throw at them as they climb into the limo that will take them to the airport. Instead of hugging Mom one last time or shaking Trent's hand before they jet across the world, I keep just out of reach. I wave and blow a kiss and ignore the worry lines on my mom's forehead.

Suspicion is better than her knowing for sure that I'm wasted at four in the afternoon at her wedding.

When the limo disappears around the corner, people start to disperse, and I zero in on Lennon. Claire, Josh, and Eric are talking about some party Claire wants to have at our house, but I grab Lennon's hand and give it a tug. When she looks at me, I nod to the courtyard, then turn and walk that way.

I know the instant she follows. I turn to face her once we're outside.

"You look stunning," I tell her honestly, and she blushes.

"Thank you." She gestures to my tux. "You look pretty great, too."

"I don't like not seeing you in free period. Or at the rec center."

She walks past me and tips her head back. I turn and watch her.

"You know why I had to," she whispers into the air, and I follow her.

"It's bullshit, Lennon," I say. "You shouldn't have been the one to quit. You can't lose painting."

She shakes her head.

"I'm not losing it. I'm just..." She shrugs, then turns back to me. "I had to."

"Come back." I reach up and trace my knuckles over her jaw. Her eyes flutter shut. "When we get back from winter break, I'll drop the free period so you can paint. And I'll have James take me off Tuesdays and Thursdays. I won't even be in the building." She opens those breathtaking eyes and locks them with mine. "Just come back."

We're quiet for moment. I give her space. Let her think it out. I wait for her to speak, but before she does, the door to the courtyard opens. I turn to see who it is and laugh when Eric fucking Masters appears.

"Everything okay out here?" he asks slowly, bouncing his eyes from me to Lennon.

"We're dandy, Masters," I say with an annoyed smile. "Family stuff. You can leave."

He cocks his head to the side. He doesn't trust me. He shouldn't, honestly. It still pisses me off when he looks to Lennon for assurance.

"We're gonna head back with Claire and Josh," he says to her. "We should leave now."

His insistence grates on my already frayed fucking nerves.

"She's not leaving yet," I tell him, and he frowns at me.

"Lennon, are you sure you're okay?"

This dick. Coming in like some fucking white knight.

"Back off, Masters," I grind out. Lennon's fingers tighten on my bicep.

"Macon," she warns in a low voice.

"You back off, Davis," Eric spits back, taking a step toward me. "I'm just here to get my date."

He tries to reach past me for Lennon, but I shove him hard and he stumbles back a step.

"Macon, don't," Lennon says louder. I ignore her and point at Eric.

"You fucking touch her, and I'll break every finger on your hand."

"Are you insane?" he snaps, standing up tall and puffing out his chest. He eyes me like I'm some escaped serial killer, then looks over my shoulder. "C'mon, Lennon."

"Don't talk to her," I grind out. "Don't look at her." I try to push Lennon behind me.

"Macon, stop it," Lennon says with a sigh. She goes to step around me and I stop her.

"This is what you want?" I ask, and she hesitates. "You want to go with this jock asshole?"

It's not what she wants. I know it, and she knows it. She just doesn't want to hurt his feelings. *But what about my feelings.*

"Just let her fucking go," Eric says from behind me, and I feel his hand come down hard on my shoulder as his other hand reaches for Lennon.

I react on instinct, throwing my left elbow back into his stomach, then turning quickly and clocking him with a right hook. He nearly falls on his ass, but catches himself and comes at me.

"Macon!" Lennon screams.

"What the fuck is wrong with you," Eric shouts, launching his fist at my face.

I'm drunk as fuck, so he lands it right on my left eye. A crunch sounds through my body with the burst of pain, but I throw out two more jabs, glancing one off Eric's jaw and the other in his stomach. My punches don't stop him. He swings on me, body shots to the stomach and sides. He catches me once more on the cheek, then the mouth. My lip splits and my face throbs. It should hurt, but I barely feel it.

He expects me to stop. I don't. I come back harder. I get him twice in the torso before landing an uppercut to his chin. He stumbles and falls to a crouch.

"I'm fucking insane, remember?" I spit out, advancing on Eric's hunched form. "I swear to fucking god—" I swing again, busting up my knuckles on his teeth, "—you don't fucking touch her."

Eric swings blindly at me, catching me in the head and splitting my eyebrow open. I can feel blood dripping down my face. Can taste the metallic tang on my tongue. Before I can land another punch, Lennon pushes in front of me, pounding on my chest with her fists. The tears on her face halt me mid-swing.

"Just stop, Macon," she pleads. "You're gonna really hurt him."

I've scared her. She's looking at me like I'm unhinged. The villain. I drop my arm, and she turns to Eric. She reaches her hands to his face then drops them to her sides.

"I'm so sorry," she says to him. "You should go."

"And leave you here with that psycho?" Eric argues, glaring at me.

Lennon puts her hand on his chest, and I want to snap again. I want to rip it off him and bust up his other eye.

"*Go*, Eric," she says more firmly. "I'll call you later."

He hesitates, and I smirk.

"Go on, Masters," I goad. "Bye-bye."

Lennon throws me a murderous glare, so I put up my palms and shut my mouth. But I wink at him with the eye not currently swelling shut, and I swear he growls at me.

He and Lennon have a whispered exchange, and then he turns slowly and leaves the courtyard. As soon as he's out of sight, Lennon whirls on me.

"What the hell is wrong with you, Macon?" she shouts, shoving at my chest. "Are you high? Why would you do that?"

She shoves me again, and I grab her wrists.

"I don't like his fucking hands on you," I say, pulling her closer. "You're not his to touch, *Astraea*."

She tries to tug her arms away, but I don't let go.

"I'm not yours either," she argues, her voice an angry, shaky whisper. I pull her harder against my chest.

"Yes, you fucking are, Lennon," I snap. "You're mine. You've always been mine."

I don't think as I bring my lips to hers. I groan when she kisses me back. It's been weeks since I've tasted her, and this is like the first hit after forced sobriety. She tightens her fingers into my now-ruined tux shirt.

My bleeding, broken face doesn't stop her. She doesn't pull away when she tastes my blood in her mouth. She doesn't run from my darkness. She puts her lips on mine and draws it out of me. She runs her fingers through my hair, calming and soothing. I bring my hand to her neck and hold her to me, afraid she'll disappear. Everything good in my life turns to ash when I touch it. I'm so scared to stop kissing her and realize this is just another drunken illusion. For her to realize how much better she deserves.

I'm not good enough. I'm not worthy. But I'm selfish, and I can't stop.

"Oh, my fucking god!" someone yells behind us. We're always getting fucking interrupted.

Lennon and I break apart, and I turn around to find Claire. Her mouth is dropped wide and she's staring at me in shock. Her hands are pressed to her temples, and she looks so...lost.

Fuck.

"Claire..." Lennon says, stepping away from me. "Claire, I can explain," she pleads, but Claire hasn't taken her eyes off me, and tears start to fall down her cheeks.

"You promised," she says. "You *promised*!"

I shake my head. I open my mouth to speak, but nothing comes out. Her face wars between disgust and betrayal. I take a step toward her. I reach for her, but she steps away.

"I'm sorry..." I say. She shakes her head.

"You have to ruin everything," she rasps out, her voice angry and broken. "You couldn't just let me have this. You just had to take her from me, too."

"Claire, it's not like that," I argue, but she doesn't listen.

"You're so selfish," she cries. "What have I ever done to you? Why do you have to fuck everything up that I love?"

"Claire, I'm not. I didn't. Would you just listen?"

I'm pleading. I'm dizzy from my rapid heartbeat. I fucked up. I fucked up because I couldn't stay away. What can I even say to defend myself? I fuck everything up. I keep breaking promises. I keep breaking people.

"I hate you," she whispers. Of all the times she's said those words to me, this time feels different. It feels final. "You *promised*, Macon."

"Promised what?" Lennon asks, and when I look at her, she's staring at me, too. She doesn't know the whole story, but she's already made up her mind about my betrayal. She doesn't have to say anything. She's chosen Claire, just like I knew she would. I take a deep breath.

"I'm sorry," I say to them both. "Fuck, I'm so fucking sorry."

Then I walk away, letting the regret and self-loathing swallow me whole.

I try to call Casper, but he doesn't answer. Neither does Julian. I don't try Sam. I drive to the hardware store, but Casper's truck isn't in the parking lot. I don't know what the fuck those dicks are doing but I need something.

Someone.

And the one person I want, I can't have.

NINETEEN

Macon

Age 11

CLAIRE IS CRYING AGAIN. DAD CANCELLED, AND IT'S MY FAULT.

He was supposed to take us out to dinner for her birthday, but I got my ass beat at school over a freakin' dodgeball game, and he got mad and cancelled.

He's been doing that more and more since we moved out. I mess up, and he punishes us both. It's not fair. Claire hates me because of it. She doesn't understand that I can't help it.

I can't sit still. I can't keep quiet. It's better now that he's not here smackin' me around anymore, but it's still not *good*.

I just get so angry...

I run my fingers over the raised, red scar on my wrist. It's been almost a year, but it still hurts sometimes. He can't hurt me now, so he hurts Claire instead. And Mom. I grit my teeth at the sound of her hiccupping sobs on the other side of the wall.

I tried to apologize, but she screamed in my face. I wanted to scream back, but I threw an action figure at my wall instead.

His head popped off and the drywall dented and I felt a little bit better. But now she's crying again, and my skin is tight and that angry feeling is swirling around in my head.

I turn on my stereo to try and drown her out. Sometime later, I hear my mom knock on Claire's door. And then I hear squealed laughter and footsteps running through the hallway. I sit up and creep to the door.

Did Dad change his mind? Did he come to get her?

I crack open the door to my room and the rumbling of a man's low voice drifts toward me. It's not my dad. The voice is warm. Kind.

I walk to the top of the stairs and hear my mom talking. I hear her laugh. I walk down the stairs, so I can get a look at who is at the door. When I round the corner, I see a large man. He's wearing jeans and a t-shirt. His hair is cut short. He's smiling at my mom. When he sees me over her shoulder, he smiles.

"You must be Macon," he says, but his voice isn't hard.

He doesn't say my name how my dad says it. Or how the teachers at school say it. Like my name is a curse word, or the word for something gross you step in. He says it how Mom says it. Like I'm worth something.

I give him a tight smile and nod, and he walks toward me and holds out his hand. I take it, and he gives me a firm handshake. I've never shook anyone's hand before.

"I'm Trent," he tells me when I drop my hand. "It's nice to meet you."

"You too," I mumble. I glance at Mom, and she's smiling at me. Her one arm is hugging her tummy, and the other is propped up with her hand on her chest.

"My daughter is staying over this weekend, Macon," he says slowly. "Could you do me a favor and look after her? She's pretty quiet, but I'd feel better knowing someone like you is keeping her safe."

My chest puffs up and I nod.

"Yes, sir," I say quickly. "I can do that."

"Great. I appreciate it." He turns to my mom and smiles. "I'm glad you called, Andrea," he says softly. He says her name different than he said mine. Shakes her hand different, too. He kind of cradles it with both hands like it's a fragile baby bird.

"I'll be back on Sunday but call if you need anything. And tell Claire happy birthday."

My mom shuts the door behind him then puts her arm around me. I'm already almost taller than her.

"He's nice, isn't he?" she says. I don't answer. It sounded like she was talking to herself, anyway.

We walk into the living room where Claire is yammering on a mile a minute about that stupid boy singer she likes, and sitting on the couch next to her is Lennon Washington.

The new girl with the fake smile and stupid hair and perfect dress.

The one with the forest eyes and the pretty face.

The one who moved here with her dad right after my family split up.

I fist my hands. Trent was *her* dad. And he's way better than mine. I told him I'd look after her, though, so I walk into the living room.

"Hey, Lennon," I say to her, and she flinches a bit.

She eyes me warily, like she thinks I'll bite. I don't blame her. I haven't been nice to her. I've been jealous and angry.

"Hey, Macon," she says slowly.

"You want a soda or something to eat?" I ask her, and Claire huffs from the couch next to her.

"Go *away*, jerkface," she grumbles, and I scowl at her.

"I'd love a soda, please," Lennon says, and when I look back at her, she's smiling. A real smile that makes her eyes crinkle. I turn around and rush into the kitchen, grab three sodas, and bring them back to the couch.

233

I give one to Lennon and she says thank you, giving me another of those smiles. When I try to give one to Claire, she smacks at it. I roll my eyes and go put it back in the fridge. When I come back, they're gone.

I walk up the stairs and hear laughter coming from Claire's room. I want to go in there. I want to laugh with them, but Claire would probably throw her lamp at my head. I sit by my door, close enough to hear them talk, and take out my drawing pad.

I flip through the pages of cartoons and stuff until I find a blank page. Then, I draw her eyes. I draw her eyes over and over. I draw them when she scowled at me that first day at school. I draw them when she smiled at me on the couch. I'm surprised how well I can do it. I didn't know I'd been paying such close attention to her eyes.

When Mom calls us for dinner, I wait for the girls. I walk down the stairs after them. I help Mom pass out plates. She tells me thank you like I'm some sort of weirdo. I even get up and refill everyone's drinks when I see Lennon's is empty. She smiles at me again. The real smile. I haven't even seen her give Claire that smile.

After dinner, I follow the girls back upstairs and hang out in my room until Mom calls up that it's time for lights out. I knock on Claire's door.

"What, Macon," Claire spits. I sigh and lean on the doorjamb. I look from Claire to Lennon.

"I just want to see if you guys need anything," I say.

"We're *fine*, jeez, go away," Claire says, then throws a pillow at me. She misses. I stay on the doorjamb and watch Lennon. I wait for her to speak. When she realizes I'm not leaving until she answers, her lips twitch up and she shakes her head slowly.

"I'm okay. But thank you."

I sleep light usually. My body still isn't used to not having to listen for Dad. Tonight, though, I listen for Lennon. Just in case.

The next morning, I hear the shower kick on. One minute later, Claire comes into my room. She doesn't even knock. She'd have a freakin' cow if I did that to her, but whatever.

"You stay away from her," she says sternly. I jerk my head back.

"What?" I laugh a little because she looks kinda crazy with her bedhead and her scowl.

"Lennon," she says. "Stay away from her. I mean it."

My jaw drops, and I gape at her.

"What the hell are you even talking about? I'm not even doing anything. I'm just being nice."

"Yeah, well, don't." She folds her arms over her chest. "She's *my* friend. Not yours. And she thinks you're weird."

I scoff. "No, she doesn't."

"Yes-huh. I said you're weird, and she agreed."

"Did she really agree, or did she just say that to shut you up because you're so annoying?"

"Ugh." Claire stomps her foot, then her face falls from anger into sadness. My heart drops. "I'm serious, Macon. Please let me have this." Her eyes well up with tears and she sniffles. "You already took Dad away. Mom never has time for me because you can't stay out of trouble, and she has to work all the time since Dad's gone. Don't take Lennon, too."

I shake my head. "That's not... I wasn't trying to..."

"She's *my* friend," Claire cries, then angrily swipes at her tears. "Just let me have her. You have everyone else."

I don't know what to say. It doesn't feel like I have everyone else. It doesn't feel like I have anyone at all. But she's right. I have ruined everything. I'm a sucky brother.

"Okay," I say softly.

"Promise," she demands. "Promise, Macon. Promise you'll stay away from her."

I nod and close my eyes.

"Fine. I promise."

She turns and leaves without another word.

I shut my door and turn on my stereo, and I don't come out for the rest of the weekend.

TWENTY

Lennon

"HOW COULD YOU DO THIS TO ME?" CLAIRE ASKS, MAKING ME drag my eyes off Macon's retreating back. I want to run after him.

"What do you mean he promised?" I ask her.

She hiccups on a sob and ignores the question.

"You know how terrible he is," she says. "You know everything he's done. How could you do this? How could you do this to me?"

"Claire, it's not about you," I snap, then wince at the way she jerks back as if I'd slapped her. I take a deep breath. "I didn't do this to hurt you. I swear. It just happened..."

"Stuff like this doesn't just happen, Lennon!" she shouts. "This is why Eric is all beat to hell? Because you're cheating on him with *Macon*?"

"For the last time, Claire, Eric is not my boyfriend," I say. "He and I are friends. We're *only* friends. You're the one who keeps pushing us together."

"Because he's good for you, Lennon," she says with a sneer. "You need to be with someone like Eric."

"That's not for you to decide, Claire! It's mine."

"And you want to choose *Macon*?" She scoffs. "Macon is toxic waste. He's going to hurt you and bring you down."

I close my eyes and shake my head. Part of that is true. He probably will hurt me. He already has. And if he goes down, I might go with him. But...

"He's not waste, Claire. He's not. He's just struggling. He needs help."

"Oh, and I suppose you're going to fix him with your vagina?"

"Claire, Jesus, grow up for a second, okay?"

"He's your brother, now, Lennon! You know how much this is going to upset our parents?"

"I know." I drop my head in my hands. "God, I *know*. This wasn't supposed to happen, okay? I tried to stay away from him. I tried to not to do it again bu—"

"*Again*? How long has this been happening?"

I take a deep breath and try to fight off the tears, but they seep through anyway. Claire asks me again, more insistent this time, and I open my eyes and look at her.

"A couple of months," I whisper, and her jaw drops.

"You're a fucking hypocrite." More tears fall. "You've been holding a grudge against our parents for sneaking around and you're doing it yourself!"

"I know." I stare at the ground and bite the inside of my cheek. I'm such a hypocrite. I'm a liar, just like Macon said. A thought circles back, and I look at Claire. "What did he promise you, Claire?"

"It doesn't matter now."

"It matters to me."

"He promised to stay away from you, okay?"

Her confession confuses me. I open my mouth to ask, but she keeps going.

"He promised you'd be *my* friend. You're mine. He promised to stay away and let you be only mine."

"Claire," I croak out, "I'm not some toy you can fight over. I'm a human who can make her own decisions."

Macon's words from just moments earlier come to mind. *You're mine. You've always been mine.* I'm so conflicted. Do I want to be claimed like that? By Macon?

"You're *my friend*, Lennon," Claire sobs, interrupting my thoughts. "He can't have you."

I shake my head against the anger and confusion. I'm worried about Macon. I hate that I hurt Claire, but I'm also disappointed in her. She's never treated me like my own person. She's always used me as a prop. As a Barbie she can dress up and manipulate however she wants. I love her, but I need some space from her.

"I need to go," I tell her. "I'll talk to you in a bit, okay? I need to think about all this."

"Are you going to find Macon?" Her voice is sad and desperate, and it hurts. "Are you leaving me for him?"

"No, Claire, I'm not leaving you for him, okay? But I need some space. And maybe you should be more worried about your brother because you're going to feel like a real asshole if something happens and the last thing you said to him was that you hated him."

I turn to leave, but she stops me.

"I'm going to tell them," she threatens. I know who "them" is. Our parents. I want to throw up. I turn around slowly.

"Please don't," I beg. "I'll tell them when I have to. But please, Claire, if you're really my friend, don't tell them yet, okay?" She doesn't say anything. Just grits her teeth and narrows her eyes at me. "Jesus, Claire, I never ask you for anything. I keep all your secrets. Just do this for me. Be a good fucking friend and do this for me."

She flinches again, and her lips part. She blinks, then nods. "Fine."

I mouth a thank you, then turn and leave.

I'm grateful Dad left the keys to his 4Runner for me. I load my bags into the back and turn toward Franklin. I dial Macon on the way, but he doesn't answer. It rings and rings and rings, until cutting to an automated woman's voice.

I'm sorry. The person you are calling has a voice messaging system that hasn't been set up yet. Please hang up and try your call at a later time.

I growl and jab my finger at the dashboard screen, ending the call and then redialing.

Ring, ring, ring, then the automated message.

I try four more times until it stops ringing and just goes straight to *I'm sorry...*

Did he turn off his phone? He wouldn't be avoiding me. I'm not Claire. A prickle of unease runs over my skin, but I push it away. He's probably at the house getting high on the roof, so I head there and try not to speed on the way.

When I get to the house, Macon's Charger is nowhere in sight.

I head inside anyway. I rush up the stairs and into his room. It smells like weed, so he must have just been here, and the window to the roof is still cracked. I rush across the floor and peer out, but all that's out there is a black notebook. No Macon.

I glance back out at the notebook. What was he doing out here with that? I open the window wider and stretch my body across the shingles, reaching for the notebook. My fingers just brush the cardboard cover, and it slips down farther on the roof.

"Shit," I mumble. I kick off my heels, hike my dress up, and climb onto the window ledge. Slowly, I ease my way onto the roof, cursing myself for not at least changing into normal clothes first.

The sky is getting darker and the wind colder. Last I checked, they were calling for snow and ice tomorrow, but by the feel of it, it could be coming early. I hope Dad and Andrea are able to fly out before the storm hits. I'd hate for them to have to postpone their honeymoon because of a nor'easter. The cold air makes goosebumps dot my skin and I start to shiver. I blow out a slow breath, and it turns to a puff of white in front of my face.

I lower my shivering body to a crouch, then sit back on my butt and use my heels to scoot myself forward. It's steeper out here than I realized. I don't know how Macon does this high. Just the thought of him making one wrong move and falling off the roof makes me shudder. I close my eyes and give my head a shake, then look back at the notebook. It's slipped to just inches from the edge. If it slides any more, it'll fall the two stories and land in the black rocks lining the dormant flowerbeds below.

Slowly, I inch myself forward, until I can just reach the notebook with my foot. I lift my foot gently and put it on top of the notebook, then bend forward to grasp it with my fingers. It's so cold that my hands and legs are trembling, and somehow, when I reach for the notebook, my foot slips and my body jerks forward. I kick the notebook in my flailing, and it disappears over the edge with my body sliding after it. I scream and dig my fingers into the shingles, turning my body to try and use my knees and toes and anything else possible to grind myself to a halt against the gritty roofing. I hear my dress rip and feel my nails scrape, and my skin bites with pain as it cuts into the asphalt tiles, but my body stops sliding after my feet hit and pass the edge of the roof.

I gasp for breath, frozen for a moment. My feet are dangling freely in the winter air and my fingers and knees burn with pain. I close my eyes and try to slow my breathing and steady my heartbeat, then slowly start to push myself back to the window. Inch by inch, I move up toward the window, then pull myself inside and lie flat on the floor in Macon's room until my chills stop.

When my breathing evens out, I open my eyes. I look around Macon's bedroom in the quiet. The bed is unmade. There are empty cans of soda on his nightstand and books stacked up by his bed. The walls are bare, which is a direct contrast to how I remember his room at his old house. Movie and band posters used to cover his walls, and a giant tie-dye tapestry was pinned to the ceiling. We've been here for weeks now, but I guess he hasn't gotten around to hanging them yet.

I turn my head to the side and my attention catches on something stacked beneath Macon's bed. I sit up and crawl over to it, then reach under the bed and pull out a pile of notebooks, similar to the one that fell off the roof. There's maybe ten of them here, and when I flip open the first one, my jaw drops.

It's a sketch of a tree. The one outside my old bedroom window. It's perfectly drawn, down to the knots in the trunk and the shape of the leaves. There's even a shadowed figure standing in the window beyond the tree. *Me*, I think.

I turn the page and am in awe when I find a sketch of James, the man who owns and runs the rec center. He's laughing, and it's so lifelike that I can almost hear him. The crinkles by his eyes brighten his face, and the shading is done so expertly that even his salt-and-pepper hair is obvious, despite the drawing being done in pencil grayscale.

I remember Macon saying he'd taken an art class every year, but I had no idea he was this talented. In a way, I'm almost offended. We've spent so much time together in the art room and he never once let me know...

The next page is a sketch of Andrea, and it breaks my heart. She's sad, lost, with her head in her hands and her shoulders bowed. I can tell from her form that she's crying.

She's devastated, but instead of feeling Andrea's pain, I feel Macon's. It's like I'm seeing her through his eyes, and my chest aches.

I turn the page slowly, and it takes me a moment to realize what I'm seeing.

Sketches of hands. Fingers and wrists, so familiar that my own twitch in recognition. He even added the small freckle on my left pinky finger, making it unmistakable that this is a sketch of my hands. I turn the page and my heart speeds to a gallop when I find eyes. Eyes I stare through every day. It's the first drawing to have color, and the greens and golds and browns in the hazel irises are like looking into a mirror.

I turn the page again.

My mouth. Smiling. Biting my lower lip. Scowling. My mouth and chin and teeth.

The next page is my profile. The next is my braid from the back.

I close the notebook and open a different one. The first few pages are random sketches. Casper on the tailgate of his truck. Sam with a lit joint between her lips. Claire scowling from across a table. A broken, bruised self-portrait that must have been drawn right after a fight. Maybe the fight with his dad a few weeks ago.

And then it's me. Every page a different aspect of me. Parts of my face. My hands. My legs. Pages dedicated to my eyebrows and collarbone. The freckle on my right earlobe. It's like this for the whole notebook. Then the next. Then the next. There are pictures scattered in and out of random other things. His mom, kids at the center, his car. But mostly, it's me.

I shoot up and run downstairs, ignoring the way my bare feet sting in places from where I scraped them on the roof. I run out the back door and around the side of the house, plucking Macon's sketchbook up where it fell in the rocks. I flip quickly through the sketches until I get to the most recent, and my heart stops.

It's not of me. It's Claire.

She's standing in the courtyard of the hotel in her bridesmaid dress. Her hair is styled, just like it was earlier. Macon even detailed the crystal barrette she had pinned into her curls. But her face—it's utter devastation. Disdain and agony, with swollen, tear-filled eyes and scowling lips. My own eyes sting as I trace my finger over the rendition of what he saw today, feeling the weight of every emotion and accusation Claire threw at him. God, he must be so broken. He must hate himself right now.

I notice the corner torn and crumpled, possibly from the two-floor fall, and when I try to smooth out the page, I realize the drawing of Claire wasn't the last one in the book. I turn the page, already knowing what I'm going to see, but it still turns my lungs to cement in my chest.

It's my face, or the start of it. No hair or ears. There's no jaw or chin. No cheeks. Just a pair of eyebrows and eyes, a nose and a mouth, and I look...

I close my eyes and shake my head, then look again.

This is what Macon thinks? This is what he saw today?

On the paper, I'm disgusted. Shocked. Angry. In this sketch, I'm nothing but hatred.

He can't be more wrong. He couldn't have misread my emotions any more thoroughly. It's like he thinks I've turned on him. I feel his loss and pain immediately. He's so used to disappointing everyone. He thinks everyone has already given up on him.

I slam the notebook shut and tuck it under my arm. I run into the house and grab my car keys, put a jacket on over my emerald green bridesmaid dress, and slip my feet into a pair of boots sitting by the front door. I think they're Andrea's, but I don't care enough to find my own. I rush to my car, tossing the notebook in the front seat and back out of the driveway. I pick up my phone.

Five missed calls from Claire and ten texts. I ignore them.

One missed call and one text from Eric. I ignore those, too.

One text from Dad telling me he and Andrea are boarding the plane now, and he'll text when they land. I text him back and tell him I love him.

Nothing from Macon.

I drive toward the rec center, making sure to pass the supermarket to check for Macon's car, but it's not in the lot. I park at the rec center and run inside, heading straight for the room with the pottery wheel. He's not there. He's not on the basketball court or hitting the punching bags, either. I run back out to my car, pulling my dress up as I go, so I don't rip it more.

I get in my car and pull up Chris Casper's contact. It rings and rings, then goes to voicemail. I try Macon again and it doesn't even ring. Just starts with *I'm sorry*, and I hang up and throw my phone at the passenger seat. I don't know Julian's number. I wouldn't call Sam if she was the last human being on Earth.

I glance at the clock. It's almost eight, which means the shops in Franklin are all still open, so I back out of my parking spot and drive to the hardware store. I heave a sigh of relief when I see Casper's truck in the parking lot, and I waste no time running inside and scanning the aisles for him.

"Lennon?" I hear Chris say, and I spin around to face him. He's eyeing me, amused with a smirk on his face, then points his finger at me and waves it in a circle. "What happened to you?"

I glance down at my ripped, dirty dress, and run my hand over my mussed, ruined updo. My makeup is probably smeared. I know I look ridiculous wearing a flannel jacket and winter boots with a green silk formal dress, but it would take way too much time to explain.

Honestly, I'm not sure I could do it, anyway. I'm not even sure *I* understand it.

"Have you seen Macon?"

His eyes widen, and he shakes his head. "Not since Thursday. He had the bachelor party with your dad an—"

"Have you talked to him since then?" I cut him off, and he shakes his head again, then waves for me to follow him.

He weaves to the back of the store and into a breakroom, then pulls his phone out of an ugly yellow locker. He clicks the screen, and his face falls.

"Two missed calls," he mumbles as he dials and puts his phone to his ear. I can hear the automated message pick up immediately. I'm starting to hate that lady. *I'm sorry. The person you are calling is MIA and probably avoiding you. You failed him. Please try again never.*

She's such a bitch.

Casper pushes call on a different contact and waits.

"Hey, Jules, you seen or heard from Macon today?" he says into the phone. I watch his face as his brow furrows. "Yeah, okay. Look, if you hear from him, can you call me? And have him call Lennon, okay? Yep. Later."

He makes eye contact with me as he dials another number. From the guilt on his face, I know who he's calling even before I hear the sickeningly sweet voice pick up on the other end. From the pause and the way his brows scrunch, I know it's a voicemail.

"Sam, it's Casper. I'm tryin' to get up with Macon. You seen him? Gimme a call when you get this."

He hangs up and then sends off a few text messages before looking at me.

"Jules hasn't seen him, and Sam isn't answering," he says slowly.

He lets the silence fill in the blanks. He thinks Macon is with Sam. I can tell from the apology all over his face. Anger and jealousy riot inside me, but I grit my teeth against the desire to yell.

"Thanks, Casper," I say, and turn to leave. "I'll text when I find him."

TWENTY-ONE

Lennon

I PARK AT THE CURB OF A THREE-STORY HISTORIC COLONIAL surrounded by a wrought iron gate. I've never been here before, but everyone in town knows where Senator Harper and his perfect family live.

There's a code at the gate, but I don't know it, and there's no way Sam would let me in if I hit the buzzer. I walk around the fence until I'm out of sight of the main road, and then I hike my dress up once more and climb. I get over it easily, considering I'm wearing a dress and Uggs. I stalk up to the front door and prepare myself for having to sweet-talk a butler or some other poor, mistreated house staff, but when I ring the bell, it's Samantha Harper who opens the door.

Her swelling is gone, and the blueish bruising under her eyes is back to her perfect, prissy peach skin tone. You'd never know now that, just a few weeks ago, I broke her nose. The moment she sees it's me, she tries to slam the door in my face, but I stick my foot out and push past her.

"What the fuck are you doing?" she screams at my back. "I'm calling the cops!"

"Where is he?" I ask as I plow through her house, walking

through two living rooms, a formal dining room, and some sort of library before finding myself inside a kitchen. She's trailing me, shouting threats as I go. I spin on her when every room on the first floor turns up empty. "Where is he, Sam?"

"He's not here, you psycho!" she shouts. "Did you finally give it up and he ghosted? I warned you—"

I shove past her and run up the stairs, tuning out her shouting. I check two bedrooms, a study, a bathroom, and another bedroom, before she's grabbing my arm and turning me around to face her. I swing on instinct, but she jumps back and throws her hands up.

"I said he wasn't fucking here," she screams, staring at me with wide, bewildered eyes. "What the hell happened?"

"I'm serious, Sam," I say quickly. "I need to find Macon. Some stuff happened and he got into it with Claire and now he's not answering his phone and I feel like something might be wrong, okay? I'm probably overreacting, but I just need to find him, so if you know where he is..."

Her face softens with concern as her eyes run over my face. She shakes her head.

"I haven't heard from him in weeks," she whispers, and the confession lifts me up briefly before dropping me right on my ass.

"Where is he?" I wonder out loud before looking back at Sam. "Do you have any idea where he could be? He was really upset. I've never seen him like that."

I clamp my eyes shut against the memory of his hunched, guilt-stricken form.

"Chase..." Sam whispers, and I whip my attention back to her. "I think I know where he might be," she says, her tone laced with worry. I nod once and push past her, heading back toward the door.

"C'mon," I call behind me, "I'll drive."

We don't talk other than Sam directing me out of our town

249

limits and to a town about thirty minutes away. I don't ask her the specifics of where we're going or what we'll find. My nerves are shot, and I'm too anxious to consider any possibilities past my next immediate move. If I even think about what Macon could be doing right now, my stomach turns, and I might throw up.

I'd rather he be back in the passenger seat of Sam's car with her straddling him than hanging out with Chase Harper.

He's bad news.

Sam directs me into a neighborhood without streetlights, and my grip on the steering wheel tightens. It's dark and overcast with the impending storm, so I can't make out much about the houses. They're just looming, haunted figures that stiffen my shoulders and speed up my heart.

Macon is probably in one of these houses.

He could be drunk or high. He could be with a girl. He probably doesn't want to see me. But I... I have to know. I have to know he's okay. I need him to know I don't hate him. I'm not angry. I don't blame him for breaking his promise to Claire. In a way, I did, too. I can't hold his actions against me if I'm guilty of the same ones.

What am I going to do if I walk in on him with a girl? Anger flares inside me. Jealousy. Hurt. I made the mistake once before assuming he wouldn't do that to me.

He would.

I hate it.

I hate that it bothers me. That I can't just let go. I hate knowing that I'll let him back in after. He'll apologize, and I'll welcome his lips, even after they've been on another person.

I turn down the next street and prepare myself for what I might see. I breathe slowly. As long as he's okay. I just need him to know how I feel, and then I will leave.

"It's the fourth house on the right," Sam says, and I nod. I count, and just as I get to the fourth house, Macon's Charger comes into view.

"He's here," I say quickly, pulling to the side of the road and jumping out of the car without turning off the engine. I run across the street, forgetting all about Sam as the low music from the house grows louder as I get closer. My breath comes out in puffs of white, but I barely register the cold.

"Wait," Sam calls from behind me. "You can't just barge in there," she says, but I'm already turning the knob. It's locked, so I run to the back, thankful there's not another fence to climb in my dress and Uggs.

I find the back door unlocked, and a cloud of marijuana and cigarette smoke blankets me as soon as I step inside. There are people standing all around with drinks in their hands. Some give me a curious, side-eyed glance, and others ignore me entirely. I turn to a girl leaning on the wall.

"Is Macon Davis here?" I ask, and she pops a brow and drags her eyes down my disheveled body. I bounce on the balls of my feet and bite my tongue against the urge to snap at her. I feel someone step up behind me and look over my shoulder to find Sam. The crease in her brow and the frown on her face stresses me out more as she types something on her phone.

"Yeah, somewhere," the girl says finally, then turns back to her friends.

I push past her into the living room. There's a girl on the couch on top of someone and I hold my breath as I close the distance. I put my hand on her shoulder and pull her back. She yelps and swats at me, but I let her go only when I see the guy she's straddling isn't Macon.

I shove my way down a crowded hallway, asking a few more people if they know where "my friend Macon" is. No one helps. No one has seen him recently. I find an empty bathroom, then a primary bedroom suite with a couple having sex. I release a breath when I see two blond heads on the bed. Not chocolate brown curls.

"The basement," Sam says from behind me. I didn't realize she'd been following me, but I don't say anything as I rush down the hall and open the door she's pointing at.

I feel sick the moment I step into the stairwell.

It's quieter down here. The music is lower and slower than what's playing on the main level, and it's colder. Like the heating doesn't work. Goosebumps explode on my skin, my heart racing faster the farther I descend into the dark, cold basement.

When my feet hit the landing, I feel like I'm moving through mud and wearing cement shoes. Like those dream sequences where you want to run, need to run, but can't. My eyes don't want to adjust to the darkness. My legs don't want to work. I worry that if I need to yell, I won't have vocal cords.

I find myself in an open room with two couches and a television. I scan over the people, bending until I'm inches from their faces. They mumble, stare at me. One guy offers me his joint. I shake my head. None of them is Macon, and I'm too frightened to ask if they know where his is. I'm close. I know it. I can feel him, and I'm scared.

I reach in my jacket pocket for my phone, so I can use the flashlight, but it's not there. I turn around and find Sam.

"Can you turn on your phone flashlight?"

She nods and pulls it out. There's a collective groan from the people in the room when she turns on the flashlight, but we ignore them. She pans the room with the beam of light.

No Macon.

I follow her as she walks toward a door. She opens it, and we find an empty bathroom. I turn around and scan the basement, once more, and my eyes fall on another door. The only other option down here.

I run. Flashes of Sam on Macon's lap mix with streaks of

mascara on cold, gray cheeks. The memory of the scent of weed blends with the scent of old vomit. I hear rain on the windows. I hear my own sobs. I hear the music blasting from Sam's car. I try like hell to ignore it all as my hand hits the cold doorknob and twists it.

When I push the door open, a soft blue light comes from a lava lamp in the corner. There's someone lying on a bed and I run to it. It's a girl. She's fully clothed, which gives me a bit of relief for a breath. Sam shines the flashlight on her and she looks like she's sleeping. The girl mumbles something, but I'm already turning away. I scan the room again and my eyes land on a heap on the floor on the far wall. Someone lying on their side with a beer can by their head.

My chest aches as I walk to him, my breath stuck in my throat as I drop to my knees.

"Macon," I force out, dropping my hand to his shoulder. He's warm, and I blow out a harsh breath. Warm is good, especially down here. I give him a shake. "Macon," I say, louder, and shake him harder.

He doesn't respond, and the relief I felt milliseconds before vanishes.

"Sam," I yell as I push Macon onto his back. The flashlight shines over my shoulder onto his face, and I release a sob. His lips are tinted blue. He doesn't even flinch at the light.

"No, no, no," I say, and drop my head to his chest. "He's not breathing," I whisper. "He's not breathing, Sam," I yell.

Tears start to fall as my body moves on autopilot. I press my trembling fingers on his neck and feel for a pulse. I hold my breath to silence my cries and close my eyes, focusing on my fingers.

"No," I cry, "I can't...I can't..."

I place one hand on top of the other and put them in the middle of Macon's chest. I lock my elbows. I recite the steps for

CPR in my head, hum the beat to "Staying Alive" as tears stream down my face, and try to count.

At least two inches in depth at 100 beats per minute. Am I even doing this right? Am I pushing hard enough? This isn't some dummy at the YMCA. This isn't a class. This is Macon. This is real. His chest feels familiar and wholly different under my hands. This is Macon. This isn't my mom. This isn't a nightmare.

This is Macon. This is real.

"I'm not strong enough," I say on a sob. *One-two-three.* "I'm not strong enough." *Seven-eight-nine.* "Please. Please don't let this happen again." *Thirteen-fourteen-fifteen.* "I'm not strong enough for this!"

On thirty, I stop compressions and bring my hands to his face. I lower my mouth to his to give two breaths, hiccupping on a sob the moment my lips touch his. My tears fall on his face, wetting his cheeks.

One-second breath.

"Please, Macon. Please, baby, please don't do this."

One-second breath.

Hands stacked. Elbows locked. *One-two-three-four.*

Ah, ah, ah, ah, staying alive. Staying alive.

I go through the motions with my eyes closed, a steady stream of tears falling on my hands, soaking Macon's shirt. I count, and I hum, and I beg.

Please, no. Please, no. Not again. Not again.

For minutes or hours or days, I count, I hum, and I beg. I don't stop. Not until hands lock on my shoulders, and I'm pulled off Macon. I trip as I'm pushed to the side. I rush forward, trying to shrug out of the arms that circle my body.

"No," I shout. "No, I need to do this. He can't die. He can't."

"He's an EMT," Sam says in my ear, her arms tightening around me. "He's an EMT, Lennon."

I stop struggling and watch.

Macon is strapped onto a stretcher and wheeled out of the house. Another ambulance arrives, and another stretcher is wheeled out. I try to see who is on it, but I hear Sam yelling at someone—her brother, maybe—and it brings my eyes back to Macon. The other stretcher, Sam and her brother are all forgotten. I follow Macon to the ambulance.

"You can't get in here," an EMT says.

"I can," I demand. "I am."

"Who are you?"

"I'm—" I swallow and say quickly, "I'm his sister. I'm coming."

The ride to the hospital is a blur. Vitals and IVs and monitors. I want to weep with joy when I hear the heartbeat monitors' rhythmic beeping. I can't see his face, but I close my eyes and imagine him with pink cheeks and lips. Smirking, leaning on the doorjamb of my room.

I can't stop crying. I don't even register the tears anymore. I just let them fall and wipe my nose on my sleeve. Someone hands me a tissue, but it's worthless. Soaked in seconds.

We get to the hospital, and they stop me in the waiting room, whisking Macon behind swinging doors. I'm told I can't follow. I have to wait. I stand and stare at the double doors until a hand is placed on my shoulder. I turn to see Sam. She pulls me into a hug, and I collapse into her arms, my body wracked with sobs once more.

"Shhh," she says into my hair, "he's going to be okay. We got there in time."

I hug her tighter. God, I want her to be right.

"You got to him in time, Lennon." She pulls me back and looks at me, her own face red and tear-streaked. "You saved his life. He's alive. He's going to be okay."

. . .

An accidental overdose, they tell us. *Accidental*. The word eases the fears that had been nagging me since I saw the drawing in his notebook. Accidental.

A "designer" synthetic drug. Difficult to dose safely. Easy to get it wrong. Lucky, we got to him when we did. Lucky, I knew to start CPR. Lucky, the EMT response was quick.

Lucky. Lucky. Lucky.

The word grates on my nerves and stings my eardrums.

They let us in to see him. He's asleep and hooked up to more monitors, but he's breathing on his own. His pulse is strong. No reason to suspect long-term damage. There's an IV in his arm, and the TV is muted on the Weather Channel. I didn't even realize it started snowing, but it looks like it's going to be a pretty nasty storm. If it had started an hour earlier....

We're told not to wake him, that he's been through a trauma and he needs to rest, so Sam and I sit down and wait. Her in the couch by the window. Me in a chair by the bed. Briefly, I realize I should call Claire or try to get ahold of our parents, but my head is pounding, and my phone is missing, so I take Macon's hand in mine and put my head down on the mattress instead.

I sleep.

I wake to muffled voices and see Sam and her dad outside of the room. I let go of Macon's hand and walk to the door.

"—it go away," Sam seethes at her father. "You can't just act like he didn't almost die."

"You're being dramatic, Samantha," Senator Harper says.

He's flippant. Annoyed. I hate him immediately.

"Your brother made a mistake, but your friend will be fine. I've taken care of everything."

"So, you're just gonna foot the bill and sweep it under the rug?" Sam hisses, and her dad sighs.

"He's getting the best care. He has a private room. By tomorrow, he'll be back to normal. The other g—"

"He almost died," I interrupt, making both Sam and her dad flinch.

They look at me, and Senator Harper's gaze is apathetic at best. I'm nothing. A nobody to him. Yesterday, I'd have been intimidated by him, standing here in his bespoke suit and tie. I've been trained from birth to respect my elders. To be nice and polite and to not make a scene.

But that feels like a lifetime ago.

Now, I want to rage. I want to set fire to everything and burn Senator Harper alive.

"Macon almost died because of your son," I growl. "He irresponsibly and illegally gave him laced and mis-dosed drugs. Your son almost *killed* Macon."

Senator Harper sneers at me.

"My son is not responsible for what that boy puts into his body." His voice is low and lethal. The hushed tone sends chills down my spine. "And it's in your best interest to not repeat those baseless, false accusations, little girl."

I grit my teeth, and his nostrils flare.

"It's in your best interest not to tell *anyone* about tonight," he says slowly, the threat unspoken yet obvious. "Not your mommy or daddy. Not your friends. Not your diary. The boy will be released tomorrow, and all records will be erased."

He flicks his eyes to Sam.

"I'm going back to the house and will be leaving first thing in the morning, Samantha. Tell your brother that if either of you ever call me for something like this again, there will be consequences."

He glares at Sam, then at me, then turns and leaves without another word.

"I hate him," Sam whispers.

I nod. *Me too.*

TWENTY-TWO

Lennon

SUNLIGHT IS PEEKING THROUGH THE WINDOW WHEN MY EYES open. Fingers are drifting up and down my cheek. I look up into the most beautiful blue eyes, and I sob.

I launch myself at him, wrapping my arms around his body and crying into his hospital gown.

"I'm okay," he says, and his voice is scratchy. "I'm okay, Lennon."

We don't talk as they discharge him.

We don't talk as Sam drives us back to my car.

We don't talk as I hug her goodbye, long and tight, then release her to get into my own car with Macon. I don't look at the house. I can't. Just being this close to it makes me want to cry.

My phone is dead on the passenger floorboard. I charge it just enough to text Claire and tell her my phone died and I'll be home soon, then I turn it back off. Macon's Charger is no longer parked on the street in front of the house, and I'm not surprised to see it already in the driveway of our house when we get there.

Senator Harper really did "take care of everything."

Macon and I walk into the house in silence. Claire isn't home. She's probably at Josh's house. I trail Macon up the stairs, then he goes into his bedroom, and I go into mine. I grab a pair of pajamas and a towel, then head into the bathroom. I turn the shower on hot, then stare at myself in the mirror as steam fills the room.

I'm still wearing the flannel jacket over my torn, filthy green bridesmaid dress. My hair is ratty, the elegant updo long gone, and my face is streaked with mascara. I haven't looked in a mirror since yesterday, and I've cried so much that I'm surprised there's any makeup left.

I stare at the streaks. It looks like someone dripped watercolor black on my cheeks. My face is leeched of all color, except for red, bloodshot eyes and gray streaky mascara. I stare until the mirror fogs with steam, until my face resembles a ghost, then I step into the shower and stay there until the water turns cold.

In my pajamas, with my hair in a towel, I step into my bedroom. Macon is sitting on my bed but stands quickly when he sees me.

"Lennon," he whispers, and my face crumples. I start to cry again as I rush to him.

"How could you," I hiss. My palm connects with his cheek, making a loud smack. "How could you do this!"

I shove his chest. I shove it again. My shoulders start to shake with my sobs.

"How could you be so stupid?" I close my fists and pound on him, my voice shaky and hoarse. I hit him over and over, and he lets me. He lets me cry and beat on him until my legs buckle and he catches me, pulling me to his chest. I dig my fingers into his shirt and press my face to his neck.

How could he do this, knowing what happened to my mom? How could he be so stupid?

259

"You could have died," I cry and cling to him. "You were *dead*, Macon. You weren't breathing."

"I know." His arms lock around me. I feel his lips on my head. On my cheek. I tilt my head to the side, so he can kiss my neck. "I'm so fucking sorry, Lennon."

He takes my lips, and I groan against him, kissing him frantically. Pulling him closer, kissing him harder. I run my hands up and down his torso, squeezing the hard muscles, digging my fingers into his warm skin.

Alive. He's alive, and he's here. This isn't the last time I'll kiss him. This is real.

He wraps his hand around my neck and holds me against him, and I want to melt into his touch. If I couldn't have this. If I'd lost this...

I move my hands to his shirt and push it up, scratching my nails on his abs, then grab the band of his jeans and pop the button. His hands close on mine, and he stops me from going any further.

I blink at him.

"You don't want to?" I breathe out, and he shuts his eyes tightly.

"I do," he says, but the pained tone of his voice keeps me from trying again. "I do, Lennon. But..."

My shoulders fall, and I shake my head.

"No," I say. "No *but*. You want me or you don't."

"It's not that simple, and you know it," he argues.

I pull my hands out of his grip and step back. He tilts his head to the ceiling. The dark circles under his eyes and the sickly pallor of his skin are a punch to the stomach, and images of the night before attack me.

"We can't do this anymore," he whispers, and anger surges through me.

Violent, unprecedented anger. After last night. After

yesterday. After *everything*, this is what he has to say? *We can't do this anymore?*

"Because of Claire," I ask. "Because of Sam?"

"No—"

"You don't get to end this," I say, my voice rising. "I tried to stay away from you, and you wouldn't leave me alone."

The sadness and reservation on his face just pisses me off more.

"I'm in it now," I yell. "I'm in it. You don't get to make me feel something for you and then drop me."

"That's not what I wanted," he whispers.

"You almost died on me! I almost lost you! You don't get to dump me now. I won't let you."

"It'll never work," he says. "It'll never work."

"You're just giving up," I rasp, and I turn to my closet. "You said not to give up."

I snatch the mug down off the shelf and pull out the sticky note. I shake it at him.

"You said not to give up," I yell at him. "I'm not! I'm not giving up!"

"Stop being so pathetic," he shouts back, and I flinch. He opens his eyes and hits me with a look I haven't seen from him in a long time. One of disdain and irritation.

I saved his life, and he's back to looking at me like I'm gum on the bottom of his dirty old Vans.

"Stop being so fucking pathetic, Lennon," he says again, as if the first time didn't cut deep enough. "We don't work. It was fun but now it's messy, and it's not worth it."

I gasp. *Not worth it?*

"You're lying," I say, shaking my head.

"Look," he says with an exasperated sigh. "Thank you for everything yesterday. I'd be dead if it weren't for you—"

I scoff. He's so casual, as if the overdose was on par with a papercut and I gave him a Band-Aid. He ignores me and keeps talking.

"—but that doesn't mean we need to keep doing this to each other. I don't *owe* you a relationship."

My jaw drops.

"That's low, and you know it," I whisper.

"We're fucking up everyone's lives. We're fucking up *our* lives. So, I'm sorry, but I can't do this anymore."

He holds eye contact with me for a moment before his face softens.

"I'm sorry, Lennon," he says, then he turns to leave.

I stay frozen to the spot, my heart pounding in my head. He reaches his bedroom door across the hall when I move without thinking. I hurl the ceramic coffee mug at the wall next to him. It smacks the dry wall with a crash, leaving a giant dent before falling to the floor and shattering into pieces.

I watch him freeze, look down at the shattered mug, then walk into his bedroom and close the door without another sound.

TWENTY-THREE

Lennon

MY EYES TRACK HIM THROUGH THE HOUSE AS HE MOVES LIKE A ghost.

He pretends I'm nothing. Like we were nothing. I watch him to make sure he's real. He's alive, and I didn't dream it all up.

It feels like it's been months. A lifetime. Like we're not the same as we were before. But when he gets close enough, I still feel that jolt of energy. We're connected whether he wants to acknowledge it or not.

I've been having nightmares. The same one, over and over. Macon's lifeless body on the dirty floor of that basement bedroom turns into my mom's as I'm doing CPR. Her face is streaked with mascara and vomit, and she's gray. I haven't slept a whole night since the hospital.

I haven't told anyone. I don't think Claire deserves to know, and Macon isn't giving me the time of day. I've never felt so alone.

"MERRY CHRISTMAS," MACON MUMBLES AS HE POURS HIMSELF a cup of coffee. I stare at him and don't speak. The kitchen smells like the cinnamon rolls Drea just put in the oven. She went to her room to take a shower and my dad is wrapping a few last-minute gifts.

Right now, it's just me and Macon, but it doesn't last long.

Claire comes and sits next to me. I feel her eyes on my face, but I don't look at her. I just stare at Macon as he fixes his coffee and takes a few sips. When Macon leaves without acknowledging either of us, Claire sighs.

I swear, every time she witnesses an awkward, stilted interaction between me and her brother, she blows out a breath of relief. It pisses me off every single time. I imagine slapping her after that sigh. She's taking comfort in my pain.

I stand abruptly and follow Macon, leaving Claire in the kitchen without a word.

"You're just going to keep ignoring me?" I seethe at his back as I follow him up the stairs.

"Would you be quiet," he hisses. "Trent or Mom could hear you."

"I don't care," I say louder. He stops in the doorway of his room, one hand wrapped around his coffee mug and the other braced on the door frame. "I'm right here, Macon. I'm right fucking here, and you're just acting like I don't exist."

"That's because you *can't* exist," he says calmly. "Not how you want to."

The meaning behind his words burns into my chest like a brand. *Nobody. Nothing. Nonexistent.*

"You're just trying to hurt me," I whisper, and he shakes his head.

"I'm trying to avoid hurting you, but Jesus Christ you just won't leave it the fuck alone." He pushes his hair back and sighs at the ceiling. "Have some self-preservation or something, yeah? You're making this harder on yourself."

"How can you be so fucking apathetic?" I ask. His words, his tone, his expressions. Everything suggests that I didn't matter to him. I am the only one in pain. "Doesn't this hurt you? Didn't you care at all? Show some fucking emotion."

"I'm trying not to make a scene." He jabs a finger at his chest and argues in a hushed voice. "I'm trying to keep from fucking anything else up."

"And what about me?" I step toward him, my eyes narrowed and my jaw tight. I'm being pathetic and I don't even care. I can't stop. "This is fucking *me* up."

"That's exactly why we gotta do this!" He points between our bodies. "This is bad for both of us. This is bad for everyone." He squeezes his eyes shut and breathes through his nose. "Just fucking accept it and move on, Lennon."

My eyes sting. I don't want to cry, but I'm so fucking tired and emotionally wrecked. I can't hold back the tears.

"I don't want to accept it," I choke out. "I don't want to move on."

His face falls and he takes a step toward me.

"Lennon, please," he whispers. "Don't cry, please." He reaches out and brushes a tear off my cheek, and I lean into his touch. God, I miss his touch.

A step creaks behind us, and Macon drops his hand, taking a step back. He glances over my shoulder and his eyes harden, then he goes into his room and shuts the door without another word.

I turn around and find Claire on the stairs. She's frowning. I choke out a humorless laugh and push past her. I don't have to be back until family Christmas dinner tonight at seven, and I can't be in this house any longer.

I storm out the door and get into my car, pulling out of the driveway without a destination in mind. I barely register the cold as I drive, and soon I'm pulling up to a three-story historic colonial surrounded by a wrought iron gate. The tension in my body loosens the moment I cut the engine.

I don't even know why I'm here.

It doesn't make sense, but I don't even care anymore.

I climb over the fence in the same place as last time and trudge up to the door. Briefly I worry I'm going to see Chase or the Senator, but something tells me they aren't here. I knock and wait. When the giant door swings open, Sam's on the other side wearing a pair of sweats with her hair in a messy bun. She pops a brow, then glances over my shoulder.

"Next time text first and I'll buzz you in," she says, then she turns and walks back into the house. I follow her.

The house is cold and silent. We pass by a Christmas tree, but the lights aren't on and there are no presents beneath it. I follow her into the kitchen, where she silently pours me a cup of coffee and slides me a bottle of French Vanilla creamer.

"Want a bagel?" she asks, and I nod. "Toasted?" I shake my head.

She tosses me a bagel and a tub of cream cheese, then puts a knife down on the counter in front of me. She waits quietly as I spread the cream cheese on the bagel, then she puts the tub in the fridge and the knife in the sink.

"C'mon," she says, turning to leave the kitchen. "I just started *Die Hard* in my room. I'll start it over and we can watch it from the beginning."

She doesn't ask why I'm here or if I want something. She doesn't try to kick me out or threaten to call the cops. She just lets me in without judgement, and for the first time in weeks, I feel less alone. I feel like I could sleep without a nightmare ravaging the space inside my mind.

I never thought I'd feel more comfortable around Sam than Claire. I never thought I'd rather be with her than my dad or Andrea. Sam and I hate each other. We have for years. We probably still do. But Sam gets it, whatever *it* is.

And after *that* night, I need to be around someone who understands.

I smile to myself as I follow Sam to her room, taking a bite of bagel and chewing. Samantha Harper is watching *Die Hard* on Christmas morning.

Then my smile falls.

Samantha Harper is watching *Die Hard* on Christmas morning, and she is alone. No family. No friends. No holiday celebrations.

She's alone.

Or at least she was.

She's not anymore. And neither am I.

It's after two as I tiptoe through the house. It's past curfew, and no one knows I left after dinner. But I had to fucking get out of here.

Dad and Drea are taking us all out to a fancy dinner tomorrow for New Year's Eve. Claire asked me to go to a party with her after, and I told her no. Then she started crying, apologizing, begging me to forgive her. I almost caved, but then she started back on her "Macon is bad for you" tirade. I'm so sick of hearing it, even if she is right.

I kicked her out of my room and told her I was going to bed.

Then an hour later, I snuck out.

I get to my room and shut the door quietly behind me. I flip on the light and about jump out of my skin when I see Macon sitting on my bed. My heart is in my throat, excitement that pisses me off surges through me. I shouldn't want him to be here so much. I should make him leave, but I know I won't.

"You need to stay away from Sam," he says, and I scowl.

No *where have you been*. No *I miss you*. No *let's please try again*.

"I don't have to stay away from anyone," I hiss, and put my hands on my hips. "I can hang out with whomever the hell I want."

I'm not surprised he knows where I was. I was with Sam and Julian, and while I know Sam wouldn't have told him, I can't say the same for Julian. Truthfully, I was hoping Julian would snitch. I was hoping Macon would show up and haul me out of there.

Macon's eyes bounce between mine and his brow furrows.

"Are you high?" he asks, shocked.

"It's just weed, Macon," I say with a shrug. "Now get out."

"You need to stop," he commands. "You can't do drugs with the Harpers."

I snort.

"It's *weed*," I say again. "I'm not fucking stupid."

I raise a brow at him and cock my head to the side. I let the implication float between us. *I'm not fucking stupid* like you. It's not like he hasn't done way worse. I'm just smoking weed, and no way in hell will I ever get tangled up with Chase. Samantha isn't her brother, and Macon should know that.

"Get out," I say again. He doesn't budge, so I shrug. "Fine."

I take my shirt off and toss it in the corner. Then slide my jeans down my legs. I'm standing in front of him in a bra and panties. I can feel his eyes on me, and it's thrilling.

I walk slowly to my dresser and pull out an oversized shirt. It's a Franklin football shirt. I grab it just to piss him off. I turn and face him, then take off my bra.

I stand there, topless, for almost a full minute. I let him stare. I watch his chest rise and fall rapidly. I watch him shift his body in an attempt to hide his growing erection. I slide my hand up my stomach, trace my fingers along the underside of my breast, then up to my collarbone, and slowly downward.

Just before I get to my nipple, Macon snaps his eyes shut.

"Put your fucking shirt on, Lennon," he spits.

I huff and pull the shirt over my head, then turn my back to him, making sure he sees Eric's football number on the back. His low growl makes me feel more alive than I have in weeks. I'm about to leave my room to go brush my teeth when Macon grabs my arm and spins me, shoving my back against the door.

"You think that's gonna work?" he hisses, pressing his body into mine. I arch against him, my breath already coming in pants. He drags his nose up my jaw. "You think flaunting your tits is gonna change my mind?"

His tongue traces the shell of my ear, and I try to swallow a moan.

"I don't know, Macon," I say, then grab his erection. I squeeze lightly and he groans, thrusting his hips at me. "Seems like it definitely did *something*."

He pulls back and shoves his hand into the front of my underwear, pressing his fingers hard onto my clit before moving down to circle my opening.

"Your tits aren't special, Lennon," he says, taunting me with his words and teasing me with his fingers. I squeeze his dick again, and he slips a finger into me. "I'd get hard for anyone's tits. But do you get wet for anyone's touch?"

He pushes a second finger into me and thrusts, using his thumb to rub on my clit. I fight like hell to silence a whimper, but I fail. To retaliate, I tug his sweatpants down and pull out his dick, swiping the precum off the tip and jerking his hard shaft in time with his thrusts.

"Your touch isn't special," I lie through my teeth as he pumps his fingers into me. He circles my clit, my thighs sticky and wet with my arousal. It makes me angry how responsive I am to his touch. I don't want to want him like this. "I'm probably still wet from earlier."

"Liar," he growls, and I smirk.

He freezes, so I move on his hand and jerk him faster, using both hands this time. One to pump his shaft and one to massage the tip.

"I've already come twice tonight, Macon," I lie again. "Are you going to give me a third?"

His expression is murderous. I squeeze him with my hands, then clench my inner muscles around his fingers. His lips part on a hard breath, and I'm emboldened by the power I have over him.

"Oh, Macon," I moan, rocking back and forth on his hand and jerking him faster. "Please make me come again."

His nostrils flare, fury blazing in his blue eyes. He wraps his free hand around my neck, pressing me against the wall harder.

"You want me to make you come a third time?" he forces out through clenched teeth and starts to thrust into me once more.

"The guy you fucked didn't do it for you? It wasn't enough, huh?" He punctuates each word with a circle of my clit, and I whimper. I can't help it. He presses his cheek to mine, drags his lips to my ear. "You're such a slut, aren't you, Lennon? You need to come some more. You need me to make you come."

"Mmmhhhm," I force out, never losing rhythm with my hands.

"Beg for it, Lennon Capri," he rasps. His voice is low, breathless. He's teetering on the edge, just like me. "Be a good girl and ask me *nicely* for your orgasm."

Be a good *girl.*

Ask nicely.

I refuse.

"Go ahead, *Astraea*," he taunts, pressing hard on my clit and making me gasp. "Be *nice* and *polite* and beg me."

Astraea.

I'm always going to be a fucking joke to him. He's always

270

going to think he has the upper hand, but *Astraea* is a goddess, and goddesses rule over mortals.

I clench my teeth and shove him away, then drop to my knees and take him into my mouth—sucking hard on the head of his dick before he palms the back of my head and shoves himself down my throat, making me gag. He pulls out of my mouth and tugs my hair hard to tilt my face up. He locks his angry eyes with mine, then pumps himself twice before coming all over my chest.

We're both panting as he lets go of my head and steps back. I'm looking at him, he's staring at my chest, my shirt covered in his cum. My thighs are soaked, my core throbbing and angry. We're silent for a moment before Macon hits me with a glare. My stomach drops and my eyebrows scrunch.

"Looks like I fucked up your boyfriend's shirt, Leonard," he sneers. I shrink under the realization of what just happened. I thought I was in charge, but it turns out it was him all along. "Should probably trash it. Wouldn't want to fuck Masters with my cum all over you."

He steps back and tucks himself into his sweats. Then he nudges me with his foot, so I fall out of the way and he storms out of my room, slamming my door behind him.

What the fuck did I just allow?

Who the hell even am I?

Claire was right. Macon is bringing me down, but I'm not so sure he's coming down with me. I stand up, strip off my shirt and drop it in the trash, then collapse into my bed. Within an hour, I'm awake and gasping from another nightmare.

This time, it's not my mom's lifeless face I see.

It's mine.

TWENTY-FOUR

Lennon

I LOOK AT MYSELF IN THE MIRROR ABOVE THE SINK AS I WASH my hands. The door opens behind me, and I lift my eyes up to see who it is.

"Hey," Sam says, and she steps up to the sink next to me. She pulls out a tube of lip gloss. "Any changes?" she asks, then takes the applicator and swipes bright red gloss over her plump lips.

I watch her in the mirror and shake my head.

"Nope," I say. I turn to face her and lean my hip on the sink. "Has he...?"

She shakes her head immediately.

"I'd tell you if he has, Len," she says sincerely, turning to face me. "If he's taking pills, he's not getting them from me."

I chew on my lip and stare at the floor. She nudges my shoe with her foot.

"If he's sleeping around, I haven't heard anything about it," she adds quietly. "I think he's just going to work, school, and home. Even Jules and Casper barely see him."

I laugh, but it's empty.

"You'd think I'd see more of him if he was spending that

much time at home," I say. Maybe he's picking up more shifts at the rec center? Maybe he's driving around and smoking weed on back roads? He's not smoking on the roof, I know that.

"What about you and Claire?" she asks. "You still don't seem very buddy-buddy."

I frown and shrug. Claire's tried to patch things up, but I can't. I look at her and see Macon. I see that sketch of her from the wedding. I see Macon's lifeless face and blue lips. I hear her hurled insults and accusations.

Next time do us all a favor and OD.

"I think our parents are about over trying to give us space to adjust." I walk to the paper towel dispenser and pull out a few, then dry my already dry hands. "Christmas was stifled and awkward and full of fake smiles, but I can tell they're getting frustrated." I toss the paper towel in the garbage. "My dad has tried to ask a few times, but I just tell him I'm stressed about school."

"Do you think they know..." she trails off with a raised eyebrow, and I shake my head.

"No," I say honestly. "I haven't told anyone. Not even Claire. And I doubt Macon has said anything."

"I don't think he's told the guys either," Sam says, and it shocks me.

I also feel a little better, though, because it's not just me he's cut off. But we're two months into the spring semester, and I thought he'd have come around by now. I avoided him for a while after that night in my bedroom, but then I caved. I tried to put myself everywhere he was. And every time, he gave me the cold shoulder.

I still see him in the hallways. I stare at him, but he never looks back. Never acknowledges me at all. Sometimes, I can feel his eyes on me, but I never catch him. At home, it's almost worse. He'll look at me. Talk to me, even. Ask about school and other surface-level bullshit, and he does it all as if I'm nothing special. I'm not a friend. I'm definitely not a sister. I'm not even a former lover.

I'm no one.

"It'll get better," she says, and I roll my eyes. She snorts. "Okay, you're right, I'm full of shit."

She laughs, then I laugh, and it feels good. Like a few rocks are removed from the avalanche crushing my chest.

"Look, it fucking sucks," Sam says after we catch our breath. "The whole thing fucking sucks. But it's not forever. You'll be in England in two months, then NYU in the fall. All this bullshit? It'll be a past life. You'll get to build a new one soon."

I let her words sink in. I try to draw comfort from them, but I fail. I don't want England or NYU. I don't want a new life. I want Macon in this one.

"When did you stop being a bitch?" I ask.

"I didn't," she deadpans. "You just became one with me."

We stare at each other for a moment before falling into laughter once more. I follow her out of the bathroom with a rare smile on my face, but stop short when I see Claire standing in the hallway with Josh.

She bounces her eyes between me and Sam. Her lip quivers. She closes her eyes. The she turns and runs in the opposite direction. Sam, Josh, and I stare after her, before Josh turns to us and grimaces.

"Hey, Lennon. Sam." He nods toward Claire's disappearing form. "I better..."

He turns and jogs away. I release a slow sigh.

"Never a dull moment, at least," Sam quips, and it starts my laughter again.

My bed dips low and it wakes me from sleep. The sheets rustle, and an arm wraps around my middle.

I'm not frightened. I don't have to look to know who it is.

Spearmint and spice.

"Macon," I whisper, but when I try to turn to face him, he tightens his hold.

"Don't," he says. "Don't make me leave. Just...let me hold you. Just for a bit."

I breathe slowly.

I know I should push him away. I should kick him out. Tell him to fuck off. He just hurts me and hurts me and hurts me, and I keep letting him.

But then he presses a kiss to the back of my head, and like every other time, I go pliant.

I let him hold me. I fall back asleep in his arms to the sound of his breathing, and in the morning, he'll be gone. We'll act like it never happened. He'll go back to superficial interactions at home and blatantly ignoring me at school.

It shatters my heart. Stabs deeper and deeper until my body is in so much pain that I become numb. Numb enough that the next time, I don't even hesitate. I just let him into my bed and curl up to him eagerly.

I wait for it. I welcome it.

It makes me question which one of us is the addict.

"You look beautiful," Andrea says, snapping yet another picture of us in our cheesy prom dresses.

Claire giggles and spins in a circle. I force a smile and try to keep my nails from digging into my palms.

It's not a truce. We're not okay. It's more for our parents' sake than anything else, but that doesn't matter to Claire. She's excited that I agreed to go with her at all. She doesn't care the reason behind it.

Andrea takes a few pictures of Claire and Josh on the front porch, and then makes me stand up there with them for a few more shots, documenting my senior prom third-wheeling for life.

It's hard to smile when I don't care about any of this.

I take a few pictures with my dad, and then with Claire and Andrea.

"I wish Macon was here for some pictures," my dad says, making me wince.

The fondness in his voice irritates me. I don't know if I want to cry or throw something. Macon's not allowed to have a good relationship with my dad, not if he won't even talk to me. In one breath, I want to hate Macon so badly, and I want everyone else to hate him, too. My dad should be on my side and should therefore hate Macon with me.

But then in the next breath, I want to protect Macon. I want to keep him. I want him to be mine, again, even if only in secret, and knowing I can't have him hurts more than anything else ever has.

"He picked up a shift tonight," Andrea says, walking back to my dad and sliding her hand behind his back. "He's been working so hard lately."

"He's a good kid," Dad says, pressing a kiss to Andrea's head.

As usual, they ignore Claire's scoff, but I don't. I sneer at her, then roll my eyes, and she turns bright red. I'm so over her bullshit. Macon might not be my favorite person, but I'm not okay with Claire badmouthing him anymore, and she knows it.

The limo Josh rented pulls up just in time. Dad and Andrea tell us to have fun. We don't have a curfew tonight, but we promise to be safe.

They think we're going to the After Prom event at the local

bowling alley, but I doubt we will. Claire will probably go to Josh's, and I'll probably find something to do with Sam.

Either way, though, I don't plan to be home until dawn.

Josh pulls out a bottle of champagne once were in the limo and hands Claire and me each a glass. I tip it back and down it all in one go. I hold it out to Josh with a smile.

"More, please," I say, and Claire giggles.

She thinks this means I'm going to have fun. It doesn't. If I have to endure senior prom in the same hotel banquet hall where Dad and Andrea got married, I'm going to need alcohol. The closer we get to the venue, the more I have to fight off the memories of everything that happened after Macon kissed me in the courtyard that day.

The limo pulls over too soon, and I look up to find Claire's guilty face.

"What did you do?" I growl, and her mouth drops open.

"I did it," Josh interrupts. "He doesn't have a date, and he's my best friend. Don't be a bitch, Lennon."

"Don't call me a bitch, Josh," I spit, and he rolls his eyes just as the door opens and Eric slides in.

"Hey, guys," he says nervously, then he smiles tightly at me. "Lennon. Thanks for letting me tag along."

Ugh. He's so freaking nice. He doesn't deserve my wrath. I send him a genuine smile.

"Glad you're here," I say, and his shoulders visibly loosen.

Two more glasses of champagne and we're pulling up to the hotel. Because I'm a little wobbly, I gladly take Eric's offered hand as I climb out of the limo. I also willingly loop my arm in his as we walk into the venue.

"You doing alright there, Lennon?" Eric asks with a laugh, and I smirk.

"Feelin' pretty good, Masters," I quip, and his brow furrows slightly. I cock my head to the side. "What?"

"Oh. Nothing," he stammers. "You just, uh, you just kind of sounded like your brother, is all."

I stiffen, then unloop my arm.

"*Step*brother," I clarify, then wander off to find the refreshment table.

The music is trash. The food is decent. The company could be worse, so I try not to complain. I keep scanning the ballroom for Sam, but I haven't found her. I thought she'd be here with Julian, but maybe she bailed.

I'm popping another bacon wrapped hors d'oeuvre into my mouth when Eric appears in front of me.

"Lennon," he says with a genuine smile, then holds out his hand. "Would you like to dance?"

I blink, then hold up my finger. I finish chewing and swallow, then wipe my mouth with a napkin. He stands and waits patiently, smiling with his dimples on display the whole time.

I drop the napkin in the nearby trashcan, then turn to face him. I smile.

"I'd love to dance," I lie, and put my hand in his.

He leads me to the dance floor, spinning me once before placing his hands on my waist and pulling me close. I loop my arms around his neck and sway with him to some 2000s pop ballad, then move seamlessly into bouncing up and down with our hands in the air when the DJ moves to a popular hip-hop track.

I stay on the dance floor with Eric for song after song, alternating between slow songs and fast ones, and I start to have fun. Soon, Claire and Josh join us, and we're dancing in one big circle, singing along to the songs we know and twirling around with our classmates. I'm tipsy and I'm a bit sweaty, but I'm smiling more now than I have in months.

For a moment, I can pretend everything is fine, that my heart isn't aching, and that maybe there is hope for healing.

The track changes, and I move toward Eric for the slow song, but a hand comes down on his shoulder before I can loop my arms around his neck.

"Mind if I cut in, man?" Macon asks Eric, and my jaw drops.

Eric looks from Macon to me and back. He narrows his eyes and I watch as a muscle in his jaw pops. His chest puffs out, but before anything else can happen, I place my arm on his bicep.

"It's okay," I say to Eric. He hesitates, then nods and steps away, letting Macon fill the empty space in front of me. Macon winks, then grabs my arms and puts them on his shoulders before wrapping his hands around my hips.

He looks beautiful, and I hate it. His curls are slicked back, and his navy-blue suit almost perfectly matches my dress. His shirt is unbuttoned at the collar and he's not wearing a tie, which somehow makes him sexier.

"What are you doing?" I ask as he pulls me close. I glance over his shoulder to find Claire scowling at us. "People can see this, you know."

He rolls his eyes, the gesture so playful that my heart skips.

"I didn't dance with you at the wedding," he says. "I'm fixing that mistake now."

I open my mouth to make a sassy remark, but the next song starts to play, and I tip my head back and laugh at the irony.

"What?" he says with a smirk, swaying me back and forth and turning us in a slow circle. "You don't like Aerosmith?"

I snort.

"I just find it hilarious that of all the songs for you to decide to dance with me, it has to be the *Armageddon* theme song." I shake my head and smile. "If that's not foreboding, I don't know what is."

His smirk grows. He takes my hand and twirls me before

pulling me back to his chest and dropping his forehead to mine.

"That movie has a happy ending," he says, and his warm breath tickles my cheeks.

"Not until after a ton of heartbreak and bloodshed," I retort.

His lips twitch, and he tightens his grip on my hips.

"Isn't that how all the best love stories play out? It's not love if it doesn't hurt first."

"I don't know if that's true," I whisper, then lie my head on his chest. I listen to his heartbeat and focus on the way his hands feel on my body.

I don't know if that's true at all.

When the song ends, neither of us move. Long seconds bleed into the next song, and when I finally try to pull away, he tugs me back.

"Wait," he says. "Come upstairs with me."

I cock my head to the side. "You got a room?"

He nods slowly.

"...For us?"

He smirks and shrugs. I glance over his shoulder. Claire, Josh, and Eric are gone.

Even though every single ounce of sense in my body is screaming NO, I say yes anyway. I'm an idiot, and I'm obsessed with him, and it's been so, so long.

The moment the elevator doors shut, he pulls me to him and kisses me. It's everything I've been missing, and when his tongue sweeps over mine, I want to cry with relief. I don't want it to end. He pushes me up against the elevator wall and drags his hands down my body, moving his lips from my mouth to my neck and biting at the sensitive spot that always makes me crazy. I moan and slide my hands into his suit jacket, then down the back of his pants.

The ding of the elevator makes us break apart quickly, and

Macon laughs when he realizes we're at his floor. He grabs my hand with a mischievous grin, and we run down the hall, stopping once we're in front of his room. He turns and kisses me once more, this one slow and deep, before swiping his keycard over the lock and pulling me inside.

He closes the door behind us. I kick off my heels and immediately pull his suit jacket down his arms.

"Did you get this to match my dress," I ask, tossing the jacket on the desk along the wall. He bites his lip in a way that makes my knees weak, then shrugs. I smirk, then reach behind my back and pull the zipper down, letting my dress fall and pool on the floor at my feet.

His eyes widen and he swallows hard. It makes my cheeks and chest heat, and I have to press my thighs together as his gaze rakes down my body.

"You're so fucking beautiful," he rasps. He reaches out his hand and trails his knuckles over my jaw, then down my neck and across my collarbone. My breaths grow ragged as he drags rough fingertips over the swell of my breasts, dipping lightly into the cups of my bra. "So fucking beautiful."

He runs his hands down my sides, then walks his fingers along the lace trim of my panties. I close my eyes and drop my head back when he brushes his hand over my clit. Even through the thin panties, I can feel the rough pads of his fingertips. From drawing, I realize. Light callouses from gripping a pencil for hours.

"What do you want, *Astraea*?" he whispers, reaching behind me and palming my ass cheeks. He squeezes and groans. "What do you want?"

"Everything," I breathe out. "I want everything."

"Have you done that before?" He drops his lips to my neck, and it tickles the sensitive skin there as he speaks.

"Once." I jerk my head in a small nod. "Like, a year ago."

He bites lightly, and I gasp.

"Did you like it?" he asks, moving his lips to my collarbone.

I shrug, and he pauses. He pulls back and bounces his eyes between mine. He doesn't ask. Just raises an eyebrow, and I blush.

"I just," I whisper, then wrap my arms around my stomach, "I don't think I was ready? I wasn't exactly excited for it."

He stiffens, and his voice slices through the air when he asks, "He forced you?"

"No," I say quickly. "No, I wasn't forced. I never said no or told him to stop or anything."

"But did you say *yes*? Did you tell him to *keep going*?"

"No..."

He stands tall and wraps both hands around the back of my neck, gently rubbing his thumbs over the curve of my jaw.

"Then that's not consent," he says gruffly, then he smirks. "I'm not touching you until you're enthusiastically begging for it."

I bark out a laugh and roll my eyes, then he drops his hands and takes a step back. I watch in awe as he starts to unbutton his shirt, then shrugs it down his shoulders and onto the floor. I drag my eyes over his naked chest, and I'm close enough that I can finally see the tattoo on his pec. It's a broken clock, cracked down the middle and without hands. And the script...

"We are homesick most for the places we have never known," I whisper, reading the inked line out loud. I want to ask him about it. I want to know why, of all the lines, he chose that one, but he slides his belt out of his belt loops and my mouth goes dry.

Slowly, he undoes his pants and pulls down the zipper, the sound so loud it seems to echo off the walls and war with the sound of my rapid breathing. Then he pushes his pants down his muscular thighs and steps out of them, until he's standing in front of me in only a pair of black boxer briefs.

I lick my lips and clear my throat.

"I didn't peg you for a boxer brief kinda guy," I joke, and he laughs. He slides his thumbs under the band of his underwear and slides them back and forth. My eyes stay glued to the movement.

"I'm usually not," he says, gripping the band, "but the suit pants looked funny with boxers. I needed smooth lines."

I nod, but don't speak, because he starts to slowly push the fabric down his thighs, inch by inch, revealing more and more of the thin strip of dark hair leading down from his bellybutton. I didn't get a good look at it that night in my bedroom. It was rushed and I was angry. I didn't pay attention to anything other than trying to piss him off and get my way.

But now? Now I can savor it.

When I see the base of his erection, I bite the inside of my cheek. Then more, thick and veiny, comes to view, and I can't tear my eyes away. I can't breathe. I don't blink until his underwear is dropped to the floor and his erection is jutting out in front of him.

He wraps his hand around it and gives it a stroke, pulling the skin back away from the smooth head. He chuckles, and I rip my eyes from where he's stroking himself and look at his face. His smile is sinful and makes my thighs shake.

"Uncut," he says roughly. "Like unwrapping a present."

It's a ridiculous thing to say, and my mouth twitches with the need to laugh, but my head is so fogged with lust that I can't do anything more than chew on my lip and stare.

"I want you," I say to him, and his eyes turn molten. "I want you, Macon. This is me enthusiastically begging."

He stalks toward me, and I rush to him. We collide in the middle, a mess of tangled, grasping, needy limbs.

I kiss him with everything I have in me as he undoes my bra, slides it down my shoulders, and tosses it behind him. He bends and takes my nipple in his mouth, and I moan. He bites, and I moan louder. As he lifts me, I wrap my legs around his waist, and he walks us toward the bed before lying me on top of it.

Macon presses kisses all over my stomach before pulling my panties down my legs and dropping them to the floor, then he covers my pussy with his mouth.

"Oh my god," I cry. He licks me with the flat of his tongue, then swirls around my clit before closing his lips around it and sucking. My body bows as I moan and bury my fingers in his hair. "Macon, yes. Yes, Macon."

He hums and slips a finger inside me. I clench around him, and I can't wait any longer. I need him now. I need to feel him inside me now. I need to see what he looks like when he comes.

I pull on his hair, tugging him up my body.

"Are you okay?" he asks quickly, and I nod and take his mouth with mine.

I hum at the taste of me on his tongue, sucking on his lower lip as he continues to pump his fingers inside me. I break our kiss and bring my hands to the sides of his face.

"I want you now, Macon," I pant out, pressing kisses to his cheek and jaw and neck. "Please. I want you now. I need to feel you."

He groans and kisses me hard. He props himself up on his forearm, so he's hovering over me, then grabs my wrist with his other hand and guides it between our bodies. We lock eyes as he wraps my hand around his hard cock, and I marvel at the way his lips part with a sharp inhale when my fingers tighten around him. He's hot and hard and satin-soft. I pump my fist over him once, and he hisses.

"Fuck, Lennon," he groans. "You have no idea how many times I've dreamed of this." With his hand on top of mine, he guides me to stroke him again. "Fucking my hand and pretending it was yours. Stroking myself like it was you. It never, ever felt this good."

He takes our hands and swipes the head of his cock over my swollen pussy, and I moan.

"Oh my god," I say. I do it again, without his prompting, this time pressing down on my throbbing clit. I close my eyes and do it a third time, then push him lower toward my opening.

"You sure?" he asks. His voice is breathy and strained. I look him in the eyes and nod.

"I'm so sure," I tell him honestly, and he slowly pushes inside me.

With every inch, my body stretches to accommodate him, my skin buzzes with need. His eyes stay on mine until he's fully seated, and then we both release a moan. He kisses me softly as he starts to move. Slow at first, making me whimper as he treats me with such tenderness.

I've never felt so cherished.

I've never felt so loved.

He breaks the kiss and presses his forehead to mine.

"You feel so good, Lennon," he says. His words ghost over my lips as he drags his cock slowly in and out of me. "You're going to ruin me. You feel too fucking good."

He kisses me again, more fiercely this time, and he starts to speed up his thrusts.

"Yes," I whisper against his mouth.

I drag my nails down his back and move my own hips, meeting his thrusts. It feels amazing, and all I can do is what I'm doing. All I can think about is him, and me, and us.

I don't care about anything else. Just him. Just us.

He reaches between us and rubs my clit in tight, fast circles in time with his movements. My body starts to tingle, similar to the time in the concession stand, yet totally different. It's erotic and fascinating and I want more of it.

"Keep doing that," I tell him, and seconds later, I come with a cry.

He kisses my chin, my lips, my cheek, as my mouth opens and my body tightens with my orgasm. My moan is strangled and blissful, and the moment my orgasm dissipates, Macon pulls out of me and comes all over my pelvis and thighs.

He drops down next to me and we lie on our backs, side by side, in silence as we catch our breath.

Once my pulse steadies, a giggle slips past my lips. Then another. Then another, until we're a giggling, giddy mess of euphoria and naked flesh.

After a shower, I lie with my head on Macon's shoulder, tracing my finger over the broken clock on his pec. His arm is wrapped around me, his hand is resting on the curve of my hip, and he lazily runs his finger back and forth over my bare skin there. I sigh. This is contentment. If I could do this every day for the rest of my life, I'd be happy.

His breathing grows deeper, and his fingers move slower on my hip.

"Why is it broken?" I ask softly, hoping to catch him before he drifts off to sleep.

His chest vibrates on a hum.

"Because even a broken clock is right twice a day," he mumbles. I smirk.

"But it doesn't have hands." I yawn and close my eyes. "It can't be right at all without hands."

He doesn't answer, and I fall asleep nestled to his chest.

TWENTY-FIVE

Lennon

I stretch my legs and arms, relishing the ache I feel between my thighs.

I smile. The ache means it happened. It wasn't a dream.

I roll over in the cool, soft sheets and reach for Macon, but my hands only touch more bed. I train my ears for movement but hear nothing. No breathing. No shower running.

I tense, and my heart starts racing. I crack an eye open and feel immediate relief when I see a sticky note resting on his empty pillow. I sit up slowly, noting my sore muscles, and pluck the sticky note from the pillow.

It's the same one from the coffee mug. The one I hurled at his head after that terrible night over winter break. I wince at the memory, then smile when I realize he saved the sticky note.

please don't give up on me

♥M

Don't give up on him, it says. Don't give up on *us* is how I take it.

Us.

Me and him. Macon and Lennon.

"Okay, Macon Davis," I say with a smile. "You got me."

I stand and dress quickly in my prom dress, wishing like hell I had something else to change into. Maybe Macon is bringing us coffee. I try to call him, but my phone is dead, and I don't have a charger.

I turn the TV on and scroll through the channels. I watch some of the morning news. Every time I hear movement in the hall, I sit up straight and stare at the door, hoping to see it open with Macon on the other side. It never does. I make a cup of the hotel room coffee, then promptly pour it down the sink.

I wait patiently for the first thirty minutes. Making excuses.

The next thirty minutes, I wait concerned, running through all the possible things that could have gone wrong. By the time eight a.m. hits, I'm bouncing between terrified and infuriated.

I make my way to the front desk and tell them I don't have the hotel key, and I need to use the phone because mine is dead.

"You okay, honey?" the receptionist asks softly. "Do you need me to take you somewhere?"

My heart aches at her kindness. I can only imagine the stuff she's seen, especially on the morning after something like prom. Alone, still in my prom dress, with a dead phone and in need of a ride? I shudder and force a smile.

"No, but thank you," I tell her honestly. "I'm okay. Really."

I dial Macon's number on the hotel phone, and it goes to the automated message. I chew on my lip, then dial Claire. She doesn't answer either. I consider calling my dad, but decide instead to punch in Sam's number, surprising myself that I even know it from memory.

"It's like eight in the morning on a Sunday," she grumbles into the phone by way of greeting. I chuckle, just grateful she answered at all, then I cut to the chase.

"Can you come and get me? I need a ride."

Sam picks me up and takes me through the drive-thru for coffee and a muffin. She doesn't ask me what happened, but somehow, I know she'd listen if I wanted to tell her.

I don't.

I'm still not sure if I should be angry, worried, or totally humiliated.

He'll lose interest once you spread your legs.

Her words from months ago echo in my ears, but I push them away. Not now. Not yet. I just need to be naïve a little longer. Sam turns on the radio and we make the rest of the drive in comfortable silence.

She pulls up to the curb of my house and idles.

"Let me know if you need anything, okay?" she says, and I nod.

"Thanks. I'll see you tomorrow." I climb out and walk slowly toward our front door.

Both Claire and Macon's cars are in the drive, and my stomach tightens with nerves. Claire took the limo. Macon could have ridden with a friend. Their cars in the drive don't mean anything.

I open the door and step inside, then freeze. It smells like coffee, which means Dad is at least awake. Andrea, too. I turn and try to tiptoe to the stairs, but my dad's deep voice stops me.

"Come in here, Lennon," he says slowly.

He sounds strange. Emotionless. It frays my nerves to ribbons. Emotionless from Dad is bad news. I take a deep breath, plaster on a fake smile, and walk toward the kitchen.

Dad and Andrea are standing at the kitchen island when I round the corner.

"Hey, guys," I say with forced brightness. "Good mor—"

I stop short when my eyes fall on my luggage. I stare at it. My pink hard-shell carry-on and my matching checked bag are sitting in the middle of the kitchen floor. Slowly, I look from the suitcases to my dad and Andrea.

"What's this?" I ask quietly. Andrea glances at my dad, her forehead scrunched, and her lips turned down. "Dad?" I say louder. "What's this?"

"Lennon," my dad says, "you're going to go stay with your aunt Becca."

I cock my head to the side.

"After graduation," I say. "I have weeks, yet."

"You're going to stay with your aunt Becca *now*."

"What? Why?" I stare between Andrea and my dad, but neither of them answers me.

"Why?" I ask again. Andrea closes her eyes. My dad doesn't take his off me, but he still doesn't answer. My nostrils flare.

"Why?" I shout, and pound my fist down onto the table, making Andrea jump.

"Lennon Capri, you show some respect," my dad commands, but I shake my head.

"No, you show some respect," I say back. "I asked a question. I deserve an answer. Tell me why I'm being shipped off to Aunt Becca's four weeks early!"

"Where were you last night?" he asks slowly.

I can tell from his tone that he already knows. I square my shoulders and grit my teeth.

"I was with Macon," I tell him honestly.

My dad doesn't flinch, but Andrea drops her head into her hands. I ignore her and keep my eyes on Dad.

"What were you doing with Macon?" my dad asks.

My eyes want to close. I want to look away in shame, but I don't let myself. I don't have anything to be ashamed of. I bite my tongue and stare back at him.

"Answer the question, Lennon."

"You already know the answer," I say through gritted teeth, and my dad flinches. It's subtle, almost unnoticeable, but I saw it. My dad doesn't flinch.

"He's your brother, Lennon," he says sternly, but I shake my head.

"He's not," I say. "He's not my brother. He's not."

"He's your *step*brother, Lennon," my dad argues, his voice rising. "I am married to his mother. That makes him your *step*brother."

"It's not wrong," I defend. "It can't be."

"And the fact that he's nineteen and you're seventeen?" he says. "That's illegal."

"Age of consent is—"

"Age of consent changes when one of the people is over eighteen, Lennon," my dad spits. He's agitated. He's clenching and unclenching his fists. "What he did was statutory rape."

Andrea and I both gasp.

"No," I threaten. "Don't you dare. You know that's bullshit. You know it is."

My dad closes his eyes, and his shoulders move on a slow

exhale. He regrets what he just said. He won't admit it, but he does. When he opens his eyes, though, all signs of remorse are gone.

"I'm being deployed in three days," he says. "You're going to Becca's now."

My jaw drops.

"You're sending me to Becca's because you don't trust me here with Macon?" I laugh. "You're uprooting me at the end of my senior year of high school because you're worried I'm going to have sex? Do you even hear how stupi—"

"He is your *stepbrother*," my dad roars, and I freeze. I have only heard him yell once in my entire life, and never at me. He points a stern finger at me. "You need to stay away from him for now, Lennon, until you can act like an adult with an actual brain inside your head. He needs help, and you need space. You're going to Becca's. Your plane leaves in three hours. You'll finish school remotely, and Andrea will ship the rest of your things in a few days."

I open my mouth to argue, but he brings his fist down on the table. The bang is much louder than when I did it, and Andrea and me both jump.

"You're leaving. That's final."

"You have to let me say goodbye," I say, panic rising in my throat. My eyes start to sting with tears. "You can't send me off without letting me say goodbye to him."

"I can, and I will."

"No," I start to beg. "Dad, no. You have to at least let me say goodbye. You have to..."

I start walking backward toward the stairs.

"He's not here, Lennon."

"I have to tell him," I say again, swiping at my tears. "I have to tell him."

"I'll tell him for you."

"Daddy, no," I cry. "Please. Please let me say goodbye. Let

me at least explain to him. He won't understand. He'll blame himself."

His face softens, but he doesn't give.

"I'm sorry, Lennon. The answer is no."

I turn to run upstairs, but screech to a halt when I see Claire sitting on them. Her cheeks are wet, her eyes swollen, but all I see is red.

She told them. She told our parents about me and Macon, even though she said she wouldn't. She said she'd let me be the one to tell them, and she lied.

"You," I seethe at her, "how could you? How could you do this to me?"

"I'm sorry," she whispers, shaking her head as new tears fall down her face.

"You're so miserable, you just can't stand to see anyone happy. You're jealous and bitter," I say, my voice trembling. "You're selfish. You've been so hard on Macon, but you're the selfish one. You're the rotten one."

"No," she chokes out. "Lennon..." She drops her face in her hands and sobs.

I walk away when my dad's hand wraps around my bicep, and he escorts me to the car. Andrea is in tears. Claire is in tears. I'm in tears. Macon is nowhere to be found.

I don't speak to my dad the whole way to the airport or when he drops me at security.

"Message Andrea when you land," he says to me. "Since I likely won't be reachable."

I bite my cheek and stare at his shoes.

"Lennon, I'm sorry," he whispers. "Just trust me, okay? This is what's best. I promise."

I hit him with a glare.

"Is that what you told Mom, Dad? To trust you? Just before you left her for six months and she killed herself?"

The pained look on his face causes a feeling of sickness

deep in my stomach. Disgust. I'm disgusted with myself. But instead of apologizing, I snatch my carry-on from him.

"Have a blast in Finland," I say, then I turn and walk away.

I don't say goodbye. I don't tell him I love him. I don't tell him to be safe.

I regret it for months after.

Three Weeks Later

"Wakey, wakey, eggs and bakey."

The pillow is pulled out from under my head and the curtains are ripped open, blinding me with yellow sunlight. I groan and roll over, tugging the covers over my face.

"You're vegan," I grumble, and Aunt Becca laughs.

"Yeah, but you're not," she says, then yanks the blankets off my bed. I yelp. "C'mon, love. You gotta eat. No more moping."

I roll onto my back and throw an arm over my face.

"I'm not moping, *Becca*."

"Yes, you are, *Lennon*."

My bed dips as she takes a seat on the edge, then she grabs my hand and pulls it down, making me look at her. Her face is sad and concerned.

"I'm not like Mom," I say quickly, and she flinches, before smiling slightly.

"I know, love," she says. "I grew up with your mom, remember? I know what that looks like." She waves her hand in a circle around my body. "This? This is just heartache and stupidity."

I snort and swat her hand away. She swats back, then takes my hand in hers once more.

"I know this hurts," she says softly. "I know it's hard. But lying in bed and ignoring the world isn't going to fix anything. It'll just make it worse."

I flutter my eyes shut.

She's right. I know she is. But...

"Why won't he respond, Bec?" I whisper, and my voice cracks. She squeezes my hand.

"I don't know, love," she says softly. "Have you tried calling?"

I shake my head.

"Andrea is the only one with the app for international calls, and I can't..." I clamp my eyes against the tears. I'm so sick of crying, but I just can't seem to stop. "I can't...not before..."

"I know," Becca says. She brushes my hair out of my face. "I know. You don't have to explain."

I sit up slowly and swing my legs off the bed, then drop my head into my hands. Aunt Becca walks her fingers up and down my back in the way my mom used to do when I was little. It's so weird, all the ways that they're similar. Some big, glaringly obvious, and others so small, you might miss it.

"Has Claire responded?" she asks, and I sigh.

"Not yet."

"Well, just sit tight. You know how you kids are with checking your email. She probably hasn't seen it yet."

She's full of shit, and she knows it. It's the end of senior year, meaning it's all college planning and correspondence. Claire is probably checking her email twenty times a day. She's just choosing not to open mine.

In a way, I don't blame her. I think back to the things I said to her the day I left.

I'd probably ignore my emails, too, if I were her.

But Macon? It just doesn't make sense.

I know he's okay, physically. Andrea has the app. She'd call and tell me if something happened to Macon or Dad, and aside from the short, weekly check-ins, it's been radio silence from her.

"I don't want this," I say into my fingers. I feel so heavy and alone. I feel discarded and lost. "I don't want to do this by myself," I say again, and I hate how pathetic I sound.

I'm scared. I'm so fucking scared. Becca wraps her arms around me and rests her chin on my shoulder.

"I know, love," she whispers. "And I know it feels like it now, but you're not alone. You have me. I'm here. No matter what, okay?"

"Okay."

She squeezes me tight, then hops off the bed, grabs a pillow, and whacks me in the face with it. I yelp and burst into laughter.

"Now, let's move, lazy bones. We're having brunch with Franco, and he's agreed to teach you how to weld."

I perk up. "Really?"

She winks. "Really."

"Wait. Why can't you teach me?"

Becca snorts and walks toward my bedroom door.

"I couldn't teach a fish to swim, love." She walks out of her old office/studio/my new temporary bedroom, then calls back, "and maybe take a shower, Len. You smell like a foot."

I get off the bed and strip out of the pajamas I've been wearing for the last week. I stare at myself in the small mirror above my dresser. My skin is pale and sallow. My eyes are sunken and bloodshot and rimmed with dark circles. My hair looks like it hasn't been washed in weeks, and honestly, I can't remember when I last showered.

I probably do smell like a foot.

I wrap myself in a towel and head to the small bathroom down the hall. I take a long shower. I wash my hair twice. I shave every inch of my body, besides my head and eyebrows.

When I step out of the bathroom, I feel refreshed and renewed.

A new Lennon.

I go back to my room for a hairbrush, run it though my hair, and twist it back into a quick braid. I haven't been wearing them lately, but it's an easy way to keep it out of my face if I'm going to be welding. When I'm done, I put the hairbrush on my bedside table and notice an email notification on my laptop. I rush to it. I don't think I even breathe as I open my email.

It's a reply from Claire.

I'm anxious and excited. This is my lifeline. This is how I get ahold of Macon. This is how I fix everything. My answers. My direction.

I click on the email, but instead of scrolling to her response, I reread my original message first.

CLAIRE,

I'm sorry for what I said. I'm still pissed you ratted me out. I feel really betrayed, but I never should have said those things. They were uncalled for, and I'm sorry.

I really need to get ahold of Macon. I've sent him like thirteen emails and he hasn't responded to a single one and now they've started bouncing back. I think his email is full. Can you tell him to check his email? Please? It's important. I just need to talk to him.

Love you. Ttys.

Len

I TAKE A DEEP BREATH. I COUNT TO TEN. THEN I SCROLL TO her reply

. . .

Lennon,

Please stop emailing Macon. He doesn't want to talk to you. Take the hint. You're being pathetic and it's embarrassing. He's doing better now that you're gone. Maybe he'll be ready to talk to you when you come home at the end of the summer.

Enjoy your all-expenses paid vacation in the English Countryside or whatever.

Claire

My eyes fill with tears, but I refuse to let them fall. He doesn't want to talk to me. Take the hint. Fine.

Fuck him. Fuck all of them. I'm done being their punching bag. I'm done with all of it. I don't need them. All I need is myself, and I need a change.

I block Claire's email.

Then I block Macon's.

I start to block Andrea's contact on the app but stop. Right now, she's the fastest connection I have to my dad. I leave her unblocked for now, but I mute her and set her to text only. In five months, when he's home and retired, I'll block her.

Then I stand and rummage through Aunt Becca's drawers until I find a pair of scissors. I take them to the bathroom and look in the mirror. I grab my braid, hold it up over my head, and hack it off. I run my fingers through the strands. All that's left is a jagged, uneven bob.

I stare at myself in the mirror.

Maybe I'll dye it too. Maybe I'll go blonde. Or red.

I smile, and it's not fake.

A new Lennon for a new life. I've outgrown the last one.

Lennon

EPILOGUE

My phone is ringing. Not the regular tone. Not the alarm.

I feel around the bedside table for it in the dark, knocking it on the floor with a thud. I leave it, close my eyes, and start to drift back to sleep.

It's ringing again. I groan and kick off the covers. The balmy air tickles my naked skin, hardening my nipples and bringing attention to my already sticky thighs.

"Who is it, *chérie?*" Franco mumbles from beside me, his French accent thicker in sleep.

"*Je ne sais pas,*" I say as I kneel on the floor and feel around for my phone. It stops ringing again. I huff. My fingers finally close around the phone, and I grin in triumph, standing up and climbing back into bed before checking the Caller ID.

My heart stops and my brow furrows when I see the name. It's been a long time since I've seen that name on my phone.

"*Qui est-ce?*" Franco asks again. I barely hear myself answer.

"Claire."

"Your sister?"

"*Step*," I correct, just as the phone starts ringing again. I let it ring six times before I answer.

"Hello?"

Lennon?

"Yeah, it's me."

It's Claire.

"I know."

Lennon. You need to come home.

ALSO FROM BRIT

Available Now

Better Love **Series**

Love You Better (Ivy and Kelley's book)
Better With You (Bailey and Riggs's book)
Nothing Feels Better (Jesse's book)

Next Life **Duet**

The Love of My Next Life (#1)
This Life and All the Rest (#2)

Coming Soon

Better Love **Series**

BTTB (A Holiday Novella)
BL #4 (Zay's Book)
BL #5 (Talia's Book)

Macon

BONUS SCENE

Age 18

"I'll see you tomorrow, Macon," James calls from the doorway as I'm rounding up all the basketballs. The kids aren't always the greatest about picking up after themselves before their parents come to scoop them up.

I look up from the ball rack with a smile and wave at him.

"See you tomorrow, James."

Tomorrow, I'm starting a new boxing class for the kids. I get dumb excited for these new classes. I've been practicing my boxing techniques for three weeks. Watching tutorials online. Reading. It's gonna be good. I think they'll like it.

I finish putting the balls and scrimmage jerseys in the closet —I'll wash the jerseys tomorrow—and head out the back doors, turning off lights and locking up behind me.

School starts in two weeks and it's still hot as fuck outside. By the time I get to my car at the supermarket, I'm already sweating again. It's fine. I probably smell like sweaty pre-teens anyway. The moment I crank my car, the radio blares and the AC kicks on.

I fucking love this car.

Black 1981 Dodge Charger. Bought it about six months ago and it was a wreck, but I've been fixing it up. She's my sanctuary. Claire bitched when I bought it because she didn't want to have to ride with me. *It's not fair he gets to drive, and I have to ride the bus. I'm the golden child, blah blah blah, he's a future felon, blah blah blah, I should have a car.*

Our father ended up giving her money to put toward a car. It wasn't enough to buy a car Claire actually wanted, so Mom had to pay the difference. I chipped in, too, but I swore my mom to secrecy. Claire'd probably light the fucker on fire if she knew I had anything to do with it.

She's such a bitch.

By the time I pull up to my house, Jules has already texted to see if I want to head out to the fairgrounds. I jump out and head inside to snag whatever leftovers we have from the fridge and take a shower, but I stop short at the stair landing when I hear laughter coming from Claire's room.

Lennon.

Motherfuck.

She was just fucking here, and now she's probably staying the night. I pull out my phone and text Casper to tell him I'm crashing on his garage futon again. Might as well move in there for how often Lennon's been at our house. She's getting harder to ignore. When the bathroom smells like fucking roses, I want to jump off a bridge.

I creep up the stairs, taking each step slowly and skipping the ones I know creak. Their voices get louder until I'm passing quietly and slipping into my room. I grab a change of clothes and head to the bathroom that connects my room to Claire's, but Lennon's voice stops me from crossing the bathroom to shut the door.

Instead, I pause and listen.

"But, Claire, I love that skirt," Lennon says with a sigh. It's her annoyed voice. Claire either doesn't notice it or doesn't care.

"Lenny," Claire says sternly. "That skirt is for preteens. For lower classmen. We're going to be juniors. You can't wear kiddy stuff like that anymore."

I creep a little closer to the door and wait to see if Lennon's finally going to tell Claire to shut the fuck up. My sister is always pushing Lennon around and Lennon just lets it happen. It's fucking annoying.

"It's not *kiddy*," Lennon says, and I stand up straighter. That's right, Len. Quit letting her fucking railroad you. Grow a fucking backbone. "I got it from *Du Jour* in Norfolk. That boutique only sells stuff that's in fashion."

Claire snorts, and I clench my fists.

"Maybe it was in fashion last year, but flared skirts aren't cool anymore. If you have to wear a skirt, it's got to be shorter and tighter."

I hold my breath so I can hear better and count backwards from ten in my head. When I get to one and Lennon still hasn't said anything, I roll my eyes. She's such a fucking pushover. I kick the door shut and it slams, making the girls yelp on the other side.

"Asshole!" Claire yells through the door, and I bark out a laugh, then turn the lock. I strip and shower quickly, washing off the rec center and the sweat.

The shower doesn't smell like roses, thank fucking God.

I throw on some clothes and shove my empty pack of cigarettes in my back pocket. I'm going to have to get more weed from Jules tonight.

I sort through my top drawer and scowl when I find it empty. I'll have to get shit from Sam, too. I check my wallet to make sure I've got a condom and ignore the churning in my stomach. I'm so fucked up. I hate it, but I swallow back the disgust too. Denial is better than the alternative.

Sam and me never planned for this. It wasn't an agreement that we explicitly set up. It just kind of...happened. I don't question why it happened, but if I were a therapist, I'd probably say it was some fucked up way to fill our needs using each other. Temporarily soothing our loneliness or self-hatred or whatever. Maybe it's a trauma response or a way to self-medicate. Can you self-medicate with sex?

It doesn't matter.

She gets what she wants. I get what I want. No one gets hurt.

I grab a second condom out of spite.

I turn off my light and pull my door shut, then skip down the stairs quietly. I don't want to attract the attention of the she-demon in the next room. When I slip out the front door, and head to my car, a shadowed form catches my eye at the curb. I can make out the braid from the light of the street lamp.

I stop walking and watch her for a moment.

She's just standing there, staring at something.

I should get in my car and go. I shouldn't engage. Nothing good ever comes from engaging with Lennon. But because I'm a fucking idiot, my feet pull me toward her anyway.

He shoulders stiffen as I approach, but she doesn't turn around.

It makes my lips twitch up at the corner.

"Leonard," I croon, grabbing her dumb braid and giving it a tug. She spins and swats my hand away. My smirk grows. "What are you doing out here by the trash can? Taking yourself out?"

"Go away, Macon," she seethes, then flips back around, giving me her back. I chuckle, then my eyes catch on something by her feet. It's a box full of shit.

I kick it.

"The fuck is this?" I ask as I study it. I see a few articles of clothing. A pair of shiny black shoes. Some scrunchies and hair clips. Some nail polish.

I recognize all of it. All of it belongs to Lennon.

My anger flares.

"What the fuck is this shit, Leonard?"

"None of your business, Macon," she spits back. "Go. Away."

"Why the fuck are you throwing this shit away, Lennon?" I say, exasperated and pissed. "You gonna let her come pick out your outfits before school, too? Tie your shoes and wipe your ass?"

She spins around and gives my chest a shove.

"Shut up!" Her voice is a low growl that makes the hairs on the back of my neck stand up. My arms get goosebumps that make me angrier, and I sneer. "Jesus, Macon, this is none of your freaking business. Just back the fuck off."

"There she is," I whisper, and she blinks. I wave my hand around her face. "Why don't you show this to Claire, huh? Why are you always such a fucking phony?"

"You bring out the worst in me," she says through her teeth.

"Nah, Len," I say quietly. "I bring out the *you* in you."

She gasps. It's tiny, but I hear it.

I fucking hear everything when it comes to her.

She opens her mouth like she wants to speak, and fuck I want her to. I want her to lay into me. To give me everything she should have given Claire. At least she's getting it out that way.

But she hesitates, then clamps her mouth shut and narrows her eyes at me. She shoves past me, knocking into my shoulder hard before stomping into the house and slamming the door behind her.

And now I smell fucking roses.

I drop my head and stare at the box, getting my breathing

under control. I scan the contents of the box once more, giving it another kick to jostle the stuff inside, when something catches my attention.

It's pink and sparkly, and because I'm curious and an absolute moron, I crouch down and pick it up. It's one of those stupid hair clips the girls used to wear. I remember when Lennon got these. She bought them at the mall with birthday money, and she absolutely loved them, but she never wore any.

Didn't go with her dumb braid, I guess.

I hate that braid almost as much as she does.

I stare at the hair clip in the palm of my hand, a pink glittery butterfly, then close my fist over it. She loved this ridiculous thing, but never wore it.

I carry it back with me to my car and shove it into the glove compartment before cranking the engine and heading to the fairgrounds.

God, I'm such a fucking idiot.

FROM THE AUTHOR

WHOA what a ride.

If you're hurting right now, me too.

If you're angry with me, I get it. I'd be angry with me also.

But I promise I'll fix it. I can't promise book two is smooth sailing, because it's not, but I swear you'll get your HEA.

Like Macon said, "Isn't that how all the best love stories play out? It's not love if it doesn't hurt first."

-J-Brit

Better
WITH YOU

Chapter One Sneak Peek

I smell like stale beer and french fries.

It's disgusting. I'll never let myself get used to it.

My shoes stick to the floor as I walk back and forth, wiping down counters and replenishing garnishes. Limes, lemons, oranges, green olives, and my favorite, maraschino cherries. I snag one before putting the garnish tray back in the ice chest.

"I'm about finished here," I call to my manager, wiping my hands on my bar towel.

"You're good, B. Thanks for coming in tonight. I know you've got a lot going on."

"It's cool." I shrug. "I can always use the money. Even if it is a slow Wednesday, cash is cash."

I grab a toothpick from the jar on the bar and steal another cherry from the tray in the ice chest. Popping it in my mouth, I wink at the guy two bar stools down. He left me a decent tip earlier. The least I can do is pay him one last bit of attention since he's likely to be back.

"Alright girl, well, head out and I'll see you on Saturday night. You're closing."

Jada pulls a draft for another guy and slides him the pint. A group of them came in to watch some live streamed coverage of the Butler University basketball team then stayed. I couldn't care less about the game, but it's the only reason I made any money tonight.

I say goodbye to Jada and head to the back of the bar to get my stuff. Switching out my hideous non-slips for my boots, I drop the shoes in my locker and grab my helmet and crossbody purse.

I should change my shirt because I know I stink like a bar, but I'm just too damn exhausted. I've been working more since Jada promoted me to lead bartender at Bar 31, my classes have been kicking my ass, and I've been spending all my free time trying to concoct the perfect cookie for the Bakery On Main cookie contest next month. My body is pissed at me and letting me know it, but if I can win that contest...the two-grand in prize money would be worth it. I don't even care about having my name and cookie displayed on their menu. Okay, that's a lie. That would be cool. But the prize money? That's the real appeal.

I duck out the back exit and walk to my bike. She's my Baby. A black 2012 Honda Rebel 250. I bought it used from the guy who owns the auto garage back home for $1500. It was a fucking steal, but I think he felt sorry for me and cut me a deal. Sometimes there are advantages to being the girl everyone pities.

Putting my purse in the saddle bag, I swing my leg over the bike, put on my helmet, and start her up. No matter how tired I am, the rumble of her engine always gives me a jolt of excitement. Something about the freedom and the danger, maybe. I rev her twice, just for fun, and then cruise out onto the street.

It's already a little past midnight when I pull into the

parking lot of Quick Stop, the small convenience store just off campus. It's late, I'm beat, and I only need one thing, so I'm braving it.

I hate having to shop so close to campus. I don't like running into people I know.

Working at one of the popular campus bars means a lot of people recognize me. Occupational hazard. Unfortunately, there are not a lot of jobs where I can make 500 bucks on a weekend fully clothed, so when I'm on the clock, I fake it. Makes me quite a damn peach when I clock out.

After locking my helmet onto the backrest and grabbing my purse, I pop in my earbuds — a whole other level of antisocial. I spent the last three hours being *on.* Any more human interaction and I might develop a twitch.

My 2000's pop punk playlist, the one I reserve for post-bar shifts, is blaring in my ears, and I head to aisle six, where they keep the baking stuff. I scan the shelf, find what I need and go to grab for it, then stop.

Shit. This store actually has pure vanilla extract. I drop my hand. I was gonna get the imitation stuff—it's what I've been using—but if I want to win this contest, I need quality ingredients.

Shit. Eight freaking bucks for two ounces? I can get eight ounces of the imitation for $1.99.

I groan. This hurts. Like actually flipping hurts.

It's that poor kid mentality. I'll probably never outgrow it.

I sigh, resigned, and reach for the pure vanilla, just as another hand snatches it from the shelf. I whip around keeping my eyes on the precious bottle—the only one this stupid convenience store has—and huff.

I'm about to pop off and put this snatchy thief in their place, but my attention is stolen by the hand that's holding the bottle. A big hand. A strong hand. *A sexy* hand.

Hmm.

I scan my eyes upward. A few woven bracelets are tied loosely around the thick wrist, and a dusting of hair covers the muscular, rigid, golden forearm.

That's a *nice* forearm, right there.

I move my gaze farther up, over a defined bicep and a broad chest covered in a blue and white baseball-style t-shirt with a silver necklace of some sort hiding just beneath the collar. The defined jaw is sporting a bit of dark brown scruff, and soft, chestnut hair feathers just above the shoulders.

I expand my focus, enough to study the whole hairstyle, to find it loose, kinda messy, with a bit of a wave to it.

Prince-haired Harry hair.

When the mouth moves, I flick my eyes down to it to find plump lips quirked in a bit of a smile, and they move again.

The hulking man is speaking.

"Huh?" All I can hear is Patrick Stump in my ears.

His mouth moves a third time, the tiny smile turning into a full-blown grin, showing off straight, white teeth.

Then I watch in slow motion as the other hand, the one not holding my bottle of pure vanilla hostage, rises up and tugs one of my earbuds out of my ear.

"You said Prince Harry," he says with a laugh.

"No, I said prince-*haired* Harry," I correct. "And I didn't realize I'd said it out loud."

"Oh," he says, voice low and playful, and raises an eyebrow in question. I raise mine in response but don't speak, and he laughs. "Are you okay?"

I bristle. "I'm fine."

"I wasn't sure. You're kinda just standing there staring."

"I was sizing up my new enemy." I tug out my other earbud.

"Enemy?" He laughs again. It's a good laugh. Deep and

vibratey. Yes, I just made up that word. The laugh is unique. It deserves its own word.

"You just stole that vanilla from me. I don't make it a habit to befriend thieves."

"I didn't steal it. I just got it before you." He's still smiling. It's an attractive smile, damn it.

"I was clearly here first. I was clearly reaching for that bottle when you jumped out of nowhere and snatched it." I put my hand on my hip and pop it out. My roommate Ivy calls it my power pose. She says it's how she knows when I'm in a 'take-no-prisoners' mode.

"You were here first, yeah. But you were standing there surveying the shelf for a pretty long time," he says with a smirk. "Some of us have places to be. It's not thieving to just sneak past ya and grab what I need."

"It's line jumping, which everyone knows is poor social etiquette, and it is thieving, because that bottle is mine."

"Poor social etiquette?"

"Mmhm."

"Is it poor social etiquette to blatantly check out a stranger at the grocery store, too?" He raises his eyebrows, grin still affixed to his mouth.

I huff out a laugh. "*Please.* I was not checking you out. I was surveying you for weaknesses in case I have to resort to violence."

His answering bark of laughter makes me lose my grip on my poker face, and I smirk.

Okay, maybe this particular social interaction isn't the worst.

"Resort to violence?" He laughs. "I'm like twice your size."

"The bigger they are, the harder they fall," I croon. "Don't underestimate me. It could be your undoing."

He watches me for a minute, eyes sliding over my face, my

body. I can actually feel his gaze on me, and I try to imagine what he sees. Tan skin, amber eyes, freckles, nose ring, ChapSticked lips, turquoise dipped black hair. The old Green Day shirt and plain black distressed skinny jeans I'm wearing are snug and show off what little curves I have, and, of course, I'm rocking my Docs (Thrift store find. Twenty bucks. Fucking treasure.).

For a brief moment, I wish I would have taken the time to change and at least peek in the mirror before I left work. I'm sure I have helmet head from the bike, and there's a damp spot on my jeans from a beer spill. Not to mention how I smell... I feel just a teensy bit self-conscious, but then it passes. If he doesn't like what he sees, screw him. The big, beautiful jerk.

When his eyes land on my lips again, I clear my throat loudly and force a frown.

"So, Butch, you gonna hand over my property or do I have to overpower you and take it myself?"

"Butch?" He jerks his head back, amused and confused.

"Butch Cassidy? Train and bank robberies? A famous *burglar*. Don't tell me you're a thief *and* uncultured."

He chuckles and gives me a shrug.

"Just a pretty face, then." I shake my head and sigh. "Such a shame."

"You think I'm pretty."

"I have eyes." I fold my arms over my chest and look away, feigning boredom. "Doesn't change the fact that you're a criminal."

"I'll tell you what." He mimics my stance and hits me with an all-business stare. "I'll trade you for the vanilla."

I purse my lips before asking, "What do I have to give?"

"I'll trade you this vanilla for your number."

Oh. Well, okay then. This is a no-brainer.

"I told you before that I don't associate with criminals."

"But if I give you the bottle, then I wouldn't be a criminal. I'm not stealing; it's all just one big misunderstanding."

"And what if this isn't your first offense? How do I know you're not trying to trick me? Get my number, then make off with the vanilla?" I squint my eyes at him. "You could be trying to set me up for a bunch of cold calling campaigns. Or planning to put my number on a billboard or a bathroom stall. How do I know you can be trusted?"

Pretty sure I've got this boy eating out of the palm of my hand. He's trying so hard not to let his smile take over his face, trying and failing, and his brown eyes are dancing with humor. He's amused. He's having fun, and I'm suddenly not tired anymore.

"You bring up good points." He pauses. "I don't suppose you'll take my word for it."

I huff a laugh and roll my eyes.

"Of course not." He chuckles. "I'll let you buy it first. You can buy it and put it in your car, and then give me your number."

I pretend to think it over.

"If we do it that way, you'll stay on the sidewalk until I've secured the vanilla, and then I'll shout my number to you."

He laughs, giving an amused shake of the head before nodding his agreement. "Deal. Shake on it?"

He sticks out his hand, and I narrow my eyes at it. Then I meet his gaze, pop a brow, and slowly reach out to take it.

It's warm and calloused. His grip is firm, but not crushing, and I have a feeling his hands could do some serious damage if he wanted them to. The thought sends a spark of lust through me. The way his eyes flash with heat tells me he noticed, so I drop his hand and head to the check out.

He follows me out the door, the bottle of vanilla and the store receipt clutched in my hand. When we're on the sidewalk, I turn around.

317

"You stay here," I remind him, pointing to the sidewalk where his feet are planted. "No moving."

"Cross my heart." He uses his index finger to draw an X on his chest, and I have to hold back my smile at how serious he looks.

I take my first few steps backward, keeping my eyes on him, until I'm a safe distance away. Then I pivot on the ball of my foot and sashay to my bike. I'm not ashamed to admit it. I might not have much by way of hips, but what I do have, I know how to work. When I reach Baby, I put the vanilla and my purse in the saddle bag, unlock my helmet, then turn back around to face the attractive almost-thief. I lean on my bike lightly and smirk at his shocked expression.

People never expect me to be riding a motorcycle. It's one of the reasons I love it.

We stare at each other for a moment, me with my smirk and him with his wide, surprised eyes. The connection creates sparks, even with a parking lot between us, and I have to breathe slowly to steady my heartbeat.

"Is the package secure?" he shouts from the curb, and I reach down and pat the saddlebag.

"Snug as a bug in a rug."

"Okay. I held up my end of the bargain. It's your turn to hold up yours."

"Hmmm, what was my end, again?" I cock my head to the side and watch as he grabs the back of his neck and smiles at the ground. It's so boyishly adorable, so magnetic, that I kind of hate him a little. This guy is *dangerous*.

"Your number," he reminds me.

"Oh yeah," I say with a grin. "Thirty-one."

"Thirty-one?" His handsome face scrunches up in confusion.

"Thirty-one." I stifle a giggle.

"Thirty-one is not your phone number."

"It's not," I respond slowly. "But you didn't specify what number you wanted." I shrug. "Thirty-one is the number you get."

As I swing my leg over my bike, I hear his rumbling laugh again. I'm just about to push my helmet on my head when he calls out.

"Sundance! Hey, Sundance," he shouts, and I can't help the huge smile that stretches over my face. That scoundrel said he didn't know Butch Cassidy, and here he is calling me Sundance. "I didn't get your name."

I look at him, smile wide, and roll my eyes. "Bummer for you."

Then I shove my helmet on my head, rev Baby to life, and cruise out of the parking lot without a backward glance.

By the time Saturday evening rolls around, I've almost forgotten about the baking-aisle boy.

I did think I saw someone similar on campus yesterday, and once Thursday I thought I heard his laugh on the quad. But, otherwise, he's just a fuzzy image, fading from my short-term memory, never to be fantasized about again.

Saturday nights at Bar 31 are always hopping. I'm closing tonight, so I can make a cool $200 at least, and it will be easy money. Rum and Cokes, Vodka Cranberries, and way too many Jägerbombs.

College kids and our distinguished pallets. Ha.

Around 1 a.m., thirty minutes before I get to climb on a stool and shout LAST CALL into the bar microphone, a familiar hand slides into my line of sight.

A sexy hand.

With woven bracelets tied to a thick wrist.

I allow myself one small smirk before meeting his chocolate brown eyes.

"You found me."

Better With You, the second standalone in the _Better Love_ series, is available now. Add it to your TBR or one-click it today!

ABOUT THE AUTHOR

Brit Benson writes romance novels that are sassy, sexy, and sweet.

Brit would almost always rather be reading or writing. When she's not dreaming up her next swoony book boyfriend and fierce book bestie, she's getting lost in someone else's fictional world. When she's not doing that, she's probably marathoning a Netflix series or wandering aimlessly up and down the aisles in Homegoods, sniffing candles and touching things she'll never buy.

f facebook.com/britbensonbooks

instagram.com/britbensonwritesbooks

g goodreads.com/authorbritbenson

tiktok.com/@britbensonauthor

Made in the USA
Monee, IL
22 December 2023

50374917R00184